Jove Titles by Lynn Bailey

FLOWERS BY MOONLIGHT
KISSED BY STARLIGHT
MAGIC BY DAYLIGHT
SPLENDID YOU

Splendid You

LYNN BAILEY

JOVE BOOKS, NEW YORK

This is a work of fiction. Names, characters, places, and incidents are
either the product of the author's imagination or are used fictitiously,
and any resemblance to actual persons, living or dead, business
establishments, events, or locales is entirely coincidental.

MAGICAL LOVE is a trademark of Penguin Putnam Inc.

SPLENDID YOU

A Jove Book / published by arrangement with
the author

PRINTING HISTORY
Jove edition / July 2000

The Penguin Putnam Inc. World Wide Web site address is
http://www.penguinputnam.com

ISBN: 0-515-12868-6

A JOVE BOOK®
Jove Books are published by The Berkley Publishing Group,
a division of Penguin Putnam Inc.,
375 Hudson Street, New York, New York 10014.
JOVE and the "J" design
are trademarks belonging to Penguin Putnam Inc.

PRINTED IN THE UNITED STATES OF AMERICA

10 9 8 7 6 5 4 3 2 1

*To my friends in the Delaware Chapter of
Romance Writers of America*

*Judith E. French, Colleen Faulkner, Linda Windsor,
Candace McCarthy, Donna Clayton, Angelica Hart,
Gaby Pratt, and Janet Cooper*

with many thanks.

One

~

Julia did not for a moment expect Simon Archer to fall in love with her at first sight. Though she imagined their meeting a thousand times, never more often than on the long mail-coach ride from York to London, she did not indulge in that pleasant fantasy. It would be enough if he liked her.

Certainly, their two-year correspondence had proved that they had many interests and opinions in common. They were united in their love for Egypt. Simon, who had spent many days there, and Julia, who had thus far never stepped foot off the British Isles, could both rhapsodize for pages about Egypt's arts, sciences and dusty charms.

Furthermore, each made no secret of their detestation of the dilettantes who plundered Egypt in search of mere trinkets, and agreed that the methods of the so-called archaeologists were hardly any better. Perhaps this was not the deepest foundation for a marriage, but she knew many happy couples who had started out with even fewer subjects to share over the breakfast table.

" 'Ere you are, Miss Hanson. The Bishop's Arms to the Bull an' Bush in just two days."

"We have made excellent time, Mr. Williams. I shall certainly write a letter to your superiors praising your courtesy on this journey."

" 'Twas a pleasure, miss," the guardsman said, touching his three-cornered hat.

The other passengers, a trio of attorneys come south for an important lawsuit, hung back while Miss Hanson descended. When they were all standing in the stableyard of the busy inn, she shook hands with each man in turn. "Thank you for your suggestion, Miss Hanson," the elder of the three said. "I will instruct my housekeeper to follow your recipe for that gargle to the letter!"

"They say the Roman senators swore by it, Mr. Galsworthy. Good-bye, gentlemen. The best of fortune to you."

The guard approached her again and pointed to where her luggage was piled. "I've told the landlord to give you a nice room, miss. If he gives you h'any trouble, you just tell me 'bout it."

"You've been so very kind, Mr. Williams. I do hope your little girl is feeling better." Gaily, Julia gave him two pounds as a tip, the coins clinking cheerfully. She entered the inn, finding it clean and well-furnished, if noisy.

Mr. Williams's good words indeed commanded the landlord's attention. She was shown to her room at once, a pleasant chamber near the back of the busy inn, and a bright brass can of hot water was already waiting on the washstand. She'd hardly taken off her hat before a knock on the door heralded a pot of tea, a plate of sandwiches, and today's edition of the *Times*. "Thank heaven!"

She could put on a cheerful face in front of people, but when alone, Julia admitted to herself that all was not well. The mail coach was astonishingly fast but surrendered in comfort what it made up for in speed. She'd been jolted and swayed, bounced and trounced over bad roads, until every bone in her twenty-seven year-old body ached like an old woman's on a rainy night.

There'd hardly been a moment at any stop to snatch a mouthful to eat. Due to the hasty circumstances of her departure from her home, she'd not thought to pack a hamper. Departing in the morning at dawn, she'd slept when she could, with her head against the frame of the coach, but she'd not slept. Even now, the bed in the corner of the room was beckoning to her with a seduction no siren could have bettered.

Julia considered lying down for half an hour but stoically put the temptation from her. Half an hour would make no dent in the exhaustion she felt, and she was all too aware that half an hour could well stretch into an entire evening. The maid who'd brought her food and taken away her crumpled gown didn't look to be the sort of stern disciplinarian who would coldheartedly wake her. Rather, she looked like a dear creature who'd let a tired girl sleep and sleep and say only, "You looked as if you needed it. . . ."

To occupy herself, she turned to the papers. The small print swam before her eyes, but in a moment, seeing a name she recognized, the black lines steadied. Simon had an entire column devoted to his discoveries at Deir el-Bahari. Julia smiled as she read, for she knew far more details of the discovery of the priestess's tomb than the reporter did. Simon had written to her twice a week during the exciting days of the season's excavation. She could hardly bear to wait any longer before seeing the treasures he had found, though that anticipation paled beside her eagerness to meet the man himself.

He was mentioned again in a large advertisement. Julia studied it, her head to the side. She couldn't understand it and decided at last that this 'Dr. Mystery' was simply using Simon's name without permission to draw people to his "fabulous exhibition of the wonders of the unseen!"

Putting aside the paper, Julia turned to the task at hand.

When she had taken out her best walking dress to give to the maid, she'd disordered her valise. It took time to excavate her badly needed hairbrush. She had not the courage to look in the mirror until she was armed for the battle ahead.

As she feared, her never very ruly hair had taken advantage of the situation to become a vastly frizzled bush. "If only . . ." Julia said, trying to force the brush through the tangles, "I had lived a hundred years ago when this was the mode! Or if I had lived in Egypt so I could have shaved it off!"

Not for her the smooth styles of the day, with little curls at the sides! She had enough to do to tame the wild mass into a neat bun at the back of her neck. When it was at last subdued, the maid had returned with her freshly pressed gown.

With her help, Julia turned to dressing. There, too, she avoided the present fashion. Her skirt was just wide enough to escape notice but she'd eliminated the huge sleeves and lashings of trimming, having no wish to resemble an overdecorated cake. Her heart was given to the slim, multitudinously pleated garments of the ancient Egyptians and nothing could be imagined more opposite to that ideal than the present craze for excess.

"Oh, miss, you do look nice!"

"Thank you, Mary. Will you ask your father to call a cab for me?" Julia buy this time had heard all about Mary's family, her dreams of marrying the butcher's son in the next street, and the time Mary's mother was sure she'd glimpsed the queen and Prince Albert driving by.

Before leaving, Julia took one last peep in the glass. Simon Archer need not love her at first sight, but neither should he look at her in disgust. She could only pray that brunettes with a certain lushness of outline appealed to him.

•　•　•

Simon Archer gazed adoringly at the most entrancing female face he'd ever beheld. Her beautiful dark hair fell in smooth ripples to either side of her softly rounded cheeks. Her deep eyes looked slightly past him, but surely their liquid gleam would soon light on his face. Then the austere mouth would smile.

"The coffin is in a remarkable state of preservation," he said. "We packed it in a case carefully padded with cotton so that there would be no scratches on the gold. It's a rather soft alloy."

The two gentlemen of the British Museum nodded politely. But the eyes of one slid repeatedly to the glitter of gold in the next case. A broad pectoral collar inset with a heavenly falcon, several bracelets of golden beads interspersed with red carnelian and blue turquoise, small rings, and the charms and amulets of a superstitious people had been placed carefully on the same pale velvet that lined modern-day jeweler's boxes.

With a sigh, Simon said, "Of course, the gold jewelry is what most people will want to see."

"Yes," said the director of the antiquities exhibit. "A queen's ransom. Quite the most complete set I have ever heard of."

His assistant, plump and prim in a high collar, added, "The ladies will be imagining themselves attired in them. No doubt, Mr. Archer, you'll be besieged with requests for private viewings."

Sir Walter Armbruster's thick eyebrows rose as he smiled. "Naturally, you'll be permitted to enter the museum whenever you wish."

"You're very kind, Sir Walter, Mr. Keene, but there is only one woman I would ever permit to handle these objects. My collaborator."

"You've a collaborator? And she is a woman?" The gentlemen of the museum glanced at one another. Simon Archer's misogyny was well-known in spite of, or perhaps as a result of, having three sisters and a charming mother.

"A certain Miss Hanson, of Yorkshire."

"You surprise me, Mr. Archer. Of what use has this woman been to you?"

With his fingertip, Simon traced a line of the hieroglyphs that were incised over virtually every inch of the coffin's polished surface. "She has an almost masculine gift for translation," he said. "She corresponded with the great Champollion from the time he was appointed conservator of the Louvre's Egyptian collection until his death. He discussed with her in detail the technique whereby he decoded the Rosetta Stone. From her letters to me, I conclude that she is a truly remarkable woman, whom age has not faded one whit of her vivacity or interest in Egypt." Smiling warmly, knowing the men must think him overly enthusiastic, he concluded, "I fancy that she and the Lady An-ket here would get on famously."

"I am very eager to meet her."

"I wish you might, Sir Walter. I did invite her to come south to see the exhibition, but it is a considerable journey even for a young lady. I should not like to see any of my sisters attempt it, let alone my mother."

"Indeed not. You shall have to write her of your triumph, Mr. Archer. And not only of your triumph *here*, I trust. Perhaps you'd be good enough to come to my offices later. I have a bottle of excellent whiskey and I'd consider it an honor to drink to your success this evening."

Simon shuffled his feet, feeling a surge of embarrassment. The gleam of amusement in young Mr. Keene's eyes didn't make him any more comfortable. "Thank you, Sir Walter. I must say I find your attitude surprising. So many other scientists seem to think I'm only lending credence to this fellow's outrageous claims by attending his demonstration."

"If science is to advance, Mr. Archer, we must be open to the truth even in unpalatable forms, and willing, too, to expose it even at the risk of our dignity. These spiritualistic *fakirs* are capable of doing great harm. This so-called Dr. Mystery seems to be the worst of the lot. I hope to read in tomorrow's *Times* that you have exposed him for the fraud he is."

Simon bowed as Sir Walter left the room. Mr. Keene lingered for a moment until his superior had gone from earshot. "Lady Armbruster is said to be very fond of fortune-tellers and others of that ilk," he said in a well-bred undertone. "I don't know whether she has been to any of 'Dr. Mystery's' performances. Although it wouldn't surprise me."

"Women are notoriously prone to attending such displays. It excites their credulity."

"Not women only, by what I've heard. There are a few highly placed ministers who are attending this fellow's claptrap sessions."

"Led there, no doubt, by their wives."

Mr. Keene said, "Yes, poor souls. God, who'd live under the cat's foot? We bachelors are the fortunate ones. Go where we please, live how we like, answer to no one." He brought out his watch from his waistcoat pocket. "Except to our superiors at the museum. Pardon me for leaving you, Archer. An important patron awaits my talent for pouring tea."

"If showing this exhibition ahead of schedule will help bring the money in . . ."

"You're too kind," Mr. Keene said with a grin. "But this patron's interest is in China, not Egypt."

"There is no accounting for taste."

"No indeed. I hope we shall meet again later?"

"I look forward to it."

Left alone at last with the exhibition displays, Simon walked around them as fussily as a housewife. He picked off a piece of nearly microscopic fluff from the extended arm of An-ket's coffin and straightened one of the cards. He drew out his handkerchief and gave a rub to the glass case, believing he saw a finger mark.

Cloth still in hand, Simon grinned at himself. No one who had ever been privileged to see the disordered masses that covered his desk would believe he could be so meticulous about the exhibition. Perhaps fame had changed him?

For there was no denying that he suddenly had fame. The fortunate loss of a goat down a ravine had led him to the treasures that had attracted the interest of the world. No one had ever found anything like what he had discovered that blisteringly hot day along the cliffs. Wild rumors had circulated that Archer had found an undisturbed tomb. The news hadn't been quite that good, but it had been good enough.

The tomb of the Priestess of Hathor had been robbed in antiquity. Impossible to visualize the riches it must have once contained, but how tempting to try to conjure from these remaining pieces the fabulous wealth of ancient Egypt. The thieves had been clever, tunneling into the living rock in search of the spoil. Yet for some superstitious reason they had stopped short of hacking the coffin apart for the gold. Neither had they opened it in order to steal her jewelry or to tear the resined bandages to search for the precious amulets such mummies contained.

Simon hadn't done that, either, though as a scientist he should have done so. He excused himself by saying that the embalmers had used so much of the precious resin that the body had become almost a solid mass. To retrieve the amulets would have entailed a violent assault. Better to leave her in peace.

Her jewelry had been loose inside the unopened coffin. The collar of beads looked as though it had been torn from her neck and then dropped onto her torso. The household objects, of no particular intrinsic value though priceless in terms of knowledge, had been scattered about the coffin as though by careless feet.

For reasons unknown, the thieves had never returned to

finish their work. The lady's cosmetic box, still with the unguents fresh in their wax-sealed alabaster jars, would have brought a fine price, yet it lay in the dust. So did forty-two *shabti*, the little figures who would do her bidding in the afterlife. An ivory cat, small enough to be cupped in two hands, and her polished bronze mirror had been found, broken like many of the *shabti*, but still recognizable.

That was all. Yet it was enough, with her nested coffins, to make him well-known. His anger against a spiritualist who had the gall to claim a direct psychic link to some phony pharaoh made him famous.

A page, dressed in blue livery, appeared at the door to the exhibition room. Despite his neat appearance, there were still black smears from his fingers on the folded note he handed to Simon.

In the neat hand he knew as well as his own, Simon read, *Miss Hanson presents her compliments to Mr. Archer.*

"Who gave you this, boy?"

"A lady. Downstairs."

Of course, she probably couldn't climb the stairs. Well, if necessary, he'd carry her up. He was more than strong enough, thanks to his labors in the field, to carry one elderly lady up two flights of steps. His exhibition wouldn't be here now without her encouragement during those dark days when nothing went right.

"Want me to tell 'er to come up?" the page asked.

"No, certainly not. A lady of her years? I'll come down." Simon flicked back the hair at his temples and settled his dark coat on his shoulders. He had to stop and straighten his clothing a second time before entering the main floor of the museum. For some reason, which he told himself was mere courtesy, he'd hurried down the flights as though rushing to meet his destiny.

The spacious main floor was rendered rather cold by the shining expanse of marble floor and high ceiling. The sun shone down through a skylight, quite brightly for a change. Of course, Simon always felt slightly chilly in England no matter how enthusiastically the sun consented to shine.

He stood there, looking about him. A group of school-boys in straw-boaters followed a schoolmaster who was admonishing them in a nasal voice not to touch *anything*. Several fashionable ladies sauntered by, attended by several gentlemen who would never take their eyes from so much living beauty to gaze on any antiquity. A decidedly unfashionable lady stood gazing about her as though she had walked by accident into some ancient temple of learning and did not now know what to do with herself. Two scholars, whom he knew by sight, were arguing some esoteric point about Babylonia on their way to tea.

Simon felt puzzled. Had Miss Hanson, exhausted by her journey and the excitements of London, retired to a cloakroom? Certainly there was no one of her age here.

Then two elderly ladies, attired alike in black bombazine, appeared at the far end of the entrance hall. One walked with a stick while the other supported her. The younger was in her fifties, perhaps, while under her lace cap the other woman showed a face lined and seamed enough to have been nearer eighty. This, then, must be Miss Hanson.

With a heart full of happiness, Simon approached more boldly. "Miss Hanson?" he asked with a bow. "I'm Simon Archer."

"What does the gentleman want, Veronica?" the older lady said in a voice that piped like an elderly bird's.

"I don't know, Mother. *Pardon* us!"

Ever more puzzled, Simon stood aside as Veronica hurried her mother away as quickly as possible. From behind him, he heard a little cough. It was the young woman who'd been standing all alone. "I beg your pardon . . ."

"The guards in the rooms are happy to answer any questions the public may pose."

The anticipation on her face faded a trifle. Simon felt ashamed of himself. He supposed even young women were permitted to be curious about the past, though he wished they could do it without continually asking foolish questions. "Pardon me, miss. You wished to ask a question . . . ?"

She had an attractive smile, her full pink lips soft over small white teeth. For the rest, she was rather plain though with a good, smooth skin. Her eyes were gray under slightly too heavy brows. "I was going to ask if you are Mr. Archer? The archaeologist?"

"Yes, I am. But the exhibition of my findings doesn't open until tomorrow."

"I know." She put out a gloved hand as if to stop him when he would have walked away. He hoped she would not turn out to be a tuft hunter, eager for a few words with the celebrity of the hour, but he was afraid she was. Why else would she so boldly accost a total stranger, merely because she'd overheard his name?

He said nothing and once again the brightness of her eyes seemed to dim a trifle as though whatever she expected had not occurred. What did she want from him? He did not have two heads, nor did he have a fund of witticisms that she could quote to her friends when she boasted of having met him. "If you'll excuse me, I must look for someone I'm meeting. . . ."

"Yes, I know. Miss Hanson." Her hand, rather large for a young lady's, fluttered toward herself.

"You know Miss Hanson?"

She nodded, eagerly.

"Where is she?" Simon asked, looking past the young lady, expecting to see his "good genius" standing behind her. "Is she your sister? No, you are too young. Your aunt, perhaps?"

"My aunt, sir, is at home in Yorkshire keeping house, or so I trust, for my father. Besides, her name is Miss Norris. *I* am Miss Hanson."

Two

ᦔ

His first reaction was as rude as it was vehement. "Impossible! You cannot be!"

Julia stepped, or rather staggered, back. "But . . . I am," she said.

Half a dozen people were staring, more or less openly. Veronica and her mother turned completely around to obtain a better look. Simon knew they were whispering about how he'd brutally interrupted them. One of the young men strolling through the museum with the young ladies turned and came back.

He looked Simon up and down as though weighing him. "Is something wrong, miss?" he said, turning to Julia. "Is this . . . person annoying you?"

"Not at all. It's a trifling misunderstanding. Thank you for your trouble."

"A pleasure." The young Galahad's eyes narrowed again as he stared at Simon. Though shorter by half a head than the other man, who was tall enough to be in the Guards, the archaeologist challenged his eyes. He wasn't about to be intimidated by some dim-witted tourist!

After a moment, the interloper turned away, though not

without saying to the girl, "Pray call on me if you require assistance, miss."

When the fellow had stalked away, Simon said firmly, "You cannot be Miss Hanson! It's impossible."

"I promise you, Mr. Archer, I am who I say. I am Miss Julia Hanson of Netherfield Place in Yorkshire."

"Then you are a liar, Miss Hanson."

"You go too far, sir! I can prove what I say is true. Then, I trust, you will make your apology."

Simon turned his head to be certain that a certain overgrown, interfering buffoon did not return as this conversation grew more heated. "If I am wrong, I will certainly tender an apology. But I am not wrong. Every word you have written to me must be a lie."

"Why do you say that?"

He looked at her smooth skin, her bright eyes, and that astonishing mass of hair. "You're a child, that's why. Your letters talked of your long correspondence with the great Champollion. But that's impossible! He died, my dear young lady, in eighteen thirty-two! How old were you then? Eight? Six?"

"If you must know, I was eleven when Monsieur Champollion died—"

"Aha!" Simon's cry of triumph was perhaps louder than he had intended, or the marble surrounding them may well have amplified it. He'd no sooner uttered it than he saw that masterpiece of elephantine gallantry returning.

Simon took Julia by the arm and hurried her away from the main entrance. It gave him great pleasure to take her through a door marked Private, as he closed it in the tree-tall fellow's face. To the girl's protest, he only said, "Hush!"

"I will not. If you have some points to raise, by all means, let us discuss them rationally." She looked back as Simon hurried her onward. "Goodness, what is that in that case?"

"It's the skeleton of a goat. . . ."

"Fancy! I would not have thought it looked like that. Most interesting. You know, Mr. Archer, I was thinking in the coach on the way to town . . ." She dug her heels in as they approached his office. It availed her nothing, and left long, black streaks on the polished wood floor.

When the door was closed behind them, he guided her with perhaps unnecessary strength into a chair. He sat down behind his desk, wishing it were neater. Putting his elbows on the papers, Simon felt more master of the situation. He gazed over the tops of his interlinked fingers at her in silence. It was one of his cardinal rules that a woman abhorred silence and would often convict herself out of her own mouth rather than sit without speaking for ten minutes together. At least, this theory worked well when it was his sisters or mother he had to deal with.

This one had crossed her arms over her not-insignificant bosom and stared at him with narrowed eyes. He noticed that her chin had a determined lift while her nose had a most pugnacious attitude. A more modest young woman would have insisted on his leaving the door ajar, rather than being shut up in a small room with a man she'd yet to meet formally. His sisters, even the silliest, would have shown that much good sense.

Simon decided that she was not only a liar, she was unfeminine. His heart, like Pharaoh's, hardened. "Well?" he said.

"Yes?"

"What do you mean, 'yes'?"

"What do you mean by 'well'?" she asked, imitating his tone even to the rising inflection of his single syllable.

"I mean, what have you to say for yourself?"

A faint, disbelieving smile appeared on her pink lips. "I don't believe that this is a school, nor do you look remotely like a headmistress. I do not believe I need account to you for anything, Mr. Archer."

"You don't deny that you have carried on a correspondence with me in which every word was a lie?"

"I have corresponded with someone calling himself Simon Archer, but I don't think it could have been you. The Simon Archer I know is a scientist, who would never accuse someone of lying without first listening to the facts."

Feeling his conscience prick, Simon leaned back in his chair. "I'm listening."

Her arrogant smile softened as she reached into the small chatelaine bag that hung from her belt. "I am indeed Julia Hanson. I have here your last letter to me, inviting me to come to see your finds."

She handed it across to him. Simon did not need to give it more than a brief glance. "Very well, I accept that you are the woman with whom I have been corresponding. Yet I still feel that our acquaintance is based upon a falsity of your manufacture."

"You are referring to my claim of having exchanged letters with Monsieur Champollion?"

"Yes! Considering that you were eleven years old when he died, I hardly think—"

"I wrote my first letter to him when I was *eight* years of age. He was kind enough to reply. I believe he must have been the kindest man in the world. When he died, I wrote a letter expressing my condolences to his brother, Champollion the elder. He too responded, saying that his brother had written of me. I continue to discuss archae-ological matters with Monsieur Champollion and hope to have that pleasure for many years to come."

Simon was impressed despite himself. "Why did you write to him when you were eight years old?"

"I had read about the Rosetta Stone and wanted to know how he, of all the men in the world, managed to unlock its secrets. He told me. At that time, I had not learned to read the language of the ancient Egyptians and so I immediately set out to learn Greek."

"You were eight and you learned Greek?"

"Yes," she said. "I already knew French, Spanish, and

Latin. Arabic has been quite a struggle as I have had little access to texts. I think once I am physically in Egypt, I shall do better. I didn't become comfortable with it at all until last year."

"So late?" he asked politely, not believing a word.

In elegant language, though with a poor accent, she replied in Arabic, *"Each must do as God wills."* She paused. When he didn't answer, as he felt rather stunned, she said, "You are right; I have left it until late. Champollion himself had mastered the chief Oriental languages by the time he was thirteen and could think in Coptic before he turned eighteen. I do not pretend to be in his class."

"No, few of us can claim that. And the hieroglyphs?"

"I am certain I have written to you about that, Mr. Archer."

"Remind me."

She sighed and shifted in her chair. Simon saw no reason to tell her that every letter they had exchanged was safe in a cabinet not two yards from where she sat. Even blindfolded, he could have pulled out the one in which she described her first fascination with Egypt. But he wanted to hear the tale from her own lips. He still had great difficulty believing that this admittedly vibrant, if irritating, young lady was his "good genius." Sir Walter and Mr. Keene would enjoy a hearty laugh at his expense if the truth came out.

"For my tenth birthday, Monsieur Champollion sent me a beautiful section of illustrated papyrus that he'd purchased in the Cairo bazaar. He did not include a translation of the hieroglyphics. It was a scene of children playing, very sweet." She smiled at the image in her mind. "I wanted to know what they were saying to each other. So I applied Monsieur's methods. After that, he encouraged me to study evermore assiduously. Then he died."

"Most interesting."

It was virtually word for word what she had written.

Yet Simon felt a strange sense of disappointment. When she'd first come forward, her voice had held a lilting warmth that pleased his ear even while his mind processed her impossible claim. Yet now her tone was flat and dry. He wondered if she was saying something she'd memorized.

Now she leaned forward, her large eyes—dark like her hair—intent. "Please, Mr. Archer, you must see that I am who I say. I'm sorry that I surprised you but there was never a point in our letters in which I deceived you intentionally. I think that you thought I was something other than what you see. I'm sorry for that, but it is not my doing."

"I suppose I am exactly as you pictured me?" Simon wanted to recall the words the moment he'd said them. It didn't matter what the young woman thought of him.

Julia blinked. She would not have thought he cared very much what anyone thought of his appearance. His hair had been bleached by the Egyptian sun, making an interesting contrast with his tanned skin. In the north, hardly anyone she knew burned brown, even in the summer. He had straight brows over a slightly humped nose while his lips were as firm as a granite pharaoh's. His blue eyes were hard, too, as he sat behind his desk disbelieving every word she said.

Julia's disappointment was more a nine-tailed sting than a straight stab. If it had been the loss of friendship alone, she might have borne it better. But this was the loss of friendship, possible marriage, and the hope of a life danced to her own piping.

"You forget . . . I have the advantage of having seen a sketch of you in *Punch*."

"Oh, that thing."

It had shown him dressed like a pantomime prince, slipping onto a three-thousand-year-old stage to awaken a princess who owed more to the artist's lurid imagination than Egypt. Like an actress in a recent production of *An-*

tony and Cleopatra, she wore the belling skirt and sleeves of modern dress and about her neck dripped countless ropes of pearls. But Simon Archer had been drawn with great exactness, if slightly larger than life. Even her friends, who couldn't be bothered with a book, had studied that sketch with avid interest.

To tell the truth, so had she. Though she was quite certain that marriage to him was her only way to become part of his research, she had not relished the idea of marrying at all. Somehow the *Punch* sketch had made her plan of marriage to him much more palatable. Now to proceed with it.

"Since we have established that I am indeed Julia Hanson," she said, "I should very much like to see your discoveries."

He did not rise to his feet. "The exhibition isn't quite ready. . . ."

"I don't mind. I'm thrilled that you found so much. Until I reach Egypt myself, seeing artifacts remains my delight."

"You are planning a voyage to Egypt soon, I take it?"

"I hope to." She took her courage in her hands and added, "If you'll have me."

"I?"

"Yes." He definitely did not look overjoyed. Quickly, Julia said, "I believe I can be of great help to you there. You know I can read and draw all one hundred and thirty four phonetic signs and most of the determinative signs. As I said, my Arabic will only improve once it is in my ears every day and I have every confidence that I will learn to speak Coptic quickly."

"But, my dear young lady, you have no idea what life is like out there!"

The moment he called her that, in an odiously patronizing tone, Julia knew she'd lost her first opportunity. Their meeting had been disappointing, but she had believed there was hope. Now she could only gather her pride and courage to try again.

"I have read your letters, Mr. Archer, and many books about the conditions in the field. I know that it is a difficult existence, but—"

"You are flayed by the wind which drives tiny particles of dust into your flesh. Every bite you eat crunches because of the sand—if not because of insects. Flies, snakes, scorpions live everywhere. The water, when you can find it, has been used as a bathing pool, if nothing worse, by the *fellahin*, their camels, and their donkeys. Fever crawls on the ground and flies through the air like a biblical plague."

She'd put on her blandest expression, the one she used when her aunts told her she should give up her dreams and marry some nice young man, halfway through his recital. "I told you, I think, that I have read your letters. You made it quite clear in them that life onsite is hard, but that it also has rewards."

"I did not write everything, Miss Hanson. I did not want to trouble the sweet, elderly lady I thought I was writing to with all the disgusting details. I find people in England have a false picture of life out there anyway. My mother believes that I retire every night to a pleasure boat on the Nile where I am serenaded by beautiful dancing girls. She thinks I eat like a prince because some general told her once that he lived like a fighting cock in the East on sixpence a day."

"You haven't told your mother the truth?"

"Of course not. I have no wish to worry her."

"So you lie to her in your letters the way you lied to me?"

"I have not lied to you. . . ."

"No, you simply softened the truth. Well, I think that's worse than what you say I did to you! At least I did not lie to you. You may have leapt to a false conclusion, but I didn't set out to deceive you deliberately!"

"The two cases are not the same. I should never burden a lady with the full details of a dig! A lady should be indulged, protected, humored if need be. . . ."

"A lady should be treated like a rational person," Julia said coolly.

"Why? You are not rational creatures."

Julia stared at him openmouthed. She blinked at him, feeling like an owl who'd blundered into daylight. "I beg your pardon?"

"Miss Hanson, I have a mother and three sisters. None of them is the remotest bit rational. They have whims, fancies, and need constant guidance. My mother has even attended one of these so-called seances at the residence of this Dr. Mystery despite my assurances that he is a fraud."

"Dr. Mystery. Yes, I saw something about that. You are going there tonight?"

"I am. My intention is to prove absolutely that this 'spirit-guide' . . . this King Rameses-Set he claims visits him . . . is nothing more than a fake, created by him out of bits and pieces of quasi-Egyptian lore and a depraved imagination."

"I'm afraid I know nothing about this. Who is Dr. Mystery?"

"No one knows yet. But I intend to find out. He has challenged me to prove he's a fraud and I will do so tonight. This spiritualism is a pernicious import from the United States of America and is doing great harm among the credulous. My mother is just one of many middle-aged women who have been taken in. She gave him fifty pounds for a message, allegedly from my late father."

"I can understand her temptation," Julia said gently in the face of his evident disgust. "I would give ten times that—a thousand times that—for a genuine word from my mother. She died when I was five. I hardly recall her at all."

The color in his cheeks faded. "I'm sorry. My father

only died five years ago. How I wish he were here now. Mother wouldn't be in this scrape if only *he* were here to watch over her."

For a moment, Julia felt a sense of sympathy with Simon Archer, as she had when reading his letters. They were two of a kind, once past the trappings of their sexes and relative positions in the world. Had she been a man, theirs would have been a friendship to rival the most famous in history. But she was not. The differences between them were as impassable as the Himalayan peaks. For the moment, Julia did not know how to circumvent them. There had to be a way.

She said, "I can only assure you, Mr. Archer, that I am very unlike ordinary girls. I don't scream, faint, or giggle. I don't take a great interest in dress or deportment and find tight lacing and dancing to be equal torture. My heart is given to Egypt. You, of all people, must understand that."

"Yes, I do understand. But as you are a woman . . ."

"As for the difficulties you mention, I admit that they are not on my list of favorite things. However, I am willing to overlook such personal inconveniences and others even less congenial. Every change in circumstances, whether a voyage or, say, a marriage, requires such adjustments. Certainly I would never trouble you with my qualms."

In an utterly shocked tone, he demanded, "Are you proposing to travel to Egypt in my company?"

She felt quite certain that nothing she'd said had improved his opinion, either of her or her sex. Perhaps this was not a good moment to mention that the first three words of his question were the truest. "That is my fondest hope."

"Dismiss it. I would not take you even if you were precisely as I imagined you to be. Egypt is no place for a gently reared Englishwoman."

"My mother was a Scot."

"Regardless." Suddenly, he smiled. A warmth and a humor appeared in his eyes that transformed him from a very good-looking man into one of great attractiveness. He looked younger, more tolerant, and friendly. It was as if the man in the letters had come to life.

He rose from behind his desk and came around to sit on the edge of the crowded surface in front of her. "Miss Hanson, the very idea of a woman being involved in a dig is impossible. On remote sites, such as where I found the tomb of An-ket, one doesn't see a European face for days, sometimes weeks. A young woman might find herself in a very unsavory position without a husband's or father's protection."

"Unfortunately, my father is a wool merchant with very little intention of ever visiting Egypt. If he were in cotton, now . . ."

"And you have no husband in mind?"

She couldn't bring herself to meet his eyes. "One day, I hope . . ."

Simon's chuckle was warm. "There's always some man in the back of a lady's mind, even if she wouldn't admit it on the rack, eh? Is he nice?"

"Sometimes."

"Ah!" He nodded in an odiously sage fashion. "Take my advice, Miss Hanson. We have had a charming correspondence but no man likes the woman he's set his heart on writing letters to another man."

"We are not to write to one another anymore? But how foolish! I may not be the eighty-year-old spinster you imagined, but I am twenty-seven! That makes me practically an antique myself! Certainly everyone at home has long since despaired of my marrying. In short, Mr. Archer, I am on the shelf as thoroughly as . . . as that broken *shabti* up there."

She nodded toward a fragment of limestone on one of a series of shelves stuffed with a variety of objects, most very dusty. Simon stood up, looking toward the shelves.

His hip nudged one thing on his desk, which pushed another, which toppled a pile of small stones. The last thing to fall was a sandwich of glass, a tattered scrap of papyrus sealed up with wax between the two sheets of glass.

With a speed that she blinked to see, Simon jumped to catch the precious casing. In a twisting slide that he must have learned on the rugby field, he succeeded in getting under it, though not without sending a stack of papers fluttering to the floor.

Julia came over to him, stepping carefully among the sheets of paper that covered the floor like a snowstorm. She took the protective glass that Simon handed her. As he stood up, rubbing his hip, she gazed on the faded letters written in brown and red ink. "Sweet sister," she read aloud, charmed as always by the tiny perfection of each symbol. "Sit with thy brother upon the river bank to discuss the exact moment when first we loved. . . ."

Simon stood before her, his hand outstretched, silently demanding the return of the papyrus. She gave it to him with a smile, hoping he'd notice that she'd translated at sight. She said, "I always wonder that they lived a thousand years before Christ and yet their voices are so fresh they might have lived and loved only yesterday."

Despite himself, Simon was impressed. He himself could read hieroglyphics, but not with such an easy familiarity. He'd put off reading this love poem, despite its beauty, because he felt slightly impatient these days with all such soft emotions.

"There's little room for such sentiment in . . ." Simon looked down at the papyrus. There were dozens of symbols yet his glazed vision saw only two sets. "To discuss" was made up of the symbol of an erect phallus over a half loaf of bread, both of which were immediately repeated, followed by a cow's ear. "Exact moment" was very similar. The Egyptians used everything in their natural world to make sure their written language and their drawings were crisply delineated, concealing nothing.

He felt a flood tide of embarrassment stain his cheeks. She apparently felt nothing of the kind. She looked at him with those big, bright eyes that seemed every moment to be asking him some question he could not understand.

Simon tried to force an avuncular tone into a suddenly rasping throat. "You may believe yourself to be beyond the age of marriage, but you are still young enough to be a bride. Take my advice. Go home to Yorkshire. Take an interest in dress and dancing and capture this fortunate man, whoever he is."

"I'm sure that is excellent advice, but I have no intention of taking it. You will see me in Egypt, Mr. Archer, where I am certain to be of great assistance to you, if only in helping you translate your papyrus."

She really had a most determined chin, but he could be determined, too. "No, thank you. I no longer find myself in need of help. I've been applying myself rigorously . . . day and night."

"You're taking my hieroglyphics away?"

"They are not yours, you know."

"Yes, but I . . ."

He laid the glass sandwich that he was hiding behind him on the desktop. "I'm sorry I shan't be able to show you the exhibition today. I must prepare myself for this evening. Would you like me to ask the porter to summon you a cab?"

"Mr. Archer, I—"

"Really, Miss Hanson, I have a great deal to do." He started to herd her toward the door. He slipped around her to hold it open.

"You aren't being very fair. It's not my—"

"Good day, Miss Hanson."

He had never been frightened of a woman before, but something in Miss Hanson's expression made him fear that she would cry. Somehow it hurt him to think that he'd brought tears to those eyes. He was glad to close the door so that he would not see her break down. There was a few moments of silence, in which he could hear his heart beating. Then her footsteps sounded, slowly moving away.

Simon told himself that he was doing the right thing. No young woman's eyes should look upon such things as erect phalli, some in the process of emitting fluids, and women giving birth—the word being the image. It might be too late to restore Miss Hanson's lost bloom, but he would if he could prevent her from coarsening herself with his connivance. Decent Englishwomen had a place in the world and it was not in a camp in the midst of the Egyptian desert. He'd swear to that.

Yet why, then, did he feel so guilty? He felt as though he'd murdered something, if only a dream. It was as well that he would never see Miss Julia Hanson again. She was much too disturbing to his peace of mind.

Three

~

This wing of the museum was not yet twenty years old, the great quadrangle beyond only just more than a plan on paper. Yet already the museum in the heart of the Bloomsbury residential district was stuffed full of the great art of the Western world, as well as a bizarre assortment of things too good to be lost on the rubbish heap of history but hardly classifiable as classical.

It reminded her irresistibly of the home of the dowager countess, Beryl of Haye, right down to the slight smell of must. That lady had left the family seat upon the earl's marriage to a young lady of whom the dowager did not approve. In addition to her personal effects, she insisted on claiming various family heirlooms—the bigger, the better. The earl had not objected, for his bride did not admire antiques. The Dower House was a charming villa set in its own grounds but no room was on the majestic scale that the dowager had been accustomed to dwelling in for the past forty years. The result had been rooms in which one moved sideways, if at all.

Julia had often visited the dowager, seeing in her the kind of gleefully unmanageable old woman that she hoped to become herself. The dowager was one of the few who encouraged her in her dreams. "Egyptology is a ridiculous profession for a woman, but if that is what you want, permit no consideration to prevent you! As for your father, men are trifling creatures, upset by the slightest deviation in routine. It's very good for them."

Perhaps, Julia thought as she maneuvered sideways between two Abyssinian lions, that was what was wrong with Simon Archer. He did not seem to be a man who enjoyed having his ideas shaken out like a mattress. She should have, she now saw, approached him much more obliquely. Rushing straight to her point had been a mistake.

She frowned up at a crack in one lion's waving stone beard. From his letters, he'd seemed so different, like a friend who would understand her. It never occurred to her that he would be so obstinate! Little did he realize that he'd met his match.

A footstep interrupted her musing. Julia froze, sweeping back her skirt so that her outline would not be visible behind the flowing toga of a stone Caesar, eternally addressing the senate from atop a half-column.

The watchman, a portly man who was lamentably pigeon-toed, passed by, the keys at his waist jingling. As he moved across the floor, he passed from square to square formed by the moonlight pouring down through windows very high up in the walls. The grids were in the shape of cutout stars and the pattern decorated the light-colored squares of the floor.

When his footsteps faded, Julia emerged from her haven, giving Caesar's sandaled foot a pat of thanks. The Egyptian antiquities were jumbled into a room of their own slightly farther down the corridor, which was itself packed with relics from every conceivable civilization from a huge copy of Hammurabi's column of laws to glass cases full of tiny ivory carvings from Japan. She passed Byzantine diptychs hung on the wall alongside Persian carpets brilliantly colored but soft to the hand. All of it was magnificent in its own way; none of it moved her.

She turned to enter the room where the Egyptian antiquities were kept. Almost everything here came from the two collections the museum had bought, at a bargain price, from Henry Salt, once British consul in Egypt. One set had been purchased in 1818 for a meager two thousand pounds. The other had come to the museum after Salt's death in 1827. Salt was one of those destructive collectors who seemed to care only for the "biggest," the most "magnificent," and never gave a thought for the damage the removal of the huge granite sphinxes and obelisks caused. But he did have taste.

For a few minutes, Julia wandered in a daze through the large room. Until this moment, the only true antiquities she'd seen had been those few statues and curiosities collected by the late earl on his grand tour. There'd been a small basalt Anubis, looking very much like an alert black border collie, which was here repeated in a statue three times her own size, its ears and collar lit with gold. The earl had owned a crudely carved obelisk, raw when he'd purchased it, hardly thirty years old even now. Dimly in the moonlight, she could see another at the back of the room, thirty centuries old. From the glass cases and from a coffin, the moonlight gently polished gold to a soft shimmer.

Julia laughed softly in the darkness. How right she had been to wait until she was alone to experience this! She pressed her hand to her heart to keep it from bursting from sheer happiness. Then she caught her breath, for she glimpsed something near the entrance that was undoubtedly the most valuable item in all the Department of Natural and Artificial Production.

It was not very interesting to look at. An irregular piece of black basalt, the surface was so covered with writing that it looked gray in some lights, brownish in others. She wished she could see it clearly but had to content herself with running her fingers over the surface.

" 'Ere," a voice said sharply. "Wot you doin'?"

A woman stood in the entrance, holding aloft a lantern muffled by amber glass. The light showed more of her than it could have revealed of Julia. The woman was somewhere between fifty and sixty. Over her shapeless black dress, she wore a reddish shawl pinned tightly up to her throat. She wore broken men's shoes that matched the greasy jockey's cap she wore on her neatly bound hair.

"Who are you?" Julia asked.

"Mrs. Pierce. I do for these deaders."

"Do?"

"Dust abaht. Pick up wot's been dropped by them wot comes to stare. Found me h'ever so many handkerchiefs. Wunst I found me a whole ell of ribbon. Naow, wot's a body want ribbon for in this 'ere room? H'answer me that, iff'n you can."

"I can't imagine. An ell of linen, now, might come in handy."

"I ain't never seen none o'this lot comin' unwrapped," Mrs. Pierce said. "An' it wouldn't be fittin'. This was scarlet ribbon! Made h'ever such a nice trim for my h'eldest's trousseau."

"You have many daughters?"

"Three. An' each one's a 'andful! The h'eldest was the worst—worrit, worrit, worrit every day that comes."

"What does she worry about?"

"Money, that's wot. She married *up*, d'you see? 'E runs a little shop for his dad. Naow she's tryin' t'keep up appearances on frippence a week, nearly. An' a baby's on the . . . 'ere! Who are you?"

"I'm Julia Hanson, Mrs. Pierce. It's a pleasure to meet you."

"Wot you doin' in 'ere so late, dearie? Your mother's bound to be worrying."

"I'm studying these artifacts in the peace and quiet.

And I'm afraid I lost my mother years ago."

Mrs. Pierce clicked her tongue sympathetically. "I know wot that's like, my dearie. 'E weren't much, Mr. Pierce, but he gave me my three luvs afore he went on to his reward. An' he did make for such a luverly funeral. Six plumes we 'ad on the horses. '*Hang* the expense,' I says, 'I'm only burying one 'usband in all me born life and it'll be done h'according to 'oyle,' I says."

"That sentiment does you great credit. If I marry, I'll be sure it's a man about whom I can say the same."

" 'Tis the only way to be 'appy," Mrs. Pierce said with a sniff that was half sentimental, half businesslike. "Well, I best get on with it." Behind her trundled a little wagon, such as children use to play 'farm.' A bucket of water slopped as she pulled it forward, while a scrub brush slipped around the inside.

"I alus says there's nothin' amiss with old images as we got 'ere that a mite of Glee's soap and a good scrubbing wouldn't cure. But them wot pays me wages won't let me do nothin' 'ere but dust. Fair goes to me 'eart to see wot a shockin' condition some of 'em are in."

Thinking of Simon, Julia said, "I imagine some of the men who run the museum could do with a good dusting themselves!"

Mrs. Pierce gave an unexpectedly girlish giggle. " 'At's right. Fair musty, some of 'em. Some of 'em are awright, I must say. Dr. H'archer, f'r instance. Gave me a whole 'arf crawn—last year abaht this time o' year."

"He returns from Egypt every May."

"You know 'im, then?"

"Yes. I've been corresponding with him for several years."

"Coo, 'e's an 'andsome one, h'ain't he?"

"I hadn't noticed," Julia lied with a sniff.

"You need specs, miss? 'E reminds me o'some of these 'eathen images; not this lot," she said with rather a dismissive glance at the Egyptians. "But that bunch o' Romans in the 'all. 'Specially them wot wears that fancy h'armor."

Julia said, "I really can't see the resemblance."

"Oh, well. Funny you being 'ere so late. Kinder nice to 'ave somebody to talk to. This lot don't say much." While she spoke, she was flicking her dustcloth over the cases that held faience and alabaster beads. "Tawdry stuff," she said. "I much prefer that lot o' pretties over there. Them gold 'uns. She must 'a' been a one, eh?"

"You mean An-ket?"

"Don't know 'er name, but you h'only gots to look at 'er to know wot I mean."

Mrs. Pierce carried the lantern over to the golden coffin that lay in the place of honor on a long plinth in the middle of the floor. Her death mask was inlaid in colored stones, smiling carnelian lips, bright obsidian eyes and brows, the eyes outlined as in life with broad black bands against the broiling Egyptian sun. The contours of her face were smooth, not as if the metal had been beaten into shape with hammers, but as though it had been formed and softened by countless strokes of a loving hand.

"Spoilt!" Mrs. Pierce pronounced. "My neighbor's girl, wot lived in the next street, 'ad just the same smile. 'Wot h'ever I wants, I gets,' she used ter say. 'Er mother couldn't keep 'er in line, bless my soul, no! But didn't the menfolk just flock 'round."

"What happened to her?" Julia asked.

Mrs. Pierce lowered her voice to a confidential register, despite the fact that nobody in the room had been able to overhear a conversation for approximately three thousand years. "Abaht two years ago, she gets 'erself a position as a dresser to an h'actress at Covent Garden."

"That must have been a great opportunity for her."

"You h'ain't from Lunnon, are you, dearie?"

"No, Mrs. Pierce. I only just arrived from York."

"York?" She might have been trying to remember if it were part of the British Empire or not.

"It's away north," Julia said before she could stop herself, and then grinned.

"Oh, there! Well, ordinarily I wouldn't say nothin' to an *h'unmarried* gel, it not being fit, but I alus says, 'forewarned is forearmed' and a gel's got to be wise to h'every rig in town if she's to get on. Maisie makes 'erself some gentlemen friends—'ow we will not lower h'ourselves to wondering! Next fing you knows she's gorn off and changed 'er name. Maisie Linstock was good enough for her mother, but not for 'er! Mind, I don't say she don't send money 'ome regular, but I'd not live on me daughter, not gettin' 'er money *that* way."

"What way?"

Mrs. Pierce pressed one finger to her lips. "She's on the stage. . . ."

"No!"

"As Gawd's me witness! An' this one 'ere might 'a' been a-lyin' in 'er box since Jesus went fishing, but you can tell she's just another o' the same."

"Actually, she lived at least a thousand years before Christ."

"Wot's that?"

"According to Mr. Archer's preliminary studies, of course. He might have to adjust the date when more information comes in."

"Ain't it written on the h'outside? Looks like a patent medicine bottle with all them symbols on it. 'None genuwine without this label,' like they say."

"No one has had time as yet to translate every inch of those hieroglyphics, Mrs. Pierce. But you see this rectangular box here, just below the enfolding wings?" She pointed, her finger hesitating above the symbols. "We know that's her name—An-ket—and that she was at least a sometime priestess of the goddess Hathor."

"Who was she, then?"

"She protected maidens, helped women in childbed, and was the most popular goddess if the number of representations is anything to judge by. She's there on An-ket's breast. The woman with the head and horns of a cow."

"A cow? That's a queer 'un!"

"To us, perhaps, used to a god who made us in his image, but the Egyptians had hawk-headed gods, and ibis-headed gods, and jackal-headed . . . that's Anubis, patron of embalming and the dead."

"I alus wondered why they 'ad that big ol' dog there. . . ."

Suddenly the char's shoe-button eyes turned away from the antiquities and she said, "Hist! Quiet!"

"What is it?" Julia asked, softly obedient. She thought of the watchman and looked toward the big opening in the wall. She hadn't remembered about him and had been talking in her usual tone.

"Somethin's not right," Mrs. Pierce said. "Didja 'ear a funny noise just then?"

"No. I couldn't hear anything but my own voice."

"T'weren't nothing, I guess. My nerves 'ave been on the jump that bad lately."

"Have they? Why?"

The older woman gave a wriggle that in France would have won plaudits as a thoroughly expressive shrug. "I h'ain't been wot you might call 'appy, since me oldest went off to get married. Seems like I can't turn my 'and to h'anything without it fretting me. Gettin' old, I 'spect."

"How long have you worked at the museum?"

"Nigh on thirty years."

"But this wing has only been opened . . . oh, you worked in Montague House as well."

"Still do, miss. I goes there first. Coo, them books want a lot o' dusting! Then I comes 'ere to do—"

A sudden crash made them both look up. Above them, a head and shoulders stood out against the moonlight, framed in the opening of one of the small windows. The star-shaped grid that should have been there had vanished.

A moment later, supple as a snake, the rest of the man's body followed. Mrs. Pierce drew breath as if to scream. Something long and silver flashed in the intruder's hand.

"Sharrup! One little sound and the tart gets it!"

Mrs. Pierce made only a strangled sound in her throat.

A rope spiraled down, weighted on one end. A moment later, the man, thin and wiry, followed. "Don't move a muscle, either of you, or you'll get my shiny friend in the back!"

"Can't you see we're obeying you?" Julia demanded. "There's no need for further threats."

"Ooh, well, pahdon me, yer 'ighness," he said, dropping to all fours on the floor. He looked like a gaunt spider, dressed totally in black, from his close-fitting cap to his black socks. In an instant, however, he stood upright once more, his motions as lithe as an acrobat.

He wore no shoes, only soft slippers. His pale face was thin and his smile good-humored, but the dark emptiness in his eyes chilled her. The glance he flicked over them stung with contempt. He obviously felt that he had them adequately cowed with his threats. Searching her spirit, Julia hated to learn that he had in fact done so.

"Who are you?" she demanded. "What do you want?"

"Never you mind. I'll just takes what I wants and be on me way. You never seen me; I never seen you. You let me 'ave ten minutes to make my escape and you can scream the place down wit' my blessin'."

"Wot you want?" Mrs. Pierce asked. "Wot's that?"

"Just goin' to prig these beauties. . . ." He reversed his heavy steel knife to smash the glass case with the hilt. Julia saw that he had tied it around with a padded cloth, and the breakage made surprisingly little noise.

A cold wind came sliding down through the broken window above them, bringing a metallic taste of ozone. Somewhere in the London night, thunder sounded. The thief knocked the jagged remains of the broken glass into the case.

"No!" she said, and he looked over his shoulder at her in surprise. "You can't steal those."

"An' whose going ter stop me, I'd like to know." He reached in to scoop up the heavy golden armlets. "Lovely workmanship," he cooed. "Pity it'll all be gorn by to-morrer."

"Gorn?" Julia echoed.

"No good to me like this. Too well-know. Melt it down and the fence'll give me the price. . . ."

"No!" Julia said again and walked resolutely forward. Lightning flashed, overpowering the lantern, followed by a rumble of thunder very close on its heels. The rain had not yet begun to fall from the faintly yellow clouds. "These things are worth a thousand times more in knowledge than in their base metal. Please . . . you mustn't . . ."

He spun about and waved the knife before her eyes. "You shouldn't never say 'no' to Billy the Wall. They're alus sayin' it, women. They got to learn, don't they?"

"She don't mean it," Mrs. Pierce said, in a quick, panicky tone. "She's quality, she is."

"Quality, eh? Never had me no quality woman, 'cept wunst when I was still a climbin' boy. Crawled down 'er chimbley, I did. Furst time I ever 'ad me a woman in a proper bed. Seventeen, she was. Cried somefing fierce." His lips turned up in a reminiscent smile that looked nothing like a human smile at all. It was as much as the sacred crocodiles of the Nile must have grinned just at feeding time. "Pity there h'ain't no bed 'ere. Still . . ."

Julia had been blinking at the horror before her in blank disbelief. From her childhood, she'd been the adored object of servants and her father. Thanks to her intellect alone, she'd not turned out to be a pampered brat, like Mrs. Pierce's neighbor's child. Early on, she had learned that she could only be happy if she gave love back as fully and as freely as she received it. Never had she come face-to-face with hatred; she saw it now on the face of the man before her.

Slowly, he raised the knife so that the lamplight glittered all along the blade. "Do wot I says, or I'll cut yer. Just a little bit at a time until you're 'appy to 'ave me touch you."

Mrs. Pierce gasped, her voice a thread of sound, "Oh, no . . . no."

Julia faced the knife and the hatred, asking herself what kind of scientist she would be if she gave in to his demands. His words crawled over her mind but she shook them away. If she lived life as she wanted to, she might face knives and hatred any number of times. Certainly far more often than some sedately married *normal* woman ever would. If she failed now, then she might as well give up her dreams for good and retreat into the life everyone said should be hers.

The wind flapped the women's skirts, tugged at the slightest looseness in the mummy wrappings, while livid lightning forked through the sky. For a moment, as Julia raised her head to look Billy the Wall in the eyes, the storm died.

Julia faced the burglar and said, "No. I'm not going to permit you to do anything to me."

"Wot?"

"And you're not taking the antiquities, either. They belong to history."

She read only blank incomprehension on his rather grimy face. Then the sound of the word "no" must have penetrated. He snarled and raised the knife high, ready to bring it slashing down into the breast of the woman who defied him.

Then lightning, ever seeking its counterpart, sizzled and struck the upraised knife. The reek of burning flesh filled the air and she heard Mrs. Pierce's scream. Just before she lost consciousness, Julia heard a voice say, "Behold! The Devourer of Souls shall have him!"

And she knew, as the world rushed away through a black tunnel, that the speech was ancient Egyptian. . . .

Four

Julia knew that she ought to be very, very dead. She recalled hearing a story of a shepherd, caught out in a fierce thundershower with his flock. Not only had the man been killed, but so had many of his sheep, lying in a circle around him, like a warrior surrounded by his slain enemies. The man who'd told her father the tale had said that he'd never forgotten the sight, for not one of the animals had been burned or scorched. They'd simply fallen in their tracks, whereas their shepherd had been horridly burned.

Yet except for her ears, which still seemed to ring with the sound of that triumphant voice, she was unhurt. Nevertheless, she couldn't help groaning a bit as she strove to stand up. Her skirt had skewed around her until she felt like a closed umbrella.

A grayish greasy fog stung her eyes, but the fresh air through the broken window seemed to be dispelling it rapidly. The thunderstorm—if that is what it had been— no longer rumbled outside. Raising her head, she could see a few remote stars twinkling in the opening.

Remembering Mrs. Pierce, Julia looked around for her. She found the charwoman lying flat on her back, one arm at her side, the other thrown across her bosom. Kneeling beside her, Julia reached for the other woman's pulse. The relief she felt when the slow beat moved under her fingers was like a prayer.

The older woman's eyes opened. She seemed dazed. Julia smiled down on her and said with forced cheer, "Well! That doesn't happen every day! Are you unhurt?"

After a moment, Mrs. Pierce made a movement as though she'd like to get up. Julia helped raise her to her feet. Her cap was askew and she straightened it with an automatic push.

Julia said, "I wonder what happened to Billy the Wall? I saw him . . . I *think* I saw him being struck, though I can't imagine why we are not dead if he was."

Mrs. Pierce pointed to the foot of An-Ket's coffin. A black mark marred the white marble floor. Julia was reminded of Guy Fawkes Day. Just such outflung half-circles of sooty grime were left behind when the boys set off fireworks on the ground. But looking at this mark gave Julia something of a chill that could not be explained by the wind through the window.

She felt instinctively that she looked at all that remained of Billy the Wall. Judging him on the evidence of his own words, it was probably no less than he deserved. Yet when had Justice ever overtaken an evildoer so swiftly? Julia was very grateful to whatever had annihilated Billy before he could carry out his threat, yet she felt unnerved by the speed of the service.

"Behold," she repeated softly, in English. "The Devourer of Souls has him. May God have mercy upon him."

She expected to hear "Coo, 'o's that, then?" but Mrs. Pierce said nothing. This struck Julia as unusual. Mrs. Pierce had not seemed like someone to whom silence was a virtue.

"Are you sure you're not hurt?" Julia asked. She had to touch Mrs. Pierce's arm before her eyes, focused on something in the middle distance, turned to her.

Mrs. Pierce spoke, in a deep yet female voice that was

oddly attractive. The sounds were swift and liquid, like water coursing through a dusty land. Julia couldn't understand a word, nor the suddenly graceful gestures of Mrs. Pierce's reddened hands, though they certainly seemed to have meaning for the maker.

When Julia raised her own hands in a gesture of incomprehension, Mrs. Pierce's lips tightened. She stamped her foot with frustration, then bent to look down at her shoe. From her expression, Julia would have thought the charwoman had never seen a sturdy lace-up boot before. A moment later, she was plucking at her blouse, rubbing the backs of her hands, and tugging down a lock of hair as if to study its mousy color.

Julia said, in some alarm, "Mrs. Pierce? Perhaps we should find you a doctor. I can't imagine where that watchman has gotten to. I could send him for somebody."

Very slowly, as though she were speaking to a child, Mrs. Pierce enunciated some words. They caught in Julia's mind the way furze bushes caught at her clothes on long walks. It was not Arabic, though the inflection was not dissimilar. Nor was it any of the other languages she knew, and yet it had a familiar ring. She looked from Mrs. Pierce to the bent triangle of the Rosetta Stone.

In the few halting words of conversational Coptic that she knew, Julia said, "I salute you and wish you joy."

At first there was no reaction. Julia knew her accent was poor, for she'd only read the modern equivalent of ancient Egyptian; she'd never heard it spoken aloud. But then a brilliant smile broke out on Mrs. Pierce's face, yet Julia knew somehow that she no longer looked upon the charwoman.

"Joy to you, daughter of Osiris. Is this the West?"

Julia did not know how to answer that. "The West" was where the Egyptians believed the spirits of the dead dwelt after their acceptance through trial into the afterlife. But how to explain that, while London was west of Egypt, there was little here to remind a woman of the Fields of

the Sun where the dead enjoyed again the splendors of
life?

Before she could frame an answer given her limited
vocabulary, Mrs. Pierce had turned to study the artifacts
that surrounded them. Julia noticed that the woman's
bearing had undergone a change. The stooped shoulders
and dragging gait of the work-burdened charwoman had
fallen from her. She stood tall and straight, stepping out
with a bold stride. Julia's spine tingled, telling her the
truth, even while her doubting mind wondered.

"Mrs. Pierce" showed polite interest in everything, but
when she reached the coffin of An-ket, her smile broke
out again. She pointed to the coffin and then, unmistakably, to herself.

"You . . . you are An-ket," Julia said in English.

"An-ket-en-re," she corrected.

Translating mentally into picture-writing, Julia decided
that it meant "Embraced by Re," or "Beloved of the Sun."
She wished her own name was as pretty.

The woman stood by her coffin, her head down as
though in prayer. Julia respected that, though she found
it hard to stand still. A thousand questions were leaping
in her thoughts. If it could only be true . . . But her native
caution spoke as loudly as her excitement.

Perhaps Mrs. Pierce's brain had been turned by the
lightning. Perhaps after thirty years of dusting artifacts,
some of their history had rubbed off. Perhaps it wasn't
Mrs. Pierce's brain that had turned, but her own. In all
likelihood, she still lay unconscious on the floor and this
was all some elaborate dream. Or her aunt was finally
right and all her learning had indeed made her mad.

An-ket caught sight of the statue of Anubis looming
above her, his black coat blending with the gloom of the
chamber. She made a peculiarly graceful gesture, her hand
raised before her face. Julia was reminded of the Arab
motion of greeting, hand to forehead, hand to lips, hand

to breast, that had been described in so many of the travel journals she devoured.

After a moment, An-ket crossed the room to stand before a statue of ibis-headed Thoth, which Julia had not taken notice of before. It was not a particularly large statue and no gold clung to its ebony surface. Again, "An-ket" stood in silent prayer before the statue.

Then she turned and faced Julia. "I've asked the Lord of the Underworld and He Who Is Wise for their 'elp, as promised in the *Book of Life*. They 'ave given me the power of your tongue, strange though it tastes in my mouth." The voice was part Mrs. Pierce's uneducated English and part the unconscious grandeur of a high-born priestess.

"I am grateful to them," Julia answered.

"You are not, I think, of The Land of the Field of Reeds?"

"I'm a living person, my lady." Somehow it seemed right, in this topsy-turvy dream, to call her that.

"That is true, for why should the Great Cow save you if you were but a thing made to serve?"

"I beg your pardon?"

Again, An-ket pointed to the dirty spot on the floor. "The Great Cow Who Nourishes the Land with Her Milk destroyed that one who menaced you. Great is her name and her glory forever!"

"I give thanks to Hathor and to you, her priestess," Julia said politely.

The priestess frowned. "You must be 'igh indeed in the ranks of 'er worshipers to use 'er name so freely."

"Pardon my ignorance, my lady. I . . . I am new to the ways of the gods."

"An initiate? Ah, from the country, no doubt."

Apparently it was not proper for even a god's servants to use their proper names in casual conversation. What a coup! So little was known about the life and customs of the ancient Egyptians that even so meager a scrap of information as this made Julia breathe faster.

She tried to gain control over her galloping thoughts. What questions should she ask first? There were so many gaps to be filled in! What would Simon Archer ask, if he were here?

The thought of Simon's skepticism steadied her. He would have no hesitation in declaring this episode the dream of a madwoman. Surreptitiously, Julia pinched herself, quite hard. She did not awaken.

Almost without her being aware of it, an idea took possession of her mind. If she went to Simon now, with Mrs. Pierce speaking in the voice of An-ket herself, what would he say? For a moment, she indulged in the fantasy of his excitement, his delight. But she knew perfectly well that he'd dismiss both An-ket and her at once, most likely without even hearing them. Hadn't he an appointment tonight to disprove a spiritualist's similar claim of bringing the voices of the dead to the living?

While she strove to ask a question, An-ket stooped to pick up the lantern. "What is this? A torch without smoke?"

"It's a candle. It smokes, but very little. What do you use for light?"

"Oil lamps. Why have you only one light in all this great temple?"

"It is night. The museum . . . the temple is closed."

"Which of these gods does it honor?"

Julia had not imagined that she would be answering more questions than she would ask. "It is a place dedicated to knowledge of all kinds."

"Then it belongs to He Who is Scribe to the Gods."

Julia thought *Thoth* but did not say it. "I suppose he has as much claim here as anyone. In this place is more than the wisdom and gifts of Egypt, but galleries devoted to every great kingdom."

"Only the Upper and the Lower Kingdoms can be

called great. All else is barbarity—excepting miraculous Punt."

"Ah . . . Punt?"

"You are an ignorant child! Come . . . show me these galleries. I will judge their worth."

"In a moment, my lady." The kindly face of Mrs. Pierce, now owned by a stronger will, frowned again, but Julia dunked the scrub brush and brought it dripping over to the spot at the foot of the coffin. Though her skin crawled at the thought of touching the only evidence left of Billy the Wall, she couldn't very well leave it.

An-ket's frown cleared. "It is fit you should purify the temple. I will 'elp with a prayer." She raised her arms. "Lady of the Heavens, Mother of Horus, thou art justified against 'im who sought to 'arm thy servant. Thine enemy is thrown down and unmade. Let none stand against thee. I, thy faithful one, declare thy power!"

The mark came up more quickly than Julia would have believed possible. There seemed to be no permanent damage to the smooth floor. She only wished she had a journal by her in order to write down the precise wording of An-ket's prayer. Memory was too unreliable. Even now, the words seemed to be fading away like a soft perfume.

As she stood up, she felt her head spin and a queer feeling settled on her limbs, so that she could not tell if she was standing firm on the ground or not. In that spinning moment, she didn't know whether An-ket had found her way to modern-day Britain, or if she herself had somehow traveled into the past. The otherworldly statues above her, the difficulty of belief, and above all a lack of sleep and decent food combined to give her a feeling of being detached from everything she knew about the world. If An-ket really *were* An-ket, then all Julia's notions about how the world worked would have to be reconsidered.

After feeling as though she'd walked off a carousel following a few too many revolutions, Julia found her equilibrium again. Whether temporary insanity, spiritualism, or fantasy, she owed it to Egyptology to treat this as reality, on the admittedly off-chance that it was real. A greater opportunity to learn could not be imagined—a fig for what Simon Archer might say!

As she followed An-ket to the exit, Julia asked, "Who is pharaoh in your time, my lady?"

"In *my* time. What do you mean? Are not all times one?" An-ket smiled, with a warmth and humor that made Mrs. Pierce's gapped teeth charming. "Yet to answer you, innocent one, I say Kheper-ka-re, son of the Great God Sehetep-ib-re."

The names meant nothing to Julia. Selfishly, she'd wanted to hear "Ramesses the Second" or "Ptolemy the Thirteenth," some king the reign of whom she knew something already. To add to the knowledge about the pharaoh who had spoken with Moses or Julius Caesar would be the fulfillment of her dearest dreams.

She must try to pin down the time of this pharaoh. She sought to frame her next question when someone else asked a question instead.

"What the de'il's going on here?"

The watchman, elderly but still burly, raised his lantern high, holding a knobby stick threateningly high in the other. A waft of alcohol came toward them. On a hiccup, he said, "Is it you, then, ma'am? Who's that with you?"

An-ket paused, glancing over her shoulder at Julia. There was marvelous grace in her pose, as though she stepped down from the frieze around a tomb's inner wall. Her nineteenth-century clothing was immaterial. "Is this another dangerous man?" she asked.

"No," Julia whispered. "He's the . . . the guardian of this place."

"Ah! Peace and 'ealth to thee, my friend."

"Eh?" The watchman looked closely at her, leaned unsteadily nearer yet and sniffed her breath. "You been havin' a wee dram, Roberta?"

Julia said hurriedly, "Mrs. Pierce isn't . . . isn't herself. I'll see to it that she goes straight home."

"An' who might you be, miss? I don't recall lettin' you in here. This is a museum, you know, not the Wayfarer's Rest. I think you'd better come wi' me down to my . . ." He peered past the two women into the room of relics. Dropping his stick, he ran into the room. "How did that window come to be open? What's all this glass . . . ?" There was a sob in his voice. "Never say there's been a robbery?"

Julia didn't want to stay to face the questions that would be asked once the constabulary was called in. She took An-ket by the arm. "We have to leave," she said firmly.

"Very well. Let us bid farewell—"

"No. Now."

"It seems discourteous."

"He won't mind. Come along."

Julia had trouble hurrying An-ket. With her graceful stride, she seemed incapable of going any faster. That, plus her interest in the objects they passed in the near darkness, sent Julia's blood pounding from anxiety. At any instant she expected to hear the watchman cry out for the police. They wouldn't find anything missing, of course, but the whole affair looked suspicious.

Outside the museum the street was quiet, though from somewhere not too far away came the sound of music and laughter. Someone in Bloomsbury besides themselves was having a late night. The trees cast deep shadows over the wetly gleaming streets. On the corner across from the museum, a large scaffolding arose—the framework of a new hotel.

An-ket turned her head from side to side. "What city is this? It is not Thebes."

"No, it's London."

"I know not London. Is it in the South?"

"It's a thousand miles west of Thebes."

"Ah, so this *is* the West."

"No, not the way you mean. It's a city like Thebes or Memphis, but newer. My country is England, as yours was Egypt."

"Was? For the second time, my child, you speak of my life as though it were in the past."

"What do you remember?" Julia wanted to know now not merely because of her own interest but because she could only imagine how she would feel waking up two thousand years after she fell asleep. What would the world be like then? She thought about St. Thomas More's *Utopia* but wondered if mankind would change so much. How much difference was there really between her and An-ket when it came to the deepest fundamentals?

"I remember the heat of the day," An-ket said, tugging at the shawl she wore. "The pure shining gold of the god as he rose above the desert on his journey through the sky. The lapis pool that reflected the statue of my goddess was warmed by his loving touch. And when the night came, how brilliant the stars above the Red Land!"

"Yes." Julia sighed. "That is how I see it in my dreams."

She looked up at the sky, dim and shifting with smoke. "We are much farther north than Egypt. It is colder here. Even now in summer, we use fires to warm our houses."

"Why do you not all move to where the Sun God is more kindly disposed?"

"Many of us do. England owns a great empire, my lady, from the Indus to the Atlantic Ocean. It stretches farther than Alexander the Great's."

"Who is he? A rival king?"

Well, Julia thought, *that is one clue.* An-ket lived before Alexander conquered so much of the pre-Roman world and became pharaoh himself, briefly.

They had walked, unknowingly, in the direction of the music. Now An-ket stopped to listen, smiling. "What a pleasant sound."

"It's just singing and a violin."

"The people must be happy."

"They do sound as if they are having a good time."

The music came from a public house. The frosted glass windows showed them only shadows moving on the inside, lit by the flickering yet continuing glow of the gas lamps.

"This is a place of drinking?"

"Yes, you can buy beer in there."

"Beer?" A thirsty gleam came into An-ket's eyes.

Julia recalled that most authorities were unanimous in agreeing that the Egyptian's main drink was a sort of sour beer, ill-filtered and, of course, without the necessary hops, which had been a late English addition to the brew. She herself had never stepped foot inside a public house, but she had grown accustomed to the taste of cider during the past few harvest festivals.

"I suppose there's no harm in going in," she said hesitatingly and found herself following An-ket.

Perhaps it was the yeasty odors of ale and apple cider that made Simon Archer look at them so strangely when they arrived an hour later at Dr. Mystery's residence.

Five

‿

Simon felt like a kettle coming to the boil. He could almost feel little spurts of steam escaping him, so he sat in the large, semidarkened room and kept his lips tightly shut. There'd been a lot of chatter from "Dr. Mystery" about waiting for the hour of midnight to begin his hocus-pocus, but Simon felt strongly that he was only waiting until the people in the room had reached the proper level of receptivity.

They were a mixed bag at best. Several were women. Two who had come in alone wore the mourning of recent bereavement and spoke only to each other, and then in whispers. Two others sat with their obviously disapproving brother, Mr. and the Misses Cross. As the hours passed, Mr. Cross went from being very much on his dignity to the schoolboy he'd probably been no later than last year. His sisters had begun by giggling and addressing such remarks as "isn't it *exciting*" to everyone whether they knew them or not. Now they sat close together, holding hands, and showing the whites of their eyes.

The men ranged from Mr. Cross to a retired admiral. One man wore a rather loud checked suit, while yet another looked like a banker in a stiff collar. A third was second cousin to an earl while his friend was engaged to the earl's daughter. One thing all the people—with three exceptions—had in common was that they smelled of money. Simon was too well acquainted with rich men, from whom he had in the past begged money to continue his excavations, to be deceived. Dr. Mystery had hooked some large and opulent fish.

The three exceptions were the members of the press. The fellow sitting closest to Simon had introduced himself as "Wilson, of the *Standard*." Clyde, of the *Record*, had a beard, while Partridge, of the *Morning Intelligencer* kept reaching for his cigar case, glancing at the women, and putting it back.

"What are you going to do here tonight, Professor?" Wilson had asked. "Ask this ghostie what goes on in Hades?"

"I want first to discover what method Dr. Mystery uses to 'call spirits from the vasty deep.' I have made an extensive study of Egyptian magical beliefs. I doubt Dr. Mystery has."

Wilson wrote that down. "That call spirits line is clever, Professor. You ever dabble with writing?"

Clyde had given Wilson a nudge and muttered "Shakespeare." Wilson nodded. "You like Shakespeare, Professor? Hey, what did you think of that play . . . er . . . *Antony and Sheba*? I'm in line for drama critic. Snuggest position on the paper. Going to plays and writing 'em up. What a doddle."

Simon tried not to laugh in the man's face. "I'm sure you'll shine there as a leading light of literary criticism."

Wilson poked Simon with the point of his pencil. "You're a grand chap, Professor. I'll tell you plainly—we of the press were planning to row you a bit on this spiritualism business."

"Row me?"

"You know . . . eminent professor chasing after spook doctor. We were going to show the funny side, hand the shopkeepers and the chambermaids a laugh at the doings of their betters. But don't you worry. The *Standard*'ll give you fair play and these other fellows'll follow my lead."

Clyde nodded while Partridge shrugged. "I'd rather make the professor hero of the day than this Dr. Mystery fellow. He gives me the feeling my grandfather used to get."

"What feeling is that?" Simon asked.

"The feeling he'd like a drink. Dusty as the grave in here. Don't suppose any of you fellows thought to bring a flask?"

Simon hesitated for a moment and then reached inside his coat. "I always carry spirits in case of emergency."

"Well, this is one." With a glance at the others in the room, Clyde took a quick drink. "That's the dandy. No doubt about *your* write-up, Professor. Here, Partridge."

The newspaper reporters all drank, once for their thirst and another for good luck. Simon did not drink. He wanted all his senses at their sharpest when Dr. Mystery began to play his tricks.

He'd no sooner slipped the flask into his pocket again when the clock on the impressively carved mantelpiece sounded the single stroke of the quarter-hour. One of the Misses Cross gave a gasp that was like a shriek cut off in the moment of beginning. The general cleared his throat grumpily. "Remarkable chap, but does like to keep people waiting."

Simon scented the faintest aroma floating on the air. He glanced about him casually. The room was lit mostly by the light of fat white candles, but a small fire burned as well. The ladies had at first complained of the stuffiness of the room but soon forgot their discomfort in favor of impatience. Now, glancing at the fire, Simon saw that a small cone of some kind of powder had built up on the foremost log. A little more sifted down from inside the chimney. Had the striking of the clock released some mechanism that caused the powder to fall? Was this the real reason Dr. Mystery waited until midnight to perform?

He walked to the fireplace. The scent was stronger here. It was familiar—all too familiar. He knew that certain drugs were smoked in the cafes of the East that were illegal or ill thought of in England. Living among the Arabs, he'd grown used to the smell of *kif,* a mild narcotic smoked in their hours of leisure. He'd smoked it himself once or twice when he could not avoid it without giving offense. He could not be mistaken in it now.

Returning to his place, he looked about him. The women in weeds had ceased to look mournful. One leaned back against her chair, smiling faintly, while the other looked half asleep. The Cross sisters leaned ever more heavily on one another, and their brother's face relaxed into easygoing stupidity. The press was in no more alert frame of mind.

Then Dr. Mystery was among them. Even Simon, who forced himself to stay alert by pinching his thigh, had not noticed his entrance, so that his sudden appearance had the effect of magic. The quite relaxed audience forced themselves to sit upright again, lifting heavy eyelids in an attempt to look attentive.

"Good evening, dear friends. Come to the table where all are equal, all are mere seekers after Truth."

Large doors on the far side of the room suddenly opened, showing them an even darker room beyond. A round table, lit with a single candelabra, stood in the center surrounded by chairs. One lonely candle burned at the head of the table. There was also a strange, square box with a small window inset on one side.

Dr. Mystery, a youngish man rather on the thin side, held out his hand as Simon began to pass in. "Greetings to you, especially, Mr. Archer. I know your purpose in coming here tonight."

"So does half of England," Simon said coolly.

"Yes, of course. I meant no imputation of clairvoyance." Dr. Mystery had a charming smile between his small mustache and tuft of beard. These, together with the

pomade that sleeked back his heavy dark hair, marked him
as something apart from the general run of Englishmen.
Yet one could overlook these personal idiosyncrasies once
under the power of his voice.

It was his voice that must inevitably make him his fortune. It was smooth and even, as comforting as the sound
of a small brook running past a cool green bank. There
was even a chuckle in it, friendly and likable. One might
follow such a brook down to the sea, never noticing when
it became a mighty current taking control of one's simple
barque.

Simon said, "I'm keeping an open mind."

"That's not quite true, is it? You hope you will convince these good people and indeed the rest of England—"

"I'm even more ambitious than that," Simon said
blandly. For an instant he saw the snap of something fanatical in Dr. Mystery's dark eyes.

But he went on smiling and whatever he felt made no
eddy in his trickling voice. "In the eyes of the world, then,
you wish to expose me as a fraud. You will not succeed.
I am no fraud. I have the power to bring Pharaoh before
you. Ask him what you will. He will answer you truthfully. There is nothing but Truth in the room beyond.
Believe me."

Everyone was waiting for them in the "room beyond"
but they displayed no signs of impatience. Simon knew
this was the drug acting on them. To someone under its
influence, with just that much of their natural doubts quieted, and their own desire to believe working in them, Dr.
Mystery's voice would have a powerful effect even without the appearance of apparitions. Whatever trickery he
had planned would seem all the more real to victims with
senses too dull to notice inconsistencies.

Fortunately the only effect *kif* had on Simon was to
give him a raging headache.

By holding him at the door, Dr. Mystery could be certain that the seats nearest to himself were already taken. Simon made do at the farthest end from Mystery.

"For those of you who have not attended one of our meetings before, permit me to explain the few simple rules I have created to make our experiments less dangerous." The Cross sisters looked worried. "Please," Dr. Mystery said with a wave of his hand. "Don't be alarmed. There is no physical danger. The spirits want only to communicate with us. The only time there is any possibility of danger is if someone among us panics when the manifestations begin."

He touched the polished wooden box on the table. "This is my invention. Notice that there is a small indicator needle inside this window. If the power of the spirits grows to a dangerous level, the needle will move to the right, into the range marked in red. If that happens, a little bell will ring. That will be our signal to stop until the level of psychic energy drops again. Will you be so kind as to keep your eye upon the needle?"

Miss Cross was eager and reached out for the box. "Ah!" Dr. Mystery said, charmingly admonishing her. "Please don't touch. It is attuned to my level. If you touch it, it will change the readings and it is a very finicky thing to put right." He placed it within eight inches of the edge of the table. To the other guests, he said, "Please hold hands with your neighbors. This is for your own protection as well as to insure that there is no trickery."

He smiled at the general. "Sir, pray blow out all the candles save this one before me." He had Clyde and Partridge to his left and right. Simon found himself holding hands with Miss Eliza Cross—slightly sticky—and the more mature of the two mourning doves. She wore gloves over surprisingly strong hands.

"Silence. Silence. Be at peace. Let your thought fly to the farthest reaches of space. There is no need for thought here. Only open your hearts to the possibilities. Count with me." With the light glowing eerily, lighting only his face, Mystery began to count backward slowly from one hundred. Some of the people at the table had been here before, for they were not taken by surprise when he started high and began to descend the number line.

Simon did not join in. The slow chanting of the numbers, each one anticipated before heard, made it very difficult to keep his eyes open.

"Hush!" Mystery said suddenly. "One comes. One . . . comes. One. . . . *She* comes."

"The needle's moving!" Miss Cross yelped.

"Who is coming?" the widow asked.

"She." The syllable was hardly more than hissed before Mystery's head dropped forward onto his boiled shirt-front. His black hair, slightly too long for a gentleman, fell onto his cheeks.

Wilson said, "I thought the pharaoh was a bloke."

"Shhh!" It was the widow to Simon's right. "He's in a trance. Don't wake him. It would kill him outright."

Would it be manslaughter? Simon wondered, tempted. He'd never taken such instant dislike to anyone as he did to Dr. Mystery. It was more than just his disdain for any kind of fraud. This was an antipathy as natural as that of cat and dog. Something about the smaller, sleeker man made Simon's hackles rise up.

Miss Cross said, "The power must be very strong. The needle is still moving to the right!"

The widow said, "Ask him a question, Mr. Archer."

"Very well. Sir . . ."

"Address the spirit, not the man." Perhaps feeling she'd been a trifle too forthright, the widow said, "This isn't my first visit to dear Dr. Mystery. Please let me assist you."

"Very well, then, madam. Perhaps you should ask the first question."

"If you don't think me too forward?" She simpered behind the veil that covered her from eyes to nose. Turning toward the still-silent medium, she asked, "We are all your friends, dear. We are eager to hear your messages of peace and love. Please, won't you tell us your name?"

The sticky Miss Cross gasped as Dr. Mystery raised his head. He moved as though someone, or something, was pushing his head upright, rather than with power of his own muscles. His mouth moved, words without sound. Then he shuddered all over and his eyes snapped open.

"Like the sands through an hourglass . . . time passes. Sand . . . sand. . . ." The voice that issued from Dr. Mystery's small mouth was that of a woman. Not a man's falsetto imitation, but the natural speaking voice of a mature female. It also lacked the liquid quality that was so noticeable in Dr. Mystery's own voice.

"Who are you?" the veiled widow prompted again.

"I am An-ket."

"Wow!" said Mr. Wilson, trying to jerk his hands free so he could write.

More loudly, Dr. Mystery said, "I am she, ravished from my tomb by unsanctified hands. My spirit cannot find rest."

Against the black velvet of the completely darkened room, Dr. Mystery's face was the only visible thing. The candle beneath him cast deep shadows into the sockets of his eyes and threw weird flickers of light over his nose and cheeks. One could hardly look away.

Simon leaned forward, constrained by the hands that held his. "What is your full name?"

"You must return my body to its tomb."

"Who is the pharaoh in your time?"

"There is no rest for a weary spirit."

"Tell me what function did the goddess Taweret serve?"

"Oh, can't you stop badgering her?" demanded the sticky Miss Cross, very much moved. "Can't you hear how dreadfully she feels? It's very bad of you, Mr. Archer, to treat her so!"

"This is nonsense," Simon said, shaking off the hands of the ladies. "Dr. Mystery promises a visitation that will

answer all my questions, and what happens? He can't
even perform what he has promised."

The general spoke up, very bluff, "You can't expect
spirits to come like a butler when you ring a bell, sir!"

"I can't expect sense from a charlatan, sir."

Suddenly, the candle in front of Dr. Mystery went out.
The room was plunged into a blackness deeper than that
inside the Great Pyramid.

"Clap your hands on your pockets, gentlemen," Simon
said wryly. "Lest you find your pocket picked."

A warm breeze began to blow through the room, carrying with it a hint of a singing voice, very faint and far
away. At the other end of the room, a white *something*
began to float in the air. Simon's eye could not quite follow it, for it seemed to fade whenever he looked directly
at it.

Simon rose to his feet. He was planning to slip along
in the darkness, using Dr. Mystery's own weapons against
him. Then he'd catch that floating scrap of white muslin—
or whatever it should prove to be—and show once and
for all that Mystery used fraud for his effects. But the
widow, of whom he was beginning to have doubts, cried
out, "Oh! Hold my hand, Mr. Archer!"

Almost at the same instant, the warning bell rang,
sounding oddly innocent in the midst of the Stygian blackness. Miss Cross began to sob, her voice rising into in-
cipient hysteria. "Oh! Oh, we must stop! The danger . . ."

Dr. Mystery, in his own voice, said, "Let us be calm,
friends."

The white "thing" had vanished. A match spluttered in
the darkness as Mystery relit the candle before him. Using
it, he lit the ones in the candelabra and sat back. "Well!
Did anything happen?"

Wilson, of the *Standard*, stood up. "Come on, boys.
We'd best get our write-ups in before the papers go to
bed." He grinned down at Mystery. "It's a good 'un.
'Priestess Begs Return to Comfy Tomb.' 'Archaeology as

Ravisher of Past Virgins. . . .' " The widow gasped in horror. Wilson winked at her, yet Simon felt that at least part of that wink was aimed at him.

He was miserably aware that he'd not cut much of a figure this evening.

"Are you going, gentlemen?" Mystery asked. "I am not tired yet. We could easily make another attempt."

Simon stood up, too. "You're a clever little man," he said. "But you are a fraud. I will prove it and then you can return to wherever it is you came from. Magic tricks for children, I think. I'll show myself out."

"I shouldn't dream of it," Mystery said silkily, though it was just possible that his face was redder than it had been before Simon had spoken. "I will escort you gentlemen personally. Dear friends," he said, addressing the others. "You each have departed loved ones you wish to attempt to reach. Give me a moment to refresh myself and I will return."

He bowed himself out to a chorus of thanks, pausing only to take the box from the table.

Outside, just enough of a breeze was blowing down the midnight streets to clear the fumes from Simon's thoughts. He vowed that when next he confronted Mystery, it would be on ground that wasn't full of his little tricks. He wanted very badly to take a hard, close look at the box that had so conveniently marked the beginning and the end of a visitation. He'd never heard of anyone measuring a spirit's appearance, although he felt that tonight's spirit could be measured by the yard.

The newspaper men said good-bye civilly enough as they hurried down the wet streets to make the morning editions. Besides them, and a bedraggled black cat with one white paw trotting across the cobbles, the street was deserted. Dr. Mystery watched the men go, his plump hands juggling a bit with his "magic box." He turned with that remote smile that made Simon want to get his hands around his neck, and opened his mouth to speak. But before he'd said much more than "Well, then . . . ," he was interrupted.

A hansom cab came tooling up before Dr. Mystery's door, a woman peering out through the lowered side window. When she saw Simon, she smiled and waved warmly. He groaned as he recognized her. "Miss Hanson, what on earth . . . ?"

She hardly waited for the horse to stop before she'd opened the door and bounded down. Simon realized something that had escaped him when they'd met before. Julia Hanson had an extremely active and attractive body. Even in the insufficient light shed by Dr. Mystery's open front door, he saw that she had a warm glow of health and an air of stimulating vigor quite unlike more conventional females. Beside him, he heard Dr. Mystery catch his breath.

"Who is she?" he asked in a tone of wonder.

"None of your business, Mystery."

"But . . . look!" He held out the box but Simon did not spare it a glance.

"I'm not interested in your absurd toy. I wouldn't introduce you to a decent woman for the crown jewels and a pound of tea."

As he advanced to Julia who was standing beside the cab, he found himself oddly relieved that Mystery was interested in her only on a psychic level. He told himself that Miss Hanson was a naive creature like all women, easily taken in by a smooth manner and passionate lies. Every gentleman owed a duty to protect the dear creatures from themselves and from predatory men like Mystery.

She was speaking animatedly to someone in the cab. "It's all right," she said. "He's a scientist. Give him proof. . . ."

Her smile dazzled in the light of the lamps. Her hair was untidy. Simon curled his fingers into the palm, overwhelmed by a wish to straighten the falling strands. He told himself that it was his sense of propriety that was offended, but a desire for proper decorum had never made his fingers itch before.

"What are you doing here, Miss Hanson?" he asked stiffly.

"I've brought you something . . . someone so wonderful!"

"I beg your pardon?" He became aware that she'd had at least one glass of wine with dinner.

She looked past him. "Will your friend pardon you?"

"He's not my friend. That is Dr. Mystery."

"Oh?" She was indiscriminate in her smiles.

"Please don't encourage him. I've had quite enough of his company for one evening."

"Didn't it go well?"

"He's even more slippery than I thought. I don't know what has happened to London that such men are allowed to prosecute their activities unchecked. . . ."

"Well, you may find it necessary to change your mind about some things tonight. Dr. Mystery may be a fraud, but—"

"Kindly show me whatever it is, and then permit me to take you home. Young ladies should not be roaming the streets of London after midnight without male companionship. What must your father be thinking with you out so late?"

"I thought I mentioned my father is at home . . . in Yorkshire."

"You mean you have come to London all alone?" He had noticed the female figure in the cab. "Is that your aunt?"

"No, she's at home, too." Holding out her hand to the open cab door, she said coaxingly, "Come out. You'll like him."

From the cab, hesitantly, emerged a patched skirt, a roughly cobbled boot, a stained shawl, and a wrinkled face. The bleary eyes blinked about her as though she had no idea where she was. A smell of beer clung to her.

Simon glanced at Julia, who was beaming ecstatically at the old woman. His native courtesy made him tip his hat to honor, if not the woman herself, at least her sex. "Good evening. Miss Hanson, are you planning to introduce me?"

"Oh." For a moment, Julia's brows drew together. "Well, that's a trifle complicated. You see, this is Mrs. Pierce. At least, it's her body. But inside—if you see—her soul is An-ket's. *Your* An-ket."

Six

~

The late Earl of Haye had died quite suddenly of an apoplexy while still a comparatively young man. For a moment, standing outside Dr. Mystery's house, Julia had been afraid that Simon Archer would do the same. His face grew red enough that the golden beard sprouting on his cheeks, not shaved since this morning, could plainly be seen glinting in the lamplight. For a moment, his eyes seemed to bulge, but then, as he caught at the tail of his anger, these signs faded. He had to clear his throat before he spoke.

"If this is your way of punishing me for my reception of you this afternoon . . ."

"Punishing you? Of course not. You were a trifle rude, perhaps." She thought there was no "perhaps" about it, but didn't wish to antagonize him further. "But then I was not what you expected and I can forgive a great deal of rudeness in someone so surprised."

"Then this is a joke? I don't accuse you of complicity with that slick gentleman behind me. . . ."

"Why would you?" She shot a penetrating glance at Dr. Mystery. "Did he . . . ? No, that would be too cruel a coincidence!"

"He affected to speak with the voice of An-ket. What

can I think but that you, too, are playing some kind of game with me?"

Julia thought she heard anguish in his voice. From his letters, she had come to know him as a man to whom self-respect was all in all. He could write of himself with humor, as when he told her of futilely chasing after a camel that would not be ridden, yet the respect of his peers for the work he did was vital to him. He would pursue Dr. Mystery because he hated lies, even if it meant making a fool of himself. But it would be unbearable if those he trusted made fun of him for his integrity.

"I know it sounds strange; I can hardly believe it myself. But when you know . . . when I tell you what has happened, you will believe me." Quickly, she told him how she'd returned to the museum just before closing, hiding from the guards after the building had emptied. She described Billy the Wall's violent end and the arrival of An-ket. Instinctively she knew that to protest her veracity would be to signify that she lied, so she told her tale as simply as possible.

Julia could not fool herself into believing that he was persuaded, though she told him nothing but the truth. He stood with his arms crossed before his remarkably well-developed chest, gazing at her with slightly puzzled attention. Her only comfort was that he had not yet called for a doctor to have her committed to an asylum.

All this while, An-ket had been standing patiently beside them, her eyes flicking between their faces. Julia was only vaguely aware, so focused was she on Simon, that the little man who'd come out of the building with him was staring in fascination at a small wooden box in his hands. She thought he was too far off to hear what she said, for she'd kept her voice low.

When she'd finished, Simon said, "How near to you did this bolt of lightning come?"

"Perhaps six feet. What has that to do with anything?"

"You seem unhurt."

"I am."

"You are very fortunate. The steel bones in a woman's corset can attract lightning. There was a woman killed in Hampshire not too long ago in that very way."

"How dreadful," she said, eyeing him. "If you are thinking that the lightning has confused my thinking, Mr. Archer, I assure you that my thoughts are as clear as ever. That may not be saying very much, I admit! But you don't ask An-ket any questions."

"I cannot think of any to ask her."

"I could. I asked her for her complete name, for the name of her pharaoh, all sorts of things about life in ancient Egypt . . . although that was later, at the pub."

"The pub?"

"She hadn't had a beer in two thousand . . . oh, you don't believe me. Ask her. Ask her."

"Very well. If that is the only way to satisfy you, I will. Then I will take you home." He turned to An-ket. Julia eagerly awaited his conversion.

"Good evening," he said, with a slight bow. He really had very fine manners.

"Good evening, sir," An-ket said. Julia frowned. When had the Priestess's voice become so flat?

"Are you An-ket-en-re, Priestess of Hathor in the city of Memphis?"

"No, sir. I'm Mrs. Pierce, Lumber Street."

Julia stared at the woman. She must have been blind not to notice that the elegant carriage, the proud turn of the head, the slow gestures had all been lost. Mrs. Pierce stood heavily, her shoulders rounded from years of carrying heavy pails and from scrubbing miles of marble stairs. Her voice, too, was different. The sounds were blurry, not bit off crisply.

Julia did not want to meet Simon Archer's mocking eyes. Yet when she did lift her chin defiantly, it was to find compassion. She would rather, now that she thought of it, have faced scorn. Though she knew it futile and pathetic, she said softly, "She was An-ket. She was."

"Never mind," Simon said as though to comfort a child. "You'll be all right in the morning. I'll take you home. Where are you stopping?"

"You needn't trouble."

Mrs. Pierce said, "Beggin' yer pardon, sir. I'm that turned 'round. Where am I?"

"Medford Square. How did you come to be in this young lady's company?"

"We met at the museum when I was cleanin'. She says she's studyin' them 'eathen images from 'Egypt. I didn't make no never mind. Nice to 'ave some company that ain't stone."

"But how did you come here with her?"

Mrs. Pierce scratched her collarbone. "Coo," she said meditatively. "I don't rightly know, sir. After the burglar come in, it all gets a bit blurry-like. There was a pub, seems to me. Oo'er, she's a nice young laidy, though. Bought me a pint or maybe two."

"Burglar?"

"Skinny chap 'o came in through a broken winder. Right ugly. 'E got himself killed, I finks."

"What happened to him?"

"Don't know, sir. I 'id my h'eyes. I finks the young laidy did somemat wid him."

"Thank you," Simon said, putting his hand in his pocket. Something clinked. Mrs. Pierce dipped a curtsey. "Ever so good of you, sir."

Dismayed and confused, Julia hardly spoke as Simon encouraged her to climb back into the hansom. He said to Mrs. Pierce, "Will you be able to find your way home all right?"

"Oh, bless you, yes! See the young laidy 'ome, sir. Never you mind 'bout me!"

Greatly confused, Julia sat in the stuffy interior of the cab and studied the situation. Was it all a lightning-induced fantasy, as Simon Archer believed? Or had she discovered proof that time meant nothing to the soul, that the division of time into past, present, and future was only a tool made by man, meaningless to those who wander between this world and the next?

Simon asked for her address. When she gave it to him, he called it up to the driver as he entered and the cab set off with a lurch. Simon sat next to her in the dimness. "Are you feeling better, Miss Hanson?"

"Oh, I am never ill." It was rather cozy in the cab, his shoulder touching hers, the skirt of his coat falling upon the stuff of her dress. As they rattled noisily over the cobbles, they bounced and swayed into one another.

"Surely, however, you must feel some nervous exhaustion. Confronting a burglar, being out so late in this great city . . ."

"I do not suffer from any irritation of the nerves, Mr. Archer. As for London, though I have not been here myself, my father visits often. We are going to his town house. My baggage should have been transferred there this afternoon. I hope my butler won't have gone to any trouble about supper. I wrote a note to tell him I might not return until late."

"Yes, locking oneself into a museum overnight would make one late for supper."

"Naturally. But as you did not seem eager to show me your exhibit after promising . . . If I thought I had a suit, I should sue you for breach of promise." Julia wondered if she wasn't revealing too much with such a joke.

"Breach of . . . ! Why?"

"I have a letter in my trunk from you, promising faithfully to show me your exhibit the moment I arrive in London. You didn't. Any jury worth its salt would give a wronged woman heavy damages."

Simon stared at her in puzzled wonder. Then, just as she was certain he had all the humor of a fish on a marble slab, he grinned. "I think I should have to vote with the jury."

"Certainly. Especially after I came all the way from Yorkshire. A most cruel disappointment; so I manuevered around you."

"By staying in the museum after closing. My word! You are a self-possessed female!"

She blinked at him owlishly. "Of course. It was the only way to get what I wanted. I really don't understand your attitude."

"My attitude?"

"Toward women. You seem to feel that we are a useless lot."

"Most women are useless, outside their natural—forgive me. I lost my train of thought."

"Outside our natural functions, would you say?"

He turned his head away to look out the window. The light was uncertain, but Julia thought he might be blushing. "Look," he said, "I think you can see the Houses of Parliament."

"Kindly don't change the subject. Besides, I saw the Thames as we were coming to find you. An-ket said it was beautiful but that she preferred the Nile."

"Quite," he said, and Julia knew he was merely humoring her. She preferred it to his previous pomposity, but her favorite of his expressions was the charmingly boyish grin he'd shown her before. She wondered how to get it to shine out again.

In the meantime, she found it strangely pleasant to be tooling through the night with him beside her. She felt comfortably tired and wondered if she dared drop her head onto his shoulder. The experiment appealed to her. She covered a yawn.

"You're tired," he said at once.

"I didn't rest well last night and it has been a very long day for me."

"That's right. You only arrived in London this morning. Well, I'm sorry you've had so poor an impression of the city."

"Poor? I think it's marvelous!"

"I meant . . . between my reception of you, and this thief. Was anything stolen or damaged?"

Julia suddenly realized that, despite his natural concern for the artifacts, he'd asked about her health a long time before asking about the priceless objects. "The case that held the jewelry was smashed, I'm afraid, but he hadn't time to steal anything before the lightning struck him. Anket said that Hathor sent it to protect my virginity."

"Good God!"

She laughed at him. "It did happen, you know," she said, still smiling. "You may have a very poor impression of me, Mr. Archer, but I assure you I am sane, if eccentric."

"I don't think you're eccentric."

"Then you think me quite, quite mad. Well, let us not quibble. I am at least unusual."

"That I will grant you. I knew from your letters that you are that. For the rest, when you are older . . ."

"How old must I be to know my own mind, if twenty-seven is not old enough?" She reached out and touched his hand lightly where it rested on his knee. "I used to want only one thing. I wanted only to go to Egypt. Now there is something else I want."

He seemed to be holding his breath. "That is?"

"I want to prove to you that I am neither mad nor dreaming. Something strange happened to me tonight. I'm not sure I believe all of it myself, but *something* happened."

Simon became aware that the cab had stopped. Instinctively he rose to exit first, to hand Julia out. Until she stood beside him on the pavement, he had not looked around. When he saw the house, he knew the responsibility he'd assumed for her was not over yet. He honestly could not tell if he was glad or sorry.

"Why are the shutters up?"

"Please take your hand from your pocket, Mr. Archer,"

she said at the same moment. "I shall pay the driver."

"You won't," he stated, turning away from the house. "A lady never pays."

"What did you say? Oh, you're right. The shutters *are* up. How queer." Glancing up at the interested man on the box, she asked, "Will you wait? I may need you again."

"Yes, miss." He flourished his whip in a salute.

"Thank you." She trotted lightly up the front steps without a moment's hesitation. Certainly she did not glance at him to see what she must do. Simon felt he had no choice but to follow her. Really, she was the most intrepid female!

She stared in surprise at the place where the door knocker ought to have been. "Dear me. Shutters up, knocker taken down, and there should not be all this dirt on the steps if anyone was here to sweep it away."

"In other words, your servants are not here."

"There's only Simpkins living here just now. We hire extra help when my father is in town."

"It seems strange to keep a house when one only visits from time to time."

"Father can't abide hotels. He finds them too interested in purely personal concerns." She was feeling in the bag she had slung over her arm. "Fortunately, I thought to bring the key."

Simon took it from her hand as she advanced it toward the lock. "You won't need it. You'll come home with me."

"Don't be ridiculous. Please give me that."

"No. And I'm not being ridiculous. It's absurd to think that a young woman can stay alone and unprotected in an empty house. I'd sooner leave a kitten alone in a kennel."

As though in an echo of his words, he heard a mew. Sitting on the step below them was a black cat. He was not at all superstitous; for an archaeologist to be afraid of the supernatural would be like a doctor to be afraid of disease. Let other people worry about superstition; to him it was merely part of his work.

For all that, there was something vaguely familiar about the cat. It wasn't all black; one paw was white as though it had stepped up to the wrist in paint.

"Is that your cat?"

"What cat?"

Simon looked again and the cat had gone down the stairs, trotting away under the belly of the cab. "Never mind the cat," he said. "You can't stay here alone."

"Why not?"

"Because it isn't done, Miss Hanson. It simply isn't done. You haven't even a maid with you."

"No, I couldn't bring her. Her mother is laid up with rheumatism." She made a highly undignified grab for the key but he refused to tussle with her. He slipped it behind his back.

"My spare bedroom is at your disposal."

"That is a far more shocking suggestion than that I should stay here alone." He could tell she was laughing at him again.

"You'll have my mother and sisters to protect you from me." He stared down at her, appalled at his own joke. The last thing he wanted was to establish a relationship based on their differing genders. If she hadn't begun it—but, no. He would not fall into Adam's excuse of blaming the woman.

She followed, as always, her own train of thought. "That's another thing. What would your mother say if you turned up in the middle of the night with a strange woman? She'd be perfectly justified in putting me out forthwith, which means I would just come here again. Why waste the time? If you'll kindly give me my key, Mr. Archer?"

"Very well." He unlocked the door for her.

"Thank you," she said, and marched inside with her head held high. Then she hesitated on the doorstep. "Yes,

well . . . the first order of business is some light, I think.
The gas is undoubtedly off. It would be unlike Simpkins
to leave it on. Candles . . . ah, the pantry, of course."

She started off. A moment later, he heard a crash and
a soft exclamation.

"Table?" he asked.

"Chair . . . I think."

A bang.

"Wall?"

"Yes. Ouch."

"Are you all right?"

"My head is hard, but the doorframe is harder." A moment's more fumbling and she asked, "Have you any
matches?"

"Have you found a candle?"

"No, but a match would give me some light. The
kitchen will be very dark indeed, being at the back of the
house."

Simon checked his pockets perfunctorily. "No matches,
I'm sorry."

"Perhaps the driver would lend us a side lamp?"

"I'll ask." He was back quickly. "The cab's lanterns are
bolted to the frame to keep thieves from making off with
them."

"A pity. Do you smell something?"

"Just mice."

There was another clatter. She made a sound of disgust.

"You don't like mice? Bats are worse, and they infest
Egypt."

"It's not the mice I mind. I just tripped and put my
hand in the fireplace. I think the chimney wants sweeping."

"Miss Hanson, come out. You must see this is folly."

"I can't *see* anything."

"Then how will you manage for even one night?"

"You could go home and bring me some candles . . .
but I suppose you won't."

"No, I won't."

"Has anyone ever told you that you are a difficult man, Mr. Archer?"

"No, never. My mother praises my sweetness of temper." He heard her mutter something and he could smile because she could not see him, either. "Come along, Miss Hanson. The later it grows the more likely you are to be right about my mother."

Would she be reasonable and give up this quixotic desire to be independent? He would not have trusted either of his sisters to find and light a candle in a pitch-black house and he was used to judging all young women by Lucy, Amanda and Jane. To be truthful, he couldn't imagine any of them entering such a house of their own free will. The mere threat of mice would have been enough to send them screaming out of the place, even without the effects of imaginations brought up on "horrid" novels.

Julia appeared in the tall rectangle of light thrown through the open door into the hall. Her eyes were dilated like a cat's and he noticed for the first time that the way her hips swayed in her quick gliding walk was very appealing. She said, "I wonder where Simpkins is."

"On holiday, perhaps. Regardless, you must come home with me."

"No, I'll return to the Bull and Bush. They were very kind to me today and no doubt my valise is there."

"If it's not stolen by now."

"You do like to look on the bright side, don't you, Mr. Archer? I trusted the landlord's son to bring my valise here. When he saw no one was home, he undoubtedly took my belongings back to the inn. When I arrive there, I shall have all I require."

"People in London are more dishonest than you are used to, Miss Hanson."

Her proud chin went up. "I am not a 'country cousin,' you know. I realize that there is dishonesty everywhere.

I can only say that I have never met with any. I expect the world to treat me well, and it does."

"Come along, Miss Hanson. We can discuss philosophies on the way to my home."

"I'm not going to your home. I want to go to the Bull and Bush."

When she'd shut and locked the door, she asked the driver to take her to that inn. Before Simon entered the cab, he told the driver his address. Hardly had the words left his lips than Julia had opened the window on her side and said, "Kindly take me to the inn first, driver."

"The gentleman's 'ouse is closer, miss."

"Yes, but I don't care to go there. The inn first, please."

"Nonsense," Simon said. "The address I gave you, jarvey, and then you won't need to go to the Bull and Bush."

"Mr. Archer, if you please! I have no intention of burdening your mother with the arrival of an utter stranger."

Suddenly a window flew up in the house across the street. The owner poked his head, topped with a white nightcap like a meringue, out the window. "Will you stop that ghastly row? People are trying to sleep!"

"Look, now," said the driver reasonably. "You can't expect me to drive me 'orse all h'over creation fer you two. Gi' me *one* place t'drive you an' I'll take you there quick as winking."

In the same breath, Simon and Julia repeated their divergent requests. The driver sighed and shook his head. The horse looked around inquiringly and blew out his breath in a long, contemptuous whiffle.

On the other side of the street, another window opened. A female voice plaintively demanded to know why drunken louts always chose her windows to argue underneath. Her voice apparently pierced the sleep of another neighbor who called out, "Is it fire? Is it thieves?"

Someone farther along the street, catching only one word, yelped, "Call for the police!"

Summoned like a genie by the sounding of the magic word, a large blue form appeared, complete with truncheon; tall hat; and blue, double-breasted frock coat. Simon realized that his bad evening was about to become worse. He foresaw that he'd next be arrested for kidnapping a woman he didn't even want.

Then, like a miracle, he heard Julia say, "I've changed my mind, driver. Please take us to the address this gentleman has given you."

"Thanks be! Come up there, girl, get on."

Simon sat back in the cab, staring at her, hardly even aware that a spring was poking him. "What made you change your mind? The constable?"

"Yes. I suddenly realized that if you were arrested I never should get what I want."

"And that is?"

She hesitated, her eyes sliding away from his. She seemed on the point of making up her mind to tell him when the cab stopped again. The constable stood looking in at them. "What's all this, then?"

To Simon's alarm, Julia slid over to sit close to him. Her hair brushed his cheek, bringing with it the faintest hint of some kind of flower. Her body was soft and surprisingly full where she pressed against his arm. He was not attracted to her, he told himself, yet it seemed that his body was not listening. Almost without realizing it, he curved his arm about her waist, so slender in contrast with her round breasts and hips.

She said in a warm, throaty tone he'd not heard before, "Just a little lover's quarrel, officer."

Simon found he had to clear his throat before he spoke. "I'm sorry, officer. We had a slight difference of opinion."

"Try not to 'ave it in the middle of the street next time." The bluecoat stepped back. "All right, get on."

As the cab drove off, Constable Number 429 noticed what looked like a cat riding on the boot between the back wheels. He'd seen stranger things during his twenty years on the force. But what sent him off-duty with a headache was the impossible, unshakable idea that the cat smiled at him as it drove away.

In Medford Square, Mrs. Pierce squared her shoulders and started off in the direction of home. A true Londoner, she could follow her nose through the streets and never make a wrong turning. But, Lor', how she wished she didn't have to walk it! But she could tell plain as plain that the gentleman, polite as he was, didn't relish sharing that cab home. Besides which, she wouldn't have liked it herself. She didn't know what had gotten into her that had made her so familiar with Miss Hanson. For she was gentry, through and through, and Mrs. Pierce had always prided herself on knowing her place.

As she walked, the jingle in her pocket where she'd stowed the gentleman's present made a musical accompaniment to the thud of her boots. When she reached a part of the city lit with gas, she tugged out the coins.

She gasped, then trembled so hard that she nearly dropped one of the golden coins. There were five of them—three months' wages. Mrs. Pierce looked hastily around her, on the watch for thieves. She thought she saw a shadow move behind her. Quick as winking, she pushed the coins into her pocket again.

Five pounds was a fortune to a charwoman keeping body and soul together on thirty shillings a month. She thought of what her daughters would say when she showed them the glittering hoard. Knowing them, they'd think of a hundred ways to spend it within the first five minutes. She could think of that many without half trying. But, being good girls despite temptation, they'd soon calm themselves.

Min would want to put it aside against the day when her mother could no longer work. Amabelle would think of a clever place to hide the fortune. Neither of them knew that their mother had saved nearly this much already, shaving a penny here and there. This nest egg had been mostly achieved by going without meals.

As Mrs. Pierce walked, she found herself wondering just how far off that rainy day of unemployment was. She knew what to dread. One day, she'd be unable to work as hard, despite the strength of desperation. The governors of the museum were kindly, yet they'd not keep her an hour past her usefulness. Then she'd be like the other old women she knew—living alone, struggling by on bread and tea, threadbare clothing creating an outward show of dignity with nothing behind it, no one caring whether she lived or died. Dreadful as that picture was, she could bear it better than becoming a burden to her children.

"But what can I do?" she asked plaintively.

Were those footsteps behind her? Mrs. Pierce didn't stop to look about her. She hurried on, making good time despite corns and bunions.

When she'd reached this point before, her thoughts had become so mired in fear and misery, she would always head to the nearest pub rather than face her future. Now, though, a new idea popped into her head as though a seed long planted had suddenly sprouted beneath the caress of a warm breeze.

No one can sack the mistress, she thought.

It came as such a startling revelation that she stopped in her hurried pace to examine the idea. She said it aloud, slowly, "No one can sack you if you're the top of the heap."

Then she laughed at herself and walked on. "An' wotcher goin' t'do? Wave a magic wand and make yerself inter a fine laidy?"

As though from quite outside herself, though still inside her head, Mrs. Pierce heard, "Take this money. Rent some shop on the street and advertise for men and maids to come work for you. Guarantee their honesty and see to it that they are well-trained. You know what salary a really well-trained parlormaid can ask an' get?"

"Who's going to train 'em, then?"

"The workhouses already train young girls to sew and cook. How much harder can it be to teach them some manners befittin' a chamber or parlormaid? You can do it. You know how."

That was true. She hadn't always been a charwoman. She'd started in good service and had given satisfaction until she left to be married. "But . . ." She could think of half a dozen objections to the plan.

She walked through a street of shops, closed now, their shutters up. Looking at the signs above the doors, she wondered how they all had started in business. One sign was especially handsome—a board covered in shiny green paint deeply scored with gilded letters.

Blinking at it, Mrs. Pierce felt as though she were visited by a revelation. Aloud, slowly, she said, "Mrs. Pierce's Domestics. Mrs. Pierce's Domestics. By the Day, the Week, or the Month."

Seven

The large wheels of the cab had scarcely completed one revolution away from the constable before Julia sat back in her own corner. "That worked," she said.

Simon, a trifle unnerved still by the way the warmth of her body lingered against him, said, "That was clever. How did you think of it?"

"I remembered that love is an excuse for all sorts of bad behavior. For instance, I adore Egyptology. That is my only excuse for taking you by surprise today." She looked down at her hands, then glanced sideways at him.

In the mobile lights and shadows of the cab, Simon was tantalized by a glimpse of beauty hitherto unseen. Julia was the kind of woman whose beauty depended very much upon lighting, her mood, and the eye of the beholder.

Right now she sat in the corner looking at him with eyes as deep and mysterious as Cleopatra's. A stray beam of light moved across her mouth like a finger brushed sensuously over yearning lips. Another gleam highlighted her throat and the lobe of her ear, just those places most likely to be kissed in the throes of passion.

Simon moved restlessly on the seat, reminding himself in a fierce mental whisper that she was just another dif-

ficult woman. "My mother knows, of course, that I had
invited a certain Miss Hanson to see my exhibition."

"You told her about me?" She smiled, pleased.

Reluctantly, Simon admitted, "She has seen your letters."

"She has? I have never shown yours, not even to my
father."

Simon found himself responding to the very slight
tinge of hurt in her tone. He'd never been particularly
sensitive to the emotional shades of a woman's voice;
they seemed to start shrilling about the silliest things. Yet
he hastened to justify himself. "I did not show them to
her. She found them while—ah!—looking for stationery
in my desk."

"Did she think my letters were blank pages?"

"Are you suggesting my mother was prying?"

"Of course not," she said, very softly.

"Well, she was. I thought your letters were safe enough,
locked in a drawer, but Mother is very clever when she
wants to find something out. I keep them in a locked box
at the office now."

Suddenly he heard a muffled laugh. On being pressed
to tell what was so funny, Julia said, "I am only thinking
. . . you must have told her I was an old woman. What
will she say when she sees me?"

Simon felt he had a very good idea, but he could hardly
say so. He was having enough trouble adjusting to the
idea that he'd just told her, to all intents and purposes a
stranger, that his mother had snooped through his desk.
He did not tell her that he'd been kicking himself ever
since for not keeping Julia's letters at his office in the first
place.

Yet why should he feel that the letters of an elderly
woman needed protecting from prying eyes? After all,
they were not love letters. He could not remember Julia
ever having written a word that could not have appeared
with the greatest propriety in the *London Times*.

"I'm afraid that she will think I have been deceiving

her, that I knew all along that you were young and . . ." He swallowed the word "pretty." "Mother likes to think she has the complete confidence of her children. My sisters tell her all the details of their lives; I do not."

"Being away so much."

"As you say, I am only home now in the hot seasons. I've only missed two years of excavation while seeking new patrons."

"Will you be able to go again in the autumn? Did Lord Quarterfoil agree to fund another expedition?"

"I doubt I'll have any trouble finding money for the coming season. I'm known as a lucky 'digger' now, thanks to An-ket."

"Thanks to An-ket," Julia echoed. She turned her head away to look out the window, leaving Simon only her back to gaze at. He'd never known how eloquent a back could be. He almost wished that he were her brother so that he could put a comforting arm about her waist. He had often offered an absorbent shoulder to his sisters, of whom he was genuinely fond, when the burdens of their lives grew too heavy.

He moved a trifle closer to Julia. "Tell me again what you saw and heard."

"You still won't believe me."

"Let me judge. I was angry at Dr. Mystery before and some of my anger turned toward you. I'm calmer now. Please, let me judge."

She drew a deep breath and faced him. Her eyes widened slightly and he realized he'd moved even closer to her than he'd intended. To cough and hasten away would be to make something perfectly natural seem sordid. So he stayed right there and said, "Speak softly. We don't want the cabbie to overhear."

This time he listened closely to more than her words. He heard the throb of sincerity in her voice and saw no hint of either mischief or madness in her eyes. When she spoke of the threats of Billy the Wall, he unknowingly sought to take her hand. Her fingertips were slightly rough, like his own, and returned his strengthening pressure. In the close darkness of the hackney, near enough to her to feel her breath on his cheek, he could not assert that she lied or recounted only a dream.

When she finished, he said, "I believe that you believe. I can't say more than that."

"Then I am happy." With head bent, she withdrew her hand from his.

Something thudded on the roof of the cab. "Ho! 'Ow long d'ya h'expect me to wait!"

As if awakening from a daydream, Simon started and stared out the window. "We're here," he said.

He opened the door with a latchkey. The hall was deep, with rooms opening to either side. Diminished jets of gas gleamed in the dark rooms like cats' eyes shown up by a passing lantern. Julia received an impression of spaciousness perfumed by the gas and by flowers.

Simon said, "I suggest I show you straight to your room. Explanations and introductions can wait 'til the morning."

"That's best. May I suggest you leave a note for your mother? It would be impolite to leave her uninformed until presented with me over the breakfast table."

A merry, youthful voice said, "But I cannot wait so long! Please, darling, introduce me now."

Mrs. Archer was much younger in appearance than Simon's age had lead Julia to believe possible. She stood at the top of the stairs, enveloped in what seemed to be several yards of foamy white tarlatan. Though entrancing, it seemed a strange choice for the mother of four grown children. A broad piece of the fabric had been thrown over her head like a mantilla and her hair was an even brighter gold than her son's, though without the accompanying tan of his skin.

She walked down the stairs with a queenly grace, her right hand floating above the stair rail. Stopping in front of Julia, she said, "Aren't you pretty, my dear. Simon, who is she?"

"Mother, may I present Miss Hanson? Due to an unfortunate confusion, she has nowhere to stay tonight. I have offered her our guest bedroom for the duration of her stay."

"Naturally! What else was left for you to do?"

Julia hardly had time to wonder what exactly was meant by that before Mrs. Archer turned her limpid blue eyes on her. "How perfectly dreadful to be homeless in a great city like London! You must have been so frightened!"

"Not at all, Mrs. Archer. And your son quite mistakes the matter. I hope not to impose on you beyond tonight."

"Oh, but the night is half over already! You'll hardly catch a wink of sleep. I know that I need all the rest I can find." She covered the daintiest yawn Julia had ever witnessed.

"I'm terribly sorry we woke you, Mother. We were trying to be quiet."

"I'm sure you were, my dear love. I do hope you shan't wake your sisters. Poor lambs were so tired, they went to bed at nine o'clock!"

"Then we must be especially quiet," Julia said. "I should not like to disturb them."

"I believe in plenty of sleep for young girls, Miss Hanson. Nothing is more injurious to a girl's freshness than late hours." As if in echo, somewhere a clock tinged twice.

"Mother," Simon said.

Mrs. Archer could not repress a smile as she looked on her son, even though she must have been displeased with him. Julia couldn't really blame her for her cattiness. No mother would welcome her son coming home past midnight with some female he'd just met. She might be anything from a prostitute to a poisoner.

Simon said, "As it is so very late, you should go back to your bed. I will show Miss Hanson up."

"No, no, no!" Mrs. Archer showed none of her teeth when she smiled, nor did her cheeks crinkle. Julia noticed for the first time that her hands were encased in soft leather gloves, undoubtedly some sort of beauty treatment. Mrs. Archer was evidently anxious to preserve her beauty, which, showing itself still so strong, must have been re- markable when she'd been younger.

"Simon, this isn't some savage, backward land! What kind of hostess do you think I am? Besides, she will need various things that you cannot give her. I shall have to wake Maria to help her."

Though tired, Julia could not imagine waking some poor exhausted maid simply to help her with her shoes and buttons. "You needn't disturb anyone. I'm used to taking care of myself."

"Of course you are! But coming into a strange house like this is fit to disorder anyone."

"Mother," Simon said again, with an edge to his voice.

Gaily, Mrs. Archer sang, "That's enough talking, don't you think? Come with me, Miss Hanson." Mrs. Archer started up the stairs. "Good night, Simon. Don't dawdle about downstairs the way you always do. I'll come in for just a moment before I go back to bed, shall I?"

Julia stayed a moment more by the foot of the stairs. She felt, perhaps falsely, that the time they'd spent in the cab had brought them into the sort of accord they should have had all along. He had seemed the man she'd come to know through his letters: kind, intelligent, and sym- pathetic. She wondered what he thought of her now, and did not dare to have hopes.

"Thank you for everything, Mr. Archer," she said. "Though I disagreed with you, I see now that you were right to bring me here with you. Returning to my inn so late would have brought me more notoriety than I want."

"You're quite certain you are well?"

She smiled happily under the lurking humor in his eyes. "Perfectly well. My admission of being wrong is not a sign of illness."

"Though unusual," he said softly. "But you are nothing if not unusual."

"Come along, Miss Hanson, do."

An hour later, she lay awake in the very pleasant room to which Mrs. Archer had conducted her. Simon's mother brought her a pitcher of water to wash with and a crisply ironed nightgown to sleep in. She made no more sweetly caustic remarks, merely wishing Julia a good sleep for what was left of the night.

The nightgown was too short, leaving her ankles and some of her calves exposed, but it would not have mattered were it not for the fact that Julia's stomach began rumbling noisily. She'd been so eager to return to the museum before it closed that she'd not thought to eat dinner, and the fly-specked boiled eggs and soda bread at the public house had not tempted her.

After an hour, she sat up. She did not know at what hour the Archers breakfasted, but it could not be less than six hours away. Remembering the proverb. "He who sleeps, dines," she'd tried to nod off but her own internal noises had kept her awake.

She slid out of bed, determined, despite the laws of hospitality, to seek out food. Perhaps there was a bowl of fruit in a drawing or dining room. What she wouldn't give for a ripe pear!

Pressing one hand against her stomach to stifle it, she opened her door and peered out into the upper hall. She would not have been at all surprised to find Mrs. Archer sleeping across her doorstep. Obviously, Mrs. Archer was concerned that Julia had designs on her son, a fear that was entirely warranted, little though she knew it.

Julia wondered which of the doors opening off this hall was Simon's. Sending him a silent wish for pleasant dreams, she headed down the stairs, her bare feet sinking into the pile of the carpet.

Halfway down, she hesitated, thinking she really ought not to have left her room. If anyone saw her, how very odd she would look in her too-short gown, and how lame an excuse hunger would prove! An extra loud gurgle from her stomach sent her onward.

Stealthily, she turned up the gaslight in each room and scanned it quickly for fruit, nuts, or even a peppermint drop. She'd settle for pemmican and hardtack! There seemed to be a few crackers behind a set of decanters in the dining room, but the glass-fronted cabinet was locked. Disappointed in the public rooms of the house, she made her way very reluctantly toward the door at the back that concealed the servants' hall.

The scullery window was open a few inches at the bottom, sending a cool breeze to dally with her exposed ankles. In the light that came through there, Julia spied a biscuit barrel and seized upon it thankfully. The three rusks she found at the bottom saved her life.

She heard a sudden clatter and turned sharply around, the last, illicit biscuit clasped in her hand. But it was only the household cat clambering in through the open window. It had knocked over a pail. "You startled me!"

The cat said, "You startled *me*!"

"She came all that way quite alone? How shocking! Oh, Simon . . . you don't suppose she has run away from home!"

"I haven't asked her that, Mother. It would not surprise me in the least."

"What a hurly-burly thing to do! Dear me, how wicked! To cause such anxiety . . . I'm proud to think that no daughter of mine would ever behave in such an underhanded fashion."

"If you are imagining Miss Hanson climbing down a drainpipe in the dead of night, you are indulging fantasy too much. It would be more in keeping with her nature, as I have come to see it, that she ordered up a gig to drive her to catch the Mail, had the maid pack her baggage, and drove off in broad daylight. Who would have the audacity to stop her?"

"So headstrong! So unfeminine!" Seated in his bedroom chair, his mother pleated the folds of her wrapper in her agitation.

"Yes, she is headstrong." His reverence for the truth would not permit him to lie to his mother, so he stopped there.

"Thank heaven she is so ordinary-looking," his mother said.

"Would you say so?"

"Oh, my dear! All that reddish hair! Like a wild beast looking out from a bush! And did you notice her hands? So brown and coarse!"

Simon looked at his own hands, tanned and callused from working in the field, and wondered where Julia did her practice excavations. He had no doubt that she worked thus somewhere. He had noticed that Julia did seem to have rather a lot of hair, imperfectly controlled. He'd glimpsed sparks of red among the rich brown waves but, like her beauty, it changed with every alteration of the light.

"And her complexion is not good. No wonder she is yet unmarried! She must be almost thirty."

"Twenty-seven."

"How, pray, do you know that?"

"She told me."

"Oh, then she is more than thirty! No woman ever gave a man her age without shaving off a few years."

"I don't believe she lied, Mother."

"Oh, it's not a lie to flatter yourself a little. I don't blame her for it. Being so old-maidish, one can't blame her for trying! But I'd be remiss if I didn't warn you, dear. You've been away from England so long . . ."

"Only six months . . ."

"It always seems longer. But you don't know what girls like this Miss Hanson are like. Any man will do for a girl who is facing permanent spinsterhood. You might find that she tries to compromise you. You should lock your door."

"Mother, I'm not a virginal maid in the house of a rake. I doubt Miss Hanson has any thought of seducing me."

"Oh, Simon! Your language!"

He stooped and kissed her softly scented cheek. "Go back to bed, you dear goose. I need no protection from the likes of Miss Hanson."

"You only say that because you don't know how handsome you are! Like an angel."

"Good God!" Simon said, revolted.

"But you are! Every woman I know agrees with me."

He escorted her to her door, kissing her forehead as he bid her good night. Her eyes, only slightly lined, looked at him anxiously but he did not try again to dispel her worries. He might as well have saved the breath he'd expended thus far.

Back in his room, he tore off his brown silk cravat and removed his collar. Kicking off his shoes, he eased his feet into a pair of red morroco slippers. It had been a long day.

Yet he puttered about his room for a little while. It was quite the largest in the house, having been his father's. The furniture was all ebony-painted wood, popular in the last century. It was comfortable enough, but made the room rather dark, even with the gas jet on full.

He smiled to think that his mother was afraid that Miss Hanson meant to compromise him in some way. Though he did not know the girl well, he guessed that such tactics were too underhanded and subtle for her.

He thought that if Miss Hanson had seduction on her mind, she would go about it in as straightforward a manner as possible. Flirtation and hints of undress were not for her—she'd drive toward her goal relentlessly, flattening everything in her path. No doubt she'd feel that the mere sight of her naked form would be enough to bring a man to his knees.

The picture that rose before his eyes sent a jet of desire flaring up in him, taking him completely by surprise. It was as if a hard crust over a stream of lava had suddenly broken, letting a burst of heat surge through. He imagined her generous mouth opening under his as he crushed her full bosom against him. His chest felt tight as his body clamored for the woman.

Then it quieted, and he told himself that Miss Hanson had nothing to do with this chaos. It had been caused by a combination of exhaustion and abstinence. He could hardly remember the last time he'd coupled, having too much self-respect to visit any brothel and his previous "dear friend" had reconciled with her long-estranged husband while Simon had been away.

He really should lie down and go to sleep. Thinking about women was not restful after so disturbed an evening. "An-ket!" he said in disbelief. "Twice!"

Usually, after his mother and sisters had retired, he would remove to the little den he kept at the side of the house. Here he kept his private papers, the manuscript for his book, and his cigars. He only smoked one a day, but the hour dedicated to the cherishing of the ash he held sacred. He only ever drank then, too. One glass of whiskey, one cigar, a few crackers munched, one hour to himself alone. . . .

Thinking of the crackers reminded him that he'd had nothing to eat since luncheon. He'd been so busy arranging the exhibit that he'd not even stopped for tea. Now as he thought about the crackers and smoked salmon the cook laid out for him every evening, his stomach made a sound like a snarling tiger.

That decided him. Very carefully, he opened his door. His mother had ears like a cat and she'd be waiting to see if there was any traffic between his room and Julia's. He'd had enough scenes for one night.

Downstairs, all was quiet. The ticking of the clock in the parlor sounded like a distant drumbeat. Simon knew the cook would not have allowed his after-supper rations to sit out in his den, but it was just possible that she'd covered the plate with a cloth and left it in the kitchen. He turned to pass through the door, but as he pressed it open, he heard voices.

One was plainly Julia's. "I almost hate to do it. He's been so kind to me this evening. I quite forgive him for thinking I'm mad."

The second voice was low, hardly more than a purring current of sound. Simon couldn't make out a word.

"If only I knew more about this sort of thing," Julia said, seemingly in reply. "Perhaps my aunt is right and girls ought to make men their study."

Again came the second voice. Simon strained his ears, not daring to open the door and stroll in. What was it that Julia "almost hated to do"?

"No," she said. "We choose our own husbands, although few girls marry without at least some thought of pleasing their parents. No one likes to disoblige them, for if the marriage turns out badly, where can most girls go but to their former homes? I haven't married yet because of my poor father."

Simon thought, *poor father*?

Apparently the unknown second person said something similar, for Julia replied easily, "Because he's hounded, poor darling. After my mother died, all the women expected him to marry again fairly quickly. Being left a widower with such a young daughter and all."

A few words from the purring voice led to the answer, "I'm afraid I don't remember her at all. I was hardly five years old when she died together with her baby, but, you know, I think I miss her."

Strange how Simon could hear her sigh so clearly, yet

the other voice remained difficult to catch. He pushed the door open a trifle farther. Perhaps he could catch a glimpse . . .

Julia said, "At any rate, soon the ladies started calling, some for themselves, and some in representation of their unmarried daughters. Father says he was nearly caught several times but he always managed to escape. He said that he wouldn't make me grow up under a stepmother. It was a long time before I found out the real reason why he didn't choose any of them."

The whisper made her chuckled warmly. "That's right. Her name is Ruth, half French, half Irish . . . not that that means anything to you! But she's fascinating. Black eyes and black hair; I'd make two of her.

"Of course, I've met her. She comes to stay at the house. Father would have married her any time these last twenty years but her husband wouldn't divorce her. Not that Ruth would be divorced, either. Her religion forbids it. It's called Catholicism and I can't really explain it all to you now.

"But I have to find somewhere else to live and something else to do besides excavate the garden midden and scare off women who want my father's fortune. Ruth's husband died a few months ago, so Father wants to marry her as soon as she's out of mourning. No, we don't shave our heads. . . ."

That was unexpected, but what made Simon fall forward, slamming the door against the wall, was Julia's calm, matter-of-fact voice saying, "So that's why I must marry Simon Archer as soon as possible."

Eight

The noise he made seemed to set up an echo; a second clatter followed hard upon it. He heard Julia's sudden exclamation as he staggered against the wall, only staying on his feet by luck. If only he could have whisked out of sight, back up the stairs or around a corner. There was no time, however, to employ discretion. The only thing to do was pretend he'd heard nothing.

But all such pretense was as irritating to him as desert sand between his toes. He shoved open the door and marched into the kitchen.

Julia sat at the big worktable, quite alone. In one glance, Simon took under consideration every corner of the room. He even pushed open the pantry door to see if anyone was hidden in there. "Who were you talking to?"

"Talking?" she asked, her eyes wide.

"I heard you talking to someone."

"There's no one here."

He leaned one hip against the table and looked down at her, his arms folding across his chest. She wore only a white nightgown of some dense material, its placket securely buttoned to her smooth throat. He could see nothing of her body, yet the very fact that she wore nothing but that, sacred to the bedroom, was enough to unnerve him. But he refused to show it. "You were talking to yourself?"

"I suppose I must have been, since there is no one here but me."

Simon took a deep breath, then let it out gustily. "Then you are barking mad, Miss Hanson. I will take you back to your room and lock you in, lest you do me or my family a mischief."

"*Barking* mad? I've never heard that one before."

"Come along," he said. He stood up and gripped her by the upper arm as though he'd pull her to her feet.

She smiled at him as though he'd just offered her a lump of sugar for her tea. "If I told you that I was talking to An-ket, here in the shape of a cat, you wouldn't change your mind about my mental condition."

"You still persist in that fantasy? First thing in the morning, I'll call Dr. MacInnes. He helped Lucy when she turned so melancholy last year."

"Why did she?"

"Blighted affection. Come along."

"Who blighted it?"

"A friend of mine. Are you coming?"

"Are you hungry?"

He released her arm. He was enjoying the feel of her muscles beneath the sleeve a trifle too much. Besides, women weren't supposed to *have* muscles. Muscles weren't built by shopping, supervising servants, or lifting teapots. These were the things women were supposed to do. They were supposed to be dainty, readily shocked, and easily led.

Simon sat down across from her. She said, "I'm sorry I ate the last biscuit. I hadn't had anything to eat this evening."

"I should have thought of that. I hadn't had anything, either."

She looked about her. He realized that she seemed quite at home in these simple surroundings. "I suppose your cook would be justifiably distressed if we made a mess of her kitchen. I know Mrs. Finch would be."

"Is she your cook?"

"Yes. A fine woman—she taught me a very great deal—but she does so hate to have anyone else cook in her kitchen. Rather the way the queen must feel about other people sitting on her throne."

Simon found the crackers and salmon in the pantry, then brought out the plate.

"You do know how to cook, then?"

"Yes," she said, then the merest twitch of her brows showed that she'd caught his tone.

"I thought perhaps you despise all the things of a woman's natural sphere."

She said levelly, "I cook very well indeed. I can also shoe a horse, if need be, and spin wool."

"Astonishing." He poured two glasses of water, setting one before her.

"Not at all. I have had many fine opportunities to learn things. I have tried not to waste my time." Then, more animatedly, she said, "By the way, I do not believe that a woman's 'natural sphere' is as limited as you apparently do."

"I confess I shouldn't like to see my sisters shoeing horses—or tramping about London at night in the company of a charwoman."

"But what would your sisters say about it?"

"They'd be even more shocked than I am."

Now, when he didn't want her to leave, she rose to her feet. "You're a very narrow person, aren't you, Mr. Archer?"

"Then you've changed your mind."

"No. I thought you were narrow from the moment we met. However, I have changed my mind about one thing. I am going to bed."

"I meant . . . you've decided not to marry me?"

She sat down slowly, as though all the stiffening were

leaking out of her knees. A warm blush suffused her cheeks and, for the first time in their acquaintance, she could not meet his eyes. "When did you guess my purpose?"

"Only a moment ago. I suppose I should tell you that I've been laughing up my sleeve at you ever since this afternoon, but it wouldn't be true."

"Wouldn't it?"

"No. It was only now that my thoughts became clear. I couldn't imagine why you would think we could travel to Egypt together, because the scandal would prevent either of us from accomplishing anything."

"Surely in a land as distant as Egypt, no one would care."

He smiled at her and tried not to sound too patronizing. "The community of Europeans in Cairo is tiny. Everyone knows everyone else's business with an intimacy only rivaled by the smallest of provincial towns. For two people of—pardon me—different genders to attempt to work together without being married . . . but you must know this, or why else would you have proposed?"

She seemed to want to protest his use of the term. He said quickly, "It was a proposal, Miss Hanson, wasn't it?"

Rather to his surprise, she said unblushingly, "Yes. It was."

"I quite realize," she went on, "the impossibility of which you speak. I believed from your letters that you wouldn't be adverse to finding at once a companion and a colleague. Often in your letters I felt that I . . . that we had much in common, not the least of which is loneliness."

"Loneliness?"

Her brown eyes looked black in the gaslight as she looked past him. She seemed slightly fey. He could almost believe she had spoken with a priestess three thousand years dead, just as she now conjured with words his own memories. " 'These desolate sands seem to echo with the sounds of the lost cities that lie beneath them. I am often aware that once, where I now walk alone, friends met, merchants haggled, and passing lovers spoke only with their longing eyes.' "

Now it was Simon's turn to blush. "Did I write that?"

"December fifteenth of last year. Of course, I realize now that you never would have revealed so much of yourself if you'd known you weren't writing to an old lady. But I am very glad that you didn't know. Your letters came to mean a great deal to me, for while you walk alone in Egypt, I am alone in Yorkshire."

"But your father . . . your aunt?"

"I have friends, too. Dear friends, really. I went to school with some of them and have known others since I was a little girl, but . . ." She shook her head, her rippling hair glinting with chestnut lights.

"But?" he prompted.

"Some are married and all they want to talk about is the servant question or clothes. They won't talk to me about their husbands because I am a spinster and mustn't know the things wives whisper about."

Simon cleared his throat. He quite agreed with those unknown matrons.

With that lilt in her voice which told him he was being narrow, she said, "They will talk to me about their babies, though it is a subject of which I know very little. I know which goddess to invoke for their health, yes, or the proper prayers to the crocodile god for easier teething, but somehow they never show much interest."

"How odd," he said, and meant it.

"My unmarried friends are worse yet. They will talk of men; what clothes will entice them, what foods one should feed them, what this word or that gesture meant, everything under the sun to do with men. And yet they never once touch upon the subject of how to embalm one properly."

When he laughed, he saw her smile in relief and realized that her friends probably never understood her when she made a joke.

"And when you raise the subject?" Simon asked.

"I don't dare. I am already thought quite the eccentric in our circle, and it is true. Sometimes I think I have no heart. Certainly it has never beaten at all for the things ladies are commonly held to adore . . . not even for a curate."

"No? Any curate in particular?"

"Oh, young Mr. Bixby was adored by all the proper young ladies in church. He sang hymns on summer evenings to a sighing crowd of maidens. I tried to sigh, feeling it obligatory, but I'm afraid they were not sighs of rapture."

"What does your father think of your interest in things Egyptian?"

"He doesn't mind it. He realizes I must have something to occupy my mind. He has the mill and Mrs. . . ." She shut her lips so tightly on the name that their edges turned quite white.

"And Mrs. . . . who?" Simon said, interested almost despite himself. She was shedding her reserve very quickly and while he was charmed, he also wished for her to protect herself against regret.

She leaned forward confidingly. Simon tried to ignore the shifting of her figure as she moved, but the quilted jacket he wore suddenly seemed both too hot and too tight. He gulped some water.

Julia said, "I may as well tell you everything. My father hasn't wanted me to leave home. So long as I am there he has an excellent excuse for not marrying again. When ladies pursue him—and they do!—he says that he feels he cannot marry until I do. Something about always having promised me a home, or that I will always come first with him. Oh, I have been stared out of countenance many, many times by frustrated women! You can't blame them, I suppose, for feeling that only my selfishness stands between them and the ownership of Father, Dalton Manor, and his twenty thousand pounds a year."

"Twenty thousand pounds?" Simon echoed, hoping his voice didn't squeak.

She nodded glumly. "The mill always shows a good profit and now that Father is trading so heavily with the Americans . . ."

Reminding himself that she was an irritating woman and that nothing, not even unlimited funding for his expeditions, was worth marrying for, Simon managed to put his feet once more on solid ground. He asked levelly, "If you are not the check on your father's remarriage, what is?"

"At first, I think it really was that he couldn't bear the thought of replacing my mother. They'd been childhood sweethearts, you see, and neither of them had ever wished to marry another."

"Very touching."

"It is rather pleasant to be the product of such a love match, Mr. Archer. I don't remember her well, but I remember them together. I want my father to have such happiness again, believe me."

"I do believe you."

"The problem," she said ruefully, "is Father's stubborn nature. If he sets his mind on something, there is no changing it short of murder. His heart is no more changeable than . . . than . . . well, than mine. Unfortunately, the lady on whom he has set his heart was married."

"To an unfeeling brute, no doubt?"

She arched one eyebrow, an infuriating habit that he had himself. "Perhaps. But then again, he could just have been one of those men who have little use for women. There are many such men, I believe. Aren't you one?"

Simon coughed and ran his fingers over his satin lapel. He realized what he was doing and stopped instantly. "On the contrary," he said. "I am very fond of women—very fond. I merely don't care to be married."

"I'm sure Mr. Very felt the same way. It is a mystery to me why, in that case, he married at all. She's much too sweet a woman to be ignored that way."

"You know your father's—"

"Of course! She often stays at the house. All quite aboveboard so long as my aunt is there. Her husband lived most of the time in France . . . in the Dordogne region, I believe. He came home to see her twice in five years. He had a . . . um . . . 'friend' himself."

"And he didn't object to your father's relationship with his wife?"

She sat back and said, "Father, I might mention, though he isn't tall or very impressive, is quite burly and very strong. He is the one that taught me how to shoe a horse."

Simon said, "Surely your father could have arranged a divorce for the lady?"

"In an instant, were she not a most devout Catholic. Religion has been her solace for so long; one would hardly expect her to abandon it merely because it had become inconvenient."

"Naturally, she has her principles. . . ."

"Naturally. However, I am glad to say that this story does have a happy ending. The husband died some months ago. The moment she comes out of mourning, Father will marry her, despite her protests. She doesn't believe herself good enough for him, which is nonsense, as Father will spend his life proving to her, no doubt."

"Provided you are married?"

"Regardless, I think. Father doesn't believe that the three of us will find it hard to live together, but Mrs. Very and I are agreed that it will not serve. My aunt is happy to retire from her position—I think I have been rather a trial to her."

"You amaze me," he said with a grin that she instantly answered with one of her own.

"She will take a pleasant allowance from Father and go

live in Bath. That has been her dream since she was a little girl."

"A strange object for a lifelong dream. Bath is very dreary now, though once it was the last word in elegance."

"It is not a dream I share, but it is hers, so why shouldn't she have it?" She looked down at her hands. "As you have guessed, Aunt Norris and I have not always existed in harmony. Yet I cannot help but be grateful to her, for if she has taught me one thing it is that I do not wish to live as she has done. I have no brother to be useful to and I will not dwindle into a mere housekeeper for my father. Or, indeed, for any other man. If we were to enter into the arrangement I have . . . proposed, I would be your partner and expect to share in both the dangers and the pleasures of our work."

As though in a vision, Simon saw what the future would be like if he were insane enough to accept Miss Hanson's proposal. She had shown herself to be impetuous, oblivious to the propriety of her actions and, taken all together, exactly the sort of woman he most disliked.

He could imagine her becoming so interested in working that his meals would never be served on time. She'd allow too much familiarity on the part of the native servants so that nothing in the house would ever be done properly. In a few years, her fresh complexion would be coarse and dark from the unrelenting sun because she was the sort who would always forget her hat, or find it too restrictive. Her figure would probably go, too, after the first few children . . . but of course, theirs would be a platonic union, dedicated to science.

Thinking of the energy and enthusiasm that seemed to infuse her every action, Simon knew on that point, at least, he was fooling himself. All else he'd imagined would probably come to pass in the life of any man shortsighted enough to marry Julia Hanson. Yet it was absurd to think that a man with blood in his veins could spend day and night in her company and not want to know what embracing Julia, passionate about so much already, would be like. He himself was already far more aware of her as a woman than was good for his peace of mind.

Yet was undoubted sexual bliss worth a lifetime of burned dinners, insolent servants, and intellectual arguments instead of peaceful female acquiescence? Simon told himself that he had—more often than not—found sex a disappointment. It was pleasant while it lasted, but it cost more in self-respect than he wished to pay.

"I'm afraid it's quite impossible," he said.

And yet . . . there were the letters they had exchanged. The woman he'd seen there had been charming, wise, and astoundingly intelligent. She'd shown a vivid interest in even the most mundane events of his daily work and given him many helpful ideas along the way. Sometimes only the unflagging confidence that she expressed gave him the strength to go on when his excavations had proved fruitless once again.

It was for this reason that Simon added, "I'm simply not the sort of man who will ever marry."

"Why not? I know I never shall, now. But why not you? You are relatively young, very good-looking . . . you don't mind my saying so, do you?"

"My mother thinks I am, but I don't spend very much time looking in the glass."

"You may believe your mother," Julia said. He was glad to see her smile. For a moment, he'd thought he'd hurt her too much by refusing her. Her eyes had seemed to wince. Now he realized she'd never expected him to accept. Perhaps she'd cherished a half-reared hope, but she would have known that any decent man would refuse her offer.

She continued, looking at him dispassionately, her head to one side. "Yes, quite good-looking, bright, fairly witty when you forget to be stern, and I think you could be, all in all, young love's dream."

"Oh, for heaven's sake . . . !"

She laughed. "So why not? I'm sure there are half a dozen friends of your sisters who would marry you with glad cries."

"If I married half a dozen, I would be arrested."

"There! You see! Fairly witty. Besides, you need only marry four to be quite *au fait* in a Muslim country."

"I know a few men with more than one wife. If your aunt is an object lesson to you, my friends are the same to me. Besides, I already have my 'harem.' They are asleep upstairs. Four women who rely on me absolutely."

"I can't wait to meet your sisters," Julia said. "What are they like?"

"Nice girls," he answered after a moment's considera-tion. "Jane can be a minx. She's the youngest, and some-what spoiled. Amanda spends too much time reading novels. She is always mooning about and tends to forget things. Lucy is the eldest and is best fitted to run the house. Mother doesn't always have the strength to manage the servants or to keep the accounts. My father did all those things and Mother never needed to learn."

"So Lucy is the one you trust the most."

"She's a very good sort of girl. Reliable."

"They have no interests outside the house?" Her tone was not provoking, yet he was slightly nettled by the tenor of the question.

"I don't think so. They go to parties when they can. Lucy was actually presented at court when she came out. The other two will make their curtsies next year thanks to my uncle."

"Ah!" In a fair imitation of his mother's voice, she said, " 'Before my marriage, I was the Honorable Miss Plimp-set.' "

He should have frowned at this show of disrespect, but he was taken by surprise and laughed instead. "I should have known she'd find a way to work it into the conver-sation."

"It was more dropped in than worked in . . ."

Simon said, "It was the greatest disappointment of her life when my uncle married and had three boys in four years. I think Mother used to plan that one day I'd be the Earl of Rexbury. I was never so relieved in my life when his wife gave him the first heir. The last thing I need in my life is a titled position!"

"It would interfere with the digs."

"It would be the very devil . . . I beg your pardon."

"Oh, don't. You should hear my father when he forgets I'm in the room."

Behind them, the kitchen clock struck four rather dull notes. Both Simon and Julia looked, in surprise, at the hands. Simon looked twice, unable to believe so much time had passed. "You must be exhausted."

Her eyes took on a faraway look for a moment. "Yes," she said as if giving the idea slow study. "Yes, I am. It has been a most unusual day."

"I'll walk up with you."

"I can find it, and . . . your mother is already suspicious of me. If she sees us together . . . and me in this . . ." she plucked at the sleeve of her nightdress and did not finish her sentence.

"Nevertheless, as your host, I will escort you."

"On your head be it."

When she stood up, he saw that the dress was too short. Her slender ankles curved away, showing off a pair of feet as small and pretty as a fairy's. Beneath her glossy skin, muscles flexed as she crossed the stone-flagged floor. Simon felt desire strike into him like a flaming arrow. He must have gasped involuntarily, for she turned, her dress flaring out slightly, to glance at him inquisitively.

Then she looked past him, with an expression of recognition in her eyes. He turned, too, and saw the shadow of a cat against the window.

Nine

An-ket sat on the kitchen windowsill, quite enjoying her balanced command of the narrow ledge. Though an adherent of Hathor, she had always been on easy terms with the goddess Bastet, Queen of Cats.

What bliss to leap lightly from the ground to the shoulder height of a man with so little effort! How delightful to walk surefooted where only a cat could trespass! She reveled in the play of her sinews and spent no less than five minutes flexing her front claws to watch them pop in and out of her paw. Oh, the pleasures of a tail wound about the feet . . . and the sensitive communications of her whiskers! Small wonder cats always bore themselves like the superior race. They were!

On the negative side, she could tell from the rough condition of her coat that she was not well cared for. And her tiny stomach grumbled at the abrupt end of the snack she'd been sharing with Julia.

Twitching an ear toward the sound of the man's voice, An-ket eavesdropped unashamedly. This strange world in which she had awakened was full of mysteries. Everything that could help her explain what she saw and heard around her must be done, even if she did not quite approve morally.

Julia had explained why she'd come to London during their drink in the "pub," so when An-ket heard her address "Mis-ter Ar-cher," she listened all the more closely. What sort of man had discovered her tomb? An-ket found herself very curious, and leaned her head against the cool, smooth surface of the window. It pleased her, this clear substance, and she was surprised to find that it was the same as the mug that had held her beer.

Perhaps it was her sharpened cat's senses that told her the truth about the two people in the room beyond. Though their language was as correct and proper as a priest's, she could hear the surge of emotions beneath the smooth surface. That Julia was already attracted to the man, An-ket had guessed, but how pleasant to learn that he had seen her friend as a desirable creature. It was also plain that they were so intent upon impressing each other with their courtly manners that neither of them would lift a finger to improve upon this moment alone.

What could she do to foster a better use of their time?

An-ket smiled as she cast her thoughts back across the centuries.

A whispering song from a blind harper had mingled with the perfumed air as the family celebrated the marriage contract between her sister Saret and the man of her choosing. Choice meats and fowls, ripe grapes and figs were spread upon the tables while near-naked servants, their bodies scented with oils, served wine to their master's guests. An-ket's father's chief's wife presented magnificent beaded necklaces to her new in-laws, while her father smiled proudly in the background, his eyes filling with tears at times when friends praised his children.

Dressed in a shining wig and a new gown of fine pleated linen, An-ket sat with the other unmarried girls, rejoicing for her sister's happiness and wondering when her own turn would come. She lifted one of the flowers from the table to tuck it behind her ear. Then—it was the merest chance that made her turn her head at that moment—she looked up to see a man enter the dining chamber. For one instant, no one else seemed to see him.

He stood looking about him with a half-smile on his firm lips, as though in expectation of wearing a broader one when his welcoming host should approach him. His shoulders were as broad as a mountain range, while his smooth, hard chest showed plainly beneath his tunic of semitransparent linen. About his throat he wore a Golden Fly, symbol of bravery in battle against Pharaoh's enemies. His shoulder-length wig displayed high cheekbones and a pair of brilliant eyes, which met hers at that instant.

She would never be the same again.

Her father clapped his hands to silence the musicians as he hastened forward. "My lord! You are welcome in our house. Come, meet my friends."

An-ket heard the other maidens whispering his name. He was Senusret, ninth son of the god-king, but his Golden Fly was not given to him because he was Pharaoh's son, but because he had himself killed an enemy general in single combat. They whispered that he was as beautiful as a red hawk soaring above the golden sands, and giggled behind their hands at their daring as they peeked at him. An-ket sniffed and said, "I do not think him so very fine."

He looked at her and smiled, though it was impossible that he could have heard her over so many other voices. She tilted her chin into the air, even while her father was offering him the finest chair and sending a servant for the mate to his own alabaster cup. Yet she could not forbear glancing at him a moment later. He lifted the cup to her before he drank. She felt her cheeks flush and turned away abruptly. Somehow the sound of his chuckle reached her.

Two days later, when she went to the marketplace to buy some hairpins as a gift to her sister, Senusret was there with several friends. He wore a short kilt, and she thought she'd never seen legs so smooth and strong. Instead of his medal, he wore a blue scarab on a thong, the stone rising and falling on his chest as he breathed. She felt her own breathing change to match his, so aware of him was she. He spoke her name and as if he had performed some spell, she stopped to hear him. His friends bowed and withdrew, taking her servant with them.

"An-ket . . ."

They stood beside a small shop that had baskets full of little statues of the gods. They were cheap things, amulets for peasants, yet their presence added a solemnity to the scene that she never forgot.

"An-ket, do you know who I am?"

"Yes," she said, but did not raise her eyes to him. The sun beat down, making the air waver between them, but it was not the heat of the sun that troubled her, but the heat in his eyes. She lifted a corner of the shawl she wore about her shoulders and covered her head. "You are the son of the Lady Meret."

"I am your husband."

She felt a warm glow inside as she acknowledged the truth of his words, but did not want to give him too easy a conquest. "My husband? One of us is mistaken, my lord. I have not chosen a husband."

"You chose me at the same moment I chose you. Let us go to your father, for my heart claims you as my own."

"My father will no doubt rejoice, but what of yours? I am not of your house."

She turned to go, but Senusret caught her hand. His fingers were strong but gentle. About his wrist he wore a gold bracelet incised with the Eye of Horus in lapis lazuli. "Before the Great White Baboon rises full in the sky, you will be mine."

With her eyes she told him that she was his already, but her willful mouth said as she freed herself, "I am not of your house, Prince. Seek among the great ladies for your bride. See how my hands are rough and sun-burnt?"

She turned her arm over so that he could contrast the pale amber smoothness of her skin to his own, darkened by long marches and chariot drives under the full power of the sun. An-ket was proud of her arms, slender and graceful, and wanted him to notice them. Her hands, too, had the long fingers and flowing gestures so prized in their arts.

"Her hands are the boats that carry my soul," he quoted, then grinned at her with an impudence that made her laugh despite her best intentions. A moment later, though, she tossed him a furious glance and hurried away, calling her servant to her. Badly flustered, she did not get as good a bargain as she might have on the hairpins. At home, she—

In her cat form, An-ket frowned, twitching her tail. Her memories were so clear, up to a point. She could recall the very shape and color of the hairpins, the ends cunningly carved and painted like lotus blossoms. Yet when she tried to remember her marriage to Senusret, she saw only the night that surrounded her. The voices of the two people inside were distinct once more.

"Nevertheless, as your host, I will escort you."

"On your head be it."

An-ket peered through the hard, clear substance and saw that Julia and the man were leaving the small room. She felt a great curiosity to know what they would do next. If they were wise, they'd forget to be so courteous and let their joyful bodies take the steps that lead to delight. There did not seem to be any reason why they should not, though An-ket acknowledged there might be constraints in this strange place of which she knew nothing.

She slipped inside the room, through a space too narrow for anything but a cat. They had left the far door slightly ajar. An-ket eased back onto her hind legs and hooked a forepaw around the door, pulling it open just enough to insinuate herself through. It was strange to be able to compress and lengthen one's body at need.

The house smelled stale, as though it had been sealed as tightly as a tomb for a long time. To a human, the darkness of the hall would have required outstretched arms and tentative fingertips brushing along a wall for guidance. To An-ket, slit pupils opened wide, all was clear and easy. She twitched an ear toward the scrabbling sound of mice in the walls. Her cat instincts went on alert, as her hollow stomach informed her that this chance of a meal was too good to miss.

But An-ket ignored her small body's needs as she halted. The two young people stood at the foot of the stairs—strange to notice how little stairs had changed— still talking. Above them, a single globe glowed with light, so that their faces were illuminated, while their feet were in shadow. An-ket could come very close to them without either person being aware of her.

"Will you return home to Yorkshire at once?" Simon asked. "If not, I would be honored to show you the ex-hibition as I had promised."

"Thank you. I don't think I will go home for a little while yet. Tomorrow I will find some servants . . . do you happen to know of a good employment bureau?"

"Mother probably will be able to give you some name or other, but surely you can't mean to set up a household in London without some decent woman to give you her companionship?"

Before she could answer, he held up his hand and said, "I know . . . I know. You will do what you think is best, no doubt."

"Yes, but at the same time, you are right. I should have someone if only to prevent my neighbors from shunning me. Do you have a maiden aunt by any chance who would care to come have a holiday in London at my expense?"

An-ket rolled her eyes toward heaven. At this rate, they'd still be standing there when the Great God of the Sun drove his chariot into the sky! Out came An-ket's claws.

"Aagh!" Simon exclaimed sharply, staggering forward. Surprised, Julia moved back hastily, only to trip over the fleeing cat. Without a second's hesitation, Simon grabbed her, keeping her from falling by pulling her into his arms. Though he'd acted on instinct to save her from harm, his body reacted as though his need was to kiss her. His hands were filled with her warmth, while the perfume of her hair flooded him. Slowly he brought her upright, his eyes fixed on hers, as he realized that kissing Julia was a very good idea indeed.

Julia had always preferred to keep her feet on solid ground, but being off-balance in Simon Archer's arms was deliciously exciting. Such excitement was dangerous. It made her head swim so that she could no longer keep sight of what was important.

Though she'd rather cold-bloodedly plotted to marry him, she'd never thought beyond the realization of her dream of a career. Now she realized there was more to Simon than science.

Looking up into his eyes, she saw his intellectual gifts change their focus. A new kind of curiosity increased the blue intensity of his eyes as they studied her mouth. With what seemed to be calculated slowness, he raised one hand and drew the back of his forefinger down the slope of her cheek. His touch was feather-light, as if he handled some fragile treasure newly exposed to the day.

She couldn't speak or move away. Her limbs felt heavy and without will. A raving need to know more of his touch had taken possession of her, but she could not form the words to ask for what she wanted. She could only hope that he knew more than she.

With each touch melding into the next, he traced the swell of her lower lip with the tips of his fingers. Julia gripped his forearms, afraid to fall if he failed to hold her. It was there she first knew that he intended to kiss her, when the muscles of his arms tightened under her hands.

He moved his hand under the heavy mass of her hair, to thrust his fingers into the cool, entangling mass of curls.

"Julia," he said, and his voice rasped as though he were engaged in a ruthless struggle.

She curled her fingers into his shoulders, closing what little space still remained between them. Along with nervous qualms, she felt an impatience with his deliberate speed. Wondering why she had hesitated to act, she lifted her face toward his. Then the light that fell around them increased as someone on the landing above turned up the gaslight. Instantly Simon stepped back, releasing her so quickly he might as well have thrown her.

Julia looked up, blinking, as dazed as an owl in daylight. She saw Mrs. Archer looking down at them, her thin brows raised. "Whatever are you doing down there so late? Simon? It's after four!"

"I had not meant to wake you, Mother. Miss Hanson was hungry, and so was I."

"Hungry?"

"We had overlooked dinner. We are going to bed. . . ." He coughed as though the words had caught in his throat. "That is, Miss Hanson is very tired."

"Yes, I am," Julia said clearly, placing her foot on the bottom step. Looking back at Simon, she asked, "What time tomorrow shall we go to the museum?"

"Sleep as late as you care to. Everything is ready and if I go in early, I'll just fuss about."

Mrs. Archer said, "You don't know what a compliment that is, Miss Hanson. Usually Simon is waiting outside his precious museum before it even opens."

To her surprise, Mrs. Archer seemed much less hostile than she had earlier. Julia wondered what had caused so sudden a change.

On reaching the landing, Julia said, "I'm not certain that I thanked you properly for allowing me to stay in your home overnight, Mrs. Archer. Tomorrow I shall open my house in Carderock Square, provided I can find some servants."

Simon, climbing toward them, said, "Yes, Mother. Can

you recommend a good employment bureau?"

"I wish that I could, but they are usually dreadful! A really good servant shouldn't require the use of such a place!" Mrs. Archer looked askance at Julia's ankles. "You must be cold, my dear. Hurry back to bed. Don't worry about tomorrow. I shall have my maid bring you breakfast in bed at whatever hour you ring."

Her new cordiality was so marked that even Simon noticed it. One fair brow rose in surprise as he glanced between the two women. "You'd better go back to bed yourself, Mother, or you'll be fit for nothing in the morning. I'll make sure Miss Hanson reaches her room safely."

Julia smiled at them both with equal warmth. "It's only a step. Good night—again!"

As she turned to leave them, she idly glanced down the stairs. There, at the edge of the pool of light, she saw the cat walking, hardly more solid than a shadow. She found herself divided between a hope that An-ket would visit her again, and a nearly overwhelming need for sleep. Her long day had been followed by a tiring night, and she wanted nothing more now than to rest her head on a pillow. Though if Simon Archer looked at her again with that vivid light in his eyes, she felt somehow that her tiredness would vanish in a heartbeat.

Behind her, Mrs. Archer caught her breath so sharply that Julia spun about, staring. The older woman lifted a shaking hand to point down the stairs. "C-c-cat!" she stuttered, the word rising into a shriek.

"Now, Mother . . ." Simon said, without effect.

Mrs. Archer shrank back, the back of her hand against her mouth, her wide eyes rolling wildly. "Chase it away! What is it doing in here? Chase it away!"

An-ket had seated herself in the center of the pool of light and gazed upwards, as still as a cat carved of ebony. Only the flickering glow in her amber eyes showed as a sign of life. To hear Mrs. Archer, however, one would have thought the small alley cat was a ferocious tiger stalking her.

"My mother dislikes cats," Simon said in explanation as he slipped his arm about Mrs. Archer's waist. His mother began sobbing on his shoulder.

"Dislikes? She sounds terrified!"

"That, yes."

All but simultaneously, three doors on the landing swung open, disgorging three young ladies into the hallway. Two were enveloped in flowery wrappers, the third was fully dressed except for her shoes. They all had long hair flowing down their backs, straight, sleek, and elegant even in dishabille. If for no other reason, Julia could envy the Archer sisters for their hair.

The smallest, and roundest, of the three stepped close to her mother, looking with worried eyes at Simon. "What's wrong?"

"There's a cat in the house. Mother saw it."

"A cat!" exclaimed the one that was fully dressed, peering about her. "Where?"

"Come, Mother," said the smallest sister. "Come with me."

"Oh, yes, Jane. Lock the door so it can't get in."

"Lucy," Simon said. "Please go down and chase it out of here. I'll help Jane tend to Mother."

"Come on," said the third sister, Amanda. "We'll have better luck if we both look."

Julia said, "I'll help too, shall I?"

The two sisters just looked at her in surprise. They were remarkably pretty girls, fair like their brother and with similarly blue eyes. But where Simon's eyes were stern and piercing, the girls' wore a milder expression. Amanda's were half-hidden behind a pair of silver-framed glasses riding atop a small nose. She smiled at Julia, both quizzical and amiable.

Lucy seemed to droop where she stood. She was fairly tall for a woman, though her bent shoulders took an inch or so off what should be her natural height. In repose, the corners of her mouth turned down. Looking at her, Julia's hands itched. She wanted to grab the girl and give her a good shaking—but that would never do.

"Why, who are you?" Amanda asked.

"My name is Julia Hanson. I am an acquaintance of your brother's."

Even Lucy's lackluster eyes widened at this. "You're Simon's mysterious Miss Hanson?"

"I seem to be."

"But you're not ninety!" Amanda blurted.

"Amanda!" her sister said, putting her hand against the other's arm. "Don't be so gauche! Please excuse her, Miss Hanson. My brother has not said a great deal about you."

"He's been as quiet as a clam," Amanda added, irrepressibly.

Lucy said, "I'm sorry none of us were here to welcome you when you arrived. Simon must have forgotten to tell us you would be staying with us. I'm so very pleased you are here."

"I hardly knew I would be staying myself. Mr. Archer persuaded me that I would not be putting anyone out by coming."

"Oh, definitely not!" Lucy was indeed much improved by vivacity. When lost in her own thoughts, the other two eclipsed her. Drawn out of herself by even so minor a conversation, she held her head up and her cheeks brightened. Of the three girls, she had the greatest potential for beauty. Her face was a piquant heart shape, her skin as flawless as peach velvet.

Jane opened her mother's door an inch or two. "Have you put it out yet?"

"No," Amanda called. "Not yet."

"Well, hurry! Mother will never calm herself until you tell her it's quite gone."

"Then tell her it is," Julia said.

"Oh, no!" Lucy looked horrified. "We never lie to Mother."

"But if it will ease her . . . oh, very well. Let us go find the cat."

Since Julia felt certain An-ket would come to her when she called, it surprised her when, after a few minutes calling "hi, puss, puss" the cat came purring up to Lucy. The girl bent and lifted the seemingly boneless body into her arms. She cuddled the cat against her bosom. "There, now."

"You like cats," Julia said, stating an evident fact.

"Yes, I adore them. Old maids are supposed to, aren't they?" Her voice was sharp with bitterness. Cuddling the cat under one arm, she approached the front door.

"Wait," Julia said, not wanting to lose her chance to speak again with An-ket. She wanted to ask her to pay a visit to Simon, to convince him, for both their sakes, that what Julia said was true. "Why not give the cat to me? It can stay in my room and then in the morning, it can leave with me."

"No. Mother would find out and she truly is terrified of cats. It's beyond reason."

Amanda hurried, in response to a glance, to unlock the door and throw it open. "Poor old thing," Lucy said, bending down to put the cat onto the stone threshold. "I wish we could . . ."

She held the position, cat still in her hands, and stared across the street. Behind her, Julia looked to see what had so engaged the other girl's attention. Judging by her rigidity and appalled expression, Julia expected to see nothing less than a sheeted spectre.

She saw nothing more portentous than a black carriage pulled up in front of a similar town house. A man was in the act of descending. He was tall, graceful, and the light spilling from the Archer home reflected from the gold braid decorating his shoulders, sleeves, and breast. Despite the lateness of the hour, he showed not a trace of weariness.

Then he, too, looked about him and saw the three young ladies posed in the doorway. He already carried his uniform hat under his arm so he could not sweep it off, yet he made a profound bow. Julia couldn't help smiling, any more than she could help noticing that the other two girls seemed stricken with paralysis. Holding up the pride of womanhood, Julia dipped a curtsey.

The cat, seeming to lose its docility, wrenched free of Lucy's grip with a wide-mouthed hiss. Lucy seemed to shake off her inertia and stepped quickly back, shutting the door with an emphatic bang.

"Did you hear . . . bells?" Amanda asked.

"I don't believe so," Julia said. "Who was that very nice-looking young man?"

With a sideways glance at her silent sister, Amanda said, "Our neighbor's son, Major Robert Winslow. He's attached to the court, you know, and always attending the most elegant parties." She giggled faintly. "His name is forever appearing in the *Court Circular*. I think the prince is quite fond of him."

She nodded toward Lucy as though to say that Prince Albert was not the only one fond of Robert Winslow. Julia thought this an interesting piece of news. She wondered if Simon knew of it.

Suddenly, she was caught unawares by a huge yawn. "Oh! I beg your pardon. Perhaps we should tell your mother that the cat is out . . . and then I'm going to retire."

At the door to her room, Julia was startled when Amanda kissed her cheek, as fleeting as a butterfly landing on a wind-waving flower. "My sisters and I are so very, very glad that you have come!"

"You are?"

"Oh, yes. We dearly love our brother, you know. He can be stern . . ." She shook her head slightly. "Well, never mind that! What I mean to say is, any friend of

Simon is our friend too. Isn't that right, Lucy?"

The solemn girl inclined her head graciously as she entered her own room. Amanda gave vent to her soft giggle once more. "Never mind *her*. She's blighted, you know. It's very sad."

Knowing she'd regret it, Julia asked, "How is she blighted?"

"Love," Amanda whispered, then shrugged. "I intend to avoid it, myself. It seems to cause nothing but complications!"

Closing her door at last, Julia could only echo that sentiment. Thinking of the look in Simon's eyes when he'd almost . . . what? Had he intended to kiss her? She certainly had been planning to do just that.

One more instant and she would have been part of an irrevocable act that would have changed them both forever. So much safer not to kiss him. So much wiser not to give in to such an unreserved emotion. Keeping a cool head was so important for a girl.

Yet, as she lay down on her pillow, she wondered what wonderful thing might have happened if they had been given just that one more instant of time?

Ten
ᴗ

Across the way, Robert Winslow stooped to cat-stealing. It was not the action of an officer or a gentleman, but of a man desperately in love. Had it really been two years since he'd last spoken to Lucy Archer? The lost time had telescoped into an instant when he descended from his father's carriage to see her at the door of her house. He had believed himself to be over her. He now knew he'd been deceiving himself.

The cat waited until the carriage had driven off before running as if on tiptoe across the gleaming street. It stepped lightly between the iron railings that separated the front steps of one house from the one next to it. Robert carefully noted the place, then entered his own home.

There were bound to be scraps from dinner. If he could just entice the cat into range . . .

He carried a plate of chosen morsels outside, carefully keeping the grease from soiling his dress uniform. Making what he hoped were alluring sounds, he laid the plate down on the concrete walk and stepped back.

The cat had no qualms about being bribed. It choked down the food with such rapidity that Robert said, "Here now. Be careful."

Capturing the creature was surprisingly easy. When its

pink tongue had given the plate a final polish, Robert simply picked up the plate. The cat stood below him, looking up. It shifted on its paws as if hoping against hope.

"Come on, then."

The cat trotted along behind, its attention riveted to the plate Robert bore away. Robert kept chatting to it, promising it all sorts of delicious viands and beverages if it would only follow him into the house. Even then, he was not sure what he was about. He had some idea that Lucy would come looking for her cat and in that way, he could again be admitted to her friendship.

"Robert?" his father called.

"Sir? I'm sorry I woke you."

"I wasn't asleep." Tying his robe about his waist, General Winslow came limping down the staircase. "I was working on my memoirs."

"How goes it, sir?"

"Well enough, well enough. What's that?"

Robert looked down to where the cat was twining itself around his ankles, no doubt making a hairy mess of his uniform trousers. "It's a cat."

"You astound me. Here, puss." Leaning heavily on the newel post, the general bent down to let the cat smell his fingertips. When it condescended to do so, the general stroked its head. Its rumbling purr stuttered and sputtered as if it had been infrequently used.

"That's a nice cat," the general said. "Is it a stray?"

"I—I believe so."

"I wonder if Mrs. Nicely could use a cat in the kitchen. She was complaining of mice the other day." The general's wrinkled, hooded eyes brooded upon the cat. "We shall call her Josephine, for she looks a bit like the Creole empress about the eyes. Don't you think?"

"If you say so, Father. I believe Josephine would like some cream."

"I'll do it. You'd better go to bed. You're expected at

Whitehall in the morning." He handed his son a white envelope.

"What on earth do they want now? I was there for hours only this afternoon." He tore the envelope open.

"Duty, my boy. The message came while you were out."

Robert read the information contained in the note. It was from his friend, Bunty Bruce, attache to some minister or other. "It's not too bad. Just another discussion of the situation as I left it in the Punjab."

"Again? You'd think they'd know that backward and forward by now. Why, in my day, we would never . . . but then, I don't want to go on forever about *my* wars. It's the modern-day battles we must fight and no one is better suited to soldiering than you, my boy."

General Winslow's pride centered around his only son having followed him into the army. He never tired of telling his cronies at the club that his boy had risen to major five years before he himself had attained such a rank. "And then," he'd say with a chuckle, "it took Waterloo to do it!"

Robert himself had only once entertained doubts about his career in the army. That had been during his last home leave, when he'd fallen hopelessly in love with Lucy Archer, then in the full flower of her debut. She had been the sweetest, gravest creature imaginable, with great blue eyes that could turn sentimentally damp over music or poetry. He'd counted a smile from her as a greater triumph than the battles he'd known. But the thought of such a delicate, fine flower withering in the heat of India, a place that destroyed even strong and healthy men, had appalled him. He'd gone away without proposing, stealing one kiss as a bulwark against a bleak future. Lucy had reacted badly, but he could not forget that one blissful instant when he'd felt her lips cling to his.

The future had proved brighter than he could have imagined. Through sheer luck—for he never gave himself credit for his military talents—he had led a charge against the Sikhs. Having his horse shot from under him, and receiving a minor scalp wound, added to his fame. He'd received a medal, too, and falling into conversation with Prince Albert after the ceremony, had the good fortune to praise one of the prince's ideas for reforming the uniforms of his battalion. He had not known at the time that it was the prince's idea, though no one believed him now. Many people found the prince stiff and formal, but no one who saw him working so hard for so little notice could fail to respect the man.

Other things had changed besides his position in the world. Simon Archer was famous; there was even talk at court that the queen and the prince would make an appearance at the grand ball given to celebrate the exhibition of his fabulous find. The two younger girls were fully grown young ladies and Lucy had become something of a recluse.

His father claimed that he had not seen her in just under two years. Before Robert had kissed her, she'd been wont to come to his door every other day to arrange the flowers or do the other duties of a daughter. Had that been the reason the kiss Robert had pressed on her lips had shocked her so? Did she regard her childhood friend as a brother only? He knew the general missed her. He did not say so, but he did.

Robert knew it was despicable to use Lucy's cat to reach her. He felt that if only they could talk for a few minutes all their misunderstandings would be cured. But how to do it? She never seemed to go out. The one time he'd sent his card in, it had come back very carefully snipped into small squares of pasteboard only fit for the calling cards of extra-formal mice.

Between the two of them, the general and Robert managed to find a warm corner for Josephine. They tipped some clean sheets out of Mrs. Nicely's clothes basket and lined the wickerwork with today's *Times*.

Then, weary right down to his bones, Robert went to bed. Within half an hour, he'd heard his father's door open and close twice. Robert rose and went to investigate. His father was creeping along the corridor to his bed-chamber at the far end.

"Father? Is something amiss? Do you feel unwell?"

Without turning, the general said, "Oh, no. All is well. God bless you, Robert, and good night."

Robert had no doubt that if his father felt ill, the proud man would do all he could to conceal it. So he walked up behind his father and asked again. A strange thrum-ming sound interrupted him.

He walked around the general, only to have his father turn away from him again. "Father?" Robert asked, torn between amusement and hurt.

The general sighed gustily. He faced his son and showed him the little black face peering out from the breast of his dressing gown. "I went down to see if she'd had all she wanted. She seemed comfortable in her nest near the stove but, after a time, I thought perhaps she'd be happier in my room. I don't need all the pillows Mrs. Nicely gives me."

Robert chucked the cat under the chin. It closed greeny-gold eyes in pleasure. "She probably has enough fleas to populate a kennel."

"I don't know about that. She seems a clean little thing. And what are a few fleas in exchange for companion-ship?"

Robert knew the general often felt lonely, especially with his only son away so much of the time. When his inevitable recall came up, General Winslow would be all the more solitary. "Wouldn't you prefer a dog, sir?"

"No. I'll never have another dog after poor old Baltha-zar. But a cat, now . . . a cat is a good friend to an old man. She stays close to warm his aching knees and there is something pleasantly meditative in the stroking of soft fur. Not that yours is so very soft, my little one. Whoever your master was, he did not pay enough attention to you. Or perhaps you were one of many, eh?"

Remembering that this was Lucy's cat, Robert tried to weaken his father's interest. "She probably does belong to someone. . . ."

"I shall watch for posted notices of a lost cat. Until then, she may as well stay with us."

In his room, Robert removed his uniform, heaving a sigh of deep relief when he unbuckled the stiff stock from around his neck. He hung up his trousers to be brushed. His throat felt scratchy and dry from the cigar smoke and whiskey that had followed dinner at Her Majesty's table. He opened his bedroom window, which overlooked the street, and stood in front of it while drinking off a tumble of water.

It was as he was lowering the glass from his face that he realized that there was someone in the street below. He would have dismissed this visitor as a policeman on his rounds, or a late-passing stranger, were it not that the man was standing there staring at Lucy's house.

Impetuously, Robert thrust his head out and shouted, "Here! What do you want?"

The figure did not start or look around. He simply turned and walked away, the long cape, such as a man might wear to the opera, swinging above his heels.

Julia awoke to a sparkling day and the smell of freshly cooked bacon. A maid was just peeking in around the door, her starched cap bobbing. "I'm awake," Julia said, stretching out all her limbs. "What time is it?"

"Now, there, I didn't mean to wake you. 'Let her sleep,' the mistress says to me. 'Went to bed ever so late,' she says. 'And them what's young need more sleep than old 'uns.' Mind you," she said, coming in at a bustle and jerking apart the curtains, "I could do with a bit of a lie-in meself this morning."

"Why? Are you ill?"

"Oh, no, miss. It's just this here ball we're all working ourselves to death on account of."

"Ball?"

"To celebrate the young master's bits of junk he found out in them heathen nations he's always traipsing off to. And a more higgledy-piggledy mess there never was!"

"How do you mean?"

The maid gave her a darkling look. "You'll find out if you stay on. This one says such and such, while her sister says 'no, it's to be thus and so.' Not to say what I shouldn't, but it's only worse when they go to the mistress. 'Tis a shambles, right enough."

She whisked up Julia's clothes. "Here, I'll have these brushed and back before the cat can lick her ear."

"The cat!" Julia tossed aside the blankets and slipped out of bed. She was forced to engage in a short tug-of-war with the maid over her clothes. "No, I don't care to have them brushed . . . they'll do just the way are."

Releasing her grip on her skirt, Julia pushed her hair out of her face and said, "What is your name?"

"Apple, miss," the maid answered, bobbing a little curt-sey while a look of consternation crept into her pretty gray eyes. She only had that much beauty. Her face was marked by tiny pitted scars over her cheeks, while her stout figure was positively brawny in the tight black stuff gown she wore. Julia decided not to pursue the tug-of-war any farther after seeing the girl's arm strength. An apron was pinned on at her waist to fall like a crisp white flag of cleanliness and virtue. Like a nun's scapular, it told everyone what she was—a menial—while at the same time daring anyone to humor her or bear with her.

"Well, Apple, I am only staying with the Archers over-night. The night is done, so I'm leaving today. My own maid will take care of my clothes, though I thank you for the trouble you've gone to for me."

"Don't you want no breakfast?"

"Breakfast sounds wonderful. Why don't you get it while I dress?"

As soon as the maid left, Julia threw open wide the window of her room. She poked her head out and looked down into the street. The sky gave a promise of a clear day and the usual vendors had already come out. Maids in caps, cooks in aprons, butlers muffled in their own aprons of green baize stood trading, shopping, or gossiping. It must be early, Julia reasoned, for in a little while all this humanity would be back behind doors or would have moved off to some other sector of the city.

She leaned her chin on her hands and watched them. One maid with pretty blond hair was flirting just as hard as she could with the knife grinder, but Julia would have bet that her real interest lay with the handsome, if older, butler behind her. He was pretending not to notice her while he exchanged courtly greetings with another man—a gentleman's personal gentleman by the look of his slightly more flamboyant waistcoat—but Julia noticed the way he frowned when he looked past his friend. She smiled, hoping it would all turn out well.

All the while, she kept a watch for the cat. If An-ket were down there, she'd find a way to show herself.

When Apple returned with Julia's breakfast, she still had not dressed, so the maid bore off her clothes with an air of triumph. Realizing she was near to starving, Julia ate everything in sight, even eyeing the daisy in the little glass vase with appetite. She drew the line there, however.

When a knock sounded at her door, she knew it couldn't be Apple. "Come in."

Mrs. Archer entered, her head enveloped in a fluffy lace cap and a straw-colored cashmere peignoir swathed around her crinolined form. "I could not understand Apple when she said you were awake and breakfasting already! Ah, the resilience of youth!"

"It was less my youth and more my stomach that woke me, ma'am." She expected at least a frown for referring to so delicate an object as a stomach, but Mrs. Archer surprised her by laughing merrily.

"You poor thing! So remiss of Simon not to feed you but there! Men always have their heads in the clouds."

"I can't blame him. He wasn't with me at dinnertime. But I must compliment you on your cook, Mrs. Archer. Such a marvelous omelette! The mushrooms were perfectly sauteed. How do you suppose she does it? Mine always come out like india rubber."

"A good cook is like a good stage magician, my dear. They never reveal their secrets." She took the tray from Julia's lap, placing it on the bedside table, and sat down across from her. "So—now. Tell me what your plans are. My son said something about planning to open your home? Hire servants and the like?"

"Yes, ma'am."

"But surely you are only remaining in London for a very short period? You don't intend to live here all year round, for instance?"

"No, indeed. I shall return home in a few weeks for my father's wedding."

Mrs. Archer paused a moment. "Ah. Your father is marrying again? How wonderful! Some sweet young creature, no doubt."

"No, a widow of maturity."

"Indeed. Well," she said with a bright, yet wistful, smile. "That lends hope to us all. Not that I'd ever marry again. My dear husband was the most patient and understanding of men. No one could ever replace him in my heart. You are, as I understand it, the only child?"

"Yes. My mother died when I was quite young."

"Poor child." Mrs. Archer patted Julia's knee. "I can at least tell myself that my children need not miss their father so much when they have each other. My girls are devoted to each other—quite devoted."

"I should have liked a younger brother or sister. Someone to look after. . . ."

"Perhaps one day you shall have them. After all, you may marry someone with siblings. Then they would become yours. My own dear brother—the earl—he was very fond of my husband, though at first he thought him not quite good enough for his sister! But they were soon reconciled with each other, and Jack has been really wonderful to the children. He has his own now, of course, but never a birthday or a holiday go by without some mark of his affection."

"That must be very gratifying." She was still at a loss to know why Mrs. Archer's attitude toward her had changed so drastically. Last night, she'd seemed most unwelcoming. Later on, and now this morning, she seemed determined to be gracious. Even more than gracious, Mrs. Archer was being positively congenial.

"He's even throwing open his house for the ball we are giving to celebrate Simon's discovery. Everyone will be there. We've even something of a promise that the queen herself . . . but there! I shouldn't even hint at such things."

"I have never seen the queen. My father is very much a queen's man, though, as they used to say."

"Oh, a little lady in stature, but very much what one would want one's queen to be. None of that loose behavior like those Egyptian queens Simon studies. I sometimes wonder if . . . but I shouldn't trouble you with a mother's worries."

For no longer than a heartbeat, Mrs. Archer's determinedly bright prattle faded along with her toothy smile. "You are very easy to talk to, my dear Miss Hanson."

"So people say. But you must call me Julia."

"May I?" She seemed inordinately pleased. "Well, then, Julia, I must tell you that Simon will probably be champing at the bit to be gone. The exhibition opens tomorrow and he will want to make some last-minute changes. Undoubtedly!"

"Would you tell him that the moment Apple brings my

dress back from being pressed I will be with him?"

Alone, Julia washed her face, hands, and the back of her neck, vowing that the first thing she would do when in her own home would be to have the bathtub scrubbed out. Then she'd soak herself in a concoction of lavender salts until all the kinks were gone. She had a secret love of long, luxurious baths, one she might as well indulge while she could. Such things were hard to come by in Egypt, she feared.

She had to face the fact that she was no nearer to that country than she'd been in her dreams while still bodily in Yorkshire. Simon Archer still wasn't certain whether she was a madwoman, or merely eccentric. Truthfully, she wasn't so sure herself. Perhaps he was right and An-ket had been a mere hallucination. "But she seemed so real. . . ."

As real as the look in Simon's eye when he'd almost kissed her last night. Julia knew now that he'd wanted to, just as she had wanted him to. It had seemed a good idea at the time, but now she was glad Mrs. Archer had interrupted. Julia wanted to go to Egypt as Simon's wife, yes, but not under false pretenses. She would not seduce him into taking her along.

"You just keep that in mind, my girl," she said, beginning the process of making her hair behave. "If you try to seduce him, you'll just make a fool of yourself. Be sensible, be knowledgeable, be friendly. Nothing else."

Yet she still felt her body tighten when she thought of the look in his eyes. He'd come closer and closer . . . his hands moving in her hair . . . Julia found herself sitting with her eyes closed in front of the mirror, her hairbrush fallen to the floor. Straightening up, she turned a rebuking glare upon herself. "That's just what I mean. No more of it, if you please."

A knock made her jump. "Miss Hanson?" Simon called. "May I see you a moment?"

"I'm not dressed," she replied, then could have kicked

herself, for she was wearing precisely what she'd had on in the kitchen when they'd talked so long.

"Oh! Ah, I'll see you downstairs then, shortly?"

"As soon as Apple brings my clothes back."

"Quite. I shall wait for you."

"Thank you."

Simon was waiting on the front step when she came out. "You look remarkably fresh for a young lady who was up so very late, Miss Hanson."

"You're kinder than my mirror, Mr. Archer. It had quite a different tale to tell."

The street, so bustling earlier, was now nearly deserted. The crowd of menials and vendors had given way to the carriage of a lady making morning calls and a pair of horsemen, on their way, no doubt, to ride in Hyde Park. Across the road, a window slid up with a bang. "I say, is that you, Archer?"

Turning, Simon pushed back his shining hat with the knob of his stick. "Ah! Good morning, Winslow! I had no idea you had returned, my dear fellow."

"Yes, I came home a few months ago on leave. Listen, Archer, there's something you should know. Last night, I came home rather late—after three, it must have been. I wasn't taking much notice, but later on, I saw a rather queer thing. An unsavory character was standing right where you are now, looking up at your house."

"That is strange, at so late an hour."

"What's queerer still is that he ran off the second I hailed him. Didn't like the looks of it, I can tell you."

"Well, thanks, Winslow. I'll ask the constable to come by a bit more often and keep an eye out myself." Turning to Julia, Simon said, "Shall we walk to the corner? We'll have better luck finding a cab there."

"Who do you think it was?" Julia asked excitedly.

"No one important, probably. A late-night reveler who'd mistaken his house, or someone looking for an ad-dress."

"At three A.M., I'd grant you the first but not the second! Who'd dream of paying a call so late?"

"Don't make a mystery, Miss Hanson. And pray don't mention it to my sisters or mother. Mother is already convinced that every burglar in England has our home address in his pocket."

Eleven

Entering the museum on Simon's arm, Julia felt like a bride coming to her new home for the first time. She had been greatly impressed with the vast cool chambers last night when she'd been an illicit vagrant in these halls of learning. Now, with the full approval of one of its leading lights, she was nearly overwhelmed. She didn't even mind his not carrying her over the threshold. People would have stared.

"Was there ever anything so wonderful?" she asked, breathing in the mysterious perfume of the air. The mingling of antique dust, camphor, and yellow soap went to her head more rapidly than champagne.

"Wait until it is complete. They say it will only take another ten years." Simon smiled at her and the dizzy tingle in her head increased. "What would you like to see first? My . . . my exhibition?"

Julia reminded him, with a confessional air, "I saw it last night."

"It looks different by daylight. Come on." He squeezed her hand under his arm. By his smile, she could tell that he was eager to have her opinion of his work, and that gave her a greater thrill yet. Was he coming to respect her, at all?

The guards saluted him as he passed, straightening up and touching their caps with two fingers. "The hardest thing was getting proper glass cases. You would not credit it were I to tell you what people are allowed to touch in here. I believe the oils on a pair of even clean fingers can do more damage to a vase than three thousand years of being buried in the ground. But even the fingers are not so bad as those fools who . . . like that one, there!"

He stopped dead, frowning. Julia followed his condemning finger to see a black-suited man pointing out the perfections of a Gobelin tapestry to a crowd of interested ladies. Unfortunately, he was doing his pointing with the steel tip of his umbrella.

Skewering a half-clad goddess, he said, "See how this figure represents the snare of carnal love by dropping burning honey into the mouth of this figure . . . er . . . Mars, is it?"

Simon walked up and tapped the man on the shoulder. "I beg your pardon, sir, please don't do that."

"Eh? Do I know you, sir?"

"I'm Archer of the museum. If you'd be so good as to not stab the tapestries. You're not Hamlet, you know."

Julia saw that some of the younger ladies had recognized Simon and were whispering behind their hands. Some cast envious glances upon her. Rather to her shame, she found being the focus of their jealousy to be quite gratifying. She tried to look unaware of their interest but couldn't help wishing she had worn a smarter frock. She must remember to have her luggage sent on to her house at once.

"Indeed, sir!" the gentleman was saying. "That tapestry and everything else in this museum was purchased by Her Majesty's government for the good of her citizens. I have as much right to poke this tapestry as any man in England, having paid for it with my taxes."

"Which is no right at all, sir. If everyone dragged steel

sticks across this magnificent cloth, how much of it would be left at the end of a year? If you are so concerned about your taxes, I suggest you preserve what is bought with them so that the government will not have to spend more to replace what you have so wantonly ravaged! Good day, sir!"

Continuing on their way, Simon said, "If it were left to me, everyone would have to check their umbrellas at the door. Walking sticks, too, unless strictly necessary for locomotion."

"That seems reasonable enough."

"The Board of Governors won't hear of it. If an Englishman's home is his castle, it seems his umbrella is his figurative sword."

"It could be worse. Men like that could still carry actual swords, as they did in King George's era. Imagine how much damage they could do then!"

"Don't, Miss Hanson. You'll give me nightmares."

He fished out from his pocket the key to the tall door of the Egyptian Gallery. "How did you get in last night? Wasn't the door locked?"

"No, it was ajar. I just pushed on it and it opened."

"Strange. I had thought it was understood that this room was to be kept locked until my exhibition opens. I shall have to have a word with the watchman."

"The Scot," she said under her breath.

"Yes, Douglas. He's a good fellow, though I suspect he drinks." He shook the door handle. "Well, it's locked now."

He turned the key and opened the door wide. Though sunlight came through the high windows, at floor level the shadows still lingered. "Let me turn up the lights."

Julia stood on the threshold while Simon went about turning up the gas jets. She felt as if she were watching him illuminate a stage on which all the history of the world had taken place. Early canopic jars gleamed alabaster white, followed by dark statues of gods and men mingled into one alien form, and everywhere the glint and gleam of gold.

"Come in," he said. "Let me show you what I found. . . ."

Julia wanted to follow him—she had come so far and thought so long about this very moment—but could not force herself to take even one step forward. She looked at him, biting one corner of her lower lip. "I'm afraid," she said. "Isn't that silly?"

He came hurrying back to her, his long strides resounding over the marble floor. "Afraid? Of what?" He gave her the kind of humoring grin one offers a nervous child. "Not of the mummies, by any chance?"

"Of course not!" she said with force. "I wandered around in here last night with never a qualm. My friends would have been terrified of the statues, let alone the mummies. I was only interested in them for their own sakes. No. This is . . . something else."

Simon took her hand and started to chafe it lightly. "I can understand your fears. Something strange happened to you last night in this very room. Naturally you are a little reluctant to enter it again. Once, in Cairo, I was attacked by a man with a very large knife. He was a madman, I think, who believed the old gods were talking to him, telling him to destroy the infidels who were digging up the ancient kings." He cleared his throat. "Your—um—visitor didn't happen to mention anything of that sort, did she?"

Julia couldn't decide whether to reprove him or to smile, so she combined the two, acknowledging his attempt at humor with a smile even while she said, "She didn't seem to care what had happened to her body. But I want to know what happened with the man who attacked you in Cairo."

"He had a heart attack shortly after I knocked him down. I think it might have been his chest pains that drove him to attack me on that particular day. But what I'm trying to tell you is, after that it was *days* before I could walk past where it had happened without perspiring like a fish. Usually the heat doesn't bother me; even that year I stayed weeks past the digging season. But as I walked down al-Qasaba, the great high street that runs through Cairo's heart, whenever I came to the tomb of Kalaoun the heat seemed to push down on me like a giant hand. I couldn't even breathe until I was safely past."

Without her realizing it, Simon had drawn her step by step into the room of antiquities while relating his story. She hesitated, then nodded. "You're right. The only thing to do is face up to it."

Somewhat cautiously, she looked around her. "What do you consider the cream of your find?"

His eyes spoke of his approval of her courage, but he said, "Oh, that's too hard to answer. But if you were to hold my feet to the fire and demand an answer, it would have to be the coffin itself. The images are really splendidly preserved—as clear as the day they were first inscribed."

"I know. You sent me a copy."

"But to see them in reality! Come here."

As they crossed the floor, he said, "One day I hope some clever man will invent a better light than gas lamps. They deposit a witches' brew of residue and dirt over everything, which is nearly impossible to remove without damaging the items. However it is still an improvement over candles. We must use them in the tombs, unfortunately."

Julia didn't listen. She was gazing upon the face of Anket. She'd been delighted by its remote beauty as revealed by the uncertain light of Mrs. Pierce's lantern, but now she was even more pleased . . . now that she knew the priestess personally. Julia raised her eyes to Simon's face. "I know you think I was temporarily insane last night. . . ."

"I never said that."

"Well, you thought I'd been thrown off my balance by the things that had happened."

"That, perhaps."

"But I tell you now, plainly and simply, I do believe that magic touched me last night. I did speak with An-ket-en-re, Priestess of Hathor. Somehow she could speak through Mrs. Pierce the charwoman."

His face had grown hard and remote. "And the cat, according to you."

"And the cat. I can't deny to you that these things happened, but I promise not to speak of them to anyone else."

"Thank you for that, at any rate. After my clash with Dr. Mystery, and all the things I have said about spiritualism, if I were known to harbor someone making such claims . . ." He almost seemed to shudder.

"It would be difficult for you to be taken seriously?"

"Impossible!"

"Therefore, by telling you the truth I have ruined my chances of ever being taken seriously by you?"

He couldn't meet her eyes. Julia sighed. "I thought so. Perhaps I should have lied to you."

"No." He put his hand on her shoulder. "Never tell me lies."

She felt again the tremulous anticipation that she had known the evening before when she'd read hunger in his eyes, not for the supper he had missed, but for her. Wild ideas raced through her mind. What would he do if she reached up to kiss him? What would he do if she brazenly drew his hand down from her shoulder to caress her body?

Julia could not say where such wild ideas had come from. Before she could steel herself to act on her impulses, she noticed that Simon was looking up at the ceiling. His eyes were narrowed against the sunlight.

"I thought you said one of the windows had broken. Which one?" His hand dropped away.

"It had." She turned and scanned the rectangles of glass. "How odd."

"And where did you say that burglar was standing . . . ?"

"Over there. By the broken display case. With An-ket's jewelry in it."

"There is no broken case. Look." He stepped over to the glass box and ran his fingers over the slick surface. "You see. Quite whole. Not even cracked. Not even scratched."

"Someone must have replaced it." Julia was aware that a pleading note had entered her tone.

"Ah! That's possible, but not very likely. As is the case with so many bureaucracies, the museum is slow to dispense funds for anything of less than immediate necessity."

"Wouldn't replacing a window and a display case fall under the heading of 'immediate necessity,' especially when you consider our native weather and how soon the public will be permitted to enter here? Even if people are allowed to handle some of the museum's treasures, surely no one would allow them to take such liberties with such rare and valuable jewelry."

"I suppose it is just possible that these repairs were made with such incredible speed. It hardly seems British, however."

Though she knew he was still disbelieving, Julia judged that any further protestations on her part would only solidify his suspicions. Instead, she turned again to the sublime example of the funerary arts before her.

Every inch of the coffin was covered with small pictures showing the reception of An-ket's spirit into the Egyptian Underworld. There, guided by some gods and opposed by others, she would make her perilous way to the chamber where Osiris awaited her. He was the judge, but there were many tests before her *ka* would reach him. Everything in the Underworld had a name. The soul must be able to address each thing—even the doorposts—by its proper name to prove its purity before the journey of the dead could be completed. Julia wondered if An-ket remembered these tests. Had she really done all the things her religion had prescribed?

She recoiled from the idea. Surely the faith she herself followed was perfect and the faith of the ancients was flawed. To doubt that would be to doubt herself, a thing with which she'd never had any patience.

To distract herself, she glanced at the small white card lying beside the coffin. In small, precise script, she read the translation of the hieroglyphics that wrapped the coffin in the same lines that linen bandages covered the body within.

"Goodness . . . that can't be right."

"What cannot?"

"This translation. Surely not."

"I don't think there's anything amiss with it. It runs in the usual style of such things. Prayers for guidance and testimony as to the purity of the dead traveler's heart."

"Yes, but it's so dreary. No poetry at all. Just the same old . . ." her voice trailed off. Something about the litany as written down in black and white seemed familiar. She scanned the rest of the card until she came to a name more familiar still.

This translation is gratefully acknowledged as the work of Miss J. Hanson.

She looked at Simon with sparkling eyes. He shuffled his feet, giving her a sideways glance. "Oh, Simon!" she said. Dropping her handbag, she threw her arms about him.

"This is the best gift . . . *everyone* will see my name and know that I . . . you even put 'Miss' so no one will dare assume that I'm a man."

He stood rigid inside her embrace. Realizing she'd gone much, much too far, she backed hastily away, feeling as though her cheeks were on fire. "I beg your pardon."

"Not at all. I understand your excitement. If I were in your place, I would be ex . . . elated, too."

"Elated. Yes. That's how I feel. And grateful."

His embarrassment seemed to grow more pronounced. "I've done nothing you need to be grateful for."

"But you have! No one has ever given me such a wonderful gift. No one has ever given me credit for my translations before. I told you how I don't fit in very well among my friends. They all think it's absurd to, as one used to say, 'mess about with dirty old stones and bits of paper.' Even my father—"

"I thought he didn't mind your work."

Julia pressed both her hands to her heart and cast her eyes upward in rapture. "My work. No one's ever called it that. 'Messing about,' 'overtaxing my feeble female mind,' 'scribbling away . . .' "

" 'Feeble female mind?' Who on earth would say that to you, of all people?"

"Our former vicar used to be employed at a school for young ladies of good family. He came away with a very poor opinion of learned women."

"But your father doesn't share that opinion."

"I think, secretly, he does. He is proud of what I have accomplished, make no mistake. But he doesn't understand it and has never made the least push to try. He's not prone to rolling up my latest work as a spill to light his cigars or anything cruel like that; he'll hardly come into my studio even with my permission. It's just that he really can't love it as I do. Perhaps it's too much to ask of anyone."

"I know exactly what you mean. He's content to leave all such mysteries to you. My mother is the same way. When I talk to her about anything, even my discoveries, she nods and smiles in the precise way she did when I first began excavating the garden at age three."

"Did you do that? I can imagine you, towheaded and intent."

"I used to bring some fairly revolting things into the house, expecting Mother to coo over them. To do her justice, she generally managed to be pleasant about my unfortunate obsession."

"Exactly," Julia said on a laughing note. "Giving orders that one may dig as much as one likes, even if it meant the gardener gave notice."

"And preventing the maid from sweeping out the corner where you kept your treasures. I was quite sure once I found the toe bone of Jack the Giant Killer's on the gravel walk in Kensington Gardens. That was some years after we moved to London."

"I found a unicorn's horn. Or at least the very tip. When it turned out to be a seashell, I cried for two days."

"I have found better things than that. Let me show you."

Julia realized the difficult moment had passed. He still did not trust her version of last night's events, yet he obviously found her to be good company. *Almost as good as he is to me*, she told herself.

She did not have to pretend an interest in the things he showed her. Even if the flash of gold hadn't attracted her attention, the lovely white cards that bloomed on every case bore her name. She felt she could never grow tired of seeing those twelve words strung out in their entirety, save one.

"Why did you put 'J.' instead of Julia?"

"Remember I didn't know you when I wrote these. I didn't want to embarrass the sweet elderly woman I thought you to be by splashing your name about."

"That was thoughtful. They look very nice indeed."

For an hour, Julia followed Simon around as he expounded on his theories of life three thousand years ago. Many of his ideas she'd read in his letters, but she found it thrilling to be able to ask questions and argue contrary views on the spot, as it were, instead of waiting weeks for an exchange of letters.

"Would you care to try on one of these bracelets?" he asked while standing over the case of An-ket's jewelry.

"Oh, no. I wouldn't want to damage it. Besides, I don't really care for jewelry. A ring or a brooch is well enough, but anything more than that is overdoing it, I find. My aunt loves to go clanking around wearing five beaded necklaces, two cameos, three bracelets per arm, and at least one ring for every finger—everything, in fact, that can be strung or hung on a person. And you should see her when there's a special occasion!"

"Did your mother like jewelry?"

"I think my father liked her to wear it. When he started making a great deal of money—they were quite poor when they first were married—he gave her a fine string of pearls. I don't think she wanted anything else."

"From what I discovered in the tomb, I don't believe An-ket would be of the same opinion. Even these few pieces show, I think, that she was very fond of adornment. Most Egyptian ladies were, it seems."

"Then you do believe the tomb was robbed at least once? Your last letter seemed to indicate some doubt."

"Didn't I tell you about the sandal mark?"

"Not that I recall."

"We found a smashed chest that held jars of unguent. All but one had been stolen, but that one had spilled, making a pool. It was quite hard and black as tar by the time we arrived, dried out and changed into something utterly different, but it must have been sticky when the robbers first broke the jar. One of them stepped in it, because a woven-sandal print was impressed into the mass."

"Amazing! To think that one could see such a thing. As though we were traveling back in time to that very moment."

"I confess, I felt something of that when my *reis* pointed it out to me. At first, it looked so fresh that I thought one of his men must have done it, but he showed me that the splotch was as hard as a stone. Entirely impervious to new impressions."

"Did you bring it with you? The shape and form of the weaving might tell us much."

"I think that in order to remove it we'd have to heat the substance, which would destroy the print. It's still there, on the floor in one corner." He sighed. "Besides which, people are not interested in the footprints of tomb robbers. Only in the gold. Frankly, I think the footprint has more to tell us than all the bangles and beads in the world. But my opinion is in the minority."

"There's a minority of two, then. When I do reach Egypt, will you show me where you found these things?"

"You are still determined to go, then?"

"If I must, I shall submit to undertaking a Cook's tour. They at least show one the most important monuments, if in the wrong chronological order."

"I pity your tour guide, if he tries to teach you anything."

"Why should you? I am willing to learn from any source willing to teach me." For some reason—perhaps it was the look in Simon's eye—Julia felt suddenly self-conscious, as though she'd unwisely said something with a double meaning.

Just then, someone rapped on the door, pushing it farther open even as he knocked. "I wondered why this door was open. Hello, Archer."

"Good morning, Keene. All's well, I trust."

"Yes, fine. Just came in for a last look round, did you?"

The young man who had come in had so schooled his features to be cool and faintly amused that he might very well have been said to have no expression whatsoever. He hardly glanced at Julia, focusing instead on Simon. She couldn't tell whether he meant to be polite, by ignoring a strange lady until introduced; or rude, by ignoring a lady who might not be a lady at all. Many people might frown on a young woman remaining alone with a man for any length of time, no matter how little patience she had with such conventions.

Simon performed the introductions.

"Ah," Mr. Keene said, taking Julia's hand. "The marvelous Miss Hanson. I've heard so little about you."

"Then we are even. I've heard nothing about you."

He bowed as though she'd complimented him. "I have the honor to be secretary, and general dogsbody, to Sir Walter Armbruster, one of the guiding hands of this establishment."

"Which means, I suppose, that you do all the work and he gets all the credit."

Mr. Keene grinned at her and she saw why he'd cultivated a mask of imperturbability. When he smiled, he looked like a particularly mischievous twelve-year-old boy. He said to Simon, "She's as perceptive as you said, my dear fellow."

He bowed again over the hand he'd held all this time. "I'm enchanted, Miss Hanson."

"The pleasure is mine, sir," she answered, tugging free.

Keene asked, "Tell me, what do you think of Archer's finds?"

"Magnificent. This exhibition, combined with his theories on the religious beliefs of the ancient Egyptians, will rock the fuddy-duddies back on their heels."

"I wish I could quote you to the newspapers." He glanced about him. "But regrettably, the fuddy-duddies can read. Speaking of newspapers, my dear Archer, have you seen the morning editions?"

"No, I didn't have time this morning," Simon said. "I suppose they've all carried stories about that nonsensical seance at Dr. Mystery's last night."

"You suppose correctly, but that story is somewhat eclipsed by the most recent developments. Permit me to congratulate you, sir. Dr. Mystery has announced his withdrawal from the spook business, effective without delay."

"What?"

"I have the newspaper in my office if you'd care to see them. Miss Hanson, would you honor me by taking tea?"

Twelve

~

Simon read the closely printed columns of his third newspaper with the aid of Mr. Keene's magnifying glass. "This is impossible," he said, turning over a leaf. "Nothing happened at that gathering last night to warrant this reaction."

"Something must have happened," Mr. Keene said, pushing a cup of tea across the table to him.

Simon shook his head. "I did not expose him as a fraud, nor offer proof of his trickery. I merely assured myself that he was resorting to tricks, including burning a mild form of a drug I know from the East in order to disorient his 'clients.'"

Julia looked up from the newspaper she was reading. "Then why is Dr. Mystery suddenly throwing his hand in? Unless he is afraid you will find out more than you have already."

"I suppose that could be it. Though I did not present much of a threat last night. I had the feeling he was laughing at me."

Julia realized that she'd never met a man before who could admit without excuse that someone might laugh at him. She could only respect him for it. "Perhaps he saw that you recognized the drug? Surely drugging people against their will must be against some law. Perhaps he is afraid you will give him in to the hands of the police. Even a minor charge laid against him would spoil his ability to draw in the credulous."

"I think you have too high an opinion of the intellect of the people I saw there last night. They were not the kind to disavow their beliefs for anything less than absolute and unarguable proof. If that. Mystery must know I don't have anything near that convincing, so why throw in his hand so soon?"

"True, he could go on bilking people until that proof was in your hands. How much did he charge to contact spirits, anyway?"

"You wrong him," Simon said with a sneer, throwing aside the paper. "He never asked for money, not directly. One of the ladies present last night—obviously a confederate—went on and on about Dr. Mystery's expenses and how unselfishly he asks for no payment. Of course, donations are always welcome."

"I wish I could feign dudgeon at Mystery's tactics, but I fear they are the same as those we employ here at the museum to open the hands of our patrons."

Julia, who liked Mr. Keene better the longer she spent in his company, said, "But for a much nobler purpose."

"Perhaps, perhaps. Well, whatever the reason for Dr. Mystery's having so suddenly decamped, it's a fine thing for the museum. The publicity will bring eager hordes through our gates, which is all to the good when it comes time for dunning our patrons." He handed Julia a teacup, for he was being "mother" on the principle that it was wrong to ask a guest to work. "Let us drink a toast to Mr. Simon Archer. Confusion to his enemies!"

"Hear, hear," Julia said, lifting her cup in salute.

"I'm the one that's confused," Simon said. His eyes went to Julia. "About so many things."

For some reason, she felt herself flush. She set down her teacup, murmuring, "So hot! I shall take cream after all, Mr. Keene."

"By the way," Mr. Keene said, pouring a dollop into her cup. "What do you think of the goings-on in Egypt Hall last night?"

"Hmmm? Did something unusual happen?" Simon asked in a casual tone. Julia felt that Simon was still looking at her, this time with his brilliant blue eyes as hard as sapphires. Yet when she dared glance in his direction, he seemed to have eyes only for the swirling tea that he was stirring.

"Why, yes. I didn't think that I . . . you really don't know?"

"I haven't heard a word about anything unusual."

"Douglas told me about it—actually called on me at my lodgings at an unearthly hour this morning, fairly panting with excitement and anxiety."

"Douglas?" Julia said wonderingly.

"Our best watchman, Miss Hanson. Terrified he'd be sacked, poor fellow. Of course, I told him none of it was his fault. One cannot blame a man for failing to prevent acts of God. Whom, by the way, I thank for your escapade last night, my dear fellow."

"But . . . Keene . . ."

"No, I say it in good faith. If the newspapers got hold of this—especially after Dr. Mystery's folderol about your mummy's displeasure over her 'violated' tomb . . ." Mr. Keene raised expressive hands high in exaggerated horror. "Well! That kind of publicity we don't need."

" 'Got hold' of what?"

"Oh. Didn't I say?"

Both Julia and Simon shook their heads. Julia was bracing herself to hear that she'd been seen leaving with Mrs. Pierce. Perhaps this cozy little tea was really the bait in a trap.

"First, let me assure you, Archer, that no damage was done."

"Damage?"

"Not even the smallest clay hippopotamus was so much

as cracked. It missed all the significant specimens, by what I can only term a miracle!"

"It? What's 'it'?" Simon pronounced each word with force, as though to compel Keene to be less murky in his suggestions.

Keene bowed before Simon's intensity. "A bolt of lightning was attracted by the metal grids over the windows. It broke the window and left a huge scorch mark on the floor. One of the jewelry cases was smashed but nothing, as I say, was broken."

"Lightning?" Julia said, for Simon sat back, drained even of amazement, his handsome mouth hanging open ever so slightly.

"Yes," Mr. Keene said. "It was a mercy the whole building didn't burn down. It's all the marble, you know. Hard for a flame to gain any headway. But think if it had struck a mummy! They're highly flammable."

"Yes. Didn't they once use mummy wrappings to burn as torches to light the tombs?"

Mr. Keene and Julia both glanced at Simon. He was frowning, as he found a flaw in the story. He said slowly, "I saw nothing of this when I was there this morning."

"Naturally not. I realize we of the museum have a reputation for being dilatory—after all, there's little point in rushing about foolishly when dealing with thousand-year-old pieces—but, by jingo!, when there's a need for haste, we shall never hold back!"

"Bravo!" Julia said.

Mr. Keene ducked his head like an embarrassed schoolboy. "Sorry. Didn't mean to make speeches. It's an easy matter to explain, old boy. As soon as Douglas told me, I came to see for myself. Then I sent a messenger hotfoot to the builders. They had a few squares of marble left over—always quarry a couple over in case of accident—and they sent them over directly with the right men for the job. For a wonder, they even had the proper tools. No sending back to the shop for this or that."

He took a sip of tea. "They had the old pieces levered out and the new ones laid before you could say Jack Robinson. Only difference is the new ones ain't as highly polished, but I doubt anyone will notice. They'll be too dazzled by the display."

Simon said, "And the window? And the display case?"

"There's a glazier's not two streets over. It's a small shop but I try to throw our business their way when I can. They were the ones who replaced the glass in the skylight that time those birds landed on it. Did a first-rate job of it in next to no time."

"Birds?" Julia echoed. "How could birds break a skylight? Unless . . ."

"Nothing gruesome," Mr. Keene hastened to say. "Merely that a whole flock of pigeons, Miss Hanson, decided that our main skylight was the perfect roosting spot. Feldspar—the glazier—estimated there must have been nine hundredweight of pigeon on it, more or less, and, of course, it was never meant to bear such a burden."

"How ever did he arrive at that figure?"

"Approximately four hundred and fifty pigeons times the average weight of one bird."

"Ah, of course. And a glazier must necessarily be fond of making measurements and calculations."

"A good thing it was not my father's profession," Mr. Keene said. "I am perfectly hopeless with figures."

Simon seemed to have recovered from his stupor. "I suggest you don't let Sir Walter overhear that confession, Keene. Don't you balance the office accounts?"

"I try," Mr. Keene said with a rueful shake of his head. "I can but try. More tea, Miss Hanson?"

Julia drank tea with the two men, her heart relieved by Mr. Keene's story of the lightning strike. It fit the facts so well, in part through its truth, and left out so much that was awkward. Simon would have to accept that lightning had struck last night. Now he had only to believe her about the burglar and he would be two-thirds of the way to believing her about An-ket. For if so much of her story was proven, then it must follow logically that the rest would be true as well.

"I beg your pardon," she said during a break in the men's conversation. "Mr. Keene, do you have the address of one Mrs. Pierce? I believe she's been a charwoman for the museum for many years, beginning with the last premises."

"Mrs. Pierce? Pierce?" Mr. Keene drummed his fingers on his somewhat prominent chin. "It sounds familiar. . . ."

"Perhaps you have her name in your files?"

"I suppose I must, but why . . . ? I beg your pardon; it's none of my business."

Julia smiled and explained, shading the truth a trifle. "I met her yesterday and discovered she does mending. I need someone reliable to do some work for me while I am in London and thought she would do."

"Ah! Of course. Pardon me a moment. I'll just ask my clerk."

Julia took a biscuit and sat back to nibble on it. Simon hissed at her from across the table. "Why do you want that address?"

"I want you to interview her. Ask her some questions."

"I asked her questions last night at your request. She knew nothing."

"Perhaps she didn't want to speak then. She might have been afraid of getting into trouble. But you could ask her about the lightning, at least, and more about the burglar. Then you'd know I was telling the truth about that, at least."

He sighed, exasperated. "Very well." He lowered his voice as he glanced toward the door through which Keene had departed. "I didn't like you lying to Keene. He's a good fellow."

"I couldn't have very well said, 'I want the charwoman's address so I can ask her what it was like to be possessed by the spirit of a dead Egyptian priestess,' now could I? Be practical."

"Lies are so often practical, Miss Hanson. It is no excuse for telling them to all and sundry."

"Do you never lie, Mr. Archer?"

"I make every effort to stand on the truth. Truthfulness is the cornerstone of science."

"Probably very true. But it is the headstone of polite society. Shh. He's coming back."

Julia thanked Mr. Keene for the tea. "You've been very kind."

"Nonsense," he answered, spluttering a little. "Everything is none too good for Archer's muse."

Mr. Keene threw Simon a waggish glance. "Isn't that right, old boy? That's what you called her?"

"Is it?" Julia asked.

"I may have said something of the sort."

"My dear, he raved about you. I'm delighted for his sake that you aren't the elderly lady he told me about, but then, he always has been the luckiest devil of my acquaintance. Just look at how he discovered his marvelous find."

"Oh, he didn't need a goat to find me, Mr. Keene. I sought him out."

Mr. Keene heaved a sigh that would have seemed extreme coming from the chest of a consumptive Romantic poet. "As I say, a lucky devil."

Simon, his face a slightly ruddier tan, held the door open for Julia. With another mischievous look, Mr. Keene bowed over Julia's hand and even pressed a kiss onto her glove. "If there's anything I can do for you while you are in London, Miss Hanson, please don't hesitate to call upon me. I'm sure Sir William would feel the same. The resources of the museum are at your disposal."

Simon said abruptly, "Don't encourage her, Keene. She doesn't need any more motivation."

Ignoring his interruption, Julia said, "I shall certainly avail myself of your offer, sir. Good day."

Simon walked briskly down the stairs. Julia, recognizing pettishness when she saw it, made no attempt to keep pace. A faint mutter came to her ears. "Are you saying something, Mr. Archer?"

"Your exhibition was disgraceful!"

"What exhibition? You are the only one here with an exhibition."

"You are flirting with Keene! I make no apology for the harshness of the term."

"No, why should you? Of course I was flirting with him. He does it so beautifully, it would be a wanton waste not to."

"You admit it?"

"Goodness, yes. He's the sort of man who simply must flirt. I especially admired the way he laughed, as if I were the wittiest woman he'd ever met. Really, he's wasting his talents at the museum. He should be in politics. I wonder if I might suggest it to him. Given the right mentor and a really clever wife, he could be Prime Minister in ten or fifteen years.

The next sound Julia heard over Simon's footsteps was the grinding of his teeth. "You shouldn't do that," she said helpfully. "A man on my father's estate used to grind his teeth at night and one morning they all fell out."

"I'm stopping into my office for a moment, Miss Hanson. Perhaps you would care to examine our treasures from Byblos?"

She did not, but thought it would be wise to give Simon a chance to recoup his temper. She'd been riding him too hard, though it gave her a strange pleasure to see him react so badly to what was, after all, nothing more than a trifle of eccentricity. She resolved to be a model of decorum for the rest of the day, no matter what the provocation.

A little while later, Julia and Simon stood outside the

museum, attempting to flag down a cab in Great Russell Street. "I doubt a cab will take us to Lumber Street, nor should you go there yourself, Miss Hanson. It sounds most insalubrious."

"Do you mean it's a slum?"

"Undoubtedly."

"You may go alone, if you wish, Mr. Archer. As it happens, I do have some errands to run. I shall accompany you next time."

"There won't be a next time."

"Yes, there will. Oh!" She waved her hand vigorously at a passing cab. "I don't think he saw me."

"Why do you say that?"

"Because he didn't stop, of course."

"No. I meant . . ." She saw him take an almost visible grip on his temper and decided to stop teasing once and for all.

Gently, Julia said, "I doubt whether Mrs. Pierce will talk to you without me being there. Certainly she will deny anything sooner than jeopardize her employment with the museum. You—in your nice suit and collar— will look like the museum incarnate to her."

"That's regrettably true." He pulled out his watch and consulted it. "What errands do you have?"

"I must return to the Bull and Bush—indeed, I think I should have done so already. They will be wondering if I mean to pay for my lodging there, or if I have run out on them. Then I must have my trunks sent to my house. Though it was very good of your sisters to lend me some necessary items, I do long to have my own wardrobe. Then I must see about sending some flowers to your mother—what does she like?"

"I haven't any idea. Violets, I think."

"Not at this season! Well, I shall think of something. A box of chocolates for your sisters, as well. They were all so kind to me, especially Lucy. What a dear girl! Reserved, of course, but interesting." She waved even more energetically at another empty cab. Her good resolutions were strained beneath the impact of her frustration. "Blast!"

"What did you say?" Simon said, startled out of his customary politeness.

"I must say something! It makes me so furious when they simply will not see one! And I don't suppose you'd approve if I said 'damn.' "

"No, I would not. My sisters never use oaths."

She just laughed at that. "Of course not." She scanned the street for another cab but there seemed to be a lull. "While waiting for my clothes to come, I shall inspect the house to see what needs to be done. Last time I was there, I rather thought the whole place needed to be freshened up. New paint, new wallpaper, and I'm quite sure I detected a funny smell in the drawing room. The carpet must have been damp, which may mean a leak somewhere. I shall have to have it pulled up."

"You're intending to refit your father's town house while you are here?"

"Yes, I'm thinking of doing it all myself as a wedding present to my new stepmother. She doesn't care for those sort of details and quite approves of my taste."

"She'd be compelled to say that in any case."

Julia looked at him through narrowed eyes. "Are you suggesting, Mr. Archer, that my wedding present will be unwelcome?"

"I can only think that a bride would like to have some say in how one of her homes shall be decorated."

"That is because you do not know Ruth. She wanted to have her drawing room painted last year and found choosing a color so paralyzing that she took to her bed and wrote me a pleading letter to come at once to solve the question for her."

Suddenly Simon laughed and Julia found the little flame of anger that had been starting to boil in her heart blew out the instant he smiled. "Why are you laughing?"

she asked, trying hard to maintain her disapproving expression.

"I remember . . . Last season, when I had written my mother a full account of my findings. . . ."

"Yes?"

"I received an express letter back and opened it eagerly, expecting to read raptures of delight. Instead, out fell two scraps of material—patterns for the dining room curtains. Of the four women living under that roof, not one of them could make a final determination between sea-green and *eau de nil*."

He stepped off the curb and raised one single eyebrow toward a cab tooling along the street. Instantly, the driver hauled on the reins and the horse trotted decorously up to where Simon waited. He turned to Julia and smiled as he opened the door. "May I accompany you on your errands, Miss Hanson? Then, after luncheon, perhaps you'd do me the honor of visiting Lumber Street in my company?"

Seated in the cab's dingy interior, Julia looked at Simon sitting next to her. "Is it because you are a man or because you are at home in the city that the cab stopped for you? None of them would stop for me."

"A lady doesn't travel alone in town. Only . . . certain 'other' kinds of women."

"Oh, I see. How marvelous!"

"You are the most unaccountable . . . What is so marvelous about being mistaken for a . . . a lady of ill repute?"

"Not very much, I suppose, only it isn't something that has ever happened to me before. At home, you know, I am quite the most respectable figure, if thought of as somewhat eccentric. I never drive without my maid, and a groom has always followed me when I ride. But to be mistaken for an erring sister!" She laughed delightedly as the cab rattled and bumped its way along.

Simon shook his head at her. "I'm sure you would not think so under other circumstances."

"No doubt it's a rather grubby way to make one's living. But as it's only a few cabbies who think it is my way, I needn't worry. There is something strangely liberating in being thought a shameless woman—I suddenly understand the professional courtesans of Greece much better than I ever have before." She saw that he was watching her, almost as though he were interested against his will.

"I've often thought I should have made an excellent member of that sorority. I certainly wouldn't have been much use at weaving or cooking, or any of the other things ancient women did to occupy their time. But as a *hetaera* I would have had the freedom to debate philosophy and politics with men, own my own property, and choose my lovers without recourse to anyone's opinion. As a young Englishwoman, I can do none of those things without being thought even more eccentric than I am at present. Yes, I think I should have been a courtesan. I would have been good at it." She sighed wistfully.

"If the prospect pleases you so much, why not pursue it? Even in our morally upright city, men still have their mistresses."

Though she was rather startled to hear "morally upright" Simon Archer mentioning such things to an unmarried woman, she was pleased as well. Was he coming to think of her not as a weak and feeble woman, but as the equal companion she wanted to be? The answer to that question might very well prove to be the same as the one he'd just asked.

Julia sighed. "Don't imagine I have not considered it!" Ignoring his shocked protest, she went on. "There are not so many professions open to a well-read woman as you might suppose. I should make a dreadfully neglectful governess, too busy reading things myself to instruct my pupils. The same objection applies to being a companion. I could marry, but a husband must be found first and my choice has made his feelings entirely plain, for which I do not blame him, being so very plain myself." She sighed again, looking at her hands, or out the window, anywhere but at Simon.

In a less bracing tone, she said, "There is the difficulty in a nutshell. It is a very good thing I have my allowance from my father and need not seek work or a husband to keep me out of the poorhouse. Even so, could I but find a 'protector' who would desire me for my mind, then I might flee to him even without marriage. But men, alas, are all too prone to wanting beauty in their mistresses, caring little whether the women can read or even speak English, let alone four living languages and one dead."

The road was growing progressively rougher as their cab penetrated into the less-well-maintained portion of London. A sudden lurch as they went through what must have been the king of all potholes threw Julia against Simon. For an instant, she was practically sitting on his lap.

She apologized and tried to return to her place. His arms had tightened around her instinctively but now he did not let go. He stared down into her eyes from only inches away. "As a man of science, I cannot allow you to carry on under an error of perception."

His gaze dropped to her mouth and she felt her lips begin to burn as she recalled the brush of his fingertips over them as they had stood together at the foot of the staircase.

"Plain?" he whispered. "Not a bit of it."

Then Simon bent his head to kiss her.

Thirteen

Simon did not know why he had chosen that moment to kiss Julia. He only knew that something in her eyes when she had said she was plain had hurt him. Inspected feature by feature, she was not pretty, yet taken all in all, she appealed to him as no woman ever had before. He could not find the words to tell her, so he kissed her.

He felt her lips quiver under his and realized she'd probably never been kissed by a strange man before. His arm was around her shoulders so that she could not have moved away, though of course he'd have let her go the instant she signaled she wanted to. But she didn't try to push him off or even wriggle away.

She just sat there, her head tilted up, as he pressed his lips to hers. They were warm and soft, sweet and tender, and Simon felt a trifle ashamed of himself for stealing a kiss that belonged properly to the man she'd marry one day.

Therefore, he put her gently away from him. He noticed that her eyes were wide open as though she had not known to close them during a kiss.

"Thank you," she said.

Simon wondered if he'd ever have the power to rock

her on her foundations as she'd been doing to him since the moment they had met. "For what?"

"For telling me you don't think I am plain." She adjusted her hat, which had somehow twisted off-center. He noticed that her hands were trembling ever so slightly. It made him feel oddly triumphant, though it was the only sign of disquiet she showed.

Ducking her head a tad, she glanced out the dirty window. "Are we there yet?"

"Julia," he said, and even the first time he said her name it didn't seem odd to do it. "Julia, a kiss isn't a compliment. You don't thank someone for it."

"But it is a very great compliment. You wouldn't have done it if you found me utterly repulsive."

"No. You're not repulsive to me . . . at least not utterly."

"May I say 'thank you' for that, at least?" She gave him her sideways smile and added, "I don't find you repulsive either, Simon."

The driver knocked on the roof and the door swung open, pulled by a string from his seat. Simon climbed out first, hoping his reddened cheeks would fade before Julia saw them.

"Will you wait?" he asked the cab driver as he dug in his pocket for the fare.

"Yes, guv'nor. If you don't mean to be too long abaht it?"

Simon looked about him. It was not as fearful a slum as some he'd seen just a few blocks farther north. The people here walked a fine line between privation and destitution. One person per household might actually have income—precarious at best, but just enough for rent and a morsel of food. The other members of the family would contribute whatever they could scrounge. In the deepest stews, there was no hope of regular income, no matter how meager, so the desperation there was bleakest, for there could be no escape.

Even here, the houses were so close together that the street was quite dark despite it being midday. Lines of washing ran haphazardly from one side of the street to the other and each terminating window had a face, a pale circle dimly glimpsed through soot, keeping a watchful eye on the shirts, skirts, and diapers. Urchins ran about, chasing some ball improvised from rags, shrieking. Older children stood in doorways, pinched faces staring in amazement at the wondrous sight of a cab on their barren street.

"Simon?" Julia said, holding out her hand.

"Are you sure you wouldn't rather wait for me?"

"Why?"

"Well, it's a bit . . ." His gesture took in the whole squalid scene.

"I'm sure Mrs. Pierce's house is neat as a new pin."

Yielding, Simon helped her to descend and guided her steps around a ripe pile of refuse. Julia said, "I wonder which is her house. Excuse me, miss?"

The girl she spoke to pointed to herself in disbelief.

"Yes, that's right. Would you be so kind as to tell me where Mrs. Pierce lives?"

The girl wrapped her threadbare shawl more closely around her shoulders. With a regal air that would have done a queen justice, she ignored the giggles of her friends and left the shelter of her doorway to approach the strangers. "Wotcha want with 'er? She h'ain't done nothing."

"No, of course not. I met her last evening at the museum and asked her to do some mending for me."

"You did? 'Oo's he, then?" the girl asked, nodding disdainfully toward Simon.

"See here," he began, but Julia put her hand on his arm and he found himself silenced. If it had been left to him, he would have offered the girl a penny to show them the way.

Julia said only, "He's a friend of mine. I'd very much

like to see Mrs. Pierce. Will you take me to her?"

These words—or possibly something in the tone of her voice—acted like a magical spell on the suspicious girl. Simon was at a loss to explain what alchemy had happened. One instant the creature was distrustful, asking all sorts of impertinent questions. The next, even her posture had softened. She smiled, showing teeth that were as irregularly spaced as the laundry overhead, and said, "I'm 'er daughter. I'll show yer."

As they went inside, the other girls were offering a half-dozen types of "sauce" to the impassive driver. Only by the pleading eyes, as those of some trapped animal, did he reiterate his wish that his passengers would not be long.

The girl said, "You'll pardon me, miss, I'm sure, fer being so rude just now. I'm a bit worried about Mum and that's all there is to that!"

"Worried about her? Is there something the matter?"

"She's been mighty queer ever since she come 'ome last night. Talkin' wild, makin' big plans and she come 'ome with all sorts of . . ." Miss Pierce stopped in the middle of the hall and lowered her voice to a mere thread. "She's got more money in her 'ands right this minute than I h'ever seen in all my life. I'm that worried, miss, that she ain't come by it 'onest."

"You needn't worry, Miss Pierce. Mr. Archer here gave her that as a tip."

"Wot? 'Im?" She gave a jerk of her head that expressed both acceptance and disbelief in one. "Why's a swell givin' money to the likes of 'er? 'Sides, it don't explain the other one."

"What other one?"

"Cove wot showed up 'ere at the most h'awful early hour. I'm an h'early riser myself but 'e was on the doorstep afore I was up. Talked to 'er for h'ever so long." Again she dropped her voice. "And gave her a mess of silver before he left. Wot's Mum done that's worth such a lot o' money to swell coves?"

Simon realized she did not want her neighbors to know about her mother's newfound wealth. Ten coppers might mean much to a starving man, and Simon knew he'd given the charwoman much more than that. Wondering how many people might be listening behind the doors, he said, "Let's not stand in this drafty hall any longer than need be."

Miss Pierce continued spilling her words on Julia as she followed the girl's thick-soled boots up a wobbly staircase. Simon wouldn't have trusted it to bear a dog's weight but he followed the two girls, expecting every instant to see the bolts pull out from the wall.

Julia's prediction had been correct. The furniture in Mrs. Pierce's rooms was cheap and shoddy, yet it glowed from the application of elbow grease. Not a speck of dust or mud was anywhere to be seen and the thin curtains and worn carpet looked newly laundered. Mrs. Pierce herself looked distracted.

When they entered, she was counting on her fingers and then making marks on a piece of paper. "Mum," her daughter said. "Mum, someone's come to see you."

Deep in concentration, for a moment it was as if Mrs. Pierce hadn't heard. Then she raised her eyes from the page that absorbed her so and was instantly all smiles. "Why, I'm that glad to see you, miss!"

"I'm happy to see you again as well."

Mrs. Pierce nodded her head in Simon's direction, but spoke to Julia. "Maybe you can tell me, miss. What's the proper pay for a 'ousemaid these days?"

"A housemaid?"

"Yes, miss. One wot knows her work through *and* through. No slackin', no flirtin', a real 'ard worker."

"Oh, for such a one as that I'd pay as much as ten pounds a year, plus a clothing allowance."

"Ah!" Mrs. Pierce wrote on her paper. "A Saturday 'alf-day once a month?"

"At least. Are you thinking of entering into private service?"

Mrs. Pierce smiled happily. "Not me, miss. Let me calcurlate 'alf a mo . . ."

Her daughter whispered to Simon, "See wot I mean? Barmy. . . ."

"You mind your tongue, girl! Rollin' in money we'll be afore you know where you're at!"

"Yes, Mum," she said obediently. But she tapped her temple significantly.

Julia ignored them both. She walked over to the table where Mrs. Pierce worked and looked over the woman's shoulder. "What are you doing? An employment bureau? What a coincidence! I need some staff myself. Just two girls to begin with, hardworking, clean, and regular churchgoers."

"Yes, miss. And their duties?"

"I'm not quite certain. At present, I shall need strong girls to do the rough cleaning. The family town house has been shut up for nearly two years."

"I know just where to put my 'and on two such girls. They'll suit you down to the ground, they will, or they'll hear from their mum. Min! Find yer sister. This laidy'll be wantin' to . . . to interview you." She slewed round in her seat to fix her gaze on her daughter. "See," she added triumphantly. "I told you I'd make a go of it!"

"Ah, Mum! That's just luck, it is, these two walkin' in orf the street!"

"I never been lucky afore," Mrs. Pierce said. Then she lifted her chin high. "I got a feeling I'm goin' ter be lucky from now on."

Min sighed and raised her eyes toward the ceiling. "I'll look fer Amabelle." As an afterthought, she bobbed a curtsey in Julia's direction.

Simon, now that these domestic details were settled,

broke into Mrs. Pierce and Julia's renewed conversation.
"I understand you had another bit of luck last night,
ma'am."

"Eh?"

Julia said, "There was a man who came to see you.
You talked for a while, then he gave you some money
before he left."

"That Min can't keep her lips over a secret so much as
a second. Don't worry, though, miss. A nice laidy like
you won't have no secrets she can spread abaht. An' she
don't never break nothin'—china nor glass. She knows
better."

"I'm sure I shall be pleased with them if they can clean
as well as you do. She's a handsome girl, too, and will
look very fine in a cap."

As with mothers the world over, Simon saw Mrs. Pierce
simper when her child was praised. "There's not a finer
pair of girls in Lunnon than my two, though I says it as
shouldn't."

"Now, about this gentleman . . ."

"Oh, he weren't no gentleman. Talked very fine and
got up regardless, but he weren't no gentleman at all. 'Ad
too much of that there pomade on his 'air, fer one thing.
And perfume, which is one thing I can't h'abide fer a man
to wear. Beards and such, I don't mind. A nice mustache
or bit of a beard sets a feller off. But I draws the line at
a man's smelling like a lot o' lemons nor flowers, neither."

Simon asked, "This man had a mustache?"

"Yes, sir, 'e did an' all."

"A beard, too?"

"Wouldn't 'ardly dignify it with the name o' beard, sir!
Just a little thing it was, hanging off the end of his chin."
She pressed her finger to the cleft in her own chin. "Just
there. Looked h'ever so comical when he talked, wagging
abaht. All I could do to keep from larfing in 'is face!"

"What did he ask you about?"

"Oh, he said he had questions to ask me 'bout things that 'appened when I was young. He wanted to know if I'd ever seen anything h'uncanny. Ghosts an' sperrits."

"And had you?"

"Love you, no! I don't believe it that sort o' rot, beggin' your pardon. Unchanciest thing I h'ever seen was me poor ol' uncle staggering home after hoisting a few down the pub."

Simon paced, a few steps either way, while Julia listened to Mrs. Pierce's plan for a grand new style of employment bureau. He'd never been so eager to discuss his discoveries with another person before, not even during his archaeological work.

He had to practice even more patience during the next delay, though he was sure Julia at least could hear his teeth grind. Then there was another delay while Julia interviewed the two girls for their positions. Though initially sulky, they each made a quick recovery and seemed eager to begin by the time Julia was ready to leave.

"I'm sorry we took so long," she said prettily to the cab driver.

"Not to worry, miss," he said, touching his hat.

She hardly waited for Simon to enter before saying, "Do you think Mrs. Pierce's visitor was Dr. Mystery?"

"Why do you suspect him?"

"The same reason you do, I imagine. There are not so many men in London who are anything but clean-shaven. Sailors and such still wear beards, I believe, but they surely wouldn't burden themselves with a cloak. Add together the mustache, his asking her about ghosts, and the fact that he saw her last night with me and could easily have found where she lived." She paused for breath and then asked, "Does Dr. Mystery care for the opera at all?"

"How would I know something like that?"

"Perhaps it was the cloak that put it into my mind. There's something so dramatic about one. Romantic, too."

"And drama and romance combined is opera?"

She gave him her most impudent grin. "Do you think it was Dr. Mystery that came here last night?"

"I doubt it. What interest could he have in Mrs. Pierce?"

"Why don't we go and ask him?"

Julia was happy to find that Simon had all but abandoned his well-meaning attempts to keep her out of things. Though his mother and sisters had not given her the impression that they were inconsequential fools, she could understand how Simon might have made a wrong assessment of their characters. No doubt they did pander somewhat to the idea of male superiority that everyone in the Archer household seemed to take for granted. She was rather glad to know that she would never have the chance to meet the late Mr. Archer. Or at least, she hoped that opportunity was past.

They stood together on the wide step in front of Dr. Mystery's door. A butler in a black waistcoat had gone to discover whether his master was "at home" or gone abroad on the town.

Looking up at the blank windows, Julia asked, "You're quite sure Dr. Mystery cannot possibly communicate with deceased persons?"

"He's a complete fraud, Julia. You have nothing whatever to be afraid of."

"Afraid? Certainly not. I simply wish to be prepared for what might occur."

"Nothing will happen. He only performs his tricks under circumstances that he can control completely. We shall not give him the opportunity to perform for us. No doubt his servant will simply tell us that we were not expected and therefore Dr. Mystery will be unable to see us. That is what I should do, if I were in his place."

Julia said with confidence, "You could never be in his place. I know how abhorrent fakery is to you. I well remember your comments on the persons who fabricate fake antiquities."

"They encourage the tomb robbers. When a villager sees what he can get for a fake, it spurs them on to find the real thing, which they can sell for a much greater price."

"I know," she said. "Thousands of pounds of valuable statuary go wandering away from their ancestral homes. I deplore the practice."

The butler returned. "Dr. Mystery can spare you five minutes, sir."

They were shown into a small, pleasant drawing room, decorated in light blue and cream, rather as though they were standing beneath a Wedgwood bowl turned upside down. Though the style hadn't been fashionable for some thirty years, it breathed serenity and charm. The windows, framed in blue silk, looked out onto a tiny square of garden, dazzling in the sunshine. The contrast between this elegantly decorated salon and the shabby rooms of Mrs. Pierce, unusual only for their hard-won cleanliness, was all but dizzying in its completeness.

Julia said, "He must be a very extraordinary man, this Dr. Mystery."

"Oh, but I am!"

Somehow, neither Julia nor Simon had been looking in quite the right direction when Dr. Mystery came into the room. He was just there, as though he had popped up out of a trapdoor. He nodded to the butler, who was behind him carrying a perfectly enormous tea tray.

"I do hope you'll take some refreshment. Won't you sit down?" His soft shoes were silent as he crossed the parquet floor and stepped onto the carpet.

"Nothing for me, thanks," Simon said curtly. "What we've come for is—"

"But surely your charming companion will take tea? Or is she also afraid of what might be in it?"

"No," she said, despite Simon's frown. "I should like

a cup. I'm more than a little bit thirsty. Riding around London is hot work."

"I also find London stifling in the summer."

"Is that why you're getting out?" Simon demanded rudely.

"Getting out?" Dr. Mystery's face was a perfect blank. Nobody could have read his feelings regarding Simon's rudeness. "But I am not leaving town. Merely postponing my work for some few days."

Julia hadn't known just what to expect. She knew Simon's prejudice against this man and had been, all unconsciously, allowing his view to color her own. Now she studied him with unbiased curiosity.

Dr. Mystery was a smaller, slighter man than Simon, and Mrs. Pierce had been right when she called his mustache and small imperial "comical." Furthermore, he wore a plum-colored suit, which even to Julia's untutored eyes looked eccentric. A glittering ring flashed from his smallest finger while another gold ring constrained his tie. He seemed foppish and inconsequential.

Then Julia met his eyes over the cup of tea he handed her and, startled by what she saw, hurriedly revised all her views.

"Oh, yes," he said, just as though he were reading her mind. "I am a true believer, Miss . . . may I know your name?"

"Julia Hanson."

"Julia Hanson." Suddenly, he smiled with warm satisfaction. "It suits you."

"Thank you. Have you a Christian name?"

"Basil. Or Randall. Or Guillermo. Once I was Bram, which means 'raven.' I lived in a quiet village on the north coast of Ireland. The Vikings ended that incarnation. With violent suddenness. But I don't like to remember that."

Julia looked uncertainly toward Simon. But he, with a woof of disgust, had turned his back to look down into the garden. "Naturally not."

"Life before our own time was so often nasty, brutish, and short. Believe me, I remember. Now, however, we can say we have reached the pinnacle of civilization."

"I would agree with you," Julia said, "were it not that every civilization says the same thing. Every government, every religion, every philosophy is certain of its own superiority."

He smiled as though she were a backward pupil who finally lucked upon the right answer. "You are very clever. I should like to find out about your previous existences. Will you permit me to feel your head?"

Simon turned around at that. "Absolutely not!"

Dr. Mystery did not flick so much as a glance in Simon's direction. Julia might have almost imagined that the spiritualist did not know the archaeologist was there for all the notice he took of him. "Does he speak for you? Are you—perhaps—engaged to be married?"

She saw Simon's back stiffen. "No to both questions, Dr. Mystery. Actually, no to all three. The bumps on my head shall have to wait until another time."

"I would actually prefer to read your palm. Phrenology is such an inexact science, Miss Hanson."

"Science? Bah!" Simon said explosively.

Once again, Dr. Mystery's ability to ignore what he didn't choose to notice was masterly. He lifted a plate. "Do you care for cake?"

Julia, who wasn't hungry for the sticky confection, took it just to be polite. It seemed to be sponge cake cut in half. The two parts were put together again, oozing a brownish-pink custard. It did not look wholesome, but Dr. Mystery ate one with every appearance of enjoyment, even licking his longish fingers when he thought no one was looking.

"I am curious about one subject, Dr. Mystery."

"It will be my pleasure to tell you whatever you want to know, Miss Hanson. Provided . . . but it is unhandsome of me to make conditions. Ask your questions and then, if you are agreeable, you will answer mine?"

She didn't answer that one. "Why did you go to see Mrs. Pierce today?"

"Mrs. . . . who?"

"The charwoman?"

"Ah, forgive me. I did not trouble to inquire her name."

"Why did you go to see her?"

"You are tenacious, Miss Hanson. That is an excellent quality."

Julia gave him one of her very brightest smiles. "Therefore, you might as well answer, for I'll not grow tired of asking."

"I thought you and your companion might be interested in why I have decided to suspend my poor attempts to help my clients."

"That, too," Julia said. "But, leaving that subject for the moment, why did you . . . ?"

Dr. Mystery raised his hands in defeat. "Don't you already know why? The reason for my seeking out Mrs. Pierce is the same as the reason I am setting aside my efforts. When I saw you last night with Mr. Archer, I felt compelled to learn all about you. You are my one interest now."

Julia had not expected such an answer. She could only stare at the strange little man. Simon, however, did not seem stunned. He walked over and lifted Dr. Mystery straight out of his chair, holding him only by his lapels.

Dr. Mystery's almost unearthly composure was disturbed at last. He clutched Simon's wrists, his dark eyes wide with fear. "What . . . what . . . ?"

Julia yelped, "No! Please. . . ."

Not listening, Simon shook Dr. Mystery vigorously, until the smaller man's head bobbled like a toy's. Then he dropped him back into his seat with a teeth-rattling jar. "That's for impertinence," he said levelly, tossing the hair out of his eyes.

Dr. Mystery's face was as red as a Turkish carpet,

clashing terribly with his plum-colored suit. He glanced at Julia, who'd watched the performance deeply chagrined. Though she had not liked the appraising look in his deep eyes when he'd said she was the reason for his talking to Mrs. Pierce, she had wanted to find out more. She feared now that the opportunity to question Dr. Mystery further was lost through Simon's impetuosity.

"I'm terribly sorry."

"It's not your fault," Dr. Mystery said, tugging his tie into place. "The man's spirit is pure barbarian."

"Don't apologize to him!" Simon said. "That's for him to do."

Dr. Mystery pursed his small red lips. "I will gladly apologize to Miss Hanson, but not under duress. I'm sorry if your 'friend' put the wrong interpretation on my words. I meant them in no infamous sense. I merely wish to express my deep admiration for the young lady."

"Admiration?" Julia asked.

He moved as though to take her hand. Julia, recalling with what relish he'd licked his fingers, evaded his touch by lifting her teacup. He settled for pressing his right hand to his heart. "Deepest and most profound admiration. If ever you need the particular kind of help I can offer, please call upon me. Day or night, at any hour, I stand ready to serve you."

"Thank you, but I don't . . ."

Simon came to stand by her chair. "Come along, Julia. We're leaving. I've had quite enough of this."

Though she'd never before seen Simon in such a temper, she could almost feel the angry heat he radiated. She should have allowed him to persuade her to stay behind while he interviewed Dr. Mystery. Then she could have come later, by herself. Now, she felt the only thing to do was to leave with him before he further alienated the spiritualist.

"Good day, Dr. Mystery," she said pleasantly. "I don't

understand you. But it has been a . . . an experience to meet you."

He rose when she did and bowed profoundly. "We will meet again, Miss Hanson. If not in this life . . ."

Fourteen

~

On the street, Simon began to walk. He set a pace that Julia could only just match. Even then, she had to make the occasional skip to keep up. She was breathless by the time they reached the park, several blocks away, and it was only there that he spoke to her.

"That pip-squeak!"

He walked on. She could imagine him striding like this across the burning sands of Egypt, working out a problem in his mind. Fortunately she was fond of a walk herself. Many were the days she'd put an apple in the pocket of her favorite homely dress and gone for a long tramp over hill and dale. If it had not been for the fact that Yorkshire is hilly while London is flat, she doubted she could have kept up with Simon at all. But her legs were in excellent condition. It was her wind that worried her. He walked so very fast.

"Simon," she panted. "If you would only listen!"

"I knew what he was like. I saw how he looked at those girls there last night. It isn't only money he wants, oh, no. He wants to get people in his power. With women the best way to do that is . . ." He shrugged his broad shoulders as Julia hung on his words. "I should be thrashed for taking you within a hundred miles of 'Dr. Mystery.' "

"But I wanted to go."

He stopped so suddenly that Julia's feet sent little spurts of gravel flying from the path as she tried not to walk slap into him. "And that's my fault, as well. I should have sent you to your house this morning."

Julia made a grab at his arm as he turned away. "Understand once and for all, Simon Archer, nobody sends me anywhere! I chose to come with you; I chose to speak to him."

"But that's absurd. No woman—"

"If you say once more that no woman can choose for herself, I will scream!"

"There. You see. No man would ever say such a thing."

"Would you prefer me to be more manly? Very well. Simon, you tell me even once more than no woman can be trusted to choose for herself and I'll—I'll punch you in the nose. Better?"

"Don't get hysterical, Julia."

"That's enough!" She reached out and seized hold of his shirt.

"Stop! What will people think?"

Though Julia was rather tall for her sex, she still felt paltry when she stood close to him. Some of her anger departed, for when he looked down at her like that she could only remember that he'd kissed her in the carriage. Nonetheless, she fixed him with as steely an eye as she could manage.

Enunciating each word with precision, she said in a ruthlessly controlled tone, "Never tell me I'm hysterical when you are being unreasonable."

"I'm never unreasonable."

"Ha!" She released him and marched past him. "And you call yourself a scientist!"

"What is that supposed to mean?"

This time, she stopped short and had the satisfaction of watching him windmill his arms to avoid running over her. "A scientist has a theory that fits the facts. When a new fact comes along, he changes the theory. You, Mr. Archer, attempt to tailor the facts to fit your theory."

"I do not! Give me one example."

"One! I have a hundred, but one will suffice. You theorize that all women are weak and feeble, unable to think or reason without a man's help. I am a woman."

"Yes, you are," he agreed with warmth.

"Don't interrupt, if you please. I am a woman. I have as loving a heart as any woman ever born. But I am neither meek nor helpless and you yourself have paid unstinting homage to my mind."

"Your translations are masterly."

"Yet you refuse to change your theory to fit the fact of my existence! I am a woman and must therefore be a fool and a coward no matter how often I prove the reverse. By not accepting new evidence, you prove yourself to be nothing more than a blind dolt who tripped upon good fortune. You don't deserve to have found An-ket's tomb."

With that parting shot, Julia strode away. It took a surprising amount of self-discipline not to look back and see, if not Simon hurrying to catch up, at least him standing with a look of baffled wonder on his face. When she heard his footsteps matching hers, she looked down just long enough to see his shoes come up beside her. Then, head up, back straight, she continued on her march.

At a rapid pace, they continued through the park. Having surged against a flotilla of nannies with children, both walking and in prams, they could not stop to continue their argument. A few heads turned to watch a man and a woman striding along as though competing for which would bring the news of Marathon.

Julia felt a prickle of sweat under her dress. It was not fair. She must have been carrying twenty extra pounds of clothing compared to his neat attire. And her shoes, while comfortable, were not as sturdy or as supportive as his. Once already, she'd nearly turned an ankle in the gravel.

But she was determined not to falter. At least, not before Simon did.

They rounded a corner and the scent of sun-warmed roses poured over them. Julia slowed her pace perforce to breathe in the aroma, sharp and sweet together. A garden of color-dappled bushes stood to one side off the path, bounded by wrought-iron fences. The Do Not Pick the Flowers notices were discreet but adamant.

"Thank goodness there's no law against smelling public flowers."

Drawn by the scent and the colors, she left the path to bend down over one pink blossom and draw its fragrance deep into her soul. "Heavenly. Simon, come smell this."

"I've never been able to smell roses. Their scent is too light for me to catch."

"You can smell these. Here—the red ones have the richest perfume. Mmm. It's enough to make one drunk. I sometimes think bees get intoxicated by the roses." She pointed to one fuzzy-bodied bee staggering out of a fully opened rose. "Look, there goes one. His flight is very crooked. I think he's dizzy."

She held the bloom steady while Simon sniffed hesitantly. "Yes, I can just catch that."

"I have some attar of roses in my luggage. I wear it on special occasions. If you're good, I'll let you smell my wrist." Her tone was teasing. Not looking at him, she leaned low to inhale once more the exquisite bouquet that attracted bee and man alike.

"Julia . . ."

His hand rested lightly on her waist. She straightened, squinting a trifle in the sunshine. He touched her cheek with his fingertips. She remembered the look in his eyes from the carriage and felt a shiver of some emotion that fell halfway between apprehension and delight. She suddenly knew how a rosebud must feel when, day by day, under the caressing influence of the sun, it began to open. Every time Simon touched her, she unfurled a little more.

She wondered what the end would be even while she hoped for wonders beyond her experience.

"Julia . . ." he said again, with an increase in urgency. His hand curled around her waist. She felt the strength in his arm as it began to tighten.

"You can't kiss me here. There's a constable coming up the path."

For one heart-clenching moment, she thought he'd ignore that and kiss her anyway. She wanted him to be so reckless even while she admitted it wasn't at all wise. But wisdom, she was beginning to sense, wasn't everything.

The constable gave them a lowering glance from under his hat brim. She supposed they did look more than a little disreputable. Her hat was tilted far back on her head again, her face hot, while her dress was bedraggled and dusty about the hem. Simon's shirt was wrenched from where she'd grabbed it and his silk cravat had twisted around under one ear. She reached up to adjust it, even while smiling brightly at the policeman.

"Stay off the grass," he growled.

"Yes, constable. Thank you."

Once more on the path, Simon said, "So tell me, what you did think of him? A mountebank, no doubt, good only for frightening the credulous."

"On the contrary, Simon. Dr. Mystery, despite his flamboyant appearance and approach, is completely serious about his spiritualism. He might even prove to be a fanatic about it."

"Come, come. How can you tell all that from a single half-hour's conversation?"

"I looked into his eyes."

"I've never noticed anything odd about his eyes."

"Have you ever looked into them? Deeply? I doubt he would let a man do it, but he was as interested in me as I was in him. Oh, not in any amorous way," she said, taking the word with a gulp. "Not even in a financial way, and I have seen both often enough. If I did not believe myself to be indulging in wishful thinking, I could almost say that Dr. Mystery was interested in me for my mind."

Simon said sourly, "In short, your perfect man."

Julia studied him. Was it possible that Simon Archer was jealous? Impossible, she thought. How could a man be jealous unless he was in love? If he was falling in love with her . . . but to her surprise, she found the idea did not elate her. Surely love that admitted jealousy was a possessive, untrusting love, not at all what she had dreamed of since girlhood.

Sighing, Julia walked on, her hands clasped loosely behind her back. Her father always called it her "sailor walk" but it served as an aid to thought like no other.

Was she asking too much of fate? Surely it would be enough for Simon Archer to take her on whatever terms. As his wife, she would have the felicity of assisting a great man in his life's work, a work that she loved as well as she loved the man.

Julia stole a glance at him, once more walking beside her. He had a remarkably fine profile, like a cameo of a Roman general. It must be a lasting wonder to her that some woman hadn't married him out of hand years ago.

Was she in love with him? Not just with the personality revealed in his letters, but with the man himself? She recalled seeing him for the first time yesterday, remembering with what anticipation she'd waited for him to notice her. Surely the butterflies in her interior had not been those natural to an applicant inquiring for a post, but the nervous flutterings of a woman meeting the man of her dreams.

She asked herself what he must have seen in that first moment. An Egyptologist, sensibly controlled, stating her case with clarity and determination? Or a man-hungry spinster, looking with covetous eyes at an eligible male? Julia wriggled with humiliation at the very notion of that second possibility.

Had she been in love with Simon all along? Had her

wild plan of marrying him been born not out of love for Egypt's ancient glories, but out of a connection to Simon himself? She could not help being uneasy about the answers.

Above all, she asked herself why he had kissed her in the carriage. Was it—horrid thought—out of pity? Had she been giving out, all unconsciously, some sort of signal that she wanted him to do it? Was she demonstrating, even now, that she wanted him to do it again? Because she wanted him to kiss her again. The first one had been too brief. She had sat there, frozen against the cushions, unable to react to this new situation. What if she never had another opportunity?

"Did you say something?" Simon asked.

"No. I have a stitch in my side from all this walking."

"There's a bench over there. Shall we sit down?"

"For a few moments. I still have much to do today."

When they sat down, Simon turned toward her and put his arm along the back of the bench. If her posture had deviated even slightly from perfection, she could have thought herself all but cuddled in his arm.

He said, "So you think Dr. Mystery is a fanatic?"

"I believe he could become one very easily. Once, after our former vicar had died, several men served our church until a permanent replacement was found. One, a middle-aged gentleman, was as merry and charming as could be, but I could never like him as well as my father and some of the other committee members did. I saw a look in his eyes that made me most uncomfortable. I wish to make no comparisons between true religion and Dr. Mystery's beliefs, mind you."

"Of course not. What happened to this 'middle-aged gentleman'?"

"We heard through friends that in his next post he became convinced that the Messiah would be returning to earth within the year. When he was found waiting for Our Lord in the middle of an icy river at Christmas, it was decided that he must be confined for his own safety. My father sent money for the man's keep and he was not sent to an asylum. But until he died, he believed that he himself had become what he'd waited for. They say he was a very gentle madman."

"And you feel that Dr. Mystery is on the verge of such madness?"

"I'm not a physician. But such a little thing set Mr. Marcham off. He'd always been very stern against swearing. Apparently when he heard a young boy take the name of the Lord in vain one too many times . . . it was too much."

"I feel sorry for him. But I'm not concerned that Dr. Mystery . . . how I hate that name! I wish I knew what his true name was so that I could use it to his face!"

"Do you hate him?"

He considered, staring off toward some distant trees, before replying, "No. I sincerely hope I have no hatred in me toward anyone. But I despise him because he feeds the false hopes of others and battens on their grief like a vampire."

Changing his warm, masculine voice to a reedy falsetto, he said, "Do you yearn to speak with those who are lost? Do you long for the touch of a vanished hand? Simply give some prating actor fifty pounds and the eternal mysteries are revealed." In his own voice, mastering passion with difficulty, he said, "It's . . . it's making a mockery of things that are too sacred to be made the stuff of commerce."

"I agree with you," Julia said, laying her hand on his sleeve. "I'm delighted that he has given it up, for whatever reason."

Simon's hand covered hers. She felt tingles run from the spot he touched to the back of her neck. Knowing her cheeks were pink, she slipped her hand from under his gentle pressure. "Dear me," she said, catching the faint reverberation of the city's church bells. "I must run away!

I told the Pierce girls that I'd meet them just a little while from now. No," she added, rising. "Don't trouble to come with me. Domestic details can never be as absorbing to a gentleman as they are to women."

"Now you are guilty of the same sin of generalization as I have been. I'm very interested indeed in your 'domestic details.'" Somehow he managed, whether by inflection or the lift of his impertinent eyebrow, to make those two words sound tempting, as though Adam were discussing applesauce with Eve.

In Dr. Mystery's bedroom, Basil Mortimer stood before his full-length pier glass mirror. Overhead, four soft balls stuffed with millet flew in an endless cascade, while the man's hands scarcely moved. He juggled without ever taking his eyes from his own reflected eyes, catching and releasing the balls using only peripheral vision. He'd trained himself to be perfect and found the appearance of looking straight ahead while carefully observing around him to be a very valuable skill.

There was no past, no future, he told himself. There is only this moment, this juggling—each ball, every ball. Catch and release, using only the springs in my fingers and the trampoline of my hand.

"'It has been an . . . experience meeting you,'" he quoted, without realizing he'd meant to say anything at all. He dropped one ball, then another. He let the remaining two fall, bounding away over the carpet.

"Damn Simon Archer," Basil said. "Damn his black soul."

He'd so nearly had her. He'd exerted himself to intrigue her, dropping hints of what he could do, and he'd so nearly succeeded. If he'd been allowed even five minutes alone with her to make another appointment! Her lovely warm brown eyes had been fascinated by him, fascinated and slightly repelled. He didn't mind that; he was used to it. So many people were put off by him on first acquaintance, but he'd made a life's work out of reversing that immediate impression.

He had always been amused that the women who were most troubled by him at first made the most passionate devotees at the last. It was as if they worked so hard to convince themselves that they'd never felt disturbed by his peculiarities that he hardly had to exert himself to seduce them. They came willingly into his bed, eager to learn from him more than mysticism.

Not that he felt any physical desire for Julia Hanson. He recoiled from the very notion. His need for her was not of the gross body, but that of a wizard who has at last found his lost familiar. No, she must remain as pure as when he'd first met her. It would be best if she fell in love with him, of course. Women in love were so easy to control.

"Better than drugs," he said to himself. The man in the mirror shrugged. "No, I won't drug her. The manifestations must be undiluted. When she falls in love with me, she'll give me what I want willingly."

He'd use the "psychic powers have crippled my manhood" story. That always went down well with a certain type of woman. He wondered how much money she had. Not that it mattered. Between her gifts and his management, they'd both soon be rich enough even for his never-ending wants.

Basil took off his clothes, hanging coat and trousers neatly over the back of a chair. His body was on the stunted side, true, but he had worked with the raw material to fashion an ideal form, in the same way that Michelangelo had found his David in the rough-hewn marble.

No one who had not seen him unclothed would have believed the extent of his muscular development. It was this that made so many of his "tricks" possible. Slipping out of knotted ropes, seeming to levitate using the arm strength no one believed he had, hiding in the top of a cabinet by the pressure of feet and hands—funny how no one ever thought to look at the ceiling of such a deceptively empty box. Just as no one troubled to look past his unappealing facade until it was too late.

It had not been lack of strength that kept him passive when Simon Archer had used him so shamefully in front of Julia Hanson. When it came to a battle of sheer brawn, he could have triumphed. Then it would have been handsome Simon humiliated in the eyes of warm, sympathetic Miss Hanson.

Basil looked at himself and sneered. Lying to oneself was pointless, whatever tales the world swallowed. He knew it hadn't been a lack of strength that kept him from knocking Simon Archer down; what he lacked was courage.

Ever since his childhood he'd been terrified of being hurt. To improve his skills and his body, he'd suffered tremendously and never grudged a pang. What he feared was pain at the hands of another. He didn't know why. He'd never been struck as a child, not even by his envious brothers. Grannie Daly had protected him, prophesying that it was this boy who'd inherited her "special gifts." Everyone had been in awe of that old woman, tiny, white-bonneted, and bent, but with an inner fire capable of scorching anyone who defied her.

She'd been the wise woman of their village, whom even the doctor consulted. Most of the local fools had been afraid of her, fearful that she could "ill-wish" them. Grannie Daly had scorned to do that, though she'd always added that she could if she would. Grannie Daly had taught him more than she knew, for no advice or herbal preparation would be offered without a suitable show of theatricality to wrap her mysteries in greater mysteries yet.

She'd warned him often never to use his powers for financial gain, showing him at the same time how to make people pay or barter without a single overt word being said. He had understood that for her, the power that her fellow villagers gave her was the real reward rather than the chicken or silver pennies they brought in trade.

He himself could never see that starving to death as a second-rate touring actor was nobler than giving brilliant performances as a medium for a select few. At least dogs didn't chase him when he walked through the streets, nor did small boys think it funny to disrupt his speeches with rude noises and cherrystones. Despite various drawbacks, he much preferred staying in one place for more than a single night, especially in such luxurious surroundings.

Herr Esbach of Mittle Berenia had been so generous to lend him this town house when he'd been so suddenly recalled to his home court. Basil had given him warning that to have less than a perfect apology prepared for the King's hearing would mean certain ouster both for the Elector and his charming mistress.

Basil patted the bed reminiscently. Elsie had been really too good for the Elector. She'd probably kill him one day with her gymnastic abilities. Basil made a mental note to ask about the Elector's future at some time when the spirits were in a good mood. With a telegram at the proper time, he'd earn both the Elector's continued gratitude and, with luck, the return of the delectable full-bodied Elsie to London.

All his difficulties arose from the fact that the spirits only came when they chose to. He hadn't wanted to create plausible effects to fool people. He'd been forced into it. When someone had paid five guineas to talk to dear departed Uncle Gerard, they don't want to hear that he's not in the mood to chat.

"I only cheat so people don't go away disappointed," he said, lighting the candles that stood on mantelpiece, tables, and shelves. "I wouldn't do it if you were all more cooperative."

Naked, he sat down in a wing back chair and opened his mind. "I want to know about Julia Hanson," he said slowly. "Julia Hanson."

Fifteen

~

Usually Julia enjoyed domestic details. Though her bent was toward scholarship, she did not believe that one must live in squalor to be intellectual. As a rule, she devoted an hour a day to ordering the menu, talking over linen and preserves with her aunt, and inspecting the maids' work. Then she turned with a quiet mind to her translations, knowing the tranquility that comes to the toiling Marthas of this world.

She realized now, inspecting all that needed to be done in the London house, the difference a full complement of staff made. With only two girls, rendering the house livable would take all of her time in the foreseeable future.

"Best get started," she said. "When did your mother say she'd have a cook for me?"

"Tomorrow morning, bright 'n' early!" Min said. Her hair was tied up in a cloth, her sleeves pushed up past the elbow. "We brung our tea in a padded basket, miss."

"I'm glad, for I doubt there's so much as a usable leaf in the place."

There'd been a strong smell of mice in the kitchen and sour grease in the sink. Though the servants had covered the furniture in great swaths of holland, the floors were dusty and the library had evidently not been aired properly in weeks. Frowning, Julia wondered if anything had been done as it should have been after the butler had closed the door behind her after her last visit.

"What can't be cured must be endured," she muttered. "But cure this I will!"

She set the girls to work in the kitchen, preparing it for the cook. Julia herself started clearing up the brighter of the two morning rooms, the one just beyond the dining room. This is where she would receive visitors, once she'd begun leaving her cards on the wives of her father's business associates. They'd think her immodestly forward in her notions, but she owed it to him not to neglect any such small courtesies.

She scrubbed the soot from the surface of the white marble fireplace. Of course, she'd brought no clothes for such dirty work, but luckily it seemed the last cook had been a woman of considerable girth. A much-spotted apron, unearthed in the kitchen, had wrapped twice around Julia. With her sleeves rolled up to the elbow and a duster tied around her hair, she fancied that she looked exactly like a maidservant and amused herself while she scrubbed by inventing a family to work for.

She'd just decided that the family governess would be the long-lost daughter of a duke—stolen by gypsies in infancy—when the front door knocker beat a tattoo. Julia stood up, brushing a wisp of fallen hair from her eyes with the back of her hand.

Going out into the hall, she called, "It's my baggage," to the girls in the kitchen. She heard an indistinct reply.

Wiping her hands on that voluminous apron, Julia opened the door. "Mrs. Archer? Amanda? Apple?"

"Good afternoon, Miss Hanson. My son told me what an enormous task you undertake and I simply had to drop by to offer my services." Mrs. Archer turned to her maid. "Make yourself useful, Apple."

"Yes, madam."

"Why, thank you, Apple. If you don't mind?"

The black-haired maid, with cheeks as round as her name, suddenly smiled and dipped a curtsey. "Naw. Where should I start?" She glanced down at Julia's hands. "What were you doin', miss?"

"Scrubbing the morning room fireplace. Oh, I beg your pardon, Mrs. Archer! I'm so at sixes and sevens, I forget my manners! Won't you come in?" She stood back to let the three women enter. "I'm afraid I haven't anything to offer you. Would you believe there's nothing to eat or drink in the house?"

"Your servants must have taken advantage of you. They will take refreshments on holiday to save on their own expenses."

Amanda said with the abruptness of uncertain adolescence, "It's a very pretty house. I like the . . . the . . . um . . ." her voice petered out.

"And such a central location! Your father must need ride hardly ten minutes to enter the City. That must be a great savings on time."

"I believe he didn't consider that when he purchased the house. He wanted a house in London; this one met his not very stringent requirements. I'm not even certain he saw it himself beforehand. He did it all through his solicitor." Julia couldn't help noticing how gratified Mrs. Archer was at these revelations. "Would you care to see over the rest of the house? It isn't quite straight yet, I'm afraid."

"I should be charmed, Miss Hanson. It isn't often one gets the chance to explore another person's house. I suppose it isn't ladylike to be curious about such things, but I just can't restrain myself."

Though Mrs. Archer's nose wrinkled in some of the rooms, she pronounced herself captivated by the overall house. She admired windows in one room, a handsomely carved oak frieze in another, the placement of the furniture in the third.

"It needs bringing up to date," Julia admitted. "There's

several weeks of work to be done just on the ground floor alone. Happily, I'm a lifelong reader of ladies' magazines and am all but stuffed with ideas I want to try."

"You must be a great comfort to your father, Miss Hanson. Would it be asking too much too see the upper rooms?"

She glanced with puzzled eyes at Amanda, walking silently behind them. Letting Mrs. Archer busy herself with unheard raptures over an uncovered portrait, Julia murmured, "There are only bedrooms upstairs. What 'upper rooms' does she refer to?"

"Mother's too elegant to say the word 'bed,' Miss Hanson," Amanda replied, confirming Julia's belief that the girl's attitude was too meek to be true. They grinned at each other and Julia felt that, no matter what happened between herself and Simon, she'd found another friend.

In the 'upper rooms,' Mrs. Archer's pleasure in everything seemed to fade. "Oh, no, no, no. My dear girl, you can't mean to reside here."

"Well, yes, I had intended to do so," Julia said.

"But the paper is peeling off the walls from damp. And the other three rooms are just as bad. You'll have to build big fires in each room and keep them roaring for a week to chase it all away. You'll stifle in the heat!"

It was true that in the bedrooms a nose with any claim to sensitivity would be assaulted with a musty, mildewy odor. "It wouldn't be practical to fix one room and then move on to the next, would it?"

"Not if you want to have everything prepared in time for your father's wedding. Yes, Simon told me what a marvelous gift you are giving them by decorating this house. But it's much too big for one young girl to do alone!" Mrs. Archer held up her hand while Julia was still planning a justifying argument.

"You must air the rooms thoroughly first, so that the smell won't come back on the first overly warm day. Then the paper must be torn off and new pasted on, or perhaps a coat of distemper, which means having the painters and the paper-hangers in." She sniffed appraisingly. "That carpet will need to be cleaned and all the upholstered pieces aired. It will take days."

"I suppose it will."

"Meanwhile, where will you sleep? What will you eat? Everything will reek of paint." Mrs. Archer put her head to one side like a bird checking which way a worm would crawl before coming down on it.

"I could go back to the Bull and Bush. . . ."

"A common staging post? Acceptable for one night when first arriving or on the day one leaves, but not for an extended stay. No. There is only one solution. You must come back with us."

"Oh, but . . ."

"Wasn't your room comfortable?"

Julia hardly had a chance to say "very" when Mrs. Archer pounced, "Then it's settled. You'll come here every day to check on the maids' progress. We'll put Apple in charge; she has the most experience."

Julia wished Simon could see his mother now. This woman, whom he complained about, saying she dithered, was now giving orders like a battlefield general, telling the Pierce girls that they were under Apple's leadership, quelling the inevitable grumble, and taking for granted everyone's agreement.

Amanda murmured, "You may as well give in. She won't stop until you do, and really, my sisters and I would love to have you."

"But why does your mother want me to stay?"

Amanda's eyes were as wide as a doe's. "Don't you know?"

Julia shook her head.

"I probably shouldn't say this . . . promise me you won't blame Simon?"

"Simon? What does he have to do with anything?" Julia caught herself being breathless at the thought that Simon might have obliged his mother to offer the invitation. Did he want her under his roof? If so, she thought a tad bitterly, it is only to keep me from seeing Dr. Mystery again.

"Late last night, he told Mother about your father, the mill owner. I know he only wanted to assure her you are respectable. But, you see, Mother wants us all to marry well . . . do you see what I mean?"

"All too well. Never mind, Amanda. I don't blame anyone. I'm used to it."

Impulsively, seeming to surprise herself as much as Julia, Amanda hugged her around the waist. "I don't care if you're rich. I like you. Please come and stay with us. We'll have ever so much fun. Not Lucy, maybe. But Jane is great fun."

"All right," Julia said, feeling rather as though she were being besieged by an army of puppies, equipped with the latest ordinance of adorability. "I will."

Once she'd made the decision to accept Mrs. Archer's kind invitation, she realized how much she'd been dreading spending the night in the town house. Neither of the Pierce girls would be sleeping there. It surprised her to be troubled by the thought of being all alone in the house. She'd never known that kind of nervousness before. Perhaps it had been brought on by the thought of vast London breathing outside her windows. Or did the memory of Billy the Wall trouble her? Perhaps it had been the expression in Dr. Mystery's eyes.

She considered that expression, trying to interpret it, to place it in a category. Men had looked at her so many ways in her life—from the proud puzzlement of her father to the ardor of a suitor interested in her money. That particular expression was mirrored on Mrs. Archer's face, though for her son rather than for herself. One or two boys had actually believed themselves at least as much in love with her as with her fortune, only to prove themselves willing to love her only with certain changes in her behavior. "Why can't you try being just a girl?" one had asked.

But that only brought her back to the enigma of Dr. Mystery.

Could he know about An-ket? Surely he'd been standing too far away the previous night to have heard her impetuous outburst to Simon. Yet he'd either followed or searched out Mrs. Pierce and asked her questions about "unchancy" happenings. That having lead nowhere, he'd gone on to the next string in his bow—Julia herself. She further recalled Simon's neighbor telling him about some man who had been loitering outside the Archer house sometime before dawn.

She found Amanda standing in the den, her attention completely absorbed in a book. "Look what I found. *Les Trois Musketaires*. When Mother heard that the Duchess of Kent wouldn't let the queen read it, she took it away from me. Do you mind if I come with you tomorrow so I can read it here? I'll work, too, of course."

"I've read it. I'll tell your mother so. It's a very mild work, really, except for Milady. By the way, Amanda, that cat from last night . . ."

Amanda's eyes had been drawn once more to the fascinating work of Monsieur Dumas. "Cat?"

"Yes, have you seen it anywhere around today?"

"No. Mother doesn't like cats."

Simon had all but convinced himself that it would be best if he never saw Julia Hanson again when Jane informed him of his mother's good intentions.

He'd been passing a restless hour in his den, having retreated there to catch up on his lost sleep with a catnap. At first, the silence had pleased him. No bright, rapid voice, no shining eyes and eager smile disturbed the blessed peace of his *sanctum sanctorum*. He told himself that he preferred women like his sisters who could be counted on to leave a man strictly alone, if such was his wish. They never challenged his pronouncements.

Spending time with Julia Hanson, he reflected, was like the day he'd visited a horse-mad friend, Luke. He had been lent, in all innocence, a steeple-chaser that Luke had only just purchased. Once out of sight of her stable, the mare had careened all over the country, beyond control of rein, of voice, of knee. Clinging to the saddle like a burr, despite plunges, switchbacks, and flat-out gallops that brought his heart into his mouth, Simon could do nothing but hang on and pray. He closed his mind firmly against the treacherous thought that he'd never had a more exhilarating ride in all his life.

No, he thought firmly, much better not to see too much of Julia. Naturally, he'd be polite should she return to the museum, but when his mother had her come to tea, he should be able to arrange to be somewhere else. During the party, he would ask her to dance, once. After all, that was using her with common courtesy, such as he would show to any young woman.

Above all, he would contrive never to be alone with her. There must be no repeat of the kiss he'd pressed upon her in the carriage. What had he been thinking of, ushering a young woman about London without his mother or some other woman for chaperon?

Julia might be an unusual young woman but the risks she took were enough to make a proper man's hair stand on end. She didn't seem to care a jot for her reputation. To his shame, he'd done nothing to help her protect it. His only excuse was that he had a very hard time thinking of Julia as just another young woman. She was Julia.

He sat down, putting his feet on the corner of his desk. He couldn't decide what he liked least about her. Was it her flat contradictions of every opinion he held? Was it the way she smiled, like a bold privateer, as she engaged him in argument?

On further consideration, he tended toward the view that the worst of her was that she didn't seem to realize that her zest for information enhanced her beauty, while any man with red blood would be distracted from his own defense by the splendid contours of her figure.

If only she'd made an obvious play of these natural attributes, he could have disliked her intensely. But she seemed to forget in the heat of debate that she was a woman at all. Yet he could never charge her with being unfeminine. She remained a lady in all she did and said, even when she'd seized him by the shirtfront. He would have liked to have kissed her then, too.

He'd been doing so when Jane woke him up to tell him that Julia was coming to stay.

Blinking at her, startled by a return to reality from a dream that had seemed even more real than life, he couldn't force even one word from his dry mouth.

"Don't be such an owl," Jane said. She perched on the edge of his desk next to his feet. "Does she have good handwriting? I ask you because you've exchanged so many letters. Do you think she'd mind helping me address all these invitations?"

"What did you say?"

"I asked you if Miss Hanson would mind lending me a hand with all these dreadful invitations? I wouldn't have thought you'd know so many people, Simon, what with spending all your time in Egypt."

Due to his parents unfortunately having lost several infants between the births of Simon and Lucy, there were almost sixteen years between himself and his youngest sister. She had been in the schoolroom until this year, under the care of a competent governess, so Simon had seen very little of her, as he'd been either at school or in Egypt for most of her life. He had not thought, however, that she'd learned to speak obscure Oriental dialects in that time, yet her words made as much sense to him as if she'd been speaking Khmer.

"Did . . . did you say that Julia is coming here? To stay?"

"I didn't know you'd taken to calling her 'Julia.' Mother will be pleased."

He sat up from his weary sprawl and tried hard to focus. "Jane, kindly begin at the beginning."

She rolled her eyes. With an almost theatrical clarity, she said slowly, "Mother sent a messenger to tell me to tell you that Miss Hanson, finding that her house needs more work than she anticipated, has accepted Mother's invitation to stay with us while the work is being done. That's clear, isn't it?"

"The fog is beginning to thin," Simon said. "Anything else?"

"No, not from Mother."

Something else she'd said had penetrated at last. "Why are you only just sending the invitations? Isn't the party in several days . . . this Wednesday, in fact?"

Jane shook her head at him, sighing an exasperated breath. "No, silly. Haven't you heard? We postponed it until next Friday. The countess has a cold and Mother won't put herself forward, as she says, to play hostess in Aunt Lucinda's absence. I'm just as glad about that! My godmother will do a much better job of it than Mother would. Mother was going to forbid the orchestra to play waltzes. Really, you know, she's almost gothic in her notions."

"While Aunt Lucinda is notoriously fast? You're dreaming, little girl. Aunt Lucinda was a bosom bow of the queen's mother and is a stickler for propriety."

"It must run in the family," Lucy muttered. "At least I hadn't sent out any invitations with the old date."

"Why not?"

"Because it took us twice as long as it need have to decide what we were going to have. No one liked the paper I chose at the printer, and Mother and Amanda kept changing their minds about the printing. And you know Lucy will agree with everyone just to keep the peace."

"Everything else is all right, though?"

"Well . . ."

"What is it?"

"Mr. Fiersole, the caterer, is still waiting to hear what we want to serve. Since the date has been pushed back, it's not quite as desperate a situation as it was."

"Why doesn't Mother just give him a free hand?"

"Because Mr. Fiersole is a dreadful spendthrift, but really the very best chef. Aunt Lucinda swears by him and, of course, he knows her house so well."

Simon stood up. "I had no idea this was turning into such a catastrophe."

"Oh, it will all turn out well . . . I hope."

"When will Mother return home? I had better have a serious discussion with her about this. She doesn't seem to realize how important this launch could be to my fundraising. If I could find just one patron to finance next year's dig!"

"Couldn't Miss Hanson's father do it? Mother hinted that he was fearfully rich."

"Jane!"

"Well, isn't she? Apple said her underclothes had to be seen to be believed."

"Jane!" Simon said again, even more shocked. "Didn't Miss Lanyon tell you never to mention certain subjects in mixed company? I thought she was supposed to be teaching you ladylike deportment as well as geography and needlework."

"I didn't think it mattered if the man was your brother. Speaking of which . . . you'd better see Lucy."

"Why? What's the matter with her?"

"Nothing, I think. You might not believe me, Simon, but when I went past her door this morning, I thought I heard her . . ."

"Was she crying again?"

"No, that's what is so strange. I thought I heard her singing. And not one of her sad songs, either. There are days when I think if I have to listen to 'The Ash Grove' one more time . . . ! Anyway, I heard her singing something happy. As she's your favorite sister, I thought you'd like to know."

Simon gave her a very straight look. "I haven't a favorite sister," he said.

"Haven't you?"

"No. There are times when I dislike you all equally."

She laughed and jumped down from his desk gracelessly. "You mustn't dislike me too much," she said. "You sent me ten pounds as a Christmas present last year and told Mother I could spend it however I chose. I bought a very fetching hat, with an eye veil, if you please." She pulled a freakishly charming face at him.

Simon unlocked the top drawer of his desk. "I suppose that ten pounds is long since spent. Could you do with, say, five pounds more?"

"Couldn't I just! Mother promised me a pair of silk gloves for the party but with one thing and another there hasn't been time."

"Tell me, Jane, isn't there some nice man who'll marry you and take you away?"

"Not yet," she said, closing her hand around the money. "But after next Friday, who can say?"

He was still smiling at her nonsense as he started up the stairs. He'd hardly put his foot on the first step when the doorbell was sharply twisted by someone outside. Thinking it might be Julia arriving already, he didn't wait for one of the servants to open it.

"Winslow?"

"Good afternoon, Archer." The soldier wore civilian dress, very point-device. Simon saw himself blackly reflected in the other man's shoes. "It's a pleasure to see you again so soon."

He might express his pleasure but Simon realized Winslow was trying so hard to see past him into the house that he couldn't be said to see the man before him at all. "Won't you come in?"

"Only for a moment. I've come about the cat."

"Cat?" Simon couldn't very well tell Winslow that it wasn't a cat at all but An-ket, Priestess of Hathor. He wondered suddenly if the reason Julia was returning to Carderock Square was neither because of his mother's pressing nor from a desire to spend more time with himself. He hoped, but did not hope very much, that she wasn't coming back to talk to the cat. She'd not mentioned her strange delusion after they'd left Mr. Keene's office; he'd foolishly imagined that she'd forgotten it, as one forgets a dream upon waking. Squelching the memory of his own recent dreams, he repeated, "Which cat?"

"I believe I mentioned this morning that I had come home rather late last night. At about the same time, I saw your sisters putting out a cat." Again he looked past Simon, this time up the staircase. "Is it her . . . their cat?"

"No, it's a stray."

"Oh. Oh, I see." Why should the cat's lack of ownership make a soldier look so downcast? He wouldn't have supposed Robert Winslow was a sickly, sentimental type.

"Perhaps that's just as well," he said. "M'father's taken a liking to the creature. Pretty thing, or would be if it were fed adequately for a while. I'll tell him that as she . . . they don't want it, he's free to adopt it."

"He's fond of cats, the general?"

"It's always been dogs, actually. Can't keep them in town very well, except for lapdogs, and m'father's always been fond of kicking that sort."

Simon tried to frame a question, but couldn't seem to get beyond, "Does your father think the cat is talking to him?" which was hardly a question to ask about a noted and decorated officer. He said instead, "Quite a rare breed, that cat."

"Did you find it so? I thought it a common alley cat, but as I say, m'father's taken to it. He's been a trifle down-pin of late, what with my posting off to the end of the world and then being gone so often at night."

"I tell you what, Winslow. There's a lady staying here with us. It may be that she wants the cat. I'll stop by with her later, if that's agreeable to you."

"A lady? A friend of Miss Archer's, no doubt."

"No. A friend of mine . . . she helps me with my work."

"Oh!" Winslow nodded as if he understood, but how could he when Simon didn't understand his relationship with Julia himself.

"Well, good day, Archer. Er . . . stop by the club one of these days. We'll have a drink, eh? Talk about—er—Egypt. I passed through there on my first posting, you know."

As Simon closed the door behind Winslow, he found himself wondering whether his neighbor had received a touch of the sun while in India. He himself had never been susceptible, but he'd known many a man who'd come back from the desert wearing just such a dazed look.

Reaching the top of the stairs, he knocked on Lucy's door. "Lucy? It's I, Simon."

"Ah. Yes, Simon?" Her voice was oddly muffled.

"May I speak to you?" He heard a faint thump and a fainter "ting" as though something glass had been struck. He rapped again. "Lucy? Are you all right?"

"I was—er—about to lie down, Simon. I have a headache."

"Another headache? I'm sorry to hear that. I'll only take a moment of your time. I wanted to tell you about Robert Winslow."

"Who?"

"Winslow. Our neighbor." He thought, but did not say, *The man for whom you've been eating your heart out the last two years.*

When she opened the door a minute or two later, a waft of perfume amounting to a gust puffed out into the hall. He coughed. "No wonder you have a headache. You should open a window, Lucy."

"I tried. It's stuck or something."

He entered to do it for her but stopped after a step or two. Her simply furnished room was, to be brutally honest, a fright. Every gown she owned lay tossed haphazardly on the bed, several sliding off even as he watched. On her dressing table, pots wore no lids, every bottle of perfume was open, her pins and necklaces strewn about as though she'd upended their boxes and shaken everything out. When he looked at her, however, she seemed unconscious of anything amiss, merely looking back with the expectation that he'd open a window.

"It's not stuck," he said, after trying it. "You haven't unlatched it."

"No? Oh, thank you . . . Simon."

"Are you all right? You sound odd."

"Do I? It must be my head. It's very bad." She pressed her fingertips against her temple but all her movements were sluggish and somehow disjointed. "I'm going to lie down for a little while."

"Not until you clear off your bed." He tried to chuckle but he was seriously concerned. He wished his mother would hurry home. "Do you want me to call the doctor?"

Her answer was slow in coming. "No. I'll be all right just as soon as I . . . rest."

"Very well," he said. She waited for him to leave with just enough obviousness that he could not press her further. "But don't you want to hear about Robert? I just saw him one moment ago."

"Did you?" she asked without any particular sign of interest. "I hope he's well."

"He looked in tolerable health. Lucy . . . are you . . . ?"

She yawned. "Oh, so tired. I had a busy night, but I can rest now. 'Bye, Simoon . . . I mean, Simon." She smiled at him sleepily, batting her golden lashes.

When Mrs. Archer came home, Simon took her aside and, without beating about the bush, asked straight out, "What is Lucy taking?"

"Taking, my dear?"

"Think, Mother. Are we missing any laudanum? Has there been an unusual amount of whiskey missing from the decanters?"

"No, Simon, of course not. You know, you haven't even greeted Miss Hanson."

He glanced at Julia. There was something different about her. "You've changed your dress," he said abruptly.

"Simon!" Mrs. Archer sounded shocked and, at the same time, pleased. "Where are your manners? Please forgive my son, Miss Hanson. He's lived among savages so long he's quite forgotten how to behave."

"I hope Mr. Archer will never need to stand on ceremony with me."

"That's very sweet-natured of you, my dear, but you mustn't encourage him to treat you like a sister. He has quite enough of those!"

"By God, I should say I do. Where's Amanda?"

"She's so good," Julia said all too sweetly. "She stayed to help the maids with some dusting."

"The books, no doubt," he said, snorting.

"Why, yes. How clever of you."

Mrs. Archer had been looking from one to the other as they spoke with the air of women fatigued by a tennis game she had arranged herself. "Dear me, what good friends you are already. You'll have the same room as before, Miss Hanson. And, Simon, kindly don't keep her up 'til all hours discussing mummies or whatever it is."

"No, I won't."

Julia laughed, and Simon felt that even the gods were conspiring against him when she said, "I can't promise not to keep him up all night."

Sixteen

~

Julia could tell that Simon was deeply worried about Lucy when he asked three times during the course of one dinner whether his sister would be joining the family. Finally, his mother diverted his mind by remembering, suddenly, that a crate had been delivered earlier in the day.

"It's from Egypt, I think. At least it had that strange writing on it. I always think, Miss Hanson, looks as though it had been written with a shoelace trailed through ink."

"Arabic is such a beautiful language, Mrs. Archer. Like Chinese, writing it well is an art form much practiced by their scholars."

"How very interesting. Simon, why don't you ever tell me interesting things like that?"

Julia met his eyes. They were seated next to each other, Mrs. Archer on his other side. She felt sure that he'd often tried to interest his mother in his work, just as she was sure Mrs. Archer had only met his overtures with politeness and a swift escape into her own doings. Her father was just the same.

"The box is most likely filled with papyri," Simon said, as he began to eat more quickly. "I asked my man out there to keep an eye out for anything that looked good. I am especially interested in rent rolls, storehouse inventories, and such."

"How mundane," Jane said. "Give me a good love poem. Or didn't your dusty old Egyptians write such things?"

Before Simon could say anything pointed, Julia said, "They wrote some beautiful and moving love lyrics, but there is so much we can learn from these other records. Things about their day-to-day lives—what they ate, what other nations they engaged in commerce—a myriad of questions solved from one scrap of writing."

Jane said, "You're as bad as Simon! I'm interested in today only. If a man were handsome enough, he might interest me in the doings of last week, but no man could involve me in things that happened thousands of years ago!"

"Except Dr. Dawley," her mother said chidingly. She explained in an aside, "The dean of St. Suplice. His doctrine is very sound."

"I'll look forward to hearing him on Sunday."

"Oh, no. He's on leave just now. Visiting the Holy Land, or Blackpool. Somewhere like that. I'm not quite sure which." She seemed to think this odd herself, and added, "It's his wife, you see. She tends to hop about from subject to subject and if it's the least bit noisy—as it was at the tea when she told me—it's so easy to become confused. I know she mentioned Jerusalem . . ."

Julia rescued her by saying, "I will look forward to hearing him another time."

Simon leaned close to Julia under pretense of retrieving his napkin. "The dean is capable of leaving for Blackpool and ending up in the Holy Land without noticing for a week. His wife is very hard of hearing and might answer a question with the first word she thinks of."

"And they rely on each other utterly, I'll wager."

"A very devoted couple," he answered, smiling into her eyes. She felt herself coloring, for there had been something intimate in his tone. Another cause for the heat in her face was the way he looked tonight. The crisp black of his formal clothes set off his topaz-golden hair and the dazzling white of his shirt gave distinction to his tanned skin. He'd been handsome enough in his everyday clothes to turn her head. Wearing evening clothes, Simon Archer was nothing less than godlike.

"Perhaps, if you are not too tired, we could open the box after we've eaten," he suggested, loud enough to be heard by the others. "Wouldn't you girls like to be present?"

Amanda said, "You forget, Simon. We've seen you open boxes like that before. They always look so intriguing on the outside, Miss Hanson, like something from a novel. They look like they should contain fascinating secrets, maps to lost treasures or something. But they never do. Such a dull way to pass an evening. But maybe you'll be lucky and find a love poem or two." The two girls giggled, while their mother looked severe.

Julia wondered if anyone in the house was unaware of Mrs. Archer's ambitions. She would have been more perturbed by them if she had not come to London with a similar intention. But of course, she'd given up the idea now.

She said, "Actually, I've often wondered if parts of the Song of Solomon weren't originally written with an Egyptian influence. So much of the imagery is the same as we see in the tomb art and papryi."

"Yes," Simon said, stroking his chin. "It seems to me I remember some reference to . . . to Pharaoh's chariots. Seems unlikely in a love poem, but . . ."

Julia said softly, " 'I have compared thee, oh my love, to a company of horses in Pharaoh's chariots.' "

She realized too late that she'd been gazing at Simon as she quoted. Hastily, she addressed the women at the table. "I don't see why a Jewish poet would think that there was anything beautiful in the chariots of his oppressors. Of course, one must allow for the errors of the seventeeth-century translation. One day, perhaps, I will try my hand at translating it myself."

"But that would take years," Mrs. Archer said. "Quite apart from everything else a woman must accomplish if she is to be happy. You'll find that marriage and the raising of your children will be sufficient challenge for an intelligent woman."

"Oh, I doubt I shall ever marry. My work will have to be my children."

Mrs. Archer tittered. "No woman ever wants to marry until the right man proposes."

"I'm quite taken with your theory," Simon said, apparently not having heard a word. "I don't remember the Song very well; I last read it when I was, I fear, a callow boy. I shall have to take another look, keeping your ideas in mind."

Julia sat with the ladies while Simon enjoyed a glass of port in lonely splendor. She would rather have sat with him, being used to remaining with her father when they ate alone, and even sipping a small glass herself, but she plainly saw that such unorthodox behavior would trouble Mrs. Archer. So she talked to her while Jane strummed a mandolin and Amanda read some improving book. Her reference to exciting novels had not gone unnoticed.

"I hope Miss Archer will feel better tomorrow."

"Oh, poor Lucy. She's so . . ." Mrs. Archer sighed. "She was never a giddy child, but she'd always been biddable. Then this sad disappointment. It's doubly awkward, living where we do. I wanted to move back to the country, but there are so many advantages for the girls in living in London."

"What disappointment? I beg your pardon; I don't mean to pry." She wished she liked embroidery so that she should have something to occupy her hands.

Mrs. Archer glanced swiftly at her two younger daughters. Jane, whose chords had been spaced with longer and longer pauses, suddenly began strumming again. Amanda, who had been absorbed in one page for the longest time, turned it over.

Mrs. Archer leaned closer to Julia. "It's the young man across the street, Major Winslow. We all thought he meant to propose to Lucy—his attentions were most marked. Then he went away without a word to me or to Simon. Or was Simon in Egypt at the time? I can't entirely recall. . . ."

"Oh, he was . . . !" Jane showed her teeth in an open-mouthed smile and broke into song. "Oh, what a man he was, he was. Oh, what a man he was!"

"What song is that, dear? Nothing vulgar, I trust."

"I don't believe so, Mother. It said 'traditional' on the music."

Amanda giggled. Looking up guiltily, she said, "Most amusing character in *Self-control*."

"Amanda loves to read," Mrs. Archer said, like one telling a deep secret.

Returning to the subject of Lucy, Julia asked, "The young man didn't address his proposal to Lucy herself, did he?"

"Oh, I shouldn't think so! He's a most correct young man and had often expressed himself just as he ought on so many subjects, not least of all the duty of a child to its parents. And I'm certain Lucy would have told me if anything of that sort had passed between them."

"But she didn't tell you what the trouble was between them?"

"Not a word. Of course, I never intrude. To force a secret from one of my girls would spoil the beautiful confidence we all share."

In half an hour, Julia excused herself and went to join Simon in his retreat. "Your mother is a wonderful woman," she announced.

"In her way, I suppose she is." He closed the black-bound book he'd been reading, placing it with some care on his desk. "But to what do you refer specifically?"

"Well, if I had a daughter and she'd spent two years moping over some young man, I would feel compelled to meddle."

"You refer to Lucy, I imagine."

"Yes. Isn't your mother even curious as to what caused the rift between them?"

"She was, in the beginning. Now I believe she has convinced herself that Robert Winslow is solely responsible for Lucy's misery."

"You don't sound convinced."

"I'm not. No one could remain this unhappy for this long without something preying on their conscience."

He stood up and went to the window. Pulling back the curtain, he looked out into the street, or perhaps he was only looking at his reflection. "You see, I like Winslow. He's a steady fellow and a brave soldier, whereas my sister has always lived by her emotions. If I had been here, I might have been able to direct each of them to find someone else. By the time I came home, however, the damage had been done."

"Damage? Because they loved one another?"

"Damage because they are each romantic fools. He is playing the suffering Lancelot while she pictures herself the grieving Elaine. Any sensible person would have solved the coldness between them without all this woe." He let the curtain fall. "You should have seen Winslow this afternoon. Pitiful. Gazing up the stairs, praying for a glimpse of Lucy. And her in her room, trying on every gown she owned, hoping one would give her the courage to face him."

"I doubt he wanted to be gone so long. Your mother tells me that he was decorated for bravery in the Punjab."

"Mother would very much like a war hero for a son-in-law." He crossed the floor to stand in front of Julia. With one finger, he tilted up her chin so that she had to look in his eyes. "She'd also like an heiress for a daughter-in-law."

Passionately, Julia prayed that he would not propose. She'd decided not to marry him after all because it wouldn't be fair to him. Purely to forestall him she said, "It's always a shame to disappoint one's mother, but in this instance, she will have to settle for the war hero."

"So you've definitely decided not to pursue me?"

"That's correct. I'm sure you're relieved?"

"Absolutely." His hand dropped to his side. "Get your hat and mantle. We're going to see a man about a cat."

Prompted by what she called freedom from the burden of her embarrassment, Julia said wickedly, "Shouldn't we arrange to send Lucy? If they met once again, they would assuredly work out their differences. Wedding bells might yet ring out."

Simon shook his head, grimacing. "Unlikely. Lucy didn't even seem interested when I told her he'd called."

"No? You would think that she'd at least be interested, no matter how badly they've hurt each other. Oh, I hate such mysteries! People should talk more to each other about the true nature of their feelings."

"You will never find an Englishman to agree with you, Julia. We have been trained from childhood not to have any feelings."

"You're not like that."

"We're all like that. Public school training. Mustn't let the side down, and all that rot."

Half an hour later, as they left the Winslow's, Julia said, "What a shame!"

"You mean that the cat didn't speak to you?"

"Partly that."

"How do you explain the events you claim to have participated in yesterday, Julia? You must have come to some conclusions."

She stopped in the middle of the deserted street. "I've been waiting for you to bring this up, Simon. As it happens, I have determined what caused the things I saw and heard."

"Shock? As I suggested?"

"Magic." Her smile held the mysterious remoteness of La Gioconda. "But that's not what caused my comment. I think it's a great shame that Major Winslow and your sister are not married. She would care for the general like her own father, and anyone can see he badly needs such care."

"Would you have her marry a man merely to be of service?"

"Isn't that why most women marry, Simon? It's better to wear out than to rust, as my aunt says. In one's own family, such attentions are taken for granted. One grows old, dwindling into a mere maiden aunt who is valued only for her usefulness. But a devoted daughter-in-law is praised to the skies."

"I know Lucy was fond of the old man. She loved to sit with him by the hour and listen to his stories. You wouldn't think it now, seeing him sitting there with that cat on his knee, but he was a real 'death or glory' man."

"I think he's adopted that cat because he's lonely. It's a stroke of good fortune for the little thing. She'll be queen of the house in another week; anyone could see that the general is spoiling it. That should have been Lucy's role."

"I doubt my sister would sit on the general's knee."

Julia slapped her hand lightly on his arm. "Lucy and the general would have each other for comfort when the major returns to his duties. As it is now, I fear he'll grow more and more lonely with only servants and a cat for company. One cannot be satisfied for long with the companionship of subordinates."

"I wonder how many of the people who go to a fraud like Dr. Mystery do so seeking a way out of loneliness." He unlocked the door and stood back for her to enter first. "One can hardly blame the poor devils. I shouldn't do it, but then I'm never lonely so long as I have my work."

"Yes," Julia said. "I feel that myself." She knew she lied. Perhaps she'd felt that way at home, but not here. Not when she saw what it was like to put forward a theory on the authorship of a biblical book and have it considered intelligent instead of eccentric. If she spent too much time in Simon's company, she would be spoiled for anything less.

Simon's hands rested on her shoulders a moment as he assisted her to take off her mantle. She'd worn a semi-evening gown for her first dinner at the Archers'. While not nearly as low-cut as the one she would wear to their party, it did leave the tops of her shoulders bare, gleaming in the gaslight. The skirt rustled intriguingly when she moved, possibly making a man wonder what exactly she wore under there. Her hair was upswept, springy tendrils falling about her ears and the back of her white neck.

Both Major Winslow and his father, still gallant despite trouble or age, had paid her several compliments. She wasn't vain enough to believe them entirely sincere, as sometimes men unused to a woman's society pay compliments merely to make conversation. Yet she did feel she looked well.

Simon said, after clearing his throat, "You should change out of that."

"Should I?"

"You don't want to get excelsior all over it. We are going to open that box tonight, aren't we?"

"I'd love to!" Then she hesitated. "But I promised Jane I'd help her with the invitations."

"You're a guest here, Julia. You needn't slave like an overworked secretary."

Flattening the fabric at her waist where she had detected a wrinkle in the tarlatan, Julia said, "I don't mind taking some of the burden off her shoulders. She told me she is starting a blister on her middle finger from all the writing."

"She should have been doing that instead of strumming that infernal guitar."

"Your mother suggested half an hour of rational enjoyment to aid our digestions." She glanced up at him. His eyes were dark in the lower light of the hall. "And it's a mandolin."

"Was it?" He reached out and smoothed his hand over her exposed shoulder. "I am always confused 'twixt the two."

His hand was not soft like an easy-living gentleman's, but hardened by labor. The contrast between her pampered silken skin and his hand sent her senses reeling. He followed the line of her collarbone to her throat and stroked the tender curve of her throat with the edge of his thumb.

Julia saw that his eyes traveled with his hand almost absently. As if he hardly realized yet that he was touching her at all, let alone caressing her so that her heart raced and her mouth burned.

"Don't work too hard. . . ."

"I—I won't."

His gaze went to her face and his hand stilled. In a mild, conversational tone, he said, "Oh, God. Oh, hell."

He yanked his hand away as though she'd turned to flame. "Julia, you should slap me now."

"In outrage?"

"You should be outraged. And I . . . I should go to my club while you are here."

"Why?"

"Can't you see? I have no intentions of marriage. One can't go about stroking girl's necks . . ." He ran out of words.

"Aren't your mother and sisters chaperons enough?"

He sighed and ran his hand through his hair, leaving it to fall over his eyes. "Apparently not. At least, I don't see any of them at the moment."

"No, neither do I. I should go find them."

"Julia . . ." He crossed his arms, more for her protection, she felt, than because he felt annoyed. "That's a very pretty dress."

She beamed at him as though he'd given her a gift. A bubble of delight rested near her heart, a feeling she'd only had when she'd drunk a trifle too much champagne at her last birthday party. "It wasn't my favorite until just now. Simon . . . I'll help Jane for a while. Then may I be there when you open the crate?"

"Yes, of course. But change first, please."

Her smile, if anything, grew more shy. But she said merrily enough, "I'll assume the habit of a nun if you like."

"No, thank you. I have enough troubles without dragging in a mortal sin."

Simon saw her puzzling over that comment until she realized his meaning. Then her uncertain smile returned and she frankly fled away. Simon retreated to his study where he had another drink while he waited for her. Only after it was gone did he remember that if they were going to open the box, he would have to bring it into his study. After all, that was the nominal reason why she'd be coming back to him tonight. Simon also thought it would be safer on the whole for the both of them to have something to focus on besides each other.

The crate was the usual sort of thing he'd often received in the off-season. Safir had a good eye for the genuine antiquities that still floated about Cairo's bazaars and backstreets. Though Simon hated the trade in Egypt's history, which belonged properly to the people of that country, he would sometimes buy things to prevent them falling into the hands of dilletantes and tourists. Though they'd lost half their scientific value by being wrenched from the ground without method, there was still much to learn from the pieces and papyrus Safir had found.

Usually he would dive into a box like a little boy on Christmas morning. Tonight he found little enthusiasm for the task. It wasn't just that he promised to wait for Julia. Handling things of reed and stone held no appeal after touching the living silk of Julia's skin.

Though he knew less of modern women's clothing than he did about the pleated linen of ancient Egypt, he knew enough to see that Julia's day dresses were marked by quiet good taste and a severity of line that boded well for her seriousness of mind. But when he'd turned to see her enter the drawing room this evening, pranked out in a dinner gown, his mouth had gone dry.

She wore white well, better than his sisters. Her skirt had been of some floating material, layer upon layer of it, with none of the overlarge fabric flowers or swags of contrasting fabric that Jane and Amanda loaded onto their gowns. He'd looked at Julia and a vision of her as Venus rising from the foaming waves of the sea sprang into his mind. Her round, white shoulders emerging from the material fed his fantasy as though that had been the dressmaker's intention.

Simon was afraid he'd been nearly incoherent during dinner, thanking God for his mother's ceaseless flow of chatter. He'd hardly ever turned to look directly at Julia, for every time he did, he was sure he saw more than there was to see. The neckline of the gown stopped well about the swell of her breasts, but dipped the merest trifle in the front. After such ceaseless efforts not to look, he could have drawn a picture of her with his eyes shut.

Objectively, he knew it was a modest gown so far as such things went. Ballgowns were almost indecently low-cut this season; he'd heard his mother complaining about it after taking the girls for a fitting. He stifled a groan as he recalled that Julia would undoubtedly be attending the party in his honor on Friday. He remembered his determination to dance with her only once, and didn't bother to stifle the second groan.

He had another drink, feeling that his head wasn't swimming from the alcohol so much as from the violent reordering of his thoughts. He hoped Julia's humor would not lead her to appear dressed as a nun after all. One erotic fantasy a night was more than enough to cope with.

His impatience to see her again grew as the hands on the clock went 'round. He promised himself that he'd be patient and not go looking for her. He'd given quite enough of his feelings away already. But when an hour had passed, his resolution failed.

Seventeen

~

Though Simon thought he entered the drawing room with a step that thundered like Jove's, his entrance hardly disturbed the women. Julia, he saw, to his dismay, was entrenched on the sofa, one of his sisters seated on either side. She had a sheaf of papers in her hand, which she was thumbing through while a counterpoint duet went on in her ears. She was nodding and dropping a word in whenever she could.

She met his eyes and made a face of helplessness. Obviously she was trapped for some time yet to come. She had changed from her awe-inspiring dinner dress into a simple morning gown scattered with a print of violets. Instead of Venus, she looked as fresh and approachable as a milkmaid. Even her hair was more casual, tumbling down from the too-severe style she'd affected earlier. He wished he didn't feel quite so pleased about that.

His mother saw him and stood up, bundling her silk and hoop into the chair. "Miss Hanson is being such a help! It seems she often plays hostess for her father, so a party even as large as ours is child's play to her. She's already organized our plans and made such a savings in the budget! It seems we may have duplicated some of the orders. A case of 'too many cooks,' I'm afraid."

As he had reminded Jane, he repeated, "Mother, Miss Hanson is our guest. We shouldn't make her slave for us."

Julia shook her head at him, and went on lending an ear to Amanda, saying something about the orchestra.

"Oh, but she volunteered to take the whole affair off my hands. I'm only too glad to give it up. You know, I attended many such affairs in my girlhood but I was never responsible for the details. Your grandmother managed it all so beautifully without my having to help—except to arrange a few flowers."

His mother put her hand on his arm, and crooked her other forefinger, beckoning him to follow her. As he did so, he glanced back at Julia. Though she raised one eyebrow to indicate curiosity, she also flashed five fingers at him. He nodded in relief. Five more minutes . . .

He followed his mother into the dining room where Apple was sweeping the floor. "That'll do, Apple."

"Yes, madam."

Mrs. Archer waited until the maid was out of earshot. "Simon, when you first brought Miss Hanson to this house in such a hole-and-corner way, I freely confess that I thought you had lost your mind. I want to apologize to you for being so unjust."

"Mother?" he said. She certainly resembled his mother in every detail, but she sounded nothing like herself.

"Yes, I apologize, and for more than you may know. Son, as dear Julia has been so rash as to come to town without her father, I feel that I must stand in his stead. What are your intentions toward her?"

"I—I hardly know." His half-formed feelings and designs were definitely not the sort of thing a man discusses with his mother. He struck upon an answer sure to satisfy her. "I believe we are becoming fast friends."

"If you will be guided by my advice, you will marry her."

"Mother, we only met yesterday!"

"But you have been corresponding for so much longer

than that. There is no better way to truly know someone, through and through, than a long exchange of letters. I wish Lucy and dear Robert Winslow had agreed to write one another when he was away doing his duty."

"Be that as it may, Mother, I can't marry the girl out of hand!"

"I don't know why not. If heaven had designed a bride for you, it would be someone just like dear Julia. Isn't she interested in Egypt, just as you are? And if she isn't nearly beautiful enough for my splendid son, I think she has a very pleasing countenance. Girls who are too beautiful are never very restful to live with, it seems."

"Mother, Julia is a very sweet girl, but I have no thoughts of marrying anyone at present. Besides, her father would never agree. I'm not a pauper, thank God, but he's certain to think I'm only interested in her fortune."

"But you aren't, so what difference does it make? As for her fortune, such things are not to be despised. Certainly no other young lady has even come near to having so many good qualities. As I say, if heaven itself had set out to create a daughter-in-law for me, I should have ordered one just like her."

"I agree that Julia has most of the qualities I would look for in a bride, if I were looking for one. But I'm not and she knows that. Please don't talk to her this way. She'd be very embarrassed."

Mrs. Archer folded her hands at her waist and put on her most earnest expression. Alarmed at these symptoms of something even more serious in the wind, Simon put his hand over hers and asked, "What is troubling you? It isn't really Julia, is it?"

"No, Simon. It's you."

"I?" His alarm increased when he saw how tense she was, her brow creased red beneath her charming cap, her eyes tearing. "I'm well, perfectly well. Never worry about me."

She sighed tearily. "But, son, I'm afraid . . . oh, I don't

know how to say it. You're thirty-three, after all, and in all that time you haven't had even one *passage d'amour*. Not even one!" It was a cry from the heart.

"Mother, as a gentleman . . ."

He saw her gather her courage, taking a deep breath as she straightened her back. "Son, I will love you no matter what depraved taste you may indulge, but I must know the truth! Do you . . . are you . . . in short, do you like girls?"

Simon's laughter was partly because of her dear earnestness, partly because of the follies of time. She would wait to spring this issue on him on the very evening he'd been plotting, if only capriciously, the seduction of a girl beneath her very roof.

He put his arm about his mother and gave her a reassuring squeeze. "Yes, I'm very fond of girls. Always have been and I foresee no changes to my opinion in the future. I may not always understand women—you at this moment have me utterly befuddled—but I find them always and endlessly fascinating."

Her smile was one of damp relief. "Oh, I wasn't sure. Sometimes it seems the only ones who interest you have been dead for a thousand years, and that's not the way to bring me grandchildren."

"Mother!"

She stamped her foot, a girlish habit she'd never outgrown. "I'm sorry, Simon, but when I hear dreadful, vulgar creatures like that Agapantha Pertwee—"

"I thought she was your bosom beau?"

"Not any longer. She came to call yesterday and once again she went on and on about her horrible son, Jeremiah, getting himself entangled with some tawdry creature out of the chorus at some music hall. Oh, she pretended to be shocked, but underneath she was all puffed up with pride that he's such a devil of a fellow with the girls."

"Mother!" Simon said again, suffering more shocks in

this five-minute conversation with her than she'd given him in years.

"And you, so handsome and strong, a thousand times more a man than her spindly son, never giving me a moment's worry that you'd bring home some dreadful, low creature like that! But never bringing home anybody else, either! Then you arrived on the doorstep with Julia so very late last night, sitting up with her 'til all hours, and I didn't know what to think. I've told her how sorry I am if I was rude."

She leaned closer and said, "I told her I'm always out of sorts if awakened in the middle of the night. And then that cat appearing out of nowhere . . ." She shuddered delicately.

"Poor Mother."

"Never mind. Are you sure you won't marry Julia?" She instantly retreated, saying quickly, "No, don't tell me. I don't want to force you into saying a yea or a nay that might bind you later."

"I can't promise to marry anyone immediately." He imitated the way she leaned to one side when imparting secrets. "Though I shouldn't say anything of it as a gentleman, I feel I should relieve your mind thus much. I have had, as you put it, more than one *passage d'amour* in my adult life."

He'd never seen his mother smile so expansively, not even in the happy days before his father had died. She closed her eyes and seemed to whisper a prayer. Then one eye snapped open. "Out in Egypt, was it?"

"Actually, Mother, mostly right here in London. I would have thought you knew everything about them, right down to their addresses, through some crony or other."

"No, I never like to pry into my children's personal lives."

"Of course not. Of whom could I have been thinking?" He kissed her. "All right now?"

Her sigh was happy. "Yes, though I'm still impatient for grandchildren."

"I'll see what can be done. Do you suppose someone in this vast city rents them by the hour?" A disturbing thought occurred to him suddenly. "Mother, wasn't it Mrs. Pertwee who first introduced you to Dr. Mystery's seances?"

Her discomfort returned. "I—I believe it was," she said, unable to meet his eye. "It's just like her to do such a thing. Always chasing the latest fad."

"I never asked you why you went. I assumed you wanted to contact Father because you missed him so."

"Oh, I do. I do miss him. He was always such a rock!"

"Why else? Did you want to ask him about . . . me?"

Biting her lip, she nodded. "But it seemed so vulgar to ask such a personal question in front of all those people! I never thought that there'd be others present. I thought it would be just me, Dr. Mystery, and *him*. But the company was very mixed. I only went a few times and there never was an opportunity to speak to him alone. I've come to the conclusion that you are entirely right. Dr. Mystery was a fraud. It's sad to think that there is so much wickedness in the world."

"Thank you, Mother. You don't know how you relieve my mind." At least he didn't have to face blackmail from Dr. Mystery. People already looked askance at him at times because he was so often out of the country. It had even been suggested jokingly in the press that he kept a harem at his camp.

When Julia finally escaped from the drawing room, she found Simon in his study. He'd taken off his long, black coat and rolled up his sleeves, exposing brown forearms covered with sun-bleached hair. His cravat lay on his desk with his collar. She tore her gaze away from the sight of his chest, glimpsed through the undoing of several buttons on his shirt. His waist was trim, seen without a concealed knee-length coat, his hips narrow but with thighs that looked strong and very male.

"Have they talked you into painting the house yet?"

"Not yet," she answered gaily. "But I expect I will if they ask me to."

He picked up a pry-bar and twirled it between his fingers as though it were a reed. Putting his foot on the end of the crate, he asked, "Ready to get started?"

"I can't wait."

He put the narrow end under the nailed-down lid and rocked the bar. "Safir doesn't trust the postal services, or it could be that he doesn't trust the postal workers. He always nails down these lids as if he's shipping diamonds."

Julia nodded, but she was paying more attention to the flexing muscles of his arms than to what he was saying. His shirt clung intriguingly to his back, draping his sides with an almost Grecian elegance. Julia had to close her eyes and lean against the edge of the bookcase because there suddenly didn't seem to be quite enough air in the room.

"You can open your eyes now."

He'd pulled on a pair of gloves and cradled in his hands a bluish statue, four or five inches long from flat feet to truly ugly face. Lines and drawings highlighted the bashed nose and fat belly. She came two slow steps closer. "Bes?"

"That's right."

"Why are you wearing the gloves?"

"I find that the oils on your hands can do damage, especially to gold and papyrus. I always wear gloves when I handle the artifacts."

"That makes sense."

"There are gloves in the top drawer, if you'd like to hold it."

"May I?" she whispered.

Julia received it into her hands. She'd seen and touched

the massive statues, admired the works done for pharaohs, gods of their place and time, and read the words of mighty men written in the hands of slaves. But nothing had ever sent such an electric thrill surging up her spine as this model of the dwarfish, ugly god Bes.

For he had not ruled the Underworld, nor held up the sky, nor strode like vengeance made flesh over a cowering world. He was the god of household things who kept sickness from the door and brought happiness to the hearts of the common people. This little statue had probably been a cherished possession of someone not so different from herself. The centuries between the making of this statue and its emergence into a gentleman's study of the mid-nineteenth century seemed to collapse, so that then and now were but two sides of the same page.

"He reminds me of my father, a little. Is it very rare?"

"No. It's a nice enough piece of faience, but nothing too unusual. It must have been part of this job lot Safir writes that he bought cheaply. There were a few outstanding pieces thrown in among the junk. Unfortunately, he writes that he wasn't permitted to send them out of the country just yet."

Julia only nodded at this hint of trouble. "May I keep this, then? I know it's asking a great deal of your principles."

He looked at her as though he understood. "I don't think history will miss it. If you want it so much, of course you may have it."

"Thank you, Simon. I shall treasure it forever."

He lifted his hands as though he'd reach for her but instead wheeled abruptly and returned to the crate. Soon curly ribbons of excelsior littered the floor together with sheets of slick Cairo newsprint. Julia was delighted by everything that emerged from the crate—beads, scrolls, a painted face from the late Ptolemic period, figurines.

Simon, however, fished about in the bottom of the crate as though expecting more. She sat back on her haunches, for she'd long since come to sit on the floor to be closer to the treasures revealed. "Didn't Father Christmas bring you want you wanted?"

"I hoped that Safir would be able to send me those outstanding pieces he mentioned. This letter might have been a blind. But he writes that the Egyptian authorities are becoming more strict about what they'll permit to leave. The present viceroy is a forward-thinking fellow who wants to protect what he can. But the *Institut d'Egypte* is hardly worthy yet of the name 'museum.' Everything is jumbled together, so they don't know what they own, and anyone who wished could walk off with the entire place. They must find someone who understands classification."

"Why don't you volunteer?"

"I can't afford to. Besides," he added, "my love is excavation. I'd be miserable without the thrill of the dig."

She rubbed the round belly of the little god. "I'd give anything to be a man like you."

"Men don't have things as easy as women like to think." He stripped off his gloves, sticking them in his trouser's pocket.

Julia said, "I suppose one sex can never truly see the world as if belonging to the other. For instance, I believe that if I were only a man I could do what I pleased with my life. Travel, adventure, scholarship. If I had enough will, then I could do it all, regardless of my birth or my status."

"And as a woman?" He sank onto the floor beside her, and idly brushed a shaving from her skirt.

Looking off into the middle distance at nothing, Julia sighed both at the beauty of her visions and the narrowness of her reality. "As a woman, I am not supposed to have a will of my own. I'm supposed to be obedient to my parents, until at last the master hand of a husband comes to mold me into a final form of a meek and still obedient wife. Read the marriage vows for women one day if you want more proof."

"It's not so easy being a man, Julia. If one is any kind of man at all, one is bound by rules of conduct as rigid as anything society inflicts on women."

"I can't see it."

"No?" His breath stirred the lovelocks beside her ear. She turned her head. She had not realized he'd come so close. All she would have to do would be to move her little finger over and she could have touched him with it.

"Give me an example," she said, scarcely daring to speak.

He ran his gaze over every inch of her body, from the ankle that peeked out beneath the sweep of her skirt, over her legs, and higher. Julia felt his gaze like a hand drawn lightly over her naked skin. He hadn't even touched her and she was already trembling.

"I want you," he said, and his desire was in his eyes as bold as if some piratical ancestor had taken him over. Her breath came fast, but not with fear.

"Yes," she said, keeping her eyes open with great effort. She longed to close them, to forget everything except Simon. She waited for him to repeat the kiss he'd given her before. This time, she would not be taken by surprise.

"As a gentleman, however, the rules of conduct forbid my taking advantage of a young woman living in my house. Strictly speaking, I should not have said even that much. Please pretend I said it only as the example you requested."

Julia said, more vehemently than she'd intended, "But many governesses and maids are seduced by the men of households every year."

"Then they're not gentlemen. Nobility, perhaps, but not gentlemen." He gathered himself together as if to rise.

Lifting up to her knees, Julia clutched his bare arm to stay him. "Doesn't the young lady have anything to say about it? Or is this another instance in which a man declares that he alone knows what is wisest and best?"

She did not have time to be subtle or seductive. Seizing his shoulders for balance, she leaned over and kissed him. She knew she did it badly, awkwardly falling forward so that she had pitched herself practically into his lap. But she felt his body rise against her as his hands came up to cup her face.

The moment Julia touched his arm, Simon knew that all the rules he'd just attempted to explain were nothing more or less than pure bunkum. Chivalry might work to restrain a man who never met any but weak and silly women, but it proved a paltry defense against a woman who knew exactly what or who she wanted.

And when she kissed him, inexpertly pressing her sweet lips to his, Simon knew that civilization was a thin shell covering the brute being who acted instantly on every desire. Right then, all his desires were concentrated on the woman in his arms.

He needed to exert no strength at all to pull her onto his lap so that she straddled him, her full skirt spreading out to either side of his legs. She followed his lead as effortlessly as though he were dreaming her response. Leaning back, he reached up to slide his fingers into her hair, then brought her face down to his. He plundered her mouth recklessly, only to find that she took just as much from him.

He knew he was driving her too fast, taking her immediately to a level that should have been achieved in deliberate stages, allowing her to become used to each step before going on to the next. She learned the ways of passion instantly and applied the lesson at once. Realizing this, he tried to catch his breath, to recapture his *savoir faire,* but the impact of her body on his senses overwhelmed him anew.

The instant he paused, Julia took over the pace, pressing such kisses to his mouth and to the sides of his neck that he could feel the prickling touch of her teeth. Had she learned that from him? He could not analyze their progress now.

She was saying his name over and over. He felt as though he'd waited an eternity to hear just that note of passionate pleading from her, remembering only dimly that he'd never heard her voice before yesterday. Then he realized that he was begging her to touch him. Had it been he or she who had pulled his shirt free of his waistband?

He seized her hands, desperate to regain some sanity before the demands of his body completely deafened his common sense. Until that instant, he hadn't known she still wore her white gloves. Looking into her eyes, he smiled. Here, too, her response was perfection, for she gave a surprised laugh. He watched her face change, however, when he took the hem of one glove between his teeth and tore it off. Then he did the same with the other hand, pausing to bite, lightly, the raised mound at the base of her thumb. His name had never sounded better than on her lips as she twisted against him.

He could not resist his need to have her hands on his body, just this once. But as each desire was satisfied, another surged in to take its place, as waves never cease driving each other toward shore.

Simon glided his hand up the length of her leg, the silken stocking aiding him, leading him higher to where the garter divided silk from skin. He toyed there a moment, vaguely astonished that there should be so little difference. Then he touched her higher still, finding the heart of her warmth.

"Simon?"

The shock in her voice brought him back to a reality gone mad. Was it possible that, in spite of every good intention, he was on the floor, his hands filled with Julia's delicious body, her taste permeating his mouth? He was appalled by his lack of control. Even at that moment, every cell in his body clamored for him to continue, to seduce her into receiving all the things he wanted to give her. He could tell from her response thus far that she would participate willingly, never even asking if he loved her.

But it was his responsibility to care for her, even if she would be an eager collaborator in her own ruin. Not just because she was a guest in his house, but because she was Julia, unique and infinitely dear. His duty to her was clear. All the same, Simon had to clench his fingers tightly into fists in order to find the will to take his hands away.

"Julia . . . my God. I never meant . . . my God."

Still atride his lap, she rose up, staring down at his heaving chest. Her hands, fingers spread wide, covered the ridges of his stomach. She met his eyes and he read the confusion there. She said wonderingly, "I liked it, Simon. It's probably wrong of me, but I liked it."

"It was wrong of me, Julia. You don't know . . ."

She closed her eyes, her head falling back, and he'd never seen anything as beautiful as her face as she examined, with the force of her fine mind, the storm of her body. Then she frowned. Shaking back her hair so that it switched back and forth, she said, "There has to be more. I feel so . . . what is the word . . . incomplete?"

He could not lie. "Yes, there's more, much more."

His knuckles hurt from clenching his hands so hard, but he dared not let go. He said, "But not for us. There's never going to be more for us, Julia."

"No?"

He shook his head. That hurt, too, for it seemed his neck dearly wanted to nod. The warmth from her thighs, open over his waist, spread through his whole body like a tide.

"Julia, please get up." He tried to smile but feared it was a dismal failure. "I'm only human, my dear. We should never be alone again if this much could happen so fast between us. Next time . . ."

Her smile was almost as blissful as he could have made

it given just a few more minutes of madness. "Next time . . ."

"No, Julia. No."

He couldn't help wincing as she rose to her feet, but there was no point in hiding the truth with a conveniently placed hand. After all, she'd seen representations of the male body more than once in the hieroglyphs. With her skirts falling naturally into place, she looked quite as usual. He, on the other hand, appeared to have been ravaged and then tossed, a helpless wreck, on the floor of his study.

She said, coolly enough, "You would counsel me to wait until I am married to learn the rest? But I never will marry now, not even you. Am I never to know what else there is?"

He had no answer for that. Julia hoped he would not. She also hoped that he'd spring to his feet, grab her, and carry her beyond the shore of the country they'd come so near to exploring. But whatever she'd done to drive him beyond his admirable self-control would not work a second time. If only she had more arts with which to entrance him!

She swore to herself that she would not be embarrassed by her near-seduction until she reached the solitude of her room. The defences she would summon to face the trial of meeting him in the morning would have to be thought out later. She sashayed a bit as she left and could have sworn she heard a muffled groan behind her. She did not look back.

On the landing, a door stood open. At the sound of her footsteps, a figure stood silhouetted against the light. Julia peered at it. "Miss Archer? I do hope you are feeling better."

"I hope you and the man have joined in love, Julia."

"Lucy?" Then something in the regal tone alerted her to the truth. She glanced down the stairs but she had indeed heard the door to Simon's study slam shut. Coming nearer, Julia whispered, "An-ket?"

Eighteen

With her body still in turmoil from the past few mad minutes with Simon, this last shock sent Julia reeling. She staggered to a chair and fell into it as if pushed.

Lucy's blond beauty was oddly accented by the arts of Egypt. Dark lines had been drawn about her eyes and her pale hair had been divided into innumerable braids. About her slender body, she wore what looked like a pleated bedsheet. With a glance at the stripped bed, Julia confirmed her guess.

She stared about the room, seeing it less as the shambles it was than as the scene of an experiment. An-ket must have explored the depths of Lucy's wardrobe, not realizing that the fashionable clothes of an ordinary woman were not designed to be put on by herself alone but with a maid's or a sister's service. Then, of course, buttons would be something of a mystery as well. Small wonder she'd at last seized upon a bedsheet to make a familiar gown.

Blinking at the figure before her, she said, "I was terribly worried about you when they threw the cat out. How did it happen?"

"This body touched the cat first and I changed into it."

"How? By what mechanism do you do these things?"

It was strange to see the proud, majestic smile of An-ket upon the pretty, entirely English face of Lucy. Even her movements were more fluidly graceful as An-ket lifted her hands, palm to palm, before her face. "By the will of the Lady who brings love and laughter to the land."

"I don't understand. The gods of Egypt are . . ." She could not bring herself to tell An-ket that her religion had died with Cleopatra thirty years before Christ.

"The gods are immortal, though you call them by other names now and have but one. All power flows from Ra. If it pleases him to make one hundred gods, or only one son, we are still their servants. I am the servant of the Great She, whether in this body or in the Field of Reeds."

Then her sternness left her and she laughed with the easy spontaneity of a young girl. "There are such marvels here in this one room, that I have played for hours. And the food!" She pointed to a tray on a chair. "Where come you by such delights as this red fruit, this apple?"

Though Julia had not known Lucy well, she'd been struck by the pervading sense of pensive sadness she gave off like a perfume. Her head drooped, her smiles were sweet but fleeting, and her eyes never seemed to shine with interest in anything. An-ket changed all that. Julia saw Lucy as she was meant to be, happy, without any shadow fallen over her.

She asked, "An-ket, where does Lucy go while you live in her body?"

"She is here." An-ket placed her hand over her heart. "I am speaking, but she is within as well. Like two people dwelling in one house."

"May I speak with her?"

"If it is her wish. . . ."

Without any outward change, not so much as a grimace, Lucy was suddenly 'there.' Lucy's body relaxed into the stance of a properly brought up girl, which was still excellent posture but nothing compared to the effortlessly regal air of An-ket.

"Miss Hanson," she said in her own accent.

"Are you all right?"

"This is the most wonderful thing that has ever happened to me! I've never realized before what Simon was always going on about, but what An-ket is telling me of Egypt is fascinating!"

"You talk to each other?"

"I know what she knows; she knows what I know. You needn't worry about fooling anyone. We'll come down tomorrow and not even Mother will be able to tell. An-ket's looking forward to seeing more of the house and the city."

Lucy frowned and shook her head as though to respond to some inner voice. "An-ket is right; we both need to work on our appearances. Why do you wear such dreadful clothes? Don't be offended, please! If you're going to marry my brother . . ."

"I'm not."

"No?" Apparently raising one eyebrow ran in Simon's family. "You were kissing him just now."

"How did you know that?" Could they see through walls?

Lucy laid a cool fingertip to the side of Julia's throat. "Look in the mirror. An-ket says that's a love bite and she would know. She was married in life to a very attractive fellow named . . . named Senusret. I now realize I was a perfect fool to carry on so about what Robert and I did."

"What did you do?" Julia asked as she examined her throat in the mirror. She hadn't felt anything but delight when Simon had kissed her there, yet there was a mark. "I suppose powder will cover it."

Lucy just laughed. "If you haven't a dress with a high collar, we can borrow one from Amanda."

"What did go wrong between you and Major Winslow?"

"I listened to foolish girls who told me what they'd

been told by other foolish girls. That if a man kisses you it's a sin. That you can become pregnant from his touch. That wanting a man to love you makes you no better than a prostitute."

"I never thought I'd be grateful for having only superficial conversations with my friends! What are you going to do?"

"Do?" Some of the new self-confidence Lucy displayed evaporated. "I haven't the faintest notion. I want to go back two years to pick up my lost chance, and not even An-ket can do that!"

"If you feel that you made a mistake, go to him. He's just across the street, for goodness sake! Throw yourself at him; I'm sure he'll catch you."

"No, I couldn't do that. Not just fling myself at him. What would he think of me?"

"You'd get what you want."

"No," Lucy said, paling. "No. Even An-ket says she made Senusret wait and work for her. She says . . ."

The voice of An-ket, deeper, fuller, older, came from Lucy's mouth. "Women, being weaker, must be craftier than men. They do not cherish what they achieve without effort."

"That is unfortunately true," Julia said. Why else would Simon have refused her just now? He must have known how much she was his, body and soul. She thought of his hand on her thigh and felt a new, completely pleasurable palpitation of her heart. She didn't know how, but there had to be a way to get Simon alone again in order to finish what they'd begun.

"So what is to be done?" she asked them. "We can't flirt, because then they think we are not serious. We can't have a simple, honest discussion of wants and needs, because that would shock the poor dears too much. Nor can we grab them and force them to love us because . . . Well, because!"

"You see my difficulty," Lucy said. "And it's even

worse for me, because I was such a little idiot two years ago. I'd still be one now if it weren't for An-ket. I want to thank you, Julia, for bringing her into today."

"I don't think I did it, did I? It just . . . happened."

There was one question Julia didn't dare ask. Strange forces were at work in this room and, though she didn't show it, she was frightened. All the same, she wondered whether An-ket was in this time and Lucy's body to stay. The Priestess of Hathor seemed to be enjoying herself all too much.

Her enjoyment increased on the following day. Early in the morning, Lucy sent Apple in to wake up Julia. It had been too early for her because with so much to think about, she'd not fallen asleep until long after she'd heard the chimes strike three. Despite her wakefulness, ears on the prick for every sound, she'd never heard Simon go past her door. Had he slept in his study, or had he followed through on his notion of sleeping at his club?

Apple answered this unspoken question as she brought in a tray. "Such a to-do, miss."

"What's that?"

"The master—I've never known 'im to do such a thing before, but he paid a call on the Winslow house last night."

"I know. I went with him. I think the blue walking dress, thank you, Apple." Julia tried to sound distant and uninterested, for she knew it was very rude indeed to encourage other people's servants to gossip about the family. But she might as well have tried to change the course of the Thames.

"Ah, the first time you did indeed, but not the second. The second time nothing went with him but a bottle! An' I seen the general's boot boy this mornin' and 'e says that there never were two men who drank faster than them two. Shocking, ain't it?" the maid said with a sniff, taking out the dress and giving it a shake. "This 'un? But it ain't got no ruffles nor nothing. Why don't none of your clothes have fancies, miss?"

"It's a whim of mine."

"Coo. . . ."

So, Simon had gone out to get drunk last night and chose Robert Winslow for a companion, of all people. As soon as she was dressed, she hurried along to Lucy's room. She knew Apple had most likely delivered the same story to everyone in the house along with their breakfast trays.

"It is meaningless," An-ket said. "All men do such at times."

"It's not like Simon," Julia said confidently, though she suffered a few doubts when she realized that for all she knew he could drink himself insensible four nights out of five. But then she remembered his clear eyes, steady hands, and sweet kisses and knew absolutely that there was no truth in it. Strange that her emotions could answer for him before her mind worked through all the ramifications.

"Robert never used to drink, either, though I hear India can change a man for the worst."

"We have to arrange a meeting between you and Robert so you can see whether he's changed that much."

"Walk in the marketplace," An-ket said. "That is how Senusret found me."

Though at first she'd found it unnerving to have two voices speaking in turn from the same set of vocal chords, Julia learned that the human mind was so wonderfully elastic that she soon grew quite used to it. Sometimes it seemed as though An-ket and Lucy spoke to each other, too, but in their shared mind. Once or twice during the day, Julia heard her companion laugh, seemingly at something heard inside.

She had a list of tasks to accomplish in pursuit of an organized party. Aided—or complicated—by Mrs. Archer having made out a separate list, Julia took An-ket/Lucy along. Mrs. Archer was so pleased that Lucy was taking an interest in something at last that she made no demur. Yet the older woman seemed distracted when Julia spoke to her.

"Is something the matter? Is it Simon?"

"He's never done anything like this before. He's always been so moderate, so abstemious! I've never worried about his falling in with evil companions in that way."

This seemed to indicate that there were other things about Simon that troubled his mother. "Oh, no," Mrs. Archer said when very gently pressed. "No. He told me . . . that is, he promised that he wasn't at all . . . well, he's everything a mother could ask for in a son. And my opinion of dear Robert Winslow was set very high as well, despite his having broken . . . oh. Have a good time."

Jane had a piano teacher coming to give her lessons while Amanda had sneaked off early to plunge again into the adventures of Athos, Porthos, Aramis, and D'Artagnan, so Julia and An-ket/Lucy went out alone.

What An-ket had seen of London thus far had been either at night or on the eye level of a cat. Riding through the broad streets, in an open landau, seeing all the marvels of the town, she caught her breath so often that the driver wondered if she had the hiccups. "Drink water out the wrong side of a glass—that'll cure 'em."

Julia might not be able to persuade Simon Archer to do the least little thing he did not chose to do, but caterers, orchestra leaders, and florists were putty in her hands. Even the formidable butler at the residence of the Earl Rexbury could not have been more helpful or courteous despite her proceeding to overset some of his most cherished traditions.

As he showed her to their carriage, she said, "You've been marvelous about all this, Tufferty. Tell her ladyship how much I appreciate all she's done."

"It is our pleasure," he said, bowing.

As the carriage pulled away, Julia marked off the second to last item on her list with a decisive flick of the tiny silver pencil she wore around her neck on a long chain. "Almost done. A visit to the wine merchants and we'll have plenty of time to see some sights before we go back to help poor Jane with those invitations. . . ."

Her voice trailed off as she realized Lucy was staring at her. It was unmistakably the English girl and not the Egyptian woman, for An-ket never let her mouth hang open. "What is it?" Julia asked.

"That—that was Tufferty," she said.

"Yes? Is there something wrong with him? Don't tell me *he* drinks?" Lucy shook her head. "Or is prone to apoplectic attacks? This ball will never go off as planned if Mr. Tufferty falls ill."

"No, I'm sure he's fine and certainly no drunkard."

"Thank heaven!"

"It's just that . . . I only . . . I've always been terrified of him. Whenever Mother brings us to see my aunt or uncle, I always hide from Tufferty's beetling eyebrows. Mother doesn't like him, either; if she's said it once, she's said it a thousand times. Tufferty takes advantage of his position. But for you, he rolled over like a dog asking to have his stomach rubbed."

"What a horrible image!"

They went off to the wine merchant's—Fobber, Harris, and Lake—where Julia ordered a much, much better quality of champagne than Mrs. Archer had requested. By coincidence, Mr. Lake had long been supplying Julia's father with his wines, having helped to lay down the foundation of his cellar with Mr. Hanson's first fortune. He immediately suggested an excellent vintage and was only too delighted to charge it all to her father's account when she explained the circumstances.

"Thank you, Mr. Lake. The only thing I know about being a hostess is to serve the very best champagne. The food may be dreadful, the music dull, and the company appalling, but giving them the best champagne is like waving Cinderella's godmother's wand. The women become more beautiful, the men more witty, and even the dancing improves."

Mr. Lake, who bore a remarkable resemblance to a red grape, being rotund and of a bright complexion, said discreetly, "I trust we'll soon have the pleasure—humm?— of supplying the champagne for a wedding breakfast, Miss Julia."

"I will certainly recommend you to any of my friends who are contemplating marriage." She stood up and held out her hand, Lucy/An-ket following her lead. "Good afternoon, Mr. Lake. When I write to Father, I'll tell him how helpful you were."

"Tell him instead I've found a new vineyard in Portugal that is shipping as soft a port as he's ever tasted."

"I shall."

Outside again, she asked, "What would you like to see first?"

There was a brief internal discussion, then Lucy said, "I've told her all about the Tower and the parks and palaces, but she wants to go shopping."

"Shopping?" Julia looked at the other girl curiously, but An-ket did not deign to appear and explain. "Very well. What's a good place?"

"Burlington Arcade?" Lucy suggested, then paused with that far-off expression that meant she heard a silent voice. "She says she only wants to go to the most expensive dressmaker. But I can't afford—"

"Perhaps she just wants to look. Do you know of any such places?"

"I've heard of someone new called . . . called . . . Madame . . . Madame something."

"They're all called Madame something."

She went to ask the driver. He pushed back his hat and scratched a mottled skull that was as bare as an egg. "I drove a laidy somewheres like that t'other day. Don't recall the name but I knows where it is."

"Will you take us there?"

"Yus. But 'ere . . . let me tighten that girth afore the horse walks right off without us." Climbing down from the box, he muttered, "Don't look naow, missus, but there's been someone follering you h'ever since I picked you up."

"Following? Us?"

"Yis. I thought at furst it were just one of them things, but that there same brougham's been behind us time an' again. Down there, by that striped awning."

With extreme casualness, Julia surveyed the busy street. Sure enough, a shiny black carriage stood idle by the curb, the curtains inside pulled down over the windows. It might have been any genteel conveyance waiting for master or mistress to return to it, yet something about it gave Julia a cold feeling. As she stared, one of the curtains moved as though someone had let it drop back against the window.

Perhaps she was imagining things. Perhaps the driver merely enjoyed disturbing people with wild tales. Glancing down into his mild, rather watery eyes, however, Julia couldn't believe that.

He drove them to a dressmaker's that was so modest on the exterior as to make certain that the goods inside were expensive. Lucy/An-ket was exclaiming over the single rose-colored dress in the window, displayed against a swath of apple-green silk. Julia's eyes were employed in a search for the same carriage.

This street was busier yet, with many different kinds of traffic rumbling along, from spindly phaetons to burly two-horse trucks. But she didn't see any broughams, though she stood watching while passersby had to press almost to the wall to go past her. At last, she turned to enter the store, but her sigh of relief was cut short when she happened to glance up toward the corner in time to see the carriage appear in the midst of other vehicles.

Unlike them, however, the brougham pulled at once to the curb and came to a stop.

The sunlight glinted off the windows so that she couldn't see if the curtains were up or down. She recognized the horses, both coal-black and glossy, and the driver, a burly man wearing an old-fashioned coat with many capes at the shoulder.

She only gave half her mind to the dresses of Madame Variska, though ordinarily they should have fascinated her. They were almost barbaric in their use of line and color, while Julia suspected that her lavish use of gold lace would cause a sensation.

Lucy and An-ket were both in agreement that Julia should arrange then and there to have the Russian lady create a gown for her. Julia demurred, for the gowns, beautiful though they were, were of the overfussy and hugely skirted variety, which made it so impossible for a lady to be anything but decorative. However, a few whispered words to Madame Variska brought forth some thread-net shawls in her favorite lace as gifts to the Archer ladies.

The brougham was still there, Julia saw, as they left the shop. While frowning at it, she missed the man who bowed before her, hat in hand, until he spoke. "Good afternoon, Miss Hanson."

"Goodness! Dr. Mystery, you startled me."

"A thousand apologies. Your thoughts are far removed from this mundane sphere." He wore a pair of glasses with small smoked lenses. This reminded her of the brougham and suddenly she knew it was he who had been following her all that day. Had he been waiting for an opportunity such as this?

"You'll have to pardon me, sir," Julia said. "We must hurry home now."

"Why run away? Come home with me instead. Send your friend to make your excuses. That is what friends are for, isn't it?"

"Julia? Who is this man?" It was An-ket who spoke, sitting upright in the back of the landau. If Lucy had asked the question, Julia would have fobbed her off with an evasion, but An-ket was a sharper article altogether. She made the introduction, using Lucy's name, of course.

Dr. Mystery kept both hands resting on the golden knob of his walking stick, but he bowed like a prince, or an actor. Julia sighed with relief that he hadn't noticed anything wrong.

"It is an honor to meet the sister of my dear friend, Mr. Archer. He isn't with you today?"

"He's not far away," Julia lied quickly. "We're meeting him now."

She identified the odd sensation crawling up her back— she didn't feel safe. Never before had she met with a situation that made her feel as though menace were breathing down her neck. She'd always had an instinctive sense that she could take charge of any given circumstance and do it well. Now she couldn't think of anything to do but hurry away from the slight man with the impeccable manners and fanatical mind.

She looked about her, eager for the sight of one of those hustling passersby who'd nearly nudged her off the sidewalk before. No one was coming. She would have given a thousand pounds to see Simon.

Dr. Mystery said with a cool chuckle, "I'm sure I can amuse you more than he. We did not have the opportunity to finish our chat yesterday. I would be so happy, so very happy, to do so now. My carriage is just there. Please say you'll accompany me."

"That's very kind of you, but I must consider my hostess . . . she'll be waiting tea."

She moved past him to put her foot on the long step. He took her hand, ostensibly to help her balance as she entered, but he clung to it. As if a last resort, he gave over using his too-bright smile, whispering hoarsely, "Please. I must speak with you. It's very important."

An-ket's eyes were narrowed. Julia assumed that Lucy was informing her guest of the feud between Dr. Mystery and Simon. "This man is a dangerous man," An-ket said suddenly. "He follows the god of evil whose name is the sound of the whirlwind."

For an instant, all pose fell from Dr. Mystery and he resembled a squashed frog with his mouth hanging open. He snatched his glasses from his face. Julia saw that the area around his eyes was speckled as though with broken blood vessels. His clutch on her hand tightened painfully. "How is this possible? I can *see* her! Who is that other woman?"

"Let go!"

The driver, alarmed, was climbing down from the box. " 'Ere now! I'm going ter call a constable! 'Elp! Perlice!"

Nineteen

~

When Simon learned that Julia and Lucy were in the hands of the police, his immediate reaction was to leave Julia where she was. While realistic memories of last night ran through his mind, the safest place for her might well be behind iron bars that he could not break through. Knowing she was on the other side of a flimsy wooden door had been one of the chief torments that had driven him to take a bottle to share with Robert Winslow.

Of all the people in the city, he had felt that only Winslow would understand what it was like to want a woman he couldn't have. They'd not bandied the names of the women between them; that would be the behavior of cads, but each had a fairly sound idea of whom the other meant.

It had taken the half bottle and most of the whiskey in another bottle Winslow had produced to allow Simon to sleep without tormenting dreams of Julia. Her name was on his lips when he awoke, though he couldn't recall what his dream had been about. But a decent man couldn't stay drunk all the time and he couldn't leave an innocent girl in jail even from the noblest motives.

Even as he hurried to the police station, he wondered that Julia had sent for him at all. She was surely equal to a battalion of policemen. He decided, on thinking it over, that she must need him to calm Lucy's nerves. It seemed a shame that something like this should happen on the first expedition that Lucy had departed on with any pleasure.

His mother had been more excited than a man with a morning head could attend to without wincing, but he'd gathered that Lucy had gone off with Julia, skirt swinging to a vigorous walk, eyes shining with new interest. Whatever quality of life Julia had, the patent medicine people could make a fortune by bottling it to sell to despondent patients.

When he entered the station, a knot of police officers formed a seething blue circle around a young woman. Ignored by the authorities, another young woman sat on a hard wooden chair in the corner, her face in her hands, the flowers on her bonnet quivering with emotion. It must have been a slow day for crime, for no felons seemed to be present to shock a lady.

Amid the laughter generated by the men in blue, Simon crossed the room unnoticed. Standing above her, he heard a small sniff and addressed her with more gentleness than he felt. "What are you doing here, Lucy?"

The girl raised her face.

"Julia!" He glanced at the laughing men who must, despite his assumptions, be gathered around Lucy. Dropping to his knee, he took Julia's hands in his.

"Oh, Simon. I thought you'd never get here."

It seemed only natural to slip a comforting arm about her waist. "I hurried, but the traffic . . . What happened? Mother said you went shopping. . . ."

"You didn't tell her where we are?"

"Of course not. I shouldn't have even if your note hadn't mentioned it. There's no point in worrying her."

"That's what I thought. Simon, I have something to tell you, and I want you to control your temper."

"Believe it or not, Julia, I am a very mild-tempered fellow. What is it?"

"We were looking at dresses . . . but that's not where it started. The driver said that the brougham had been behind us since we'd begun. And then . . . and then . . ." She put trembling fingers against her hot cheeks. "I don't know what's the matter with me!"

By now, Simon was thoroughly alarmed, with his imagination boiling over. With an effort, he kept from catching Julia against his heart, but the strain showed in his voice when he said, "You've had a shock. The second one in three days. Your nerves—"

"I haven't any nerves," she protested. "At least, I never have had."

One of the officers noticed him at last. He detached himself from the laughing group, still wiping his eyes, and said, "You'd be the young ladies' brother, sir? Mr. Archer?"

"That's partly correct," Simon said, rising. "I'm only a brother to one of them. What's the trouble, officer? Nothing serious, I trust."

"Might have been, sir. Some bounder accosted this young lady on the street. Nat'rally she got a bit scared."

"Julia? You're not hurt?"

"I'm quite well now, Simon."

The police officer, who wore a chevron on his sleeve, said coaxingly, "Now that your brother's come, you'll make that statement, won't you?"

"Oh, I'm not her brother. The other one is my sister."

The police sergeant glanced from Julia to Lucy, and then smiled benevolently. "I think I understand, sir. You'll do us all a favor, sir, if you'll persuade your young lady here to give us the information we want."

Julia said, "I really have nothing to add to what I've said already, Sergeant. I don't know the man and I cannot give you a better description than I have done. He ran away as soon as our driver called for the police. A crowd formed and I lost sight of him among them."

Simon frowned at her. She gave her unsatisfactory evidence as woodenly as though she were participating against her inclination in amateur theatricals. Where was her sparkle, her spontaneous ability to make people like her? The sergeant showed signs of impatience.

"Surely you remember more than that?" he asked, receiving a grateful nod from the sergeant.

"I'm sorry; I don't. Perhaps Lucy saw more than I."

"She says she didn't even know aught was amiss 'till the driver started in shouting. She saw the back of this feller's head but a fat lot of good that's going to do us. Now we'll not catch the son-of-a—" The sergeant coughed. "You put it to her, sir. If we don't catch him now, next time he could give some poor old lady enough of a shock to kill her. Now you don't want that, do you, miss?"

"I don't believe he'll search for another victim. Perhaps he thought I was someone he knew and I panicked. Anyone might run away in those circumstances. Yes. That must be what happened."

From this story, the sergeant could not budge her. As it was none of his duty to bully young ladies of quality, he washed his hands of her a short time later. Simon, who didn't believe a word she was saying, stood by silently while he questioned her. He could never imagine Julia panicking, therefore the whole tale must be false. Who was she protecting? Lucy? Or the unknown man? Simon wrestled with jealousy, even while reminding himself that he had no claim on her at all.

The sergeant moved onto a happier subject. "That Miss Archer's a one, sir, and no mistake! The tales she tells! You might not believe it, but I'm a well-read man in my way. I've not heard nothing like 'em even in Mr. Lane's *Arabian Nights*. You must've taught 'em to her, eh, Mr. Archer?"

"May I see my sister, Sergeant?"

" 'Course," he said, snapping to. "Here, lads, step aside."

Lucy—shy, frail, melancholic *Lucy*—sat on the edge of the sergeant's desk, her feet swinging while she munched on an apple. Several of the younger police constables had plainly lost their hearts to her. When she prepared to jump down, half a dozen hands were waiting to assist her.

She started talking without a word of greeting. "We'd better get Julia back, Simon. She's been more frightened than hurt, but still! Good afternoon, gentlemen. I feel that I shall sleep soundly tonight knowing that it's fine men like yourselves who patrol our streets."

Climbing into the closed carriage he'd ordered, the two young ladies seemed to regain a measure of their own personalities. Simon still found something faintly unnerving in his sister's smile as she sat back. It seemed cooler, more remote, as though he glimpsed the smirk of the Mona Lisa on her lips of English rose.

Julia captured his attention by uttering four words the sergeant would have loved to hear. "It was Dr. Mystery."

Simon's head snapped around. "What!"

"On the street. It was Dr. Mystery. He wanted me to come with him and was not in the least interested that I had a different use for my afternoon."

"Lucy, did you see him?"

"Of course," she answered promptly. "Julia isn't deranged, you know. What she says she sees, she has seen. What she says is truth, *is* truth."

"Then why, in the name of all that's holy, didn't you tell the police that?"

"I doubt they'd have believed us."

"I'll see to it that they do. We'll turn around at once."

"No," Julia said, pushing down his hands as he reached for the speaking tube. "Don't you see? Dr. Mystery, if I'm any judge, ran home and created an alibi. Or it may be that he ran home, jumped into bed, and pulled the covers over his head. I don't know."

"What does it matter?"

"It matters to me. You and Dr. Mystery have a quarrel that is taking place in the press. You seem to have won it. But if you accuse him of assaulting a woman who is a guest in your house . . ."

"You're concerned about your reputation at last, Julia."

Lucy said, "Don't be a fool, Simon. She's thinking about your reputation."

"Mine? Ladies, I can take care of myself. I do it all the time."

They looked at each other and Lucy shrugged. "Male pride digs deeper than the claws of lions."

Julia said, "You have a reputation as a just and fair man. If you make an unsupported charge against a man who has already lost, you will look vindictive, as though you are trying to destroy him completely."

"I want to destroy him," he said savagely. "He attacked you in broad daylight. The man's a menace!"

"He only wanted to talk to me."

"If that's the case, why did the police come?"

"The driver—"

Again, Lucy spoke from her corner. "Tell him the real reason, Julia. You were afraid. Something about that man frightened you."

"Yes," Julia said, hanging her head. "Yes, I was afraid of him. I don't know why. He doesn't look strong enough to hurt me."

Simon, his better judgment swamped in the need to comfort her, drew her close to him on the seat. "Everyone is afraid sometimes, Julia."

"Not I." Her voice was muffled by the wool of his coat. He saw that Lucy had leaned her head back against the cushions, discreetly closing her eyes. He hoped her ears were closed as well.

He murmured into the edge of Julia's bonnet, "The first time I kissed you was in a moving carriage."

"No, we'd stopped." She stayed against him during the entire drive homeward, as relaxed and warm as a sleeping child. He sensed there were things she was not telling him, yet he felt a great reluctance to disturb this peaceful moment with the same questions the poor sergeant had asked. He stroked her back through the smooth cashmere of her mantle, trying to quiet his own mind as well as soothe her. Their breathing space lasted only until the hired carriage stopped at the Archers' front door.

Julia sat up and said, in her old tone, "Simon, you mustn't tell your mother what happened."

"I won't lie to her."

Lucy said, "You needn't tell her everything. She'd be horrified to learn I set foot in a police station. She thinks the police are low spies."

He reiterated, "I won't tell lies. If she doesn't ask, I won't say anything. That's as far as I'm willing to go."

The two girls exchanged a glance that soon turned into an eye-rolling session. As they left the carriage, Lucy looked toward the Winslow house. In An-ket's voice, she muttered, "I have told her that in the morning after a man drinks strong beer, he has no heart but too much head. She longs to run to him, but my counsel is to wait."

"That's very wise. Maybe that's why Simon is so out of sorts."

She'd almost grown used to seeing Lucy's pretty blue eyes blink slowly and deliberately while An-ket made use of her body. She did it now. "This Simon of yours is strong from digging in the earth of Egypt. He can bear the pain with fortitude. I will go to that hole you call a kitchen and prepare him a remedy of my house. We gave it to Pharaoh's son when he'd lowered the level in the wine jar too far."

She paused and looked hard at Simon, who was paying off the driver. "It was destiny that called him there. . . ."

"Where? What destiny?" Julia said. But she'd already gone into the house.

Julia started to follow, but Simon called to her as she put out her hand to open the door. Her fingers fell away from the knob. She should have known he'd not let the matter rest.

"Simon," she began. "I'm not going to tell the police it was—"

"Did he hurt you?"

Her heart melted. "No, and I don't believe he wants to. He keeps saying he wants to talk with me. Perhaps I should have gone with him. A five-minute conversation to clear the air would probably explain everything."

"Why didn't you go? Not that I want you to. I want you to stay as far away from Dr. Mystery as possible. But—if you'll forgive me—it's never been your way to take the prudent path."

"What do you mean? I'm very prudent. I'm the most prudent person I know."

"You must have an extremely limited circle of friends." He held up a hand for a truce. "Yes, I know. I started it."

"Are you going to perform both sides of an argument now?"

He looked at her as though he wanted to kiss her. That expression in his eyes made her feel like soft-centered chocolate. "I'm a better advocate for you than you know, Julia. I find it unexpectedly difficult to remain angry with you."

After such a handsome admission, Julia could no longer spar with him. She said, "I didn't accompany Dr. Mystery because I was frightened, just as Lucy said."

Simon's jaw jutted out like a ship-killing rock. "Were you, indeed? Well, now it's his turn to be frightened."

Julia ran down the steps to scurry around in front of him, blocking his path. "No, Simon. If I can't go, you can't."

"I'm not afraid of any pip-squeak medium."

"I'm afraid for you. I'm afraid of Dr. Mystery. I try to convince myself there's no reason to be, that he's just a trickster, but against all my logic is a great mass of fear that I cannot seem to throw off."

"Julia! You've gone white."

"I won't faint. I never faint." Nonetheless, she clutched his arm, glad of the strength beneath his sleeve. She'd back Simon in a standup brawl against anyone up to the heavyweight champion of England, but Dr. Mystery attacked souls, not bodies. She said, "He seemed so desperately anxious to talk me. But I wouldn't tell him anything even if I knew the answer."

"I know there are things you are not telling me."

"In response, I can only say what you have said yourself. I won't volunteer any information, but I won't lie to you." She released her clutch of his sleeve, brushing it off apologetically.

She added, "I'm leaving Saturday morning."

"Saturday?"

"Yes. My first stop today was to book my passage on the mail coach returning north. I would have left already if it hadn't been for your celebration. Your mother has pressed me to stay for it. I intend to have a very good time."

"Even though you are doing all the work."

"I don't mind. I want it all to be perfect for you. I'm so proud of you." She started up the front steps again. "You should be grateful to me, you know."

"I am," he said with such a tender look in his eyes that Julia could almost fool herself into believing he loved her. Then he asked, with a return to wariness, "Why today in particular?"

"Because I managed to talk Jane and Amanda out of persuading your mother that your celebration should be a masquerade ball with everyone attending dressed as—and I quote—'your favorite pharaoh or concubine.' "

He indulged in a trifle of eye-rolling himself and then said, "Remind me to worship at your feet when I next have a spare moment."

"Later will do. It would be a shame to ruin your creases on this rough walk. The police station floor didn't do that

one any good, either. You look like you've been proposing to a girl in a pub."

Simon inspected the brown spot on the knee of his left
trouser leg, and growled. Julia laughed as he dashed up
the steps. He paused only to shake his finger in her face
in mock anger. "Just you wait, Miss Hanson, just you
wait!"

Following in his wake, Julia sighed and said aloud,
"What else can I do?"

From that afternoon on, whenever Julia had an errand
to run, Simon went with her. Sometimes he was helpful,
but other times he was very much in the way. She
couldn't help but be glad that she'd taken care of the
champagne question earlier, for he did not allow her to
pay for anything. She was afraid the price of some things
shocked him.

"There's going to be several hundred people there,
Simon. You can't do a party like this for a pound a head."

"I suppose not. It's just that I hate to see so much being
spent on this, when the museum needs every penny for
research and exploration."

"The museum? I thought you and your mother
were . . ." She remembered that a lady didn't discuss personal finance with any man outside her family, unless it
was a debt of honor. But since she'd already broken that
cardinal rule, she asked, "Aren't you paying for this personally?"

"No, of course not. All the bills are to go to the museum—within reason."

More than ever, Julia thanked goodness that she'd had
sense enough to order the champagne billed to her father.

Despite the time they spent together, the constraint between them grew. Knowing how he hated evasion, Julia
felt guilty for not telling him of An-ket's return, but
couldn't see that there was very much point in telling him
things he would not believe. By not telling him the truth,

she avoided having him think she was telling him lies—
a neat moral dilemma.

Her guilt sharpened every day. Simon would change from
a friend with whom she shared jokes and so much of
interest to a brooding figure who stared at her from time
to time but hardly spoke. Sometimes he'd shake her hand
when she retired for the night, while on other evenings
he would escape to his study as soon as she started from
the room. No doubt, she reasoned, these abrupt changes
in mood came on when he recollected that she told neither
him nor the police all she knew.

She expected Mrs. Archer, who also noticed her son's
mercurial mood swings, to be more troubled by them then
she was. When Julia tried to explain that his behavior was
caused by trouble between them, the older woman only
smiled sagely and nodded her head. "Very natural. I remember his dear father when first we met. . . ."

On the whole, Julia's lifelong gift of being interested
in other people to the point of making fast friends of the
most unlikely types, her enjoyment of food, and her ready
sense of humor all seemed to have deserted her. About
the only pleasure she seemed to have came from doing
the sort of hard, physical cleaning that a lady never did.
Scrubbing floors, washing down walls, and beating carpets at her father's town house exhausted her enough so
that she could sleep without dreaming of Simon.

Otherwise, every night she found herself kissing him
on the carpet in his study, smells of dust and his skin
mingling, while his hands traveled to places only the bris-
tles of a bath brush had touched before. Waking from
these dreams, she found it difficult to look him in the eyes
when they met.

She should have been glad to know that soon she'd be
home in Yorkshire, never to be troubled by him again,
but the remembrance of her reservation on the coach only
gave her a grinding sense of depression.

An-ket and Lucy, strangely enough, seemed to be as happy as a couple of grasshoppers singing on a summer evening. Julia couldn't imagine what it must be like, sharing a body with another being, but Lucy didn't seem to mind at all. An-ket seemed to lend her the fortitude she needed. The day after their run-in with the police, Lucy dressed in her finest day gown and crossed the street to the Winslow house. She did not return for several hours.

When she did, her sisters and Julia were loitering casually in the hall. Mrs. Archer stood at the top of the stairs, ostensibly straightening a picture, but no picture ever took so long to level.

Lucy's step was light and the three girls smiled at one another. "Whatever are you doing there?" she asked.

Julia, nudged by Jane, asked the question they were all dying to have answered. "Did you see Major Winslow?"

"No, he'd been called away to the Foreign Office."

Something that sounded like a muffled curse came from the upper hall.

Amanda said, "But you've been gone for ever such a long time."

"I sat with the general. He has adopted a cat."

Another half-heard sound from upstairs.

"It's a dear little thing, but I think it will grow very fat. He's forever feeding it morsels of this and that. He's had a special cushion made for it beside his desk. He's writing his memoirs at last. He read me the first chapter—I think it will be very exciting."

Jane took her sister's mantle and bonnet as Lucy took them off. "So you didn't see the major at all?"

"Not today. But the general has asked me to come back tomorrow to listen to chapter two."

The sound from upstairs was a rhythmic tapping as though of someone dancing a jig. "Don't hurt yourself, Mother," Lucy called.

The next day, she had seen him. She answered their questions graciously but shortly. "Yes, he was there. Of course I spoke to him. He didn't say anything but 'how do you do?' and he looked just as he always has. A trifle thinner, perhaps."

"But that can't be all!" Amanda said, as if protesting a great unfairness.

"Life isn't like your silly storybooks," Lucy said, scoffing. "Did you expect him to propose? Or to fold me in his arms, covering my face with kisses?"

"If you must know," the bookish girl answered, "yes, I did!"

"So did I!" Lucy wailed and ran up the stairs.

There Julia found her, weeping on her bed. Wordlessly, she sat down and smoothed the tumbled hair. She felt that the Archer girls were like her sisters. She'd never realized quite how lonesome her childhood had been until she came into this house.

"Never mind, dear. It's only the first day. Things will be better tomorrow."

"Oh, Julia," Lucy said, sitting up and blowing her nose. "I'm not a child coming back from her first day at school! Robert just doesn't love me anymore! I was a fool to think . . . to dream . . ."

"He gave no sign of even being glad to see you?"

"Oh, he thanked me for visiting his father, but he was so polite, so cold. You must understand that Robert only behaves like that with people he dislikes. To the rest of the world, he's like a big friendly dog, jumping up with muddy paws on your best dress but not meaning any harm."

"That's not the impression I had. . . ."

"I might just know him a little better than you do!" Instantly, Lucy apologized.

"Never mind. You're overwrought, and it's perfectly natural. I'd be disappointed, too."

"It's my own fault for raising my hopes so high. But I did think he'd at least be glad to see me! But he just bowed. Even when we were alone for a few moments—"

"Oh, you were alone together?"

Lucy said, "An-ket told me what to do if I had the chance, but I don't think it worked."

Julia thought of Simon's varying mood and asked without any extra emphasis, "What was that?"

"Oh, you try to . . . to make him aware of your femininity. Subtly, of course, nothing overt or vulgar. But I can only think it must work better in transparent linen than in a tartan walking dress."

"What about in a ballgown? Is the major coming to the party?"

"Yes, he told me both he and his father would attend. He even bespoke a dance."

"Come, that's encouraging at least. A waltz?"

"No, the boulanger. We won't even be able to talk!"

"Then sit it out with him."

"And have him go to fetch me a glass of punch and not come back until it's time for another partner? No, thank you, I'll dance with him sooner than that!"

Julia thought Lucy was taking an unnecessarily grim view. "What does An-ket think?"

"I don't know." Lucy stared at herself in the mirror. "I don't blame him, you know, I really don't. I look a perfect hag. Why was I such a fool?"

"What do you mean, you don't know? You must know what An-ket thinks."

"Oh, Julia!" Lucy said impatiently. "I haven't heard from An-ket in two days. Not since we came home from the police station."

"Is she gone?"

"No. She's still here. But she doesn't seem to want to talk. Frankly, neither do I."

"It is strange that you have found it so easy to accept that you have the spirit of an ancient Egyptian princess living in you."

"Is it? I don't see why. I've rather enjoyed it. She has such a lofty point of view, though I must say the goddess she served must have been one of the touchier ones. Some of her stories are bloodcurdling." Lucy pinched her cheeks to bring out the color. "Perhaps I should go sit in the park for a while today. I have no roses left and I won't go to the ball looking like a ghost!"

"Can you tell what she is thinking about?"

"Of course. She's thinking about her son."

"I didn't know she had one."

"It's very sad." Lucy turned away from the mirror. "Thank you for reminding me of it. It makes my own little troubles look very insignificant."

"What happened?"

"She married Senusret, one of the king's sons. The pharaohs had quite the cozy home life, didn't they? This one had half a dozen wives." She shrugged. "I'm glad husbands and wives come in sets these days. I shouldn't like sharing my husband with a crowd."

"What happened?" Julia asked.

"Well, An-ket and Senusret were very happy when they found out they were going to have a baby, and when it turned out to be a son! Well, some things never do change. His name was Thoser and she knows no one in all of Egypt ever had a more splendid son. All the girls were wild about him, especially one who must have been some sort of cousin because she was the daughter of his grandfather's sisters. I don't know; they seemed to marry anyone they took a fancy to, even . . ." Lucy blushed.

"I know that pharaohs married their sisters," Julia said. "Some archaeologists think they might have married their daughters if no other bride of the right lineage was available."

"That's dreadful! I'm glad Mother doesn't know about it. She already thinks Simon's work has made him too radical."

"Actually, it's a very conservative idea. Blood royal

could marry none but blood royal. Go on, about An-ket's son."

"This girl was already supposed to marry some powerful man—a magician-priest, or something. But she loved Thoser and they ran away together. The magician caught them. She made the magician promise that if she went with him, he'd leave Thoser alone. He vowed by all the gods, then killed him anyway. An-ket's husband died soon after of grief. Then she died. . . ."

"Then what happened?"

"I told you. She died. There's nothing after that."

Julia realized she'd been hoping to hear the tale of An-ket's journey through the Underworld. Had she answered all the questions correctly? Had she seen Osiris, the dead-but-living god, face-to-face in some endless cavern? Had Anubis the Jackal taken her by the hand and spoken of her life?

"The undiscovered country," she whispered, "from whose bourn no traveler returns. . . ." Shaking off her wonder, she said, "But she did come back. Or is this all just some strange dream of my own devising?"

Twenty

His sisters and his mother worked harder the day of the party than they had yet. Jane and Amanda had been serving as Julia's aides-de-camp, while his mother fluttered about making suggestions. Hers might not have been the most vital role, but it was the most fatiguing to watch.

Lucy had been busy with her stalking of Robert Winslow, which consisted of standing very still and letting him come to her, like a honeybee seeking the lily. Simon knew of her designs on the major but did nothing either to help or hinder her. Whatever alchemy had created the lightning change in her, he didn't feel she needed any interference from him. Only if it all ended badly would he act, even if it meant taking her to Egypt with him, to prevent her suffering again as she did when Winslow left the last time.

As for Julia, he could hardly bring himself to think of her. Even though he did his very best to stay out of her orbit, she swam into his thoughts at odd moments. He'd be authenticating one of Safir's artifacts and find himself smiling at memories, magnifying glass suspended in his hand. Or he'd lose his place in a conversation and answer at random, thinking of something she had said or done. Remembering the mad moments in his study had no cure except hurrying out for an exhausting walk, which sooner or later always brought him home to where she waited.

Even if she'd been in Yorkshire, he would have found her distracting. Having her present physically in his house sent him wild. Yet, to be fair, she didn't do anything to trouble him. She never interrupted him when he was working. If he spent an hour with his family, she did not sit too close to him. At dinner, she passed him bread or salt or what have you without permitting her fingers to so much as brush his. She was never vulgar or overt.

All the same, he was aware of her in a whole new way. He'd always admired her mind, even on paper. He had felt that they could be friends. When she arrived, he'd found her unexpectedly attractive, more so as time passed, as evidenced by those out-of-control moments in his study.

Now, however, he was aware of her as a woman, as the consummate woman. He couldn't be in the room with her without noticing the slightest exposure of an ankle, or the graceful lines of her body, or the way she turned her head when someone spoke to her. Every smile that was not given to him made him jealous. If he heard even a murmur of her voice, he strained his ears to catch the words. He watched her reading a note with the sunlight streaming in through a window behind her, and bit a pencil in two.

He told himself that tomorrow couldn't come quickly enough. The moment she left London, sanity would return. Lucy would marry Winslow. He'd find a rich patron to finance a return to Egypt, while his mother settled down to find husbands for Amanda and Jane. Then she'd travel to visit her married children and he would be alone at last.

How much work he'd accomplish then! That would be the best of all possible worlds—himself, alone, independent, liberated. Julia Hanson would be a memory, or it was even possible they'd return to their former relationship. One day their letters would peter out naturally when she married at last and pursued other interests.

Simon tried to forget how often he'd traveled miles to the bank of the Nile when he'd heard a boat had come, hoping that the post would be aboard. How often had he sorted eagerly through a cache of letters, only to drag himself dispiritedly homeward because no envelope had been graced with her handwriting. He put from his mind the recollection of how he'd smiled at the setbacks and disappointments an archaeologist was heir to, knowing that at night he'd be writing her an account of what the day had brought.

Half-dressed, his tailcoat still hanging over the wooden valet, Simon pulled open a drawer of his bureau. A japanned box with a lock in the lid reposed there, the top jammed down tight. He wrestled with the key and at last it sprang open, spilling over with letters. It contained only this season's exchange; many more than there'd been the year before.

He poured them out onto his bed, an avalanche of paper. Sorting through them, Simon tried to imagine, for the first time, what his letters had meant to Julia. Where had she waited for the post? Had her heart begun to thump harder when the postman came by in his gaudy uniform, only to crash to her shoes when nothing came with an Egyptian cancellation? Did she keep every scrap as he did, giving in all too often to the need to savor each word again?

When his mother came into his room, he only half listened to her. As hostess of the evening, his mother would be dressing at the Earl of Roxbury's house. The countess had recovered from her cold in time to hold a small dinner party prior to the evening's festivities. Simon's sisters and Julia were invited to that, too.

As the nominal guest of honor, he himself was not supposed to arrive until enough guests had collected to make the applause satisfactorily loud. "Yes, Mother. I'll be there in two hours. And yes, I'll make sure my cravat is straight and my hair is brushed. I am more than seven, you know."

"I know. So excited, I don't know what I'm saying. I'd better fly! The girls are waiting. Just beautiful. . . ."

Simon listened to them gabbling away like swans as they trotted down the stairs to the coach the countess had sent. He tried to be happy for them as they achieved a state of nervous delight. Then he settled down to do some serious brooding.

How long had he been in love with Julia Hanson? He had firmly believed her to be an elderly lady when their correspondence began. True, an elderly lady of a particularly lively wit and vivid mind, one of those whom age did not whither but rather enriched, yet still far too old to be thought of as a desirable woman.

Thinking of the way Julia was, Simon revised that opinion. If she lived to be a crone and he with her, then he doubted he'd ever give up wanting to touch her, to hold her, not so long as he kept the memory of a thousand nights of passion to fan the embers.

Thinking back to when he'd first seen her, he wondered now if his reaction had been due more to shock than anger. All his ideas about her had been thrown into revolution. He'd had no time to adjust, so he had lashed out. Everything else that had happened—her hallucination, her danger, her nearness—had come from that reaction to the sight of her face, so young and alive that she seemed to radiate waves of energy. The air around her had seemed to ripple with it, the way the desert writhes in the heat of the sun.

Without her warmth, the future would be a bleak place indeed.

Suddenly in a hurry to get to his uncle's, Simon rushed his clothes on. He'd just finished giving his hair a final brushing when he heard a loud a thump that shook the floor, followed almost at once by another. He came out into the hall to listen. All was silence.

Then a moment later, something shattered in another room with a crash like an ice floe breaking off a floating iceberg.

Simon galloped down the hall. He suddenly wanted the noise to be Dr. Mystery up to more mischief so that he could use the fists God gave him. He almost ran the young woman down.

"Simon!"

"Julia!"

"I wondered who was pounding along up here like a herd of wildebeest! Whatever are you doing?"

"What are you doing here? You left with others."

"No, I didn't. I stayed behind to put some few last things in my cases."

"Why?" He glanced into her room, where two valises lay open on the floor.

"Because I'm leaving tomorrow. Or had you forgotten?"

"I've never forgotten anything you've told me, Julia." He drew back as though from a crumbling precipice. "I meant—why are you doing that instead of Apple?"

"No one is going to be here, the maids are having an evening out. Didn't you see the cold supper they left for you?"

"No." Her dress was in the latest mode. About all that could be said for it was that it wasn't actually transparent. The neckline exposed her shoulders in their entirety, running straight across her swelling bosom. Three gathered tiers of lace descended from there, old cream over a pale pink body, giving the impression that one glimpsed flesh beneath the lace.

The rest was a full satin skirt decorated with roses, but he hardly noticed anything beyond the fullness of her breasts, gleaming white. A strand of pearls, worth as much perhaps as the entire cost of his last expedition, was looped three times about the base of her neck, but they were lusterless compared to her glowing skin.

Simon turned away, his eyes burning as though he'd stared too long at the sun. "What was that crash?"

"Oh, I dropped a mirror. I was about to clean it up."

"Did you cut yourself?"

"No. It must have fallen by itself. I put it down carelessly on the edge."

He saw the shining shards on the floor beside her dressing table and knelt to gather them up. "Do you have something I can put the pieces in?"

She pulled open an empty drawer, saying, "Put them in here. I'll leave a note for Apple."

"You're not worried about bad luck, I take it?" he asked, trying to keep their conversation light.

"What else can happen to me?" She stood beside him while he picked up the pieces one by one. The pink slippers on her feet were tied with ribbons that disappeared under the swaying bell of her skirt. She rustled delectably when she moved, leaving a faint scent of roses behind her. He remembered how she had promised once to give him the experience of breathing attar of roses on her wrist.

He reached for her hand as he came to his feet. "Julia, what has happened to you that makes you say that?"

"Don't you know?"

He forgot her fashionably shameless gown, her scent, everything but the sorrowing look in her eyes. "You love me," he said.

"Yes." She turned away. He caught her by the shoulders, soft and powdered.

"Is that a tragedy?"

"No," she said bitterly. "Nothing but folly. I love you and you won't ask me to stay." She covered his hands with her own, pressing them against her warmth. "You touch me and you don't ask me to stay. You know I'm the perfect wife for you but you will let me go without saying a word."

"I want you to stay," he whispered, and kissed her.

He meant to stop at that. Just one kiss, then they'd

separate, for there was still more than enough to divide them. But her lips were soft and parted under his touch, while his hands screamed with the knowledge that they could so easily slip under that line of lace.

Julia reached up to put her arms around his neck. Everything under his hands shifted. He clenched down on the groan that wanted to burst from his throat. She looked up at him with radiant eyes. "Kiss me again, and again, and again. . . ."

"I don't dare. Oh, God, Julia. . . ."

Then he did hold her hard against him, her skirt billowing out, and took her mouth as he wanted to. She met his thrust with her own, opening freely, giving everything back. Her arms were stronger than he'd guessed. The gray emptiness inside him vanished, burned away in a heated, mindless chaos.

For one instant, only to save his self-respect, Simon tried to stand against it. "Julia, we ought to wait . . . but let's not."

Her laughter had a new sound, ripe and womanly. Her clever hands yanked savagely at his carefully arranged cravat. "I've already waited two years for you. I wanted this from your first letter."

She tugged his shirt out, the studs popping off. Throwing his shirt into the corner, she suddenly pressed her hand against her own burning face. "I—oh, my."

"Julia. . . ."

"No. It's all right. I—I won't think anymore. A friend told me to seize my opportunity if it came. Kiss me, please, and make me forget."

Simon know that was the moment for him to walk out, to hold to his principles. Instead, he kissed her until neither one could form the words that would stop them.

He drew her to the bed. The crisp white covers crinkled beneath him as he sat down, bringing her to stand between his thighs. "Turn around."

She obeyed, and sighed deeply as he undid the tiny

buttons that ran from between her shoulder blades down to the dimple of her back. Simon pushed apart the opening and pressed his mouth to her shoulder as he slipped his hands inside the dress. He found her breasts through the corset and felt her tight nipples push through his spread fingers. The shudder that ran through her as he touched her was his reward.

Julia turned and saw the raw male satisfaction on his face. She'd never seen that expression before but she felt she recognized it. She had caused Simon to look like that. She wanted to laugh with delicious triumph.

From that first kiss, her sense of herself had been over-turned. Always she'd been an intellect first, her woman-hood a long way second at best, a nuisance at its worst. But as her body softened under his touch and her response grew, she found that being a mere female was enough to hold a man spellbound.

Instinctively she'd crossed her arms in front of her body, keeping her dress up and her modesty safe. Now, watching his eyes, she writhed from side to side and let the gown slide down an inch at a time. He reached for her, but she stepped back.

"What are you doing?" he asked, his voice very deep.

"I want to please you, my way."

"I have no say in this?"

She laughed lightly. "You have the advantage of knowing what you are doing, Simon. I don't."

"You're doing just fine. Come here. I'll let you run things."

"I am running things, whether you like it or not."

"Oh, you needn't worry. I like it," he said, his eyes everywhere.

Blushing because it was her first time, but otherwise feeling very confident because Simon was there, Julia stepped out of the billowing mound of her dress. She bent down, giving him a view like no other, and scooped up the material to throw over the end of the bed. It wouldn't be fit to wear again tonight, but some things were more important than parties.

"Go on," he said, lying on his side, his head propped up on one hand. His eyes were like two burning sapphires. Julia had never felt more beautiful than under his gaze.

One at a time, she untied the lace-lavished petticoats and slipped them off. She stepped out of the last of four, standing up only in a brief-skirted chemise and stockings. She felt his gaze trace the length of her silk-clad legs, which no man had ever seen before. Julia felt she had to know the truth and, of course, Simon would never lie to her. "Do I please you?"

He made a sound deep in his throat, like the rising growl of a hungry lion. "Women wear too many clothes," he said. "Come here."

Julia hesitated, holding on for one single instant to the person she'd been up until now. Whatever happened now, she would never be the same. Simon's kisses had been the spells to begin the transformation; his embrace would mold the final creation. Then Julia laughed at her pompous fancies, for whatever happened, would happen to them both.

She came to him with a smiling joy that was still on her lips when they kissed. Then his hands were on her, moving with sure purpose over areas she herself hardly knew. And suddenly she understood why young women were hedged about with such strict rules of conduct. "If once they knew . . ."

"What?"

She shook her head, then moaned aloud as he kissed her ever more deeply.

Simon didn't strip off her chemise, though it was in his way. He wanted to leave her that much modesty. So he eased it down from where it echoed the line of her gown across her chest. At first, he only kept on kissing her lips and throat. Her pearls were as warm as her skin.

He gave her every chance to conceal her breasts if she

wanted to. Then he took one in his hand, admiring the smooth, cool weight of it; and she tensed, but not with apprehension.

She ran her fingers over his hand and seemed proud to have him see her whole body. He looked at last, and thought he'd surely die right then and there. The glimmering white was crowned with duskily ripe roses, already budding. He kissed her there, gently at first, and felt her fingers clench in his hair.

Things were getting beyond him. He tried hard to control his reactions, to give her time, but the pounding rhythm of his blood was driving him hard, like a rider urging on a horse. She was worthy of poetry and singing, but all he could do was make love to her and hope she understood.

Julia wrecked all his preconceptions about virgins. She did not lie idle while he worked. She clutched his back, rising and falling beneath him like waves embracing the shore, while her scent, woman and roses mixed, dizzied him like incense. Dragging his hands to her mouth, she kissed them again and again, calluses, sensitive interstices and all.

He found the words to tell her, after all. "My love is sweet as sycamore figs, her breasts like white doves nestling in my hands. She awaits me on the river bank, her hair streaming like the water. Her embraces give life to my heart."

"Simon, speak English . . . ," she gasped. "I told you . . . my Arabic isn't very good yet."

"I'll show you," he said.

This time, when he reached the top of her stockings, he untied the garters and threw them, one at a time, over his shoulders, to lie where they would. Kneeling between her legs, he met her gaze while he drew the stockings down. She bit her lip, but looked steadily into his eyes as he ran his hands back up her legs to reach the sweetest part of her.

Suddenly she wriggled away, struggling to sit upright. He sat back, disappointed but resigned. He knew loving her was too good to be true. He half expected all this to be a dream. "It's all right, Julia. I understand."

His eyes grew wide with surprise and pleasure as she sat up, pulling the chemise over her head. The rosebud-topped hairpins that decorated the dark waves of her hair tumbled out, littering the pillowcases of her bed. Naked and unashamed as a goddess, she lay back, offering him herself. "Simon? I think I know what happens next. Please . . . hurry."

He shoved off his trousers and underlinen in one gesture. She didn't seem to have qualms about using her eyes. She gazed and, though Simon would have found it hard to believe, his body responded with even greater enthusiasm. But he almost lost all semblance of control when she reached out and stroked him with one delicate hand.

"I always thought the Egyptian scribes were exaggerating when they drew pictures of this. I wonder if measurements might be taken and comparisons made."

He caught her hand and said, with heartfelt emotion, "At any other time, my love, I will be happy to talk about Egyptology until the sun dances into the sea. But not now."

Her smile held the eternal charm of woman. "Forgive me."

She opened her arms to him, gasping at the renewed heat of his skin as their bodies came into complete contact. He kissed her again and again, and Julia relished the thrust of his tongue against all the newly sensitized areas. But not as much as she had a few moments ago. He'd lost none of his skill, but she wanted something more now than kisses, sweet though they'd been.

She couldn't tell him what more she wanted, for her words had all fled. She pushed a hand between their bodies to touch him, pressing his hardness into her, there where all the heat seemed to come from. He said her name in a voice she'd never heard from him, hoarse and urgent. If the earth had a voice, it would sound like that, she thought.

Then his fingers went under her, tightening on her roundness, and lifted her up to meet the firm, insistent length of him, the complement to her soft, welcoming need. She dug her nails into his shoulders, rigid, silent, astonished by the joy that flooded through her, sweeping away the pain.

"Oh, God, Julia . . . I . . ."

"Hush. Wait." Tentatively, she flexed her hips and saw his eyes close. His lips moved as though in silent prayer. She felt the tension coil in him as he tried so hard not to take her mindlessly, to give her this moment. She needed it badly, making the adjustment to his superabundance filling her so completely.

She found it more comfortable to rest her feet on the backs of his legs. He threw his head back, biting his lips. Experimenting, she moved the arch of her foot up and down from his calf to his upper thigh, hearing his teeth grind. She chuckled, glad to know that there was more she could do to please him. Lying around while others sweated had never been her way.

"You find torture funny?" he asked, leaning his forehead on hers.

He began to move, too, adding the harmony to her own rhythm. Caught up in the rapture that seemed to bloom and grow with every second, she lost her place and could only follow the pleasure wherever it lead.

Faster and faster, they came together, fusing in the sweat and the heat into one being, someone new, separate but equal. Julia felt Simon everywhere, not just inside her, but all through her, and knew that she'd never be free of him again. Instead of feeling trapped, she felt gloriously alive. She wanted to tell him about it, but all she could gasp out was an "I love you" that came from her soul.

The flash of realization was lost in a powerful wave of

pure feeling that knocked her sideways. Before she knew it, she was drowning in it, calling out to him, not to save her but to dive in, too. His arms tightened around her, the twisting, swirling whirlpool of desire sucked her down, and the sound of their voices rose to heaven.

Julia awoke from a heavy sleep when Simon withdrew his arm from around her waist. She sat up, still boneless from release and asked, "Love?"

"I didn't mean to wake you."

"Where are you going?"

"Just down the hall. Stay there. I don't want you to go anywhere."

She smiled at the possessiveness of his tone, forgiving him because of the wonder that was mixed in. She watched through half-closed eyes the powerful flexing of his back and rear muscles as he walked away. Then she lay back, arms spread wide, marveling at the gifts of the human body. She'd never known there was so much pleasure to be had from the flesh. This hour with Simon had explained a very great deal that had always confused her, so that her mind was as satisfied as her physical self.

When he came back, his dressing gown over his arm, she tried to talk about that. He laughed and said, "I've never met anyone like you. Even now, you formulate theories."

"Of course. New experiences widen the mind."

"You've been an experience for me." He touched her face with such caring in his eyes that she felt a little shy. Not because they were naked together, but because she loved him so utterly. He said, "I don't know if you are ahead of your time or just unique. But I can't imagine my life without you. . . ."

"Oh, Simon," she said, reaching out. Then she winced at a strange new pain in her lower back.

"Are you all right?"

"I think so."

"Shall I bring you some water? Or would you like to be alone for a little while?" He held out the dressing gown.

"I suppose. But actually . . . I'm hungry. I didn't eat much at tea what with last-minute details and packing."

"I want to talk to you about that, Julia. You won't leave . . . what the devil . . . ?"

Someone pounded at the front door. Even here, they could hear a frantic note in the rapping. "It's probably just a late post. Let's ignore it," Simon said. "Julia, I want you to—"

Outside, someone began calling his name, on a frenzied note. "Archer! Archer!"

"You'd better go see," Julia said.

Simon shoved his arms through the dressing gown's sleeves. Tying it, he threw open the window and looked down into the street. "Who's there?" he demanded. A moment later, he said wonderingly, "Winslow?"

"Archer! Thank God. Come down and open the door."

With a glance at Julia, Simon said, "It's not a good time right now. Why aren't you at the party?"

"Archer!"

"I'm here! In heaven's name, what's amiss, man?"

"It's Lucy! Oh, God, Simon! She's been abducted!"

Twenty-one

Robert Winslow was far too distressed to notice that Simon's formal clothes were rumpled and creased, or to see that Julia's dress was a simple morning frock that showed all the signs of being hastily flung on. Julia herself didn't realize she had misaligned the buttons down her front for quite some time.

Simon pushed Robert into a chair in the parlor and mixed him a stiff whiskey and soda. The major held the drink in his hand, hardly seeming to understand what it was. "We'd agreed during our dance that we should meet in a little while in the conservatory. I wanted to ask her ... I wanted to propose. I wanted to make things right this time."

"What did she say?" Simon asked.

"She wasn't there. I waited, pacing, then I saw it. The cactus quills came through it." He opened his other hand, revealing the crumpled paper.

Simon took it, spread it out flat. Tiny blisters showed where the spines had poked through. Julia came to read it with him, her hand on his shoulder.

"Dr. Mystery has made all arrangements. 'If J. H. does not present herself before midnight, this girl will be carried out of the country tonight.'"

"Mystery!" exploded from Simon's lips like a curse.

Major Winslow said, "Miss Hanson was the only woman with those initials that I know of. I came here at once. I—I think I ran."

Rounding on Robert, Simon asked gruffly, "Did you look first to be certain Lucy hadn't merely gone back into the ballroom?" He smacked the paper with the back of his fingers. "This could be a hoax or a joke."

"It's no joke. She's been stolen away. I don't understand how. The house was crowded, servants everywhere. If she'd cried out, someone would have heard it."

Julia said, "Someone's always crying out at a ball. A girl with an amusing lover, a dowager losing at cards. . . . And servants wouldn't interfere if they saw a young lady leaving with some man. It's not their place."

"Then you think she left of her own free will?" Robert exclaimed.

"That would be the easiest way."

"But why would she go with someone like this Dr. Mystery? It doesn't make sense!"

Julia went to him and guided the whiskey to his lips. His hands began to shake as he smelled it. But when he put the emptied tumbler down, he was calm.

Julia said, "She'd go with him if he told her someone she loved was in danger."

Simon rejected that. "She saw him that day when he accosted you. She'd never go with him after that."

"I don't know whether she saw him or not."

"You said she spoke to him."

"No, that was . . ." Suddenly the motive for Lucy's kidnaping came over her. She wanted to explain it to Simon but he was barking out orders to the major like a born military commander.

"I won't risk Julia, too. You and I will break down the door and—"

"He'll be waiting for you to use force," Julia said. "He'll have traps prepared. It might not be anything more than a constable stationed outside. If you're caught, you're both ruined. Simon, you might be able to avoid attending a party for yourself, but you mustn't break the law."

"Well, you're not going!"

"Of course I am." She smiled at him, knowing he wanted to protect her. But he might as well learn that she would never stand by and let him run into danger without her by his side. Alone, they only had ordinary strength. Together, they could defeat giants—or devils.

Ignoring Simon's further protests, she said, "You can't storm a citadel in those clothes. We have some time. You should change into something plain and dark."

Perhaps it was the military discipline. Major Winslow seemed on the brink of snapping her a salute. Instead, he stood and said, "Yes, ma'am. I'll be ready in five minutes."

She walked with him to the door. "Better make it ten. I'll need time to argue with Simon."

When she came back, Simon stood beside the fireplace, drinking. Julia asked, "May I?" and took the glass from his hand. She sipped, coughed, and said, "It's smoother than the kind my father likes."

Simon said, "Mystery's mad. He kidnaps my sister and now he's trying to get you into his hands as well. All to strike back at me."

"I'm sorry, Simon, but this has nothing to do with you. Oh, perhaps your quarrel with Dr. Mystery began it all, but that's not why he's doing this. I wonder how he knew I was leaving today; one of the servants, I suppose. I wonder why he didn't just wait until I was back in Yorkshire. My father?"

She realized Simon was trying to make her sit down. "Julia, you've been through too much this evening."

"I'm not making sense, am I?" she asked, smiling up at him. "I'm sorry. That happens when I'm thinking very fast. Listen, please, Simon. It's not Lucy who was kidnaped. It was An-ket. Or rather, An-ket and Lucy both."

"I thought we were done with this nonsense about An-ket. Julia, you know that the dead don't come back."

"But the Egyptians believed that the soul could visit the living, flying like a hawk over those they loved in life."

"Superstitions . . . they also believed the sun was pushed across the sky by a giant dung beetle! Let's get a telescope and I'll prove that one isn't true."

"I cannot answer for astronomy, Simon, but I do know something about a woman's heart. An-ket wanted to come back, and she did. She's been inside Lucy for the better part of a week. Haven't you wondered why your sister suddenly emerged from her chrysalis? An-ket."

"Are you saying you've convinced my sister that she has the spirit of an ancient Egyptian priestess inside her? Are you mad? Preying upon a weaker mind. . . ."

Now they came to it. "Simon, Lucy was unhappy because she believed her life was blighted. Thanks to An-ket, now she has her lover back and a—"

"An-ket is dead! She's been lying in a coffin for thirty-five hundred years. There's no such person anymore."

"But don't you believe the soul is immortal?"

Simon threw up his hands. "I'm not going to stand here arguing esoteric points of theology with you. I am going to Dr. Mystery's house and get back my sister."

"He won't give her to you without me. I can't be sure, but he may believe that I am the one who brought An-ket here."

"Then he's as mad as you are."

"Simon, you really must make up your mind about me. You can't go from making love to me to hating me in half an hour!"

"I don't hate you," he said. "But I'm damned if I understand you!"

Julia sighed. "Well, that's something at any rate. Now, listen to me, please. Whatever else you believe, you may as well believe that I am coming with you to Dr. Mystery's. You'd best make up your mind to that before Major Winslow comes back."

"You're not."

"Let's not argue about it. I don't want to see Lucy carried out of the country any more than you do."

"I don't believe a word of this fellow's threats. He wouldn't dare."

"You know, I think he would. He believes I have the secret he's been seeking: the secret of how to bring back the spirits of the dead."

Simon did not appear to be convinced that her presence was necessary. Julia added, "And if you try to lock me in my room, I'll still get out and follow you."

"I'm willing to take the risk," he said, unfolding his arms and starting toward her. He could have picked her up, tucked her under his arm, and walked away with her, without her being able to do anything to stop him.

Julia stood her ground, her eyes narrow. "Not to mention that I'll never forgive you for it." Then she melted, holding out her hands to him. "Simon, trust me."

"I do, but not with your life."

"Then you don't at all. Major Winslow and I will rescue Lucy ourselves. You—go to your party. It's almost time for them to honor you." She paused in the doorway. "When you hear the applause, know that I'm right there in the front row, cheering for you."

It would have been a wonderful exit line if he had not come out of the house two steps behind her.

Fifteen minutes later, the three of them stood outside Mystery's house. "I think I see a light at the rear," Major Winslow said. "How do you want to do this?"

"You're the military mind," Simon said.

Julia said, "I'm going to walk up to the front door and . . ."

"And what?"

"Knock. Coming?"

They tried to talk her out of it as she crossed the street,

hissing in whispers that to approach directly would be ruinous. "He already knows we're coming," she said. "I saw someone look down from that window a moment ago. The longer we stand here arguing, the more foolish we shall look."

She strode up the walk to the black-painted door and tapped the brass lion's-head knocker smartly. It opened at once. Dr. Mystery was there, looking smaller than ever in a loose peasant's shirt and knee-length trousers. His face gladdened when the gaslight fell on Julia's features.

"Miss Hanson, come in. I hardly dared hope . . . come in!" He stood aside, sweeping an eighteenth-century bow. He straightened with a spine-snapping suddenness when he beheld Robert and Simon behind her.

"Guests?"

"Your note said nothing about coming alone. I thought you wouldn't mind a pair of unprejudiced witnesses?"

"Ah, yes, very wise."

Once inside the hall, with more room, Robert made a grab for Dr. Mystery's throat. "Where is Lucy?" he barked, but before his fingers could close, Dr. Mystery jerked up a pistol to point just between Robert's eyes.

"Your guests mustn't interfere," he said, as gently chiding as one who admonishes playful children. "Come, Mr. Archer, you must keep your acquaintances in line during the seance. Come this way."

As he indicated the proper door with a short but commanding flick of his pistol, they did as he had asked. The back of Robert Winslow's neck was scarlet as a grenadier's uniform. Julia hoped he wouldn't do anything rash, like charge for the pistol. She glanced at Simon. His rich blue eyes were half hidden behind lethargic lids, but she saw them flick here and there, taking in everything without seeming to do so.

Then they were all in a room dominated by a large table. The bare wood gleamed under a many-globed chandelier. At the head sat Lucy in an upholstered chair, her cheek resting on her shoulder. The jeweled pins scattered through her ringlets caught the light. She looked like a girl returning home from a ball, fallen happily asleep in the corner of her carriage, dreaming of the dancing she'd done and the hearts she had broken.

"Lucy!" Robert was by her side in one bound. Dropping to his knees, he began chafing her hand. "Is she dead?"

"No, merely sleeping. I was thoughtful enough to bring her a glass of punch to which I'd added a heavy burden of champagne as well as a little something extra I brewed myself. An old family recipe. She was asleep on her feet before she could remember where she'd seen my face before. Evening clothes do make such a difference, don't you find?"

The only things on the table were a small box and a thin brown cigar burning in a dish. Never letting his pistol's eye waver from Lucy's head, he took a long pull at the cigar. "You see, I don't mean harm to any of you."

"Then put the pistol down," Simon growled, his first words since Dr. Mystery had opened the door.

"No, I can't do that, Mr. Archer. This pistol is the only thing between myself and your natural impulses. We are quite alone here. My—er—staff departed upon learning of my change of heart. They were mere confidence tricksters, while I—"

"You set yourself up as something nobler, no doubt?" Simon stood beside Lucy, his hand on her shoulder. Julia might not have existed, for all the notice he took of her.

Dr. Mystery said, "Before now, I have always had faith in the unseen, but no proof. I could hear their voices from my earliest days, but I'd never seen one until I met Miss Hanson and your sister on the street."

"You were following us," Julia said.

"Oh, yes. I knew you were the one I'd been waiting for." He smiled at her, a warm, welcoming smile that assorted ill with the black-iron and red-wood pistol in his hand. "You have the power I seek, Miss Hanson."

"I have no powers."

"But you do. You have the power to bring the dead from the far reaches of eternity. You did it with this priestess."

Julia noticed that Dr. Mystery might point his pistol at the others, but it never came around to her. She started to think how she could turn this fact to her advantage. It might be true that he didn't want to harm anyone, but at any rate, he especially did not want to hurt or alienate her. He wanted her for something, not for love or money, but for something else.

"An-ket came to me by pure chance. I had nothing to do with it."

"I see I shall have to prove my point even to you. But once you understand, then the universe will be ours. You see that box? Open it."

Julia obeyed. Inside was a carved chunk of wood, with some sort of register on the front. It looked so prosaic that Julia couldn't imagine a use for it, except perhaps as a doorstop.

"You see that? I had it from a German I met once. He used it in his act."

"Act?" Julia asked.

"The theater was my former home. But poor old Adolf didn't realize what he had. Turn it over."

A word was burned into the bottom of the wood. The characters were deeply ornate, Gothic in their twists and incomprehensiblity. Julia puzzled it out. "Englespracht?"

"Englespracht! The name of a famous astrologer who spoke, they say, with the angels." Dr. Mystery fairly danced with excitement. "As soon as I saw that, I knew I had to possess it! It is the key to speaking with the unseen spirits who wait for our invocation."

"What are these wires?" Julia asked, moving her finger over them.

"Ah . . ." He stood still and looked directly into her

eyes without blinking. "The spirits are not always as co-operative as one could wish while bill collectors are always punctual. Therefore, it became necessary for me to . . . shall we say 'improve' the box. I place it on the proper spot on the table, give a few turns to an unseen crank, and lo! Static electricity makes the indicator jump."

"Fraud," Simon said in a tone of deep disgust.

Dr. Mystery did not seem to hear. "Miss Hanson, I tell you in all truth. The box works without my interference. It worked that night when you came in search of dear Simon."

"Why are you telling me all this?"

"Don't you see? Can't you imagine what we can do together?"

Simon surged forward. Instantly Dr. Mystery turned to cover him. "Back. I won't be interfered with!"

Desperate to get that pistol to point at herself, Julia said, "Yes! I see." She walked toward him. "You know so much more than I do about these kinds of things. I want you to teach me."

"Julia," Simon said from deep in his chest.

Dr. Mystery said, "Yes! That's what I want. All you need is training. Learn to put your mind under my control. I will help you rule your talents. If you can bring back this one creature, who else could you bring back? Cesare Borgia?"

"Marie Antoinette?"

"Robespierre?"

"Not at the same time, though," Julia said.

"No, that would be disastrous. But think of all you could learn, Miss Hanson. Sit at the feet of Cleopatra and hear how she won both Caesar and Antony. Listen to the librarian at Alexandria describe the scrolls that were burned."

"Now you tempt me," she said, and no one there could have doubted the sincerity in her voice. "Let the others go. You are right. I do have the power."

"Julia, no," Simon said.

She rounded on him. "Enough! This is what I want. You with your foolish digging in the earth like a hungry dog after a bone! What can you learn of history? Only the rubbish they've left behind. I . . . I will know them as they know themselves."

She glanced toward Dr. Mystery as one who has discovered the bright lodestar of existence. "He's the only one who can help me."

Hardly listening to Simon's protests, she walked up to Lucy. Julia steadied the girl's head and lifted one eyelid with the edge of her thumb. No one heard the faint chimes, as of many tiny bells shaken in a desert wind. Cutting across Simon's voice, Julia said, "She'll be asleep for a while yet. One of you will have to carry her out."

Robert Winslow looked like a sleepwalker himself. But he stood and picked Lucy up into his arms. "May we have leave to go?"

Julia looked at Dr. Mystery. He was holding the pistol very negligently. He waved it at Robert Winslow, giving him permission. "You won't inform the authorities. Miss Hanson is staying with me of her own free will and no one will believe you if you say I kidnaped Miss Archer. Why would I kidnap a woman I don't want?"

Robert carried Lucy out. Julia hoped he'd have sense enough to take his beloved to a place of safety before returning. She had no doubt he'd be returning, and with reinforcements. She simply had to keep Dr. Mystery busy until then. She knew only one way to do that.

He firmed up his grip and pointed the pistol at Simon. "You can go, too. There's nothing for you to stay for now. Miss Hanson has me."

And I also, said a voice inside Julia's head.

"I'm staying," Simon said. "You'd have to shoot me to get me to leave, and I don't think you want that."

"My servants and staff are gone. I could shoot you and no one would find your body until Julia and I are long since out of the country. But I won't shoot you unless you make it impossible for me not to. I don't want Julia's vibrations obstructed. Violence is very bad for vibrations."

Julia herself was too overwhelmed to pay attention to the men. A thousand thousand images were flooding her mind—golden sand brilliant under a blazing sun, cool ponds filled with lotus and fish that nibbled toes in ornate sandals, a house built of mud brick that yet achieved elegance, sounds of harp and bells, a warm cone of perfumed fat that melted into one's hair, the laughter of friends and family, the eyes of a beloved husband, and the face of a son. Suddenly, Julia understood why An-ket had come and what she must do.

"Enough!" she said, and Julia admired the snap of command in her own voice. Only it wasn't her voice, because she wasn't using it. She drew back the chair where Lucy had been sitting, and Julia saw that her body was straight and moved with a regal grace. Only she had never moved like that in all her life.

"Let us be seated."

"You can't be serious," Simon said. "Julia . . ."

"Hush, you fool. This is not Julia." The magician came closer, committing the impudence of waving some block of wood under her nose. "My God . . . ," he said. "Look at it! It's . . ."

An-ket raised her head and stared the magician out of countenance. He stepped away, fear whitening his face, and tripped over a chair. The block of wood flew from his hand and smashed on the floor.

"No!" he cried out and fell on his knees to gather up the pieces and nurse them to his chest.

Paying no more attention to him, An-ket placed her hands flat on the table. Nothing was as it should be. There were no pyramids of fruit or bowls of red-dyed beer to offer the goddess. No music or incense sweetened the air. Instead of chanting priests, their leopard skins sweeping over chest and back, there were only these two men who seemed to know nothing about religion. Yet An-ket had been a faithful worshiper even before she'd been made a priestess, making many sacrifices in the great temple, and the Lady of Love would not forget her.

In a low voice, she began, "The children of Ra's tears disobeyed his law and plotted his destruction. Ra, grown old, was angered by his children. He sent forth darkness to cover the face of the earth which he had made."

Suddenly, the gas jets above their heads blew out. Simon looked instantly at Dr. Mystery. He could only see his shadow against the slightly brighter windows where a streetlamp sent out an uncertain glow. Through Simon knew the only answer to the extinguishing of the lights was a trick of Mystery's, he had to admire the skill with which the other man had acted. Simon hadn't seen him move so much as a finger.

The voice that was Julia's yet not Julia's went on. He hadn't realized she was such a good actress. "Ra summoned the Ennead, the nine first gods, to ask what he should do. On their advice he sent his daughter, the lovely one, the divine mother, to punish them. She who is the Eye of the Sun took the form of a lioness. . . ."

Out in the room, something moved in the darkness. At first, Simon thought it might be Robert come back. But Robert did not pant hot breaths that stank of raw meat. Nor did he snarl on an interrogative note.

"In the White Land, the sand turned red as the Eye of Ra stalked the earth. In the Red Land, the sea and the earth were the same, turned to blood by Hathor's passing. The treachery of man was rewarded as befitted the deeds he had done."

Simon heard a great thud. The table beneath his hands began to shake with the tremors of impact. Something huge was walking on the table. From across the way, he heard Dr. Mystery whimper.

From very close, something sniffed at Simon. He felt

the stinking breath ruffle his hair. He tried not to move, even as he told himself that this was not happening. There could not be a large and hungry lioness—avatar of a goddess—standing on a table in a house in the heart of London.

Then the hot breath turned away from him. He heard not more than two padding steps. Then Dr. Mystery screamed.

Simon jumped to his feet. "Enough! Julia . . ."

But the voice was still the voice of the other, telling the story, making it real. "And Ra saw what his Eye had done and grieved for the children of his tears. He called on his ibis-headed scribe, Keeper of Wisdom, and the hawk-headed one who sees the horizon, husband of the Eye, to bring the Lady back to herself. They gave her beer to drink, colored with ochre, red as blood. Drunken, she slept, and Ra forgave the children of his tears and shone his divine light once more upon them."

Slowly, slowly, light came into the room, pale and yet clear. Dr. Mystery sat still in his chair, his eyes dazed. Then they widened, as realization came back into them. He rose to his feet as though drawn upwards on wires.

"No!" He said it firmly, as though to be completely clear. "Go away! No." He pointed, his hand trembling wildly, past Simon's shoulder. Then his eyes rolled back in his head and he dropped to the floor like a puppet whose strings are cut.

Simon felt a great reluctance to learn what was behind him. But even greater than that was his need to understand. It was this need that had lead him to An-ket's tomb, as well as to Julia's bedroom tonight.

Simon turned. He saw a tomb painting come to life.

Both men and the woman had ideal bodies, firm of flesh, gleaming of limb. The men wore pleated linen kilts, bright with stripes. Many-rowed collars of gold and gems encircled their necks, but above that . . .

It was easy to look at a painting on a wall and see the

fancies of days gone by. If the ancient Egyptians chose to portray their gods as monsters with the bodies of men and the heads of the creatures they saw around them, then it was simply one of the things that made them unique from other cultures, where most gods were portrayed as wearing human form.

Simon had never wondered whether the images on the walls and coffins represented literal truth. The heads of living saints do not bear halos; the gods of ancient Egypt with their blended forms had not been real. Believing anything else marked one as a crackpot. And yet . . .

Horus, the warrior who had defeated his evil uncle, Seth, to avenge his father's murder, carried his hawk head in silhouette just as in the representations, the black markings on the white feathers the clear inspiration for the sacred eye. He wore a striped headdress in the same colors as his collar, surmounted by the double crown of Egypt. Simon could not see, and did not want to see, the place where hawk's head joined man's body.

Then Horus turned his head, staring at Simon with the clear, unblinking yellow-rimmed eyes of the hawk. The pure white feathers ruffled under his throat. The black beak opened. A hawk cannot smile, yet Simon felt that he saw approbation in the eyes that only seemed to be those of a beast.

Between the grotesque gods stood a beautiful woman. She, at least, was human in appearance, though faultless in a way that no mortal woman could match. Dusky of skin with eyes as black and liquid as ink in a crystal jar, she was surrounded by a gentle glow like moonlight. On her head she balanced a great silver circle bounded by two curving gold horns. Too amazed to feel more astonished, Simon noticed that the only light in the room came from this headdress. She nodded her head graciously and Simon felt as though the moon had bowed to him.

Then the third figure stepped forward, right foot first.

He saw the thin, long beak of the ibis open and close,

the supple neck curving as though oiled. It wore a black wig coming well down over the strong shoulders, the ends tipped in gold. Its eyes were deeper and kinder than either of the others. Since Thoth was known as the inventor of writing and numbers, as well as the keeper of wisdom and magic, Simon had always had a secret preference for him.

Thoth raised his hand. In it, held by the loop, was a golden ankh, the symbol of life. Simon hesitated, then unwilling to make Thoth wait, took the object in his hand.

As though that were the signal, the three gods faded away as shadows do when the sun rises.

Simon blinked as though he woke from a dazzling dream. He heard an odd buzzing sound and turned, expecting to see anything from the Devourer of Souls to a cobra. Instead he saw Dr. Mystery, arms thrown back, sleeping and snoring in his chair.

Julia sat in the same place, her hands flat on the table in front of her. She met Simon's gaze, her eyes filled with a strange tenderness that told him more clearly than words that Julia had not yet returned to her body. Julia fought with him, laughed with him, made love with him, and would marry him. When she looked at him, she saw a lover, a colleague, and a friend. She did not look at him with the sadness of loss mingled with everlasting, undying maternal pride.

"Who are you?" he asked.

"Once I was your mother. Once you were my son. You were murdered."

Simon did not know why he glanced at Dr. Mystery. The woman who wore Julia's body nodded. "Yes. Our lives make patterns like the weaving of cloth. A thread may pull or snag, a length unravel, but the pattern goes on."

"Why are you here now?"

There were tears in Julia's eyes. "I had vowed before all the gods that if you were not in the West when I came to die, I would not stay there. I would wait for thee by the Doorposts of Eternity. But thou came not. Again and again through the centuries I would hear thy spirit hungering for the woman thou had loved and lost to treachery. Then at last I felt thee near me and called to thee. And this has been the result."

She stood up and reached out to wrap him in a motherly embrace. An-ket cradled the head of her son against herself rocking him as women have rocked their children since the beginning of time.

"Thou art taller than I remember," she whispered and laughed through her tears as all mothers must when they let their children go. She wiped a tear from his face. "Take thy woman unto thyself and be happy, oh my son. And when at last you pass into the West, seek for me. I shall still be waiting by the doorpost."

Simon suddenly knew that another god had stepped out of the mists of time: Anubis the Jackal, who guides and guards the spirit on its journey. He saw Julia's body waver and sway but that could have been from the tears in his eyes.

The gas jets spluttered and flared, bathing the room with light. Julia had her hand on his shoulder. "Are you all right? You look . . ."

He sank down onto his knees. Opening his hand, he found that the ankh Thoth had given him had dwindled into a small golden ring, no bigger around than the circumferance of a lady's finger. He gazed up into Julia's eyes. They were the same; they were utterly changed. The light of unending joy sparkled there and he knew the secret of her vitality. With her by his side, she might teach him how to find bliss in every passing moment.

"Julia, will you marry me? I'll ask you in Greek, Coptic, hieratic, or in mime if that's what it takes."

She gazed around the room, confused. She laughed at the sight of the sleeping spiritualist. "This isn't exactly the place I'd have chosen. Or the witness." Then she smiled down into his eyes. "But wherever you ask me and in whatever language, the answer is still yes."

Before Simon could even slide the ring on Julia's finger, the door crashed open. As though propelled by a powerful shove, Robert Winslow stumbled into the room, followed by a short, extremely burly man with bowlegs. Sharp, hard eyes took in the scene, including Simon just rising off his knees.

"Proposal, eh? Damn well better be. C'mere, girl."

"Now, just a moment . . . ," Simon barked, having had quite enough sudden appearances for one evening.

"It's all right, Simon. That's my father."

For some reason, Simon looked at Robert. The soldier brushed off his coat. "I met him on the street as I took Lucy home. He seemed to feel that if he came with me, the police would be superfluous."

Mr. Hanson gave his daughter a shake. "What the devil do you mean by it, eh? Runnin' off in that hole-and-corner fashion? Scared poor Ruth into fits, thinking you'd been abducted or murdered or some other damn-fool thing."

"But, Father, didn't you get my note?"

" 'Course I did. Din't need it, either. I knew where you'd gone, sure as a gun! But Ruth would have it that I come after you. Hell! I told her that if I started chasing after you at my time of life, I'd soon find myself run off my legs! An' I ain't got enough of them to start with."

Simon recovered enough of his wits to shake hands. The mill owner's hard eyes appraised him rather as though Simon were a horse Mr. Hanson considered buying. He half expected to have his arms and chest felt over. "Hmphf. Marrying her for my money, are you?" he demanded suddenly.

"That's right, sir."

Mr. Hanson looked grim for half a heartbeat. Then the

gruff face lightened and, for an instant, a resemblance to the little god Bes flashed across the brutish face. He chuckled, a sound like lava flowing down a mountain. "You'll earn it if you do, by God!"

Epilogue

For Julia, Cairo was a toyshop of delights. Nothing dismayed her, not noise, not smells, not beggars. Her instant affection for the city seemed to be requited. She traveled into places where no other European woman would go and came out not only unhurt but untarnished, even honored. Simon had not yet grown used to seeing the most knavish *fellahin* treating his wife like a cherished daughter.

The word flew around the bazaars and coffeehouses that the Sitt of Archer-effendi spoke Arabic like a native, though always with the phrasing of a princess. For, as she had predicted the first day they'd met, her Arabic had improved astoundingly fast once it was in her ears every day and every night.

"Oh, thou art a cedar among reeds! Let me drink again from thy lips!" She bent down to give him the kisses she had demanded—panting, broken kisses, but sweet nonetheless.

Simon tightened his hands on Julia's hips, trying to slow her motions before they drove him completely over the edge. He'd already had to shut his eyes, for the sight of her, head thrown back, breasts forward, had pushed him to the verge of completion. He'd always heard that married men soon lost interest in making love to their wives. Simon counted a day as lost if he didn't see Julia with just such an expression of ecstasy.

Her body had changed in the last eighteen months. Her arms and legs showed signs of the hard work she never shirked. Despite all precautions, her skin had toasted to a gleaming gold that reminded him of the small figures of goddesses they'd found that season. If her white hips and bosom were more generous than they'd been on their wedding night, he had no complaint to make, especially as the cause had been his doing.

Julia pushed up straight, her nails scraping lightly over his chest and stomach. "My beloved. . . ."

He forced himself into a sitting position, drawing her knees closer to his waist. She gasped and broke into shudders, her body so tight around him, her face so astoundingly beautiful that she brought him into the maelstrom with her.

He was awakened by her pulling aside the mosquito netting to bring him a tray with coffee and sweet almond biscuits. She wore a long, loose caftan of sheer white, decorated with twining embroideries of green leaves. He tried to block out the knowledge that she was naked underneath.

"Write on my tombstone that I died a happy, exhausted man," he said.

"Very well. I'll leave instructions in my will to inscribe mine, 'Here lies the woman who exhausted him, permitted to sleep at last.' "

The room was filled with the soft colors of sunset and the yodeling cry that called the faithful to the fourth prayer of the day. He lay against the pillows, nibbling on the sweets, while she busied herself about the room with the task he'd interrupted. He never could watch her packing without remembering the first time they'd made love.

Since then, he'd learned the facilitating power of money. Once Mr. Hanson had been convinced that Simon did not love Julia for financial reasons, he was as open-handed as Father Christmas. If it had been left to him, his only child would have had a wedding to rival Victoria and Albert's. But, with Ruth's connivance, Simon and Julia were married six weeks after they met at a quiet church near Hampton Court. Done out of the wedding of his dreams, Mr. Hanson found other things to spend his money on.

Having adopted Simon as a son-in-law, he seemed to extend his benevolence to the Archer girls. He and the general drew lots for who would have the privilege of giving Lucy away. Military strategy won the day, but it was Mr. Hanson who gave the bride a rope of pearls almost as fine as Julia's own. On the morning of the wedding, however, Julia lent Lucy her strand, saying, "I had great good fortune the last time I wore these."

"The day you married Simon?"

"Then, too."

Prince Albert found he could not part with his friend, the major. So though Robert's information was valuable to Lord Dalhousie, who had just annexed all the Sikh territory, he himself never returned to the Punjab. The queen was quite taken with Lucy, since she was interested in just those domestic details that so entertained Her Majesty. Both Amanda and Jane were presented at court, an event entirely beyond their mother's wildest dreams. But what quite put the lid on her friend Mrs. Pertwee's insufferable boasting, Mrs. Archer wrote, was when she herself was invited to take tea at Buckingham Palace.

Mr. Hanson even had fortune enough to arrange a restful trip to New York for a would-be actor named Basil Mortimer. Mr. Mortimer's nerves had been shattered by an experience that no one seemed able to describe. Before long, his acting career at a standstill, Mr. Mortimer turned his hand to writing. His blood-and-thunder epic, *The Mummy's Heart*, played to sold-out houses through 1851 and did very well in the provinces after that. He'd been bold enough to send an inscribed copy to Julia who had read it before Simon could stop her.

"It's a trumpery thing," she said at the end. "But I could see how it well would play, especially with the right makeup and stage effects." She laughed. "He's a much better writer than he is a spiritualist, but then he'd almost have to be, wouldn't you say?"

Simon himself had not read the former Dr. Mystery's play. Those moments in the seance chamber were still too vivid to be considered lightly.

For several weeks, memories had disturbed him at odd times and places. Not all the memories were of the life he'd known thus far, the life of Simon Archer. Strange images would flash through his mind, set off by the taste of honey or the scent of balsam. He saw himself, a small boy, running naked beside a reed boat, begging to be taken along. He saw a strong man with a hawklike profile who could deny him nothing. And his mother, dressed in her finest robes and jewels, going to the temple with her maids. Her long, tapering fingers touched his shaven head, and three thousand years later, Simon could still feel the great love in so incidental a caress.

The images themselves stopped the morning after he married Julia. The dreams stopped when he found himself waking two and three times a night to draw her close. The laughter and passion of their bed left no room for phantoms.

In a year, he'd grown far too busy to dwell on the residual memories. Mr. Hanson decided he was interested in Egyptology after all: "I thought it was just a whim of my girl's, but if a man takes it seriously, there must be something in it, eh?"

So his expedition was funded on a more lavish scale than was usual and the results were also greater than usual, as though heaven beamed on him. Three golden goddesses on an empty chest, smiling at nothing, led him to a cache of papyrus in the desert, the largest yet discovered.

Mr. Keene was going quietly mad trying to find scholars to translate them. He estimated it might take thirty years to read them all. The newspapers called it the find of the century. Julia and Simon smiled at that. There was a lot of century left yet.

A cry from the adjoining room made Julia look up from her packing. "Dinnertime," she said with a smile at her husband.

She came back to sit beside him under the netting, the greatest discovery of their lives nestled to her bosom. Simon stroked his son's sticky cheek. "He's greedy."

"He takes after his father."

Simon gazed in wonder at a sight he'd never grown tired of witnessing. Everyone had said Julia was mad to take a sickly, wheezing infant into Egypt, where infection rode the air like an evil witch. Mr. Hanson, who was not a religious man, had taken to quoting vast chunks of Exodus. But she had, perhaps foolishly, decreed that nothing in Egypt would harm her or her son. Adam had begun to thrive from the moment their boat docked and now, at nearly eight months, was as rosy and plump as a baby in a Pond's advertisement.

"Julia?"

She stopped humming to the baby. "Yes, darling?"

"Do you think it's safe to take him home?"

"I think so. And we'll bring him back with us in the autumn. Just imagine how much he'll enjoy it! He'll be digging his own excavations by then." She cooed down at the oblivious infant. "You'll find a better mummy than your daddy did, won't you?"

"He couldn't possibly," Simon said gallantly. Then he asked, hesitantly, "Julia? About An-ket . . ."

"Yes?" Her eyes showed no consciousness that the

name was anything to her beyond a well-known discovery of her husband's. She began rocking and singing again, an Arabic lullaby about roses and rabbits.

"Keene writes that the mold degeneration is slowly but surely destroying the remains. I wondered what you would think if we brought her back here next season."

"Yes, if you think that's best. The climate at the museum is not all I could wish." Julia began to discuss the various steps that might be taken to improve the dampness, short of moving the entire foundation to some more salubrious spot, like Spain.

Simon only half listened. For here, in a nutshell, was what puzzled him most. None of the women whom An-ket "visited," whether for a few minutes as she had Julia or for the better part of a week like Lucy, remembered her. Julia knew, of course, all that had happened to her— her arrival in London, the dangerous appearance of Billy the Wall, her pursuit by Dr. Mystery. But all was as though An-ket had never come forth, had never been the motivating factor in all these events. And all the women were better off now than they had been before An-ket's advent.

Mrs. Pierce's employment bureau was singlehandedly rescuing the reputation of such firms. Her budding business had been given a boost, admittedly, when the new wife of the Yorkshire millionaire had gone to Mrs. Pierce's for her entire staff. But not even that would have helped her were it not for a growing recognition of Mrs. Pierce's probity and good common sense. Her daughters were now partners in the firm rather than employees, though they still worked by special arrangement when extra staff was required.

Lucy had Robert and seemed happy, running between Osborne House on the Isle of Wight and her own home. With all the activity in his house, the general had quite rejuvenated and expected to see the completion and publication of his memoirs sometime in the next ten or fifteen years. Even the cat had her own cushion by the fire, all the milk and fish a feline could desire, and the satisfaction (presumably) of having a human at her beck and meow.

Simon looked at Julia, now with his child against her shoulder, and asked, "Are you happy?"

He could tell that she intended to return a light answer, but then she paused and, meeting his eyes fully, said, "There is no happier woman in the world—no, in the history of the world—than I at this moment. Does that satisfy you?"

"Satisfy me?"

"You have been worried ever since we married. I have never spoken of it, but I have known it. Can't you tell me why?"

He shook his head. "There's too much to tell. And I don't know the full tale, anyway. Perhaps it's just that there are so many questions. . . ."

"Questions?" She laughed softly, patting her child's back. "Why are we here? Where are we going? What about life, death, love, art?"

"Yes. I wouldn't have thought that you . . ."

"I'm not a philistine, Simon. I may seem only to be interested in three things, but I do occasionally stop to ponder the eternal questions of the universe. And what I think is . . ."

"What three things?"

Her smile held a trace of familiar tenderness as she moved her sleeping child into her arms. "Him, you, and Egypt. And I hope you don't mind that ordering."

"No. At least I come before Egypt."

Now her smile was wicked, with a sideways glance that sent a thrill straight to his loins. "Perhaps the ordering changes depending on circumstances. But as for the other things you mention, they have been taking care of themselves for millions of years. So long as we love each other, they can go right on taking care of themselves."

Before he could argue that this was a narrow-minded

view, she carried Adam back to his cradle, where the nurse waited for him. On her return, Julia closed the bedroom door.

Watching her walk toward him, bare feet lending a kind of hunting quality to her steps, Simon knew that he'd still have questions should he wake in the middle of the night. But as he folded Julia once more into his arms, feeling his passions warm to her again, he knew that the only important magic was the one they made together.

DO YOU BELIEVE IN MAGIC?

MAGICAL LOVE

The enchanting series from Jove will make you a believer!

With a sprinkling of faerie dust and the wave of a wand, magical things can happen—but nothing is more magical than the power of love.

□ ***SEA SPELL*** by Tess Farraday   0-515-12289-0/$5.99

A mysterious man from the sea haunts a woman's dreams—and desires...

□ ***ONCE UPON A KISS*** by Claire Cross

0-515-12300-5/$5.99

A businessman learns there's only one way to awaken a slumbering beauty...

□ ***A FAERIE TALE*** by Ginny Reyes   0-515-12338-2/$5.99

A faerie and a leprechaun play matchmaker—to a mismatched pair of mortals...

□ ***ONE WISH*** by C.J. Card   0-515-12354-4/$5.99

For years a beautiful bottle lay concealed in a forgotten trunk—holding a powerful spirit, waiting for someone to come along and make one wish...

VISIT PENGUIN PUTNAM ONLINE ON THE INTERNET:
http://www.penguinputnam.com

TIME PASSAGES

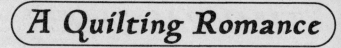